A B O U T   T H E   A U '

Rae Stewart is a former journalist who has travelled extensively in India. He first visited Goa in 1993 and has returned many times since, including a spell of several months researching and writing the first draft of this novel. And eating more pork vindaloo than was strictly necessary.

After more than twenty years working as a reporter for ITN, GMTV, Sky News and Scottish Television he became a civil servant in 2009. He lives in south west London with his family. The Vibe is his first novel.

If you'd like to find out more information about Rae, his writing, and his random thoughts on a variety of subjects, please visit:

www.facebook.com/TheVibeFiction/

Or follow Rae on Twitter @MrRaeStewart

THE VIBE

Rae Stewart

Ashburn Press, London SW19

Book layout © 2016 BookDesignTemplates.com
Cover design by Simon Avery at idobookcovers.com

The Vibe/Rae Stewart. - 1st ed.
ISBN 978-1481026499

It's all connected.

Contents

CHAPTER ONE

Anjuna

The party's over. Not that you'd guess it by looking at the people still bounding around like maniacs between the palm trees, kicking up clouds of golden dust in the early morning sunlight. They'll keep caning it for another couple of hours at least, feeding off the music, feeling every last vibration until it all gets too much and too bright and everything turns tired and sour.

But to those in the know - the long-timers, the party veterans, the old heads, whatever you want to call them - they know it's over.

They know that something can be finished long before it's ended, that past a certain point an experience is in danger of becoming little more than an ever-fainter echo of itself.

They know that trying to sustain a moment doesn't always improve it, that it's often best to quit while it's still fresh and joyous.

Then again, sometimes they're so off their tits they forget.

Jez is sprawled out on a palm-frond mat down by the beach, his head in girlfriend Nat's lap, his feet twitching to the rhythm pounding out from the giant speakers. Nat's half-consciously playing with Jez's dreads, rolling them between her fingers. She's starting to flag.

'Come on then, girl,' Jez says to her, pushing himself to his feet with slow, aching effort, surveying the party's human carnage crashed out all around him. 'This is doing my head in.'

Jez drapes his bare arm over Nat's shoulders as they trudge along the path through the palm trees towards their ramshackle rented room ten minutes to the north.

'Something about last night,' Jez says. 'It just wasn't right. The vibe. Y'know what I mean?'

Nat shrugs but says nothing. She's too numb to think about it. The party was fine as far as she's concerned, although it didn't really feel like a proper Christmas, not a *real* one.

She fiddles with the bangle Jez gave her yesterday, wondering if it's real silver. She doubts it, but doesn't mind. After all, it's the thought that counts, isn't it.

They walk in silence for a while, plodding through the long shadows.

Around them, Goa stirs into life.

Women in bright green saris set fire to small piles of dry leaves and brittle sticks of wood, sending spears of dense white smoke up to the palm-leaf canopy overhead. Men in shorts wash at square cement troughs, lathering their thin, hard bodies in preparation for another tough day of fishing, farming, climbing trees to cut down coconuts or tapping the trunks for toddy sap.

The pulse of the party fades in the distance as the air fills with the ugly, grating rattle of crow-song and the last anxious barks of scrawny nightwatch dogs.

As the dirt path reaches a narrow tarmac road, Jez and Nat hear the rasping diesel roar of a bus.

As it comes around the corner into view, Jez sees that it isn't a bus at all. It's a coach. A Shivaji Travels of Panjim, Goa, Deluxe Coach, according to the brightly coloured lettering painted on the side.

It still looks pretty much like a bus to Jez.

They watch as it putters by, catching quick glimpses of pink, nervous faces staring out from behind the glass.

Jez's tired jaws crack into a grin as he sees one woman recoil at the sight of him, the half-naked, dreadlocked, tattooed vision greeting her arrival in Anjuna.

'Sweet,' he says, rubbing his hands together. 'Fresh package tourists. Yum yum.'

*

Steve Harrison hears the woman in front of him shriek, and looks out the coach window to see what's shocked her. Just a hippy couple. He's heard there's some in Anjuna. Not exactly scary. Mind you, the woman seems a nervous sort. She's already yelped at the sight of a couple of animals on the road. And it's not like they were tigers or rhinos or anything particularly frightening. Just cows.

Steve relaxes again, continuing to check out both India and the other guests on the coach.

First impressions of India weren't great, which worried him. A run-down, chaotic terminal building made of stained, crumbling concrete, staffed by grim-faced officials and khaki-clad soldiers swinging battered old rifles. After that, the grubby outskirts of a town which he guessed was Panjim, the state capital. Then across a wide river on an outrageously ugly bridge, probably made of the same dubious batch of concrete as the airport.

But as the coach eased further north and the urban sprawl gave way to greenery, he started to enjoy himself.

This was more like it, this is how he expected India to look. Banks of tall palm trees, wide open rice fields with raised earth walkways, muddy ponds with water buffaloes sunk up to their chins, the spires of blinding white churches poking through the lushness of it all.

And there are the unexpected things, like the hand painted adverts on the sides of buildings for unfamiliar brands of cigarettes and whisky. Minor glimpses of a strange world, but enough to get a worm of excitement wriggling in his belly.

And then there are the other tourists, the people destined

for his hotel. He thinks he's got them all worked out. It's just a little game he plays from time to time, a way of keeping his professional instincts honed.

Take that couple sitting at the front, for instance. Both in their fifties. He thought a beard would make him look less skinny, she goes to self-assertiveness classes and wears the trousers in the house. Intelligent, dependable, law-abiding members of society.

Two seats behind, the fat young woman and fatter young man. The man with cropped dark hair and tattoo on his forearm, the woman with a short, permed bob. Low-paid working class. Probably don't earn enough to come here just for a holiday, so it could well be their honeymoon.

By the look of him, the man may be involved in petty crime of some sort.

And across from them. More fat people. A middle-aged couple, migrants from working- to middle-class. He's probably a sales director who cheats his expenses and drives over both the drink and speed limits, while she's a golf-club regular who drinks gin and tonic in public, but rum and coke at home. Not above a bit of graft and tax evasion.

Behind them. The fat girl, late teens or early twenties, probably the daughter of the fat couple in front of her. A face without any expression at all.

Probably too stupid to break the law. Or be let out the house by herself.

And that's it. Simple enough to figure out. Oh yeah, there's one more.

Middle-twenties female, medium height, good-looking, well-dressed, shoulder-length dark hair, bright blue eyes. Excellent figure, married about three years, wants a big house and two children, one boy, one girl, likes spending money on clothes, holidays and the home, likes the idea of status, goes to aerobics, single-minded, Capricorn, called Karen, sitting next to him, the wife.

Too easy. Inside knowledge. Doesn't count.

*

'That's it! That's them! Them's *exactly* the Goddamn ratbastard assholes I'm *talking* about! Wasn't I just saying to you? Wasn't I just saying? And there they are, the very same. Now, you tell me that ain't some kind of *sign*, because if *that* ain't a sign I sure as shit don't know what *is*. That there's a sign, a sign that every word of what I'm saying's *true*.'

The Doc's half out of his chair on the verandah, old eyes blazing with life, long white hair wild and flowing, pointing at the Shivaji Travels coach as it struggles around a tight bend in the side road at the end of the garden. Palm trees lean in over the tarmac, making turning difficult.

'It's exactly them assholes,' the Doc goes on, looking between the coach and Cyril. 'Coming here, smogging up the vibe, souls sick with money and brand new shiny automobiles. We get tainted by it, all that shit. Toxic head-waste, man.'

Cyril Rodrigues shifts his mid-life bulk on the wide wooden chair beside the Doc's. He looks over to his old friend.

'Susegad,' he says softly.

'Yeah,' the Doc says. 'But can't you feel it? Can't you just feel all that negative, poisonous shit just seeping outta them? Feel them twisted *vibes* coming outta there? Goddamn poisonous rat-ass *bas*tards.'

Cyril jerks one of his blubbery shoulders in a half-hearted shrug.

'They come, they go,' he says.

'Yeah, yeah, they *go*. I mean, *sure*, they *go*. Once they've consumed their pretty little boxed-up neat and tidy two week vacation, they *go*. But not until they've fuzzed up that vibe and tuned it out so it's crackling like static on a TV. And then more of them come, and more of them come, and they keep coming and keep coming, and one day the vibe's gonna be so whacked out ain't nobody be able to tune it back in. Sonofabitch ratfink shitkicking poisonhead *bas*tards! They don't know *nothing*. They don't know what it was like in the old days. Now *that* was a time. You remember that? When it was just you and me? Now that was a genuine time - that was *real*! The vibe was still *pure*, then. All them years, brother. All them years.'

There's a pause in the Doc's rant, and Cyril looks back over at him. But he sees that the Doc's slipped inside himself, as he does so often these days, watching some internal picture show.

Cyril has always meant to ask the Doc what he sees when he daydreams. Is it the old days? Is it all those young, wild hippies with their hair all over the place, running around and living in fishermen's huts? Is it the old full moon parties, with all those guitars and bongos and people shouting things they called poetry, and all those people dancing like they were trees swaying in the wind?

Or maybe he's just thinking about naked women. He'll ask him. One day. Now is not the time.

Cyril's thoughts are interrupted by rapid horn blasts from the road.

A dirty minibus veers around the coach, overtaking it on the bend, swerving sharply at the last second to avoid an oncoming scooter.

The rucksacks strapped to the minibus's roof strain against their fastenings, threatening to spill all over the road. But they right themselves as the minibus straightens and speeds off, leaving the coach to trundle on at its careful pace.

Quiet descends on the verandah again.

All them years, thinks Cyril. It occurs to him, and not for the first time, that the years haven't been kind to the Doc. That long, thinning white hair, the straggly beard.

When the Doc first arrived from America, knocking on Cyril's door looking for a room to rent all those years ago, his hair was dark and rich and healthy. His face was tanned, but not the cracked leather it is now. The sharp blue eyes once shone with joy and optimism.

Nowadays they flared with hatred and anger.

All them years.

Cyril looks down at himself, at the sturdy paunch beneath his shirt, feels the jowls hanging from his jaw.

For a moment he considers that maybe all them years have taken their toll on *him* too.

Then his shoulder twitches again, shrugging the thought off.

'Susegad,' he says softly, not wanting to disturb the Doc. 'Susegad.'

*

Never again. His back feels like some-one's been chipping away at each one of his vertebrae with a blunt, rusty chisel. Never, ever again.

Iain McMillan catches his rucksack as it's thrown from the minibus roof, keen to get away from the other Westerners he's been crammed up against for the last twelve sweaty, bumping, sleepless nightmare hours. Bombay to Anjuna direct by luxury private vehicle, the poster in the Colaba travel agent's office had said. Six hundred rupees, about half the price of the train. Iain shakes his head. He's just risked his life in a clapped-out minibus for the sake of saving a few quid. Smart thinking, Batman.

The driver, a ragged older man with stained teeth and blood-red eyes, stands smiling with his hand held out, hoping for tips.

'Cheers,' Iain says, shaking the man's hand but not leaving any money in it. 'And thanks for all that marvelous Hindi film music, by the way. Especially that tape we heard eight times. Don't think it was quite loud enough, though. My ears are hardly bleeding at all.'

Iain looks around. He's in a dusty, stony square bordered on three sides by open-air restaurants, telephone booths and moneychangers' offices. Beyond that, behind swaying palms, the endless, shining sea.

So, he says to himself. This must be it. The famous Anjuna. That's where they said they'd drop us anyway. Mind you, they could have been lying. This could be the middle of nowhere, for all I know. Or a small village just next to it. The outskirts of nowhere.

He picks the restaurant that looks busiest - six people slouched at different tables - and sits down on a white plastic chair in the corner so he can take in the whole courtyard as well as the other customers.

He reaches into the smaller of his two bags and pulls out a hard-backed black notebook. On the first page, in bold letters, it says;

IAIN McMILLAN'S GREAT HINDUSTAN ADVENTURE

He opens the book about a quarter of the way in, jots down 'Saturday 26th December '98', then 'Anjuna, Goa'. He thinks for a moment, soaking up the scene, then starts to write.

Happy Boxing Day. It feels like I've gone the distance in a couple of bouts already, losing on points both times. But at least I've finally made it to Anjuna, which didn't seem all that likely for a while.

During the night we nearly crashed into three buses, four cars, a couple of tractors and a big bastard of a truck, all because our psycho driver insisted on overtaking when there was something huge, dangerous and made of metal hurtling towards us. Our man seemed to think that as long as he kept honking his horn and flashing his lights at the other drivers everything was going to be okay, that we were somehow magically protected from ending up as charred, mangled, unidentifiable lumps beside the road. On three occasions my life flashed before my eyes. Unfortunately it wasn't all that interesting the first time round.

Anyway, I'm here. And in one piece. Peace. Man.

But now that I've got here, after unnecessarily risking my life, I find that there doesn't seem to be all that much to Anjuna. Mind you, I've only been here about two and a half minutes so far, so it's not like I'm some huge expert on the place.

A worn-out waiter in shorts and dirty white t-shirt flip-flops up to Iain's table.

'You like something breakfast, drink,' the waiter says in a tired monotone, stating rather than asking.

'Er, aye. Is this Anjuna?' Iain points to the floor.

The waiter looks at him a second, then nods.

'Anjuna, Anjuna,' he says.

'Tea, then. Black tea.'

'You want milk, sugar?'

'No, no milk. Just black. Please.

'You want something eat? Toads, omlat, froods?'

Iain toys with the idea of ordering toads, or maybe even toad omlat with froods on the side, just for the hell of it, but he isn't really in the mood. His back aches too much.

'Nothing, thanks. Just black tea.'

The waiter slopes off and Iain grabs his journal again.

Maybe it's too early to judge (and it's only 8.30 in the morning, after all) but I don't think I'll stay here long. A week, maybe. Just see in the New Year, maybe go to one of these infamous all-night parties, then get on further south. It's not very pretty, the people look dull and wasted (at least, going by the clientele of this particularly charming cafe), and it's far too Westernised from what I've heard. It's not really the sort of place to hang around in for long. After all, it's not real India, and real India is what I came all this way to see.

No, I'll just use it for sun, sea, sand and (please, God, please) sex. A few days' rest, then hit the road again. Rock 'n' roll.

He shuts the book and slips it in his bag, looking up to see the waiter shuffling towards him holding a glass of cloudy black tea.

Iain examines it suspiciously as it's put down in front of him.

It's not *black* tea exactly, not officially.

More a kind of dark brown, muddy, murky tea. With swirling foreign bodies in it.

And it's far too early in the morning to think about what they might be or, worse still, actually identify them.

'Cheers,' Iain says. 'Any milk?'

*

'Well, I don't think much of the furnishings,' Karen says, screwing up her face, scanning the sparse hotel room. A bed, two small bedside tables, a fridge, a chair, a scruffy wardrobe. Steve's still at the door, trying to communicate with the hunched old man who'd struggled up the stairs with their suit-cases. Steve had tried to take one of the cases off him because he was worried the man might keel over with the effort, but he'd been brushed aside.

'No money. No rupees. I don't have any rupees,' Steve says again, slowly, holding his hands out by his sides and putting on an apologetic face.

'Rupees, rupees, acha,' the old man says, nodding, smiling a toothless smile.

'I don't *have* any,' Steve says, starting to get irritated. 'Not been to bank yet. Yes? Only English money. Understand?'

He holds up a five pound note, trying to make the point as clear as he can. He's about to put the note back in his pocket but the old man's eyes and hand are following it. Steve hesitates, then gives it to him. The old man tips the note to his forehead, smiles wider, and then he's gone. Steve closes the door.

'Fiver for the bags,' he says. 'Would you believe it? Bloody fiver.'

Karen's standing by the window, lips pursed, weight balanced on one hip, arms folded. It's not a good sign, and Steve knows it.

'So much for the double bed,' she says. 'Smaller than the one we've got at home, that is.'

'Yeah, love, but we've got a king-size at home, haven't we,' Steve says softly, trying to cool the brewing trouble. 'It didn't say king-size in the brochure. Just double. It's what they said.'

'Well, I think they could have afforded something a bit bigger, the price we're paying.'

Karen drops her arms and sits down on the mattress.

'Bloody hell,' she says. 'Have you felt this? Hard as bloody nails, this is. No way. We can't sleep here. Be crippled by the end of two weeks.'

Steve sits down next to her and bounces up and down a bit. Firm-ish, he thinks. 'Nah, that's alright, love,' he says, smiling. 'Good for your back, a firm bed. Some people would pay a fortune for a mattress this firm.'

'Well, we've paid a fortune for our holiday, and I'm not bloody sleeping on *this*,' Karen says, pointing a dagger-straight finger down at the bed as if she was accusing it of insulting her. 'Go on,' she says sharply. 'Get hold of the Rep before he disappears. Tell him we're not sleeping on this. Get him to find us another room.'

'C'mon love, we're on holiday. Relax a bit. Anyway,' he says, putting on his best cheeky grin, 'we'll just have to make sure we get so tired nothing'll stop us from sleeping.'

He moves closer to her, aiming an affectionate kiss at her cheek, but she jumps up and folds her arms again.

'I'm not happy, Steve. And you know what I'm like if I'm not happy in a place. I can't settle. Simple as that. Go on, get the Rep. I'm not happy, and it's his job to make sure I am.'

For a second Steve considers trying to reason with her some more, but dismisses it. They're on holiday, their Christmas present to themselves. They're on holiday and Karen's unhappy. And if she wants a new room, a new room's what she'll get. He smiles at her - a firm, reassuring smile - and trots back down to reception.

CHAPTER TWO

Not even in Goa

'Fuck's sake, wake up! Lazy bastard,' Nat says, shoving Jez on the shoulder as he lies flaked-out on their bread-thin mattress.

'Easy, girl,' he says back through a sticky, sleep-ridden mouth. 'Time's it, anyway?'

'Past five. Wanna get down the Sun Temple, don't I,' she pleads. 'Meeting Scabs and Ricky there. We said.'

'Fuck! Five? Hang on a mo, girl.'

Jez launches himself off the bed and grabs a pair of torn, patched trousers, yanking them on.

'Got to see Hassan about something. Before he pisses off. Back in a sec.'

He shoves his feet into battered flip-flops and makes for the door while Nat moans at him, and then he's outside, striding fast, scratching at his arm, the reared cobra tattoo on his naked breast giving off a dark sheen in the low, evening sun. Along a narrow mud trail between rough clay brick houses, through the widely set palm trees, then onto a broader red dust path, the one leading down to the beach.

The path is flanked by stalls selling chillums, bongs and brass figures, or sarongs and blankets patterned with zodiac signs, Hindu gods, aliens and dolphins.

About six stalls along, there's Hassan, a light-eyed, middle-aged, pot-bellied Kashmiri. His wholesale dealer.

Hassan sees Jez coming, winks to him and nods towards a smaller path going off to the side. Jez already knows it. The path leads to the shack where Hassan does his real business, in a room shared with two other stallholders so they can cut deals away from curious eyes. As they get to the door, Hassan sweeps Jez in, casually checking around to make sure no-one's looking, no well-dressed undercover cops lurking by the palms. Satisfied, he follows Jez into the room, closing the door behind them.

A single, dull bulb lights the naked cell, illuminating faded whitewashed walls and a bare packed-earth floor partly covered by palm frond mats. Hassan gestures at Jez.

'Sit, sit, my friend,' he says, settling down cross-legged, his round belly straining against his shirt. 'Okay, now I have for you something special. Very special. Quality ektazy. Top ektazy. This is top. No bullshit. Top merchandise.'

'Bleedin' better be, Hassan, 'cos that last lot you give me was pony. Shit, they were. These no good? I start getting from somewhere else, yeah?'

'No problem, no problem. My friend, I am telling you before, that was not my fault. Supplier problem only. What to do?'

'Get another bleedin' supplier, that's what to do. Simple, innit.'

'No problem, you no worry. This is no problem this time. This is top quality I am offering you. You want?'

'How much?'

'How many you are wanting?'

Jez lets a few beats pass. He feels an unfamiliar butterfly of nerves flutter in his guts. It's the biggest deal he's ever done with Hassan. Maybe he shouldn't bother. Maybe it's too risky. Still, with New Year coming up. Think of the profit. Enough to fund another few months at least.

'Okay,' he says, keeping his eyes steady on Hassan's. 'Here's the deal. I want four hundred.'

Hassan just stares back at him for a few seconds. Then his eyes flash as he jumps to his feet.

'What you are saying to me?' he spits out. 'You think I am

THE VIBE   15

stupid man? You think I am not understanding?'

'Chill, Hassan, man. C'mon, chill, sit down,' Jez says, although his own heart's racing. He's in danger of fucking this up. Hassan stays on his feet, pacing in front of Jez.

'You are thinking you can be competitor, yes?' Hassan says, prodding his finger at the air. 'Yes, I sell you ten, twenty, for you, your friends. Okay, okay. But now you are saying four hundred? You are talking like a crazy man. You are wanting to put me out of business, this is what you are wanting. Who is buying my ektazy when they are buying from you? Buying my ektazy from you? And you are having profit. Where is Hassan's profit? I am businessman. This is not good business for me. No, this is not possible.'

'But wait, Hassan, wait,' Jez says, getting to his feet, pacing up and down alongside him. 'Think about it. You're getting your profit as well. From me, yeah? And it means you don't have to piss about selling ten here, twenty there. You're selling four hundred at the same time, getting all your profit at once. It's simple. I'm not trying to do you out of nothing. It's good money for you.'

Hassan stops, seems to think for a moment. Then he shakes his head.

'This is not possible. Where I am getting four hundred ektazy?'

'It doesn't need to be today, does it. Three or four days, fine. Don't mess me about, Hassan. You know as well as I do you can get your hands on them.'

Jez starts to feel more confident. Hassan's mellowing. He might just go for it.

Hassan sits back down, motioning for Jez to do the same.

'Okay. Okay, but this is not easy for me. Okay, I can do this. But now we are talking price.'

They haggle for fifteen minutes. It's a battle, but Jez holds out for a substantial reduction on what he usually pays. Three quid a pop, twelve hundred for the lot. Not bad when he knows he can sell them on for between a fiver and a tenner each, depending on the customer and how many they buy. A sweet profit, in anybody's book. But then there's the matter of paying up front. At first Jez refuses, but Hassan insists, threatening to break off the deal. He wants two hundred pounds in advance. Jez gets him down to a hundred and fifty, all that he's brought with him. The men shake on it. Jez is about to leave when Hassan catches his arm.

'Where you are going tonight?' he says, almost in a whisper. Jez is wary of saying too much, just in case he's being set up. Good dealer and everything, but trust him?

'Dunno. Just around, s'pose. Vibe Bar, maybe. Why?'

'You go Lucky Star?'

'Dunno. Doubt it. Why?'

'Do not be going Lucky Star. Not tonight. You and your good friends, you are not going there. I am hearing things. Police trouble, maybe.'

'Nice one, Hassan. Appreciate it.'

Jez strolls back the way he came, his veins fizzing with the buzz of the deal, but not wanting to look like he's in too much of a rush. It's Goa, after all. Nothing gets done in a hurry.

So, he thinks, Luckies getting raided tonight. Some naughty boy ain't been paying their bribes to the cops, then. Or someone else, some rival or something, has bribed the cops more to turn the place over. Or the cops need a soft target for drug arrests so they can pretend they're making an effort. Or all of the above. Bleedin' happens, dunnit. Fucked up country.

When Jez gets back to the room, Nat's sitting by the door waiting for him, ready to go.

'Right, girl,' Jez says, pulling her gently inside. 'I'd say it was about time for a wake-up spliffy.'

'Oh, Jez!'

''Oh Jez' what? They're not going nowhere, them lot. Where they gonna go? They'll still be there in five minutes.'

'That's not the point.'

'What's the point, then?'

'The point, right, is that I wanna see the sunset, don't I. The bloody sun's not gonna wait for us an' all. Though you probably think it will. Won't go down without Lord God Jez's permission.'

'*I* wanna see the sunset. We'll *see* the bleedin' sunset. Got loads of time. Now come on,' he says softly, tugging at her cut-off top, grinning. She can't resist the grin. She knows it, he knows it. Nat gives in and smiles, sitting down on the bed next to Jez while he skins up.

'And if we get this smoked sharpish,' he says, face aglow, 'I might even have time to slip you a quickie. If I really go for it. What? What?' he says, face frowned, as Nat marches out the door.

*

Steve was tired from the plane journey, the bus ride, all the dealings at the hotel, but he hasn't slept well. The combination of bright daylight blasting through the thin curtains and being worried about the restless form of Karen beside him on the firm bed denied him deep sleep.

He stares at the yellow ceiling. Three other rooms they showed them. Three bloody rooms and they all had the same quality of mattresses. Was she happy? No she was not. They eventually chose the second one because, Karen had said, the mattress was 'slightly softer'. Feels just the same to Steve. Firm, but it'll do.

Inch by inch, as carefully as he can, Steve slides out of the bed, desperate not to wake Karen. She deserves a rest. After all, she didn't get much sleep on the plane, and it's best they start their holiday refreshed. He pads across the polished stone floor towards the bathroom. The door squeals at him as he eases it open. Karen's eyes screw up and she tries to speak, yawns, and then tries again.

'Didn't sleep a wink,' she says. 'Did you?'

'Yeah, got a couple of hours, I think. It's just the light. Body clock and all that.'

'It's this bloody mattress,' Karen says, but not like it matters that much to her any more.

'Thought we might go down to the bar,' Steve says, smiling. 'Check the place out.'

'The bar? Shouldn't you have some breakfast first?'

Steve laughs.

'It's evening. I think they stopped serving breakfast about eight hours ago. May as well get used to the time difference as soon as we can.'

'You go down,' Karen says, settling into the pillow again. 'I'll maybe come down in a bit.'

Steve goes into the bathroom and thinks about shaving. Instead he just washes his face and rubs a damp hand over his short brown hair, then sniffs his armpits to check his deodorant's still working. He puts on some more, just in case.

Back in the bedroom he searches through one of the suitcases for some clean clothes. Karen had wanted to unpack at once but changed her mind when she looked into the drawers in the wardrobe. Dirty, she'd said, though Steve couldn't see anything wrong with them.

He puts on beige shorts and a fresh white t-shirt with a tiny dark blue polo player riding over his nipple. Karen bought the t-shirt for him. He hadn't dared ask how much it cost.

Before leaving the room, he bends over and gives Karen a delicate kiss on her forehead. She murmurs, but doesn't stir.

The hotel bar opens out onto to the gardens, overlooking the swimming pool. Steve can see the fat couple and fat young girl flopped out on sun-loungers beside it, dead to the world, like bloated carcasses found washed up on the beach. About half of the sunbeds have guests on them, but Steve doesn't recognise anyone else. He decides to have a seat in the shade rather than out on the lawn, even though the nearly-set sun isn't very strong. It's the heat he's concerned about, and the bar's ceiling fans draw him in with their hypnotic swirl.

'Beer, please,' he says to the barman, a teenage boy in an ill-fitting purple waistcoat and tie.

'Which beer you want?' the barman says, sounding bored.

'What beers you got?'

'Big one? Small one?'

'How big's small?'

'You want small one?'

'No, no, no. How big is it?'

'Big one? You want big beer?'

Steve nods reluctantly, accepts what the barman gives him, and sits at the bar with his chilled glass, trying to wake up, trying to believe he's really in India with its easy heat, its strange and complex odours and the feeling of utter foreignness. He finds it all rather overwhelming, but not in a bad way. More than any-thing, he'd like to get out there, start exploring, breathe in the atmosphere. But Karen might get up at any time and he doesn't want to be too far away when she does.

What a girl. He's lucky to have her. She's strong, forthright, gives him a bit of steel. And as he's first to admit, he needs a bit of a push every now and then. Just as well he's got Karen onside to give him that support, that back-up. She could have had almost anyone she wanted in Workington, but she chose him. Certainly a girl who knows what she wants out of life and is determined to get it. Sets high standards, demands the best. He feels a surge of pride at knowing he has it within him to live up to her expectations.

The surge doesn't last long. Instead, worries about the holiday start coming to the surface, worries he's had almost since he booked it. She'd left the organisation of the holiday in his hands. As long as there's sun and sand involved, she'd said, she didn't mind. A bit of winter warmth. But Goa's a bit of a controversial choice. It's India, after all. He'd done a good selling job on her, emphasising the palm trees and the white beaches, but maybe she'd have been happier going to Mauritius or the Seychelles, or even back to the Caribbean, where they went for their honeymoon.

But if he's honest with himself, it was him that wanted to go to India, a throwback to his younger days when he had notions of travelling.

He hasn't mentioned it to Karen, of course. What'd be the point in that? But God, if she doesn't enjoy it, his life won't be worth living.

He drinks his beer slowly, just looking out into the garden, trying to erase the worries, trying to acclimatise, until he turns at the familiar sound of Karen's heels click-clacking on the tiled floor.

She's walking towards him in a tight, dark blue dress that cuts off mid-thigh. Steve's not sure it's really the weather or the occasion for that particular dress, but he doesn't say anything. After all, as Karen often reminds him, what does he know about fashion?

'You look gorgeous,' he says smiling, slipping a hand around her back and drawing her towards him.

Karen winces, stiffening his embrace.

'God, me back's killing me after that,' she says sourly. 'Bloody torture chamber our bedroom is. Expect more for our money than that. What's the use of having a hotel if you can't sleep on the beds? No way are we going to last two weeks on that. And the bathroom. Now I've had a closer look at it.....'

Steve sometimes wishes Karen would draw breath a bit more, slow down, consider things.

When she's on her high horse there's absolutely no stopping her. She can go on and on and on, as if a problem's going to get solved by her talking it to death. Still, that's just her way.

He gently guides her away to a table in the garden near the pool.

Maybe a spot of dinner will cheer her up. Or at least let her forget about the room for a little while.

*

It might have been a dolphin, but then again she can't say for sure. It was only in the corner of her sight, and when she'd tried to look at it properly, stared right out where she'd caught the glimpse, there was nothing there but bronze-tinted waves.

But Sophie wants it to be a dolphin, so she decides that it is one.

Nobody else on the beach around her seems to have noticed anything. They're too busy lying on their fronts smoking and chatting or trying to juggle cloth balls or crashed out with books or personal stereos. But it doesn't matter that they didn't see it, that they can't verify it. In a way it makes it even better. It means it's her own private dolphin, a dolphin only she was meant to see.

Sophie smiles and keeps searching the sea. She gives up after a short while. No more dolphins. The sun is low, the crowd at the Sun Temple bar behind her is swelling, the trance music's easing up louder. Henrik will come soon to take her away from the beach. She doesn't mind too much. But for now, all she wants to do is smile into the warmth of the orange sun and tune in to her private dolphin vibes.

*

Iain wakes from an emergency afternoon crash-out to the sound of thumping. At first, he's not sure if it's in his head or not. He takes a few seconds to shake sleep off, then stands up and snaps on the light, a bare bulb hanging in the centre of the room. His room. Two hundred rupees a night for an earth-floored, mud-bricked, tin roof shed. He's stayed in palaces in Rajasthan for less. Well, maybe not quite less, and maybe not exactly palaces, but not far off it. It's the principle, though.

A wooden bed knocked up out of off-cuts, a pathetic mattress that's more like a thin duvet, a screened off area with a sink and a Western-style toilet, and that's about it. No fan. No window. No way is he staying here for long. Okay for a night or two, but that's it. And then there's the thumping to consider. He resolves to go room-hunting as soon as possible. Well, as soon as he's thought about it for a bit longer over a cold beer.

The room's attached to the side wall of the Vibe Bar, down at the sea front. The techno's thumping out as the bar gears up for the evening. A handful of customers sit inside the bar, which opens out onto a path running parallel to the sea. On the other side of the path, a square patch of rough ground with tables and chairs set between the palm trees, looking over the rocky shore. Six people are sitting down at the front, all facing the water as the sun sinks towards the sea.

Iain shuffles into the main body of the bar. The walls are crowded with painted day-glo images of elves, gods, spacemen, and something which Iain doesn't recognise. Maybe it's a dragon, he decides. A very badly-drawn psychedelic dragon.

A tiny Indian man in a smiley alien t-shirt swaggers up to Iain.

'You wan' somtheen? Mazic mus-roomsh?'

Iain blinks at him.

'Eh. No. Bit early for me. Got any beers at all? In this bar.'

Iain chokes back a giggle at what he's just said, knowing it sounds ridiculous but finding it stupidly funny anyway.

'Kinfisser, Kins?'

'What? Oh. Kingfisher, please. Rather than that second one. Definitely Kingfisher. Kingfisher's fine.'

'One Kinfisser?'

'Yep. One Kingfisher. Please.'

The man brings his beer and takes his money, which is more than Iain thinks it should be but he doesn't argue, not having experienced any other beer prices in Goa to measure it against.

He considers where to sit. Either in the shade of the bar itself, with the very pale junkie, the long-haired man slouched half-comatose in a corner, the fat girl with hundreds of rings in her eyebrows, and the two men who look like they're not taking the medication they're supposed to when they're released into the community. Or he can sit in the sunshine by the shore. Oooh, choices, choices, choices.

He takes his beer out to a spare seat facing the sea. He drags the dirty plastic chair up to a low wall which he uses as a table while he takes in his surroundings, trying to adjust to seeing so many Westerners - and so many weird ones - after a couple of months of hardly seeing any in the towns and villages of Northern India. Next to him a couple of older hippies with matching

beards and mirrored sunglasses are staring straight ahead, waiting for the nightly free entertainment to begin. The colourshow.

Iain settles back in his chair, takes a sip of Kingfisher from
the big, cool bottle, and digs out his precious Marlboro Lights,
bought in Bombay after weeks of Classic and Gold Flake and the
dreaded, rope-flavoured Four Square cigarettes.

The sun's now slipped very low in the sky, past a straggle of
thin clouds lying just above the horizon, and is about to dip itself into the water.

The bottom half of the sun turns a distinct deep crimson,
then changes shape, coming to a point at the bottom so it's almost as if light's being poured into the sea. Then lower and
lower, the sun oozing away until there's only a bright sliver left,
a glowing spaceship far out in the ocean. And then it's gone.

A stunning sunset, a peach of a sunset, one of the best he's
ever seen. Iain feels like applauding for a second, but reckons
it's not the cool thing to do. Just not the done thing in Anjuna,
although he's not really sure what *is*. He looks over at the two
hippies next to him, trying to pick up some clues. They're still
staring straight ahead, not moving.

Iain looks back out to sea. There's more?

The thin clouds above the point where the sun set suddenly
get brighter, as if the sun's about to rise again.

No way, Iain thinks. No way, not even in Goa. I don't care
how many drugs they've taken to believe they can make the sun
rise again, it's just not possible.

But the sun doesn't rise. Instead, the clouds turn from peach
to gold, slip to rose, then bleed to orange and a raging fire, as
the nearly-full moon cuts a bright white hole in the turquoise
sky overhead.

The sky fades to a deep grey-blue as the clouds lose their

glow, burning out to a blurred violet, musky purple, then merging into the dusk and the dull sea at the edge of the earth.

The whole show has taken the length of his beer. Iain glances over to the old hippies, seeking some indication as to what happens next. They haven't said a word in all his time there, perhaps twenty minutes or so.

Suddenly one of them looks at the other.

'Well, I suppose we'll call it a day, then,' he says, before they both break out in wrecked sniggers.

*

Jez is loving it, leaning back against the wall of the Sun Temple bar. The sixteen-stone, shaven-headed man-monster figure of Crash Mary is crouched next to him, wooden beads around his neck rattling as he nods to the music. The sun's long gone, the Sun Temple's raging, there's dancing on the beach and Jez feels euphoric.

'That French bird Sophie,' he says, pointing over at where she's sitting cross-legged on a seat off to the side, all serene and glowing with happiness, long, curled, honey blonde hair pulled back from her smiling face. 'She's definitely got to be one of the horniest girls ever, y'know what I mean? You don't get much more seriously beautiful than that, do you.'

'Eh?' Crash Mary grunts at him. 'Wouldn't let Nat hear you say that.'

'Yeah, whatever,' Jez sneers, then goes back to people-watching.

Nat's over there, dancing on the sand with Ricky, seeming happy enough. What she got the hump about earlier he can't work out for the life of him. Anyway, she's fine now, which makes for an easier life all round.

He leans back and takes a swig of warm beer. The vibe's

right, the girls are moving, the bottle's in his hand. Yeah, life could be worse.

*

Sophie's happy just to sit and watch too. Henrik came to the beach as promised, they had a couple of drinks, now he's gone up to Vagator with a couple of his friends, but he'll be back eventually to take her home. She's happy either way. Happy that she's got a couple of hours to herself, happy that he's coming back.

The dancers are having a good time. She can see it in their faces, all of them rapturous in the flickering light from the beach fires. Some of dancers are really going for it, some are just shuffling, bouncing, getting into it any way they feel. Sophie gets a kick out of them all, but doesn't need to join in just yet.

Nat and Ricky break off from dancing down on the sand and skip up the steps to the bar. Sophie sees them and smiles.

'Hi Sophe,' Nat says as she reaches Sophie's table. She doesn't know Sophie very well, but she likes her anyway. There's just something about her. Nat would expect girls who looked like Sophie to be dead vain, really uptight, but she's not.

'You're looking really amazing tonight,' Sophie says, happiness shining in her face.

'Yeah? Really?' Nat says, suddenly smiling, pleased but a bit flustered.

'You're glowing. It's like you have a bright aura around you. It's very beautiful.'

'Yeah? Aw, thanks, Sophie. That's really nice of you to say that. Really cheered me up, that has.'

Sophie just smiles, and Nat ambles over to where Jez is sitting against the wall. She slides down next to him, unable to stop grinning.

'You know what that Sophie just said to me?' she says. 'Said I was looking really beautiful. I mean, what a lovely girl. She didn't need to say that, but she did. Wasn't that, like, really nice? She's such a sweet girl, that Sophie.'

'Yeah,' Jez says, looking over at Sophie's exquisite profile. 'Need's her bleedin' eyes tested, but then nobody's perfect, are they. What? What?'

Sophie notices Nat scurrying back down the steps to the fire-lit beach. Probably decided she hasn't danced enough, she thinks. A nice girl. A good, pure heart. It's very important in a person. Sophie feels the warmth of the night, the vibration of the music, the careless joy of the people around her. She thinks about her dolphin, and the way Henrik's arms feel when they're wrapped around her. She smiles. Right at this moment, there's nobody in the world happier than Sophie.

*

'You alright? You alright, love?' Steve says, his voice coated in concern. He gives the toilet door a couple of tentative taps. 'Love?'

'I'll be out in a minute,' Karen rasps back at him. Steve gets back into bed and checks the digital travel alarm on the table beside him. 2.33 am.

After a little while the toilet flushes and, after some splashing noises from the sink, Karen emerges from the bathroom. She closes the door and walks slowly over to the bed.

'I think I'll leave the light on in there,' she says.

'You alright, love?'

'It's nothing. Just a bit of an upset stomach.'

'Upset? It sounds absolutely devastated. I could hear everything from in here.'

'Steve! Don't be so crude,' Karen says, and slaps Steve lightly on the arm, although he suspects she probably wanted to do it a lot harder. She's not happy. He can tell.

'I'm just saying, love. You should maybe take something for it. Don't want it to ruin your holiday.'

'Humph,' Karen says into her pillow. 'Ruined already.'

'What d'you mean?' Steve says hurriedly, immediately defensive, getting up on one elbow and looking down at Karen. Her eyes are closed.

'This bloody place,' she says. 'Worst bloody place I've ever stayed in.'

'Come on, that's a bit harsh isn't it? Anyway, thought you said you used to go caravanning with your parents in Norfolk. That couldn't exactly have been up to much.'

'I don't want to stay here.'

'But we've paid for here. We've been through all this. I've tried to get us upgraded or swapped to somewhere else. I've tried, but they can't do it.'

'I don't care. With the money we've paid, I don't expect to end up in a, a shit-hole like this, if you'll pardon my French.'

'But they told us to expect different standards. It's India.'

'And whose bloody idea was that?'

'What d'you mean, whose bloody idea? You wanted to come too, if I remember rightly. Anyway, this isn't a 'shit-hole'. It's perfectly adequate, it's....'

Maybe it's the term 'shit-hole' that triggers it, or maybe it's just the mysterious workings of the lower intestine. Whatever the reason, Karen suddenly leaps out of bed again and bolts for the toilet, barging through the door but careful to lock it behind her.

Five minutes later, after more echoed burbling and parps and gushes, Karen limps out of the toilet door.

'Must have been something you ate, love,' Steve says softly, holding out a hand to help her into bed.

'I think I've guessed that by now, thank you very bloody much,' Karen snaps at him. 'And I'll tell you what, I know exactly what it was. It was those bloody tiger prawns, that's what did it. It's all your bloody fault. You know what spicy food does to me, but you let me go ahead and eat them anyway.'

'But they weren't spicy. I tried them.'

'Well believe me, they feel very bloody spicy now.

Looking is free

'Are you sure you don't want me to stay with you?'

'For the hundredth time, Steve, no,' Karen says, her voice strained, trying to hide her face from the sunlight. 'I'm just going to lie here a while. See if a bit of rest doesn't sort me out. You go. No point you hanging about being miserable.'

Steve looks down at Karen curled under the single sheet on the bed. She must be exhausted, he thinks. Back and forth all night. Surprised there's anything left to come out.

'I could get them to send up some food at lunchtime. Yeah?'

'Food's the last bloody thing I want.'

'You should eat something. Got to keep your strength up, especially if your system's taken a knock.'

'Steve, for God's sake just leave. I can survive perfectly well here by myself, thank you very much. If I want food, I'll phone down for it.'

Steve reluctantly leaves Karen to her illness, and gets directions to the beach from a smiling man at reception whose lapel badge proclaims him to be Mr A K Bandodkar, Asst Mgr, Client Services.

A five minute walk, Mr Bandodkar assures him. Not far at all. Steve tells him that Karen's unwell and shouldn't be disturbed, but insists that if her condition gets worse the hotel should send someone down to the beach to get him.

Once he's happy that everything's under control, Steve walks out of the hotel compound and down a rutted asphalt road winding through dense palm trees. His stride slips into a slow, easy stroll as he adjusts to the heat.

He passes small restaurants and cafes serving breakfast - pancakes, muesli, curd, fruit - some with signs in Hebrew and Japanese as well as English. Only rarely does he see anything written in Hindi, but he hardly notices. He delights in the unfamiliarity of it all, the tidy little houses with brightly painted porches, the oddness of the old-fashioned Ambassador cars, the Tata trucks, the puttering black and yellow rickshaws, the smell of spicy cooking drifting on the dusty, late morning December air.

Soon, way ahead, he can make out the sea. The shimmering Indian Ocean. Or maybe it's the Arabian Sea. He must check later.

At the end of the road he cuts down beside one of the cafes and follows a rough path through widely-spaced palm trees. Cows loll in the shade. Thin dogs skulk out of his way as he nears them. The path becomes more defined, running parallel to the rocky shore, a few restaurants and bars on one side, alert Kashmiris at stalls on the other.

'You look my shop? Nice things. You want sarong, lungi, good bag I have, what you like.'

Steve stops, examining the first stall. A couple of collarless shirts, a row of cloth bags in dull stripes hanging from a bamboo pole at the front, large squares of cloth printed with gods and goddesses or abstract patterns, small brass figures, pipes and chillums.

'How much is that over there?' Steve asks, pointing to a large sarong with Sanskrit lettering on it.

'You like this? This is best quality. Feel, feel,' the Kashmiri says, putting the sarong into Steve's hands. 'Best quality. I make you good price.'

'How much?'

'How much you like to pay?'

'Depends how much you're offering it for.'

'Friend, for you I make special price. You are first customer for me today. You are good luck for me. I give you special price. Six hundred rupees only.'

'Six hundred?'

'Very good price. I make special for you. This your first time Goa?'

'Yes. Yes it is.'

'My friend, everywhere you see in Goa this type sarong. But not six hundred. People asking you seven hundred, eight hundred, one thousand rupees. Too much money they are asking. They are cheating, these people. I am giving you best price. Okay,' the man says, and starts folding up the sarong, handing it to Steve.

'Hang on, though. I don't think I've got much money on me,' Steve says, rooting around in the pocket of his shorts.

'How much you have?'

Steve counts it out, checking the unfamiliar notes twice.

'Seven hundred and forty,' he says finally. 'But I don't want to leave myself too short.'

'Okay, okay,' the man says. 'You give five hundred now, then one hundred after. Today, tomorrow, this is okay. Okay?'

'Are you sure?' Steve says, grinning in surprise. He hands over the money, three grimy hundreds and two newer, crisper ones with Gandhi's face peering out.

'This is no problem,' the man says, grinning, revealing a shiny gold tooth.

He claps Steve on the shoulder. Then he leans in closer.

'You want something smoke? Hassees? Good grass?'

'What? Drugs?' Steve says, taken aback, saying it too loudly.

'Shh,' the man says quietly, hushing him, pulling him nearer. 'Best quality. Good price.'

'Don't think so, mate,' Steve says with a firm, stern face.

'Listen friend, no problem,' the man says, 'good smoking, nice feeling, best quality.'

'Thanks but no thanks,' Steve says, giving the man a curt nod goodbye, then hurrying along the path towards the beach.

Other stall-holders try to grab his attention but he marches past them, past the Guru Bar, the Vibe Bar, more stalls, then up to the San Francisco restaurant. He jumps down some makeshift steps and suddenly he's on sand. The beach.

And not just any beach. Steve's never seen anything like it before. He can't help himself, he just stands and stares.

It's a forever of a beach, stretching maybe a mile or more down to a forested headland sticking out into the water. Light golden sand, gentle waves, clusters of palm trees with leaves rattling softly in the warm breeze, sounding for all the world like they're applauding the sea for being so cool.

And no people. Well, not no people. Some people, but hardly any. An absolute hero of a beach, with almost no people. And only three or four cows.

*

Iain's trying to be subtle about it. He's checking out Sophie, lying twenty yards away, and the best view he can get and still pretend he's reading is on his side, lying diagonally across his towel. He's not exactly what he'd describe as comfortable, but he's prepared to put up with it for a little while at least.

Mind you, he's aware that his back's continually facing the sun. He has visions of it becoming one big red blister if he stays like this for long, so he tries to enjoy looking at the girl while he can.

Great hair. Long and wild in curls and waves. Blonde, of course. In some places a darker, dirtier blonde. Natural blonde?

Who cares.

And her skin. Honey. Definitely honey. He's heard descriptions of a honey skin before, but never seen anything which matched it so perfectly. This was it, this was the standard by which all other honey-tone skins were set, the golden honey skin to beat all others.

And how well it suits those long, smooth-toned - oh my God - those legs. Legs legs legs legs legs.

And not just her legs. Her whole body. Gentle, curving muscles, taut, but without harsh definition. Covered by a layer of softness. Oh, and the full, rounded, pert....oh for fuck's sake!

Iain gives his face a mental slap.

Get a grip, for God's sake, McMillan. You can't let it get to you.

But it's been *so* long. Far, *far* too long without sex. I certainly didn't expect India to be a celebration of celibacy. I might as well have left my penis at home.

Two whole months in India, and not a hint of a peck on my cheek, never mind a cheek on my pecker.

Got to stop it getting to me. Don't think about it. Put it out of my mind. Forget about it.

Do what Gandhi did. Get into all that sanyasi stuff he was going on about in his autobiography, deny the evil onslaught of impure, destructive, soul-sapping sexual urges.

Or maybe I should just wank more.

Maybe that's the answer. A nifty juggle before breakfast, another midway through the afternoon - possibly during a break from the beach - then a sly chug before dinner. With another swifty before bedtime if the urges continue. That ought to just about keep a lid on it.

Oh bastard. She's started talking to someone now. A good-looking bloke. A bit pale, though. It can't be her boyfriend. It just can't be. Please, God, please. I know I don't believe in you, but please, don't do this to me.

*

'It'll just be for a minute. Just while I pop in for a dip.'

Sophie looks up at the man who's just spoken to her. He's a good man, she decides. She can tell these things. She can feel it from him.

'You want me to...?' she says slowly, her soft French vowels buffing the hard edges off the consonants.

'Oh, I'm sorry,' Steve says. 'I thought you were English. You look ... anyway. Um. Leave my things? Go swimming? You watch things? I come back, five minutes?'

He feels like he's half mimed it out. Sophie's smiling at him.

'Yes, of course, that would be absolutely okay,' she says.

Steve smiles back at her. He was right, she seems like a nice enough girl. Trustworthy. He didn't fancy leaving his stuff with some of the people he's walked past on the beach so far. Wouldn't trust them as far as.

He dumps his bag, towel and new sarong on the sand a few yards away from Sophie, kicks off his flip-flops, strips down to his trunks, and jogs to the cool, curling waves of the Indian Ocean. Or the Arabian Sea. He'll check later.

*

Good. He's pissed off for a swim. Don't go getting cramp, now.

Iain shuffles back into prime viewing position again. To hell with his back.

Oh no, she's standing up. Don't go! Don't go! What's she doing? Oh my God, she's bending over. Would you look at that! Who cares if medical science says you're supposed to bend your knees when you pick something up. The medical scientists obviously haven't seen this girl in action or they'd re-write their textbooks pretty damn sharpish. With pictures. *I'd* buy one. Oh for fuck's sake, what's *this*?

Iain's view is blocked by a young girl aged nine or ten, standing three feet away in his direct line of sight. A beach hawker from Karnataka.

'You like something?' she says in a sweet trilling voice, sitting down in the sand, her red and green sari crumpling beneath skinny legs.

'Yes, but I can't see it now. Sit somewhere else.'

'Yes? You like something? Plenty thing, good price. You like sarong?'

She starts laying out a pile of sarongs, silk scarves and shirts, then starts digging into a small cloth pouch, pulling out bangles, bracelets and ear-rings.

'No, nothing. I don't want anything,' Iain says quickly, waving his hands at her. 'What I want, what I *really* want, is for you to go away and leave me in peace.'

'Only looking,' the girl says. 'Looking is free.'

'No, no looking. Don't want looking. Don't want anything.'

Iain's annoyed that he's getting annoyed, but it's about the tenth time he's tried to get rid of one of the beach sellers.

'No looking?' she says, putting big, sad eyes on.

'No looking.'

Her face suddenly switches back to happy.

'You very white,' she says, pointing.

'I'm from Scotland. We're very, very white in Scotland. It's our national sport. Being pale whilst eating fried food.'

'Your first time Goa?' she says, remembering the script she's been taught.

'Yes,' he sighs. 'First time Goa. Look, I'd love to chat, I really would, but I'm a bit busy, so why don't you go and take your stuff over there a bit. '

The girl pauses, biting her lip.

'You give me little business? No good business today. No eating today. You give me fifty rupees business only. Something this,' she says, pulling a couple of brassy bangles from her cloth bag.

'No. No business,' Iain says firmly. 'Look, I've got five more months left in India. I can't go around buying things just because someone wants to sell me something. I buy when I want to, not when someone else wants me to. Okay?'

'Little business,' the girl pleads, pouting, putting her very best sad face on. 'Me very thirsty. Ten rupee business.'

'Oh, for God's sake,' Iain mutters, pulling a tattered ten rupee note from the pocket of his shorts. 'Okay, ten rupee business. Give me whatever you want, give me nothing if you like, but leave... me... alone.'

'Good business,' she says, smiling, taking the note and putting a bangle in Iain's hand. She stands up. 'You are good luck for me.'

The girl takes a couple of skinny strides towards a beach shack, then spins on her heel, grinning.

'You looking tomorrow?' she says.

'No. No looking tomorrow.'

'Maybe tomorrow?' she says, as if she hasn't heard him.

'Okay,' he sighs. 'Maybe. Maybe tomorrow.'

As soon as he's satisfied the girl's definitely gone, he looks back over towards Sophie.

Oh Christ, what's this!

Another man, lightly tanned and thin with longish, floppy brown hair, has walked into the no-man's land of beach between Iain and Sophie and started to set his things out, laying a frayed sarong down on the sand. Iain's view of Sophie is ruined.

Bring back the beach seller. All is forgiven. At least you could see past her a bit.

*

Jez counts out his money, adding up the mixed pile of pounds, US dollars and rupees. He thinks there should be more, but then again, Christmas was a bit heavy.

It was the coke that hit hardest, the couple of grammes he got from that geezer down in Baga. He knows he shouldn't have spent so much, but at least he had a white Christmas, even if Bing wouldn't have been too impressed.

He checks the cash again, then hides some of it in special places around the room. He decides to keep most of it on him, stuffed in various pockets. After all, you don't want to just leave money lying about. Can't trust no-one round here.

Nat's gone down to the beach with Sasha, but he doesn't fancy it. Maybe he'll take a wander down to the German Bakery, see what's happening, see if any of the crowd are there. Then again, it's usually full of Italian ponces, and he's not sure he can handle them today.

The money's bugging him. He locks the door and starts walking through the trees, dodging the cows crashed out in the shade, past an old, whitewashed church standing proudly in a clearing, then onto the road up towards the village. He needs to get more money. He owes Hassan just over a grand, but he's only got four hundred. Nat's bound to have some hidden away that he doesn't know about yet, and it shouldn't be a problem getting some advance-order cash, but still. It's going to be tight.

A plan, that's what he wants. Just needs to apply himself a bit. Stop being such a lazy bastard. Lots of money out there if you know where to look for it. The Italians have got it, the Germans have got it, the Japanese have got it. It's only fair that he should have some too. Even if it's some of theirs. After all, he's been behaving himself for the past few weeks.

Jez swaggers along in the rising heat of the day, a new scheme forming in his dreadlocked head.

*

The cool, clear water. Steve revels in it. He stays in longer than he'd meant to, swimming along for a hundred yards or more, stretching the tiredness out of his muscles. It's good to be active, get his body working, feel the blood pumping around his system. He swims into shore and starts walking back along the beach, invigorated.

When he gets to where the girl is, he's surprised to see that she's laid out all his things. His sarong's flat out, held down by his flip-flops at the bottom corners, his bag at the top, his t-shirt and shorts folded beside it. He'd been planning to go much further along the beach, find his own secluded space, before the temptation of the sea had beaten him. As it is, his sarong's only a few feet away from hers.

'Thank you,' he says as he walks up to her, smiling awkwardly, rubbing a hand through his short, wet hair.

'I didn't think you want to deal with all this when you are soaking wet,' Sophie says.

'That, that's brilliant. Thank you very much,' he says, a bit embarrassed, still standing there looking down at Sophie.

'It's nothing.' She smiles, dips her head, but then her blue-green eyes glance back up at Steve again. Something in the way she does it, something in the rich colour of her eyes, in her smile, in her voice, makes Steve's mind flip out for a second. He can't explain it. He doesn't know why it happens, but he finds it unsettling.

'That's very good English you've got,' he says, lying back on his sarong after brushing most of the water off his body with his hands, preparing to let the sun do the serious drying.

'Thank you,' she says, with a hint of an 's' in the 'th', a big enough hint to make whatever happened to Steve's mind happen again.

Very unsettling indeed.

'Where you from?'

'Bordeaux,' she says. 'France.'

'Ah. Wine country. Bordeaux, I mean,' he says hurriedly. 'Well, I suppose all of France is really when it comes down to it. But Bordeaux. One of the best.'

The words are just spilling out of him, trying to cover up his unease.

'I don't know,' Sophie says with a pout and a half shrug. 'I don't drink wine. Straight whisky and beer chasers, that's me.'

'Really?'

'No,' she says with an easy, natural laugh. 'Not really. I like wine, sure. I am only joking with you.'

And there it was again. The spark, the snap, the chord, the shift inside him. Steve laughs, a little nervously, although he can't figure out what's causing the nerves.

'Of course,' he says. 'Sorry.'

'And you? You are from England?'

'Yes, north west. Cumbria. Place called Workington.'

'Is it very beautiful there?'

'Beautiful? Well, I don't know about beautiful. Yeah, there's some nice hills and that. Then a bit further south there's the Lake District. Lots of lakes and mountains and forests. I suppose it can be pretty beautiful.'

'Just pretty beautiful?' Sophie says, smiling.

Steve laughs, a short, self-conscious chuckle.

'Beautiful, then. Definitely beautiful. That's what everybody says, anyway.'

'But you do not think so?' Sophie says. Steve catches a mild note of concern in her voice.

'I dunno,' he says. 'Sometimes it all looks like it's been planted. You know, landscaped. Trees, hills, water, all in the right position, like it's a big garden or something. And there's loads of tacky tourist shops and tearooms all over the place as well. It's all a bit too ordered, I suppose. All very organised. The things that I find beautiful, they tend to be a bit more raw. Do you know what I mean? I'm not very good at explaining myself sometimes. The Lake District seems like it's been neatly put together. Does any of this make any sense?'

'Of course. We do not all find the same things beautiful. Just because other people find a thing beautiful, does not mean that you will find it so. For you, it is not beautiful. That is okay.'

'You're right, you're dead right,' Steve says, nodding, grinning. 'I mean, you hear about 'the eye of the beholder' and all that, but you don't really think about it. If loads of people are saying something's beautiful, but you don't think so, then you might wonder, well, maybe it's just me, maybe I'm not looking at it properly, maybe it really is beautiful, so in the end you just go along with the rest.'

'And that is what you do? Go along with the rest?' Sophie says, but it doesn't sound to Steve as if she's accusing him of anything. She just seems interested. Raptly interested, like she's focused and fascinated, hungry for every word, every detail.

'Christ, this is a bit full-on, isn't it?' he says, but smiles. 'Only just sat down, and I'm getting interrogated.'

'I'm sorry,' Sophie says. 'You think I am rude.'

'No, no, it's not that,' Steve says, worried he's offended her. 'It's just not the sort of conversation you expect when you go to the beach. Anyway, to answer your question, I don't want you to think I'm like a sheep or anything. But I mean, take things like classical music or modern art. You get people who know far more about these things than I do. So if they're saying this composer or that artist is a genius, who am I to say otherwise? It's not like I just go along with the rest all the time. It's just maybe that sometimes I don't know enough about something so I bow to their better judgement.'

Sophie smiles.

'I do not think you need a diploma to judge whether something is beautiful or not,' she says.

Which is when it hits Steve that Sophie's beautiful. He doesn't understand why he didn't notice it right away. She's completely, utterly beautiful.

It's not just the prettiness, the obvious physical aspects. There's something more to her, something which intensifies her, making her one of the most incredible girls he's ever seen.

Hang on, he says to himself. What the hell am I thinking that for? I'm a married man, for God's sake. I don't go around ogling other women. Karen's quite enough for me, thank you very much.

But then again. He decides that he's not 'ogling' this girl. That would make it sound seedy, furtive, as if he's some dirty old man getting his kicks. That's not what he's doing, not by any means.

He searches for a word or a phrase, something that more accurately reflects the way he's feeling.

Appreciating her, is the nearest he can find, but it still doesn't sound right.

His conscience gnaws at him. He knows what he should do, what Karen - poor, ill Karen - would want him to do.

He weighs it up.

Let's face it, would Karen prefer him to be lying somewhere on his own? Or would she think it was perfectly fine for him to be lying next to - and talking to - a beautiful French girl?

'So,' he says. 'How long have you been in Goa?'

*

The Doc's on the verandah, rocking backwards and forwards in his chair. His eyes are dull, almost hidden in the shadows of his wide-brimmed hat. He's watching the slow, uncomplicated life of Goa as it passes by on the road at the end of the garden.

Goddamn sonofabitch rat-ass bastards. Ain't got no soul. Ain't one o' them worth a hair of Mountain Man Mannix, Swiss Dave, Screamin' Joe Petrowski, sweet Amber Moonchild, Humper, Lazy Dee, wild-eyed Violet Rosenberg, Juju Lord, Montana Slim. Not one Goddamn hair. They was the cats. They was the high-tailed nevergone cats who dug what was happening. And just the sweetest vibe, like the pristine wash of a spirit stream on the highest peaks of Shang-ri-la.

Xavier Rodrigues drives up to the garden gate on his new motorbike, a gleaming red Royal Enfield 500cc he's just bought at a heavy discount from a beer and spirits supplier who owed him money.

He notices the Doc sitting in the shade of the verandah as he kicks the bike back on its stand. He'd prefer to avoid talking to him if possible. He's had a long, hard day sorting out the accounts at his hotel, firing a thieving waiter, paying backhanders to the phone company to get more lines put in, and forcibly ejecting a tourist who was too blatant about smoking opium on his balcony. He can't be bothered humouring the Doc, not today.

The mad old man.

There he is. Cyril's boy. Back from the fishing. A man's life, a hard life, a life you know you've lived. Honesty and purity, man and the elements, nature as she's meant to be, not dressed up like some cheap whore the way them rat-ass bastards got her.

There he is, young and strong, following on his daddy's work, reaping the sea come rain or storm.

Xavier plods up the wooden steps to the verandah, keeping his head down, trying to get into the house without having to acknowledge the Doc's presence.

'Proud of a life,' the Doc says loudly, his old voice croaking and raspy. 'Ain't nothing finer a man got to do. Taking the fruits by the strength of your own. You're a real gone cat, boy. Real gone cat.'

Xavier stares at the Doc with open contempt, then makes for the cool sanity of the house.

*

IAIN McMILLAN'S GREAT HINDUSTAN ADVENTURE

Sunday 27th December '98, Anjuna, Goa

A less than superb day on the beach, unless you count having a pink back as some kind of worthwhile achievement. Everything was going so well until this guy came and sat down right between me and this extraordinary girl I was eyeing up. He couldn't have got more in the way if he'd set up a Punch and Judy show. I hardly got a peek at her from then on.

Okay, I did try sliding up the sand on my towel, inch by inch, but I stopped before I could get a better vantage point because I suddenly realised it was a bit creepy. They've probably got laws against it. The Stalking Incredibly Subtly Act 1952. The Sad Scottish Perv on the Beach Act 1975.

I need sex. It's not funny. This is getting beyond urgent.

And if I can't have sex, at the very least I need to go out and have some five-star, unbridled, stupidly-happy fun. I realised today that I haven't been laughing an awful lot recently. The last time I can remember having a decent, full-throated chuckle was when I was bhang-lassi'd out of my gourd in Jaisalmer listening to the World Service. The farming programme, I think it was.

So tonight I'm going to hit the bars and see what's happening. It'd be nice to bump into this girl too, of course, although I probably don't stand a chance. She left the beach with a bloke she was talking to, a fit, good-looking bastard with short, clean hair, who smiles a lot and looks like he'll live forever.

They went off to sit at a table in one of the beach shacks, and after half an hour or so I went over there too. But there were only four tables and they were all taken, so I just kept walking and went to another place further down the beach. The gorgeous girl and her chum were both laughing at something as I passed. Probably at my withered, twisted self-esteem hanging out my arse.

CHAPTER FOUR

Most thrilling chilled

'And this is like me, right, this beer,' Jez says, holding up the bottle of Kingfisher that BJ's just bought him. 'Exactly what it says on the label. "Most Thrilling Chilled". And that's me, right, innit, because I'm at me most thrilling when I'm, like, completely chilled out. Know what I mean?'

'No,' Crash Mary says, his round face benign and blank. He turns to BJ. 'You think Jez is thrilling?'

'What you talking about?' BJ says, confused. He hasn't been paying attention.

'Is Jez - him there,' Crash Mary says, pointing an unnecessary finger at Jez, who's grinning from under his dirty blond dreads. 'Is he, in any way you can think of, actually thrilling?'

'What? Like, now?'

'Anytime. But especially when he's chilled.'

'Definitely not when he's chilled.'

'Exactly,' Crash Mary says, and turns back to Jez. 'Thought so. You're talking ballocks again.'

'Yeah, but I only do it to drown out you two boring bastards.'

'We're deliberately trying to bore you so you'll piss off,' BJ says with a sneer, bottle raised to his lips.

'Yeah, yeah, yeah, and the rest,' Jez says, but he's annoyed that he can't think of a decent comeback.

They're in the Vibe Bar, hunched up on a concrete bench beside a long, shabby, battered wooden table. Sunset's gone, the music's ambient, and the Ket-heads are slouched in the corner staring at their feet.

Jez is relatively happy. Advance sales are going well. He's been round a couple of Japanese guys, three Germans, a Norwegian, two Italian couples and a Dutch trancehead. They're just people he's bumped into or knows through the scene, but he's sold to them all before and they know he'll deliver. At a price, of course. He hasn't even started on the English yet, the bigger market. They can wait until tomorrow.

He can't be bothered doing any more of his salesman lark tonight, though. He could easily pop up to Pandora's, get a few more orders in, but he's taken about two hundred quid's worth of deals, all cash in advance, and there's no point spoiling a good evening with business. After all, he didn't come to Goa to work his arse off. He just wants to sit and chill, drink some more beer.

Mind you, he doesn't feel right carrying so much money on him. He's still got the cash he took from his room, as well as the wad from the foreigners. Maybe he should hide it after all.

He peels himself off the bench and heads for the door.

'Back in a minute,' he says to Crash Mary and BJ. 'Got to get something.'

He heads out into the gloom, unconsciously tapping the hidden pocket in his trousers as he walks, making sure the wad of notes is still there.

His eyes struggle to adjust to the dark after the Vibe's striplit glare. As he tries to make out exposed roots and sleeping cows on the path, he goes through the figures in his head. Another ten to fifteen decent sized orders and he should have enough cash to pay Hassan. Everything after that will be pure profit. His mood soars, and a swagger returns to his step. As he passes an unlit house, two torches snap on and shine in his face.

'What the fuck's...'

Hands grab him, shoving him against the wall.

'Police check,' a deep, serious voice barks. Jez can just make out uniforms and peaked caps. Panic rises in his throat.

'Show what is in your pockets,' the voice says.

Play it cool, Jez thinks. Play for time. Think of a way out of this.

'Which pockets, man? I got loads of pockets, me. On me combats. Look, they're everywhere.' He does a 360 degree turn, talking all the time. 'Got so many pockets, don't know what to do with them. Don't remember what I've got in 'em half the time.'

'Stop playing with us,' the voice says. Jez can't make out their faces in the dark. 'This one.'

The policeman taps Jez's right thigh with his stick, the infamous bamboo lathi used to keep order and dish out punishment.

'Nothing in there, I don't think,' Jez says, reaching down to unbutton the pocket. 'At least, don't remember putting nothing in there, which doesn't mean to say I haven't, because you forget sometimes, don't you. And there I go, look. Forgotten I'd put some money in there. Silly me.'

'Give, give,' the policeman says, snapping his fingers, snatching the money from Jez. It's some of the cash from tonight's advance orders, all in rupees, a thick wad of it.

'This is much money,' the voice says as he counts the notes roughly. He points the torch back into Jez's eyes. 'Why you are carrying so much money?'

'Don't trust banks, do I,' Jez says, grinning into the beam, trying to appear confident. 'Banks get robbed, don't they. Can't trust anybody these days.'

'This is too much money for carrying. You are lying to us.'

The policeman orders the other officer to search the rest of Jez's pockets. Jez tenses. He's got half a dozen E's in his back pocket, left over from the speedy batch he got from Hassan. But the officer goes for the pocket on his left thigh instead. He undoes the buttons, puts his hand inside, but doesn't find anything. He then moves up, sticking his hand in the left hip pocket, just as Jez remembers.

'Charas,' the policeman says, bringing out a stubby finger of dark brown hash covered in cellophane. Jez's nerves start juddering.

The first policeman takes the drug, examines it.

'This is tola of hashish,' he says. 'This is very big problem for you, very serious. Ten years jail time.'

'Come on,' Jez says, beginning to really sweat now, sinking into a defeated slouch. 'Just a little bit of hash. Look, a friend gave it to me. I tried it, didn't like it. I was going to throw it away anyway, but I forgot. To be honest, you're doing me a favour taking it off my hands.'

'This is very serious,' the policeman says again, his voice sharpening. 'We are arresting you for this.'

'Nah, nah, look,' Jez says, shaking, heart in his mouth, waving his hands in front of him. 'Look, tell you what, you just keep the money. There's a few thousand there. Take it. Split it. Call it a fine or something. I know I did wrong, but there you go, that's my punishment.'

The policeman laughs, a sour, derisive laugh that Jez doesn't like the sound of at all.

'This is big crime,' the other policeman says.

'Ten years prison time, one lakh rupees fine. One hundred thousand rupees,' the first officer, the boss, says. 'One tola, very serious.'

'But that's all I've got,' Jez says, whining, pointing to the money.

'It is not enough,' the boss says, putting the money in his pocket anyway. 'You are coming to police station.'

The second policeman grabs Jez's arm and pulls him.

Okay, time for serious bargaining. The rupees didn't work,

and the E's are still in his pocket undiscovered. So far. Time to move up a gear.

'Hang on, hang on,' Jez says. 'I've just remembered, I've got some more.'

He reaches inside his trousers quickly, digging his hand into the secret pocket, grabbing some notes.

'Look. Look,' he says, fanning the notes, glancing at them. 'English pounds. Good exchange rate. Seventy rupees to the pound, they are. Seventy. This must be, what, maybe ten thousand rupees worth there.'

He holds the money out towards the first policeman, the voice. The policeman takes it and starts flicking through the notes.

'I mean,' Jez says, 'you don't want to spend your night filling out forms, all that paperwork and everything. Just a waste of your time, that is. Much better for us all if I just pay a fine. I mean you can't say fairer than that, can you.'

The first policeman counts the money again, then says something to his sidekick in Hindi. The other officer leans forward and stuffs his hand down the front of Jez's trousers, searching for the hidden pocket.

'Oi!' Jez says, but he can see the man is serious and doesn't fight him.

The policeman retrieves the rest of the money. At a bark, he hands it over. The senior officer counts it quickly.

'This will pay fine,' he says, his voice set and final, arrogantly satisfied.

'Ah, no way, man. No way,' Jez says, getting stroppy despite his fear. 'That's a lot, that is. That's about forty thousand roopsworth you've got there. Nearly half a bleedin' lakh. That's way over a fine, that is. Way too much. Tell you what, we'll split it. Fifty fifty. Twenty thousand for you, and leave the same for me.'

'If you cannot pay the fine, you must be arrested,' the officer says, his voice low and threatening. 'And then we can search you more carefully in a cell. Maybe we can find something else.'

Jez thinks fast, about sitting in Aguada jail awaiting trial for a couple of years, about the undiscovered E's in his pocket, about the money he's got stashed back in the room, about all the potential trouble.

'Fine,' he says, his voice sullen. 'Take it. It's yours.'

He's shaking, from nerves, from anger, from frustration and helplessness.

The policeman pockets the money and they start to move off. Then, as an afterthought, the sidekick turns around and cracks his lathi across the back of Jez's legs, the blow forcing him to his knees with a sharp cry.

The two policeman disappear in the dark, laughing, joking to one another in Hindi. Jez wants to go after them, kill them, get his own back, get his money back. He controls the rage. He knows when to stay down.

*

Steve feels guilty. Or rather, he thinks he feels guilty, but he's not sure if he's feeling true, deep-down guilt, or whether he just feels bad because he should feel guilty and doesn't. He doesn't believe he's done anything really, seriously wrong. But then, maybe the guilt's not about that at all. Maybe it's about something else.

'All I'm saying is you should have some consideration for others,' Karen says. She's sitting on the edge of the bed wearing tight white shorts and a blue t-shirt with the Chanel logo on the front. 'Me stuck in here all day with you off gallivanting around.'

'You said for me to go. You forced me out, more or less,' says Steve, aggrieved.

'That's not the point,' Karen snaps. 'The point is that I've been lying here for seven hours while you've been off enjoying yourself, not giving a damn for how I'm feeling. Seven hours, Steven.'

'More like six hours.'

'More like seven, you mean,' she says back sharply. 'What if I took a turn for the worse? Where would you have been then?'

'But you're feeling a bit better now, aren't you love,' Steve says, trying to sound reassuring.

'But I might not have been, that's what I'm saying.'

'Come on, love,' Steve says softly. 'Let's go down and get a bit of dinner, eh? You've got to eat. Even if it's just a bit of rice or something. Got to keep your strength up. Come on.'

'Yeah, maybe,' she says, quietening, calming down again, the short storm blowing itself out. 'Might do me a bit of good.'

She gets up from the bed, walks past Steve to the door and opens it. Steve follows, clicking the light out, making double sure the door's locked, then pocketing the key.

They walk along the bleak, bright corridor, Karen's slingbacks clip-clopping in front of Steve. Just before they get to the stairs, she stops.

'Ooh, hang on,' she says. 'Key. Quick, the key, the key!'

She grabs it from Steve's hand and retreats double speed towards their room. With one fluid swish she unlocks the door, then slams it behind her.

Steve stands looking down the empty corridor. He sighs, and his head drops as he troops back to the room. Guilty? Why on earth should he feel guilty?

*

Iain's sitting alone at a table in the Vibe Bar, trying to read a battered copy of 'Red Earth and Pouring Rain' by Vikram Chandra.

He's almost managing it, winning the battle against the dim lights and trance music, when he suddenly becomes aware of a figure standing over him.

He looks up to find it's the floppy-haired man from the beach, the one who got in his way.

'Enjoy the view today, did we?' the man says in an expensive English accent.

'Sorry, what?' Iain says, confused.

'Oh, I do beg your pardon,' the man says politely, but with a grin. 'I was under the impression that you kept trying to look past me so you could peek at that girl's breasts.'

Iain splutters an embarrassed laugh.

'Was it that obvious?'

'Only because it's exactly what I do every day too. She always goes to the same place, you see. So do I. Except you were lying there today, so I had to go a little nearer. Too near, actually. Meant I couldn't look at her directly, because she'd probably notice and become uncomfortable. And that would spoil everything.'

'Absolutely,' Iain says. 'Sorry about nicking your spot, then. I didn't realise.'

'May I sit down?'

'Absolutely. I'm Iain, by the way,' he says, as the other man pulls up a chair.

'Barney.'

Iain catches the barman's attention and orders a couple of beers.

'So what do you know about that girl, then,' he says, turning back to Barney. 'The one on the beach.'

'Very little. I haven't talked to her as such. I've just been indulging in simple adoration from afar. In fact, I was delighted to discover you doing the same thing. Because for a while I thought you were trying to check me out.'

'Oh God, no. Nothing like that. I'm not, like, gay or anything. Not that there's anything wrong with it, of course,' he says quickly. 'I mean, some of my best friends have been ... well, maybe not strictly best friends. People I was friendly with. Acquaintances, really. Fuck it, I hardly knew them at all.'

Barney laughs, a deep, throaty chuckle.

'So you're quite taken with her, I trust,' he says.

'The girl on the beach? Very pretty. But to be honest with you I don't care all that much,' Iain lies. 'You saw her boyfriend. Fit bloke with short hair. There's no point lusting after someone else's girlfriend. It's a total waste of time and emotional energy.'

'Yyeeeess,' Barney says, drawling the word out, infusing it with uncertainty. 'Well, I can sympathise to an extent. But that's not her boyfriend.'

'No? Right,' Iain says, clapping his hands together. 'In that case, I do care. You sure he's not her boyfriend?'

'Almost positive. Never seen him before. Seen her many times, but not him. And you'll have noticed how very pale he was. Compared to her delicious tan.'

'Delicious. That's the word.'

'Well? Doesn't that tell you something?'

'He's not her boyfriend,' Iain says brightly.

'Exactly. As far as I can gather, they just met.'

'Excellent.'

'Yyeeess. Her boyfriend's completely different. Tall, blonde, muscular, with eyes so piercingly blue they could stab you in the kidneys from twenty paces. Like a Norse God, I believe the phrase goes.'

'Bastard.'

'That's pretty mild compared to what you'll say once you see him.'

*

Steve is bored and restless. Karen insisted he go down to eat dinner by himself, since she wasn't too keen on him hanging around the room listening to her explosive motions.

He'd refused at first, knowing he'd only be in for more ear-ache later for leaving her all by herself, even if it was at her insistence, which she'd no doubt conveniently forget. But he gave in eventually.

Now, downstairs in the hotel restaurant, he's bored and restless and in the company of the Fat Family from Macclesfield.

The expense-fiddling sales director from the airport coach turned out to be Arthur Matlock, owner of a small private car hire firm and proud of it. He doesn't speak very often, most of the communication in the family conducted instead through Mrs Matlock, Maureen, a busy, talkative woman who'd more or less dragged Steve to their table when she saw he was sitting alone.

Also at the table out in the middle of the garden, Kim and Angela Matlock, 24 and 21 year old sisters, and Clive, Kim's Welsh boyfriend, the tattooed, crop-haired, potential petty criminal. Or apprentice plumber, as it turns out. Now that they're all sitting together, Steve can clearly see the strong family resemblance. Fat is the predominant characteristic. Even Clive, the boyfriend, looks like the Matlocks in a roly, bloated way.

Barely seconds after the introductions and small-talk, Steve regrets joining them. This, he says to himself, is not going to be a fun night. He almost wishes he had Goa Gut too. When the food arrives, he realises they're the sort of family who don't talk while they eat. And they like to eat a lot. Jaws grind. Time drags.

'So, your first time in Goa then, love?' Maureen says to Steve, breaking the silence once the small team of waiters has collected the empty plates.

'Yeah, first time. You?' He's still moored in tedium and isn't really interested in sailing into a conversation with them.

'Yes,' Maureen says. 'Thought we'd try something a bit different. We like to go away every winter, business permitting, don't we Arthur. Last year it was Tenerife, the year before that was Tenerife, and the year before that was Tenerife. Oh, it must be six years we've been going to Tenerife. Or is it seven? No, I'm lying. We first went to Tenerife the year Frances got married to that nice young fella from Altringham, the butcher's son. Remember that, Kim? So that'd make it six years, because they were together five years, and he only, you know, went off last year. So we thought about Tenerife again for this year, but we thought, no, let's try something a bit different. Not that we don't love Tenerife. We do. It's just that, what with the kids growing up a bit now, we thought maybe we should see a bit more of the world. Kim suggested Lanzarote, didn't you Kim, but I've heard it's a bit common. You've heard that, haven't you Angela?'

Angela grunts.

'Yes,' Maureen says. 'So I saw this brochure in the shop, and it was the same company we always go with, so I thought, you know, they've got their standards. So we looked at the brochure and we finally decided we'd come here, just for somewhere a bit different.'

'Well, it certainly is a bit different,' Steve says, wondering if he's been with them for a polite enough length of time that he can now make his excuses and leave.

'I'll say,' Maureen says. 'Very different if you ask me, in't it

Arthur. I were just saying that earlier, weren't I? About how different it is.'

The older couple who were sitting a few seats in front of Steve and Karen on the coach pass the table, the tall, skinny man with the beard and the self-assertive wife.

'Oh look, there's the Robinsons. Coo-ee,' Maureen calls, waving at them even though they're only a few feet away. 'Enjoying ourselves, are we?'

Mr Robinson shakes his head. Mrs Robinson looks down at the ground.

'We're going home t'morra,' Mr Robinson says in a broad Northumbrian accent. 'It's the cows. Beryl doesn't like the cows. Never has done. That's why we had to move to Leeds.'

Mrs Robinson looks up shyly, tries a brave smile, then shakes her head. They both walk away through the tables in the garden, back to the safety of indoors. Steve watches them trudge all the way to reception.

'Still bloody starving after that,' Clive says, picking at his teeth with his nails. 'Need to have a kebab later, most likely.'

'Don't be such a pig,' Kim says, her voice pinched and acidic. 'Anyways, you're not going to find a kebab shop round here.'

'Rubbish, woman. Hundreds of them, probably. Bound to be. It's bloody India, innit? Kebab shops everywhere.'

'I think she's right, you know,' Steve says, not sure why he's bothering. 'I don't think the Indians are too big on kebab shops, not in Goa anyway.'

'Rubbish, man. My local one in Swansea, the Istanbul Palace, packed with Indians it is.'

There's a pause.

'You sure they're not Turks?' Steve says warily.

'Same bloody difference, innit?' Clive says. 'All bloody Indians, aren't they? Doesn't matter what their religion is, Turk or whatever. Hundreds of kebab shops, there'll be.'

Steve leaves as the table orders more lager, saying he's off to check on Karen. Maureen issues sympathetic noises.

He means to do it, he really does, but when he gets to the bottom of the stairs he has a flash of her giving him a hard time for leaving her helpless while he's off lording it up in the restaurant.

Might as well get hung for a sheep as for a lamb, he says to himself. Beer. He'll have a couple of beers. But not with the Fat Family.

And then, as he heads back towards the bar, he finds himself drawn to the darkness on the other side of the compound walls. Out there in the gloom, in the heavy, muggy night, India is waiting. He changes direction and walks straight out of the main gates and into the unknown.

CHAPTER FIVE

A sign

Barney and Iain sip warm beers in the Pandora Cafe, the late-night, open-air drinking den a short, torch-lit stroll along the road to Vagator. The bar's half empty, the hard-core crowd yet to show.

In-between chatting with Barney, Iain's been eyeing up a short girl with brown dreads. She's pretty, but not intimidatingly so. He thinks he might be in with a chance, because she doesn't seem to be with anyone - well, no-one obvious. And, if he's being completely honest with himself, she's on the plain side of pretty. Okay, pretty plain. And, hopefully, desperate.

'We should go and sit over there,' Iain says, nodding towards a table near the girl. 'We're a bit out on a limb here. Too far away from the action. You know, just in case there's some mingling potential.'

'I'm not sure I'm up to mingling,' Barney says, stifling a yawn. 'The night has taken its toll.'

They've had seven or eight beers by now, and although Iain's enjoying Barney's company he feels there's something missing. Something with breasts.

'I'm not saying we actually have to mingle,' he says. 'Just having the potential of mingling is fine. Or at least be within touching distance of a girl. Honestly, the mingling aspect in itself isn't important.'

'But won't that girl you've been staring at find it a bit spooky if we suddenly go over and sit next to her?'

'Not next to her. Just near her,' Iain says, getting defensive. 'Anyway, I wasn't staring.'

'Glancing, then.'

'Okay, I'll admit the glancing. But I wasn't staring. I don't do the 'stare' thing. Staring's strictly for psychos. And I may have been on the road for three unbearably, outrageously frustrating months, but I'm not ready to give up my sanity just yet. Unless it's a condition of some girl agreeing to juggle my knackers, of course. In those circumstances I'd willingly admit to hearing voices telling me I'm the bastard lovechild of Napoleon and Shirley Bassey.'

Barney laughs, then cuts off when he notices Sophie walk into the bar.

'Venus alert,' he says softly.

Iain spins around in his seat so he can see her, banging his knee on the metal table leg. He yelps, rubs the sore spot and quickly tries to regain some outward appearance of cool. And there she is, walking slowly in a lazy hip-sway up to the bar. Iain gawps.

My God. Is it possible she's managed to become even better looking? Is that actually humanly possible?

Iain realises he's blatantly staring and stops himself. Then, losing a half-hearted battle against his weak will, he finds his eyes drawn to her bare midriff.

The most perfect bellybutton ever. A perfect soft curve into it, the stomach muscles not too toned, but not a trace of flab either.

The bare midriff. The killer. Nothing sexier on the right kind of girl. A cropped top, silk hipster hippy trousers, and a bare, honey-gold midriff. Perfect.

The boys turn to look at each other.

Barney's face is blank.

'Looking a bit rough tonight, if you ask me,' he says, then beats Iain to the guffaw.

*

Just a couple of beers. A couple of beers, a break from both the Fat Family and the prospect of Karen's sharp tongue, and then back to the hotel. That's the plan anyway.

Steve takes another sip of his lukewarm Kings beer. He's sitting in a small empty cafe near the crossroads, not far from the hotel entrance. He's trying to relax, trying not to think, hoping the beers will loosen him up and take the edge off the day. But no matter what he does, his mind keeps churning.

What a day. What a very strange day. The strangest of days. The strangest of feelings.

Steve finishes his drink and pays the sleepy young waiter. A walk's what he needs. Just a short stroll to clear his head.

He wanders down to the crossroads. A few shops and restaurants are still open, naked strip-lights trying to draw in the late-night trickle of passing business.

The Pandora Cafe, she said she was going to later. She'd mentioned it unprompted. He hadn't asked.

He shouldn't go. He shouldn't even think of going.

'Where's the Pandora Cafe?' he asks the group of young Indian men lounging on cheap motorbikes and scooters by the side of the road.

'Pandora?' one of them says, springing up. 'Right-side, right-side,' he said, gesturing with his arm towards Vagator. 'I take?'

'What? On your bike?'

'Bike okay,' he says, kicking the motor into life. 'Sit, sit.'

Steve gets on the back, suddenly feeling nervous. He shouldn't be doing this. He grabs the metal bar behind the seat and they set off. A couple of minutes along a dark road and they're there.

'Fifty rupees,' the young man says.

Steve gives him the money, not even bothering to haggle.

64   Rae Stewart

The man roars off, leaving Steve hesitating outside Pandora's, his mind fluttering.

He shouldn't go in. He should just turn right around and go back to the hotel. After all, it's getting late. Karen will be wondering where he is. Maybe she's taken a turn for the worse. Maybe she needs him.

He takes a deep breath and walks in. Techno pulses out from the speakers, but he doesn't find it unbearable.

Druggies, Steve thinks, examining the people scattered around the tables and benches. He can smell the dark, spicy tang of hash-smoke hanging in the air. A bunch of wasters and hippies and God knows what else, probably all off their faces.

And then he sees her, standing beside a table near the bar talking to another girl. She's in profile, looking more beautiful than ever. His chest aches as she laughs at something her friend says.

He sits at an empty table near the entrance and tries to unjam his malfunctioning mind.

*

Jez has stopped shaking. He's sharing a smoke with Crash Mary at a table towards the edge of the Pandora Cafe. Manali grass. Sweet and mellow. A joyful, sparkling high that's better than life. Crash Mary always maintained that it wasn't better than life, that it just made life better. But that's Crash Mary for you.

Crash Mary slips the joint back to Jez. He doesn't bother trying to hide it. This is Pandora's, after all. If you can't do it here, where can you do it?

'Hear about Loco,' Crash Mary says. 'The geezer what organises the parties?'

'What about him?'

'Been stung three times, all for the same party, the New Year one. First the cops from Anjuna come and want their slice. Then another lot comes from Mapusa asking for more, and he doesn't want to pay it but he does anyway, you know him, anything for a quiet life. And then a couple of them come up from bleeding Panjim wanting dosh. And Loco's saying, fuck this, I've already paid me bribes twice, and he tries to tough it out. But they're saying, nah, different office, mate. Head office. This is for the high-ups. Fuck all he could do about it. Had to pay, didn't he. More than a hundred thousand roops he's out of pocket. A hundred bleeding grand.'

'Bastards,' Jez says, taking a long hit on the joint. 'They're getting fucking greedy, I'm telling you.'

He hasn't told Crash Mary about being turned over. He hasn't told anyone, not even Nat. For a start there's the embarrassment and the shame. After all, getting stung by the cops is what you expect with tourists and two-week hippies, not long-termers like him. And then there's the business aspect as well. It's not a good move to let your customers know you've got no cash. Especially when they've given you lots of it.

'Carries on like this,' Crash Mary says, 'who's gonna put on the parties? Who's going to bleedin' come here if the cops is gonna start getting heavy with everyone?'

'It's just fucking stupid,' Jez says. 'It's Goa, for Christ's sake. If there's no parties and no drugs, then Goa's got no fucking point. Cops'll kill this place if they're not careful. People got to take a stand on this. Tell the cops where to go. Seriously, them pigs try anything with me, I'll take them to the fucking cleaners.'

Jez's mind fills with visions of him taking on the two cops. Should've gone for the big one first, the boss. A kick to the crotch, a jab in the eyes. Then the other one, the one with the stick. Heel of the hand to the bridge of the nose. A stamp on the knee, a knife to the back.

Yeah, he should've left them there eating fucking dust. Bastards. This is not over. This is not over by a long way.

*

'It is so good to see you,' Sophie says, reaching out to touch Steve's arm. 'I did not think you would be here.'

'I was just passing,' Steve says, his heart hammering. He couldn't bear just sitting there not talking to her, not being with her. 'Can I get you a drink?'

'Thankyou. A soda. I am not drinking tonight,' she says, matter-of-factly, not apologising for it.

They sit at a table near the bar, away from the vibrating speakers. Steve looks at the people around him and starts to feel self-conscious. He doesn't fit in. He's wearing light cotton trousers and a green, short-sleeved polo shirt. Adequate for hanging around the local golf club on a summer's night, maybe. But not here, not amongst the tie-dies, the day-glo, the tassels, tattoos, dreads, nose-rings and beads. He feels like the clean-cut, idealistic teacher sent into a crumbling inner city school who's given a class of the real difficult ones to sort out.

'I feel a bit out of place here,' he says to Sophie, smiling weakly, tugging at his shirt.

She shrugs and pouts, staring at his chest.

'They are just clothes,' she says. 'It is the person inside them that matters.' She raises her eyes to his. 'Clothes are just surface. They are fashion. It is nice to have them sometimes, clothes which you like. But it is not so important, I think.

'I suppose so,' Steve says, feeling a little reassured. 'Appearances can be deceptive.'

'And sometimes they are meant to be. But I think you should look through the clothes. Don't think about the clothes, about the hair, the fashion. Look through them. See the person inside.'

Steve's turned on. He can't deny it. Sophie is making him very horny, but not in a way he's used to. It's a strange sensation, somehow more than just a physical reaction.

'But it's understandable if that doesn't always happen,' he says, trying to concentrate, trying to fight the urge. 'First impressions are important.'

Jez is lolled behind them, restless. Crash Mary's talking to Becks, but he can't be bothered joining in. Instead he decides to check out this straight geezer chatting up Sophie, so he slides along the bench a bit, trying to listen in.

'Important? Maybe,' Sophie says, unconvinced. 'But only because they are a first impression. Maybe not so important for what you can find out about a person later.'

Steve thinks for a second. Jez cranes harder, a newly-lit joint hanging from his mouth.

'Still, you can tell a lot about a person from first impressions,' Steve says finally. 'How they look can tell you if they're healthy, fit, rich, poor. And the way they stand, the way they hold themselves, that shows you whether they're confident, meek, aggressive, submissive, quick, slow. And you can get an impression of whether they're intelligent or not. And that's just for starters. There's even things like the hands. You can tell a lot about a person just from their hands.'

'Let me see,' Sophie says. She takes his hands in hers. A dart of joy thuds into his chest. Jez slides over further, getting really interested.

'You have nice hands,' Sophie says, tracing her fingers across his palms, then turning his hands over and brushing her palms over his knuckles. 'They are strong, but not savage hands. You do not work outside, I think.'

She smiles, gently letting go.

'No. Not really,' he says, grinning back. 'I'm a policeman.'

Jez chokes on his joint, spewing out a massive cloud, and scrambles over to Crash Mary and Becks, urging them to move to another table.

'A policeman?' Sophie says, interested. It wasn't something that had come up earlier. If Steve's honest with himself, he'd deliberately not told her, worried about her reaction. Now it doesn't seem to matter. He feels he can tell her anything.

'It's not exactly what you'd call heavy work,' he says. 'Not any more. Tend to let the constables do all that. I sit at a desk, mostly. It's in a very quiet part of the country.'

'How long have you been a policeman?'

'Eight years. Straight from school.'

'That is very young. You must have always wanted to be a policeman.'

'Not really. Just for a couple of years before I joined. It wasn't like a boyhood dream or anything.'

'So why did you join?'

Steve feels a little uncomfortable. It's not something he's talked about before. Anybody who knows him from back then didn't need to ask. Anyone he's met since hasn't bothered to put the question. He hasn't thought about it for years. For a moment he struggles to find the words, then sees Sophie's eyes.

'Bit of a long story, really,' he says, smiling awkwardly. 'It's to do with my dad, you see. He was a policeman. He wasn't brilliant. He didn't jump up through the ranks, become chief inspector or anything. He was just a decent, ordinary copper. He had good judgement. Knew when to punish, knew when to warn. He was pretty well respected round our area. Everybody says so.'

Steve knows he's drifting from the point, moving away from it as if trying to establish a safe distance. He takes a drink of beer, feeling nervous and not knowing why.

'Well, the thing is, you see, my dad died when I was sixteen. When he was on duty. He wasn't doing anything heroic, he wasn't chasing after anyone or anything like that. It was just a simple heart attack, just like that.

'Of course, my mum was absolutely destroyed by it. It was completely out of the blue, no warning or nothing. And a police widow's pension's not much, not when you've got two young ones to bring up as well. As I said, my dad wasn't very senior.

'So that's what made me decide. That and the fact that everybody said what a great policeman my dad was. And they weren't just saying that because he'd died and everything. He was fair. Honestly. That's why everybody respected him.

'I mean, there was no way I was going to let me mum go out to work. What would she have done? She'd been a housewife the best part of twenty years. She was far too old to start looking for a job. So I made me mind up. Did my A levels, then the police exam, and that was that. Went in straight from school. Meant at least there was a decent wage coming into the house again.'

'So you did all this for your mother and father?'

'And my little sister as well. Jennifer. She was doing well at school at the time and we had to make sure she'd be alright. I'm pretty pleased about it, actually. She's done well for herself. Went to university, got a degree, in a good job now. Lives in Manchester. We're both really proud of her, me and my mum.'

'But what about you? What about what you wanted for yourself?'

'Oh, don't get me wrong. I'm not trying to make out I'm a saint or anything. It wasn't like I gave up everything just for them. It's a good job. An important job. The other things, they were really big factors in my decision, but yeah, a part of me definitely wanted to join. I mean, maybe if my dad hadn't have died, then no, maybe I wouldn't have joined, but you can't really say that now. What's done is done. You can't change the past.

The fact is, it was the right decision, and that's what matters.'

'Maybe,' Sophie says, not so sure. 'What did you want to do before?'

'What, like before my dad died?'

Sophie nods.

'Well, it was a long time ago. I mean, yeah, there were a couple of things I quite fancied doing, but I hadn't made up my mind. Actually, it might sound a bit stupid now, the way things have turned out, but one of the things I quite fancied doing was going to art college. I was quite good at it at school, really enjoyed it. I don't mean to sound like I'm boasting or nothing, but I got A's right up to A level. Although by that time it was just for fun because I'd already decided about the police.'

Sophie takes a sip of her soda.

'I think you have the heart of an artist,' she says, putting her glass down on the table, peering slightly at Steve, examining him. He feels naked, stripped of pretence and protection. 'I can feel this. You have a good heart. A warm heart, I think.'

Steve laughs, but his warm heart is boiling beneath his polo shirt.

'No, really,' she says. 'I think you are probably very decent. Decent and fair.'

She smiles, then her face turns serious. 'Your father would be proud of you I think.'

Steve blushes. He tries not to, but his face reddens anyway, aided by the soft, damp heat in the air. Sophie lays her hand on his arm. He burns.

*

'How difficult can it be?' Iain asks, waving a drunken hand in the air. 'Lots of gorgeous, hippy-type women. Unattached. Like me. In this heat, in this, the whatsitcalled, the thingmy.'

'Bar.'

'Environment, that's the word. This environment. Christ, maybe it's not environment. Some other word. Anyway, I mean, I'm not a bad-looking bloke, that's what I'm saying. Not George Clooney, grant you that. But, you know, not repulsive or anything. No major defects worth mentioning. How difficult can it be to get one of these girls to go to bed with me? I mean, what's stopping them?'

'Do you mean apart from the fact that you haven't actually talked to any of them and that even if you did you'd find you had nothing in common with them?' Barney says, raising an eyebrow.

'Yeah,' Iain says, not really taking the point. 'Exactly. I mean, I can be sensitive. I can. I can be in touch with my feelings. I could be in touch with theirs if they'd give me half a chance. They may be kind of, whatsitcalled.'

'Crusty.'

'Alternative. But I can do the new age thing. I can. Just 'cause I don't have as many piercings as them, or the clothes and stuff, doesn't mean I'm not, whatsit.'

'Deranged.'

'Sensitive. I can be as sensitive as the next guy.'

'Well maybe you should try out some of your sensitivity before you get too numb.'

'I will. You know, fuck it, I will.' Iain stands, a little unsteadily. 'Tonight, my friend, I am going to pull. I am a good person, there's nothing wrong with me. I have depths. I have needs. And I am going to pull, because I can't stand it any longer.'

He sways slightly as he looks around the bar. In the far corner he sees the short, plain-ish girl he spied earlier. He nods at Barney, nods towards the girl and grins. She's standing talking to two of her friends. Iain takes a deep breath and sets course for her.

He navigates the dancefloor with intermittent difficulty, only bumping into three people. None of them seems to mind too much. Eventually he arrives next to the girl and her mates. She's English. He can tell. The accent kind of gives it away.

They ignore him. They're talking about some festival or other, and Iain can't quite pick up the thread. He's standing right beside them, invading their space. Suddenly the other two girls turn and head for the bar. Iain's alone with her.

'Hi,' he says. He was going to say something more interesting, but forgot what it was.

She looks at him, her face blank. She's quite attractive, he thinks. More attractive than he'd given her credit for earlier. Very attractive. The most beautiful woman in the world.

'Hi,' she says back, like it's a question. She looks at him warily.

'I'm Iain, by the way.'

'Leah,' she says, after too long a pause.

'Nice to meet you Leah.' Iain's not sure what to say. 'So, um, how long you been here.'

'What? In Pandora's?' She screws her face up.

'Yeah. No, I mean in Goa.'

'Three months,' she says, looking away, bored already.

'Yeah? That's great, that's great,' Iain says, nodding, being enthusiastic. 'That's really great. It must be really great to be here for that long. Like, for three months. You know, in the one place. I'm travelling, by the way.'

'You don't say.'

'Yeah. Um, so Lee...'

'Leah.'

'Yeah, Leah, right. So, um, so what you doing here?' Iain tries to take a nonchalant swig of his beer but discovers the bottle's empty. 'You, like, over here finding yourself or something?'

'Yeah, like I came all this way just to get my horoscope done,' Leah says, her voice soaked in irony.

'Yeah? That's great. That's really great,' Iain says, swaying, sweating, missing it all. 'So, um, so what's your sign?'

Leah gives him a long, steady glare.

'No Entry.'

*

A large black motorbike crawls along the road outside Pandora's, the engine growling low and deep. It stops outside the main entrance. The driver gets off, a tall man wearing a cotton waistcoat over his broad, bare chest. His arms are tanned and thick with muscles, his long, dirty blond hair falling in sun-bleached waves around his shoulders. He strides into the bar, straight up to Sophie and Steve's table.

'Come,' he barks to Sophie, holding out a large, strong hand to her, not even acknowledging Steve. 'We are going.'

Sophie gets up immediately. Steve sees a change in her eyes when she glances down at him, a flash of something, maybe concern. He's not sure what to do. She seems to be going of her own free will. He's about to say something to the man, to Sophie, get up and do something, but he stops himself. Surely if Sophie wanted him to, she'd let him know, give him a sign. Steve suddenly feels he's intruding in a place and situation he knows nothing about, doesn't belong in. Sophie gives him another quick backward glance as she goes, but Steve can't read her expression. And then she's gone.

'Is that him?' a retreated, defeated Iain says to Barney as the man marches through the tables, leading Sophie by the hand. She almost has to jog to keep up.

'The God of Thunder himself,' Barney says.

'I have no words,' Iain says. 'I have no words at all that will begin to describe how much I hate that man. The words don't exist.'

Barney laughs as Iain's head drops into his hands.

The blond man gets on the bike but doesn't start it.

'Who was that?' he says, flicking his head back towards the bar.

'Just someone I met.'

'Same man you met on the beach?'

Sophie falters, thrown, then tries to explain. But he cuts her off, his voice harsh and loud.

'Don't try to tell me anything, any bullshit lies. People tell me things. I know these things.'

'Henrik, there is nothing for you to know. You know there's nothing,' she says, her voice breaking.

He kick-starts the bike, roaring it. He doesn't look at her. Just waits. Sophie hesitates for a second, but then gets on behind him, linking her arms around his waist. They take off, the bike's front light slicing through the dark, eventually fading into the distance.

Steve's incredibly uncomfortable. He's pretty sure people are staring at him now, but he doesn't try to catch anyone's eye. He finishes his beer quickly and walks out of Pandora's into a night humming with insects and questions.

'You want taxi?' a young Indian man sitting on a motorbike says.

'No. No thanks,' Steve says back. 'Think I'll walk. Do me head good.'

He tramps back along the poorly lit road. His head spins. His chest aches. He hates himself.

He should have done something, instead of just sitting there like a dumb animal. Or like a guilty man caught in the act.

But what? What could he have done? What right did he have? And who says Sophie would have wanted him to do anything anyway?

He thinks about her as he walks, thinks about nothing else, thinks about what it's like just being with her, talking to her, thinking about how he feels now she's not there, now that she's gone off with some-one else.

But what does he really know about her? She'd never mentioned a boyfriend. Maybe it's her brother.

Fat chance. Maybe it's something he can't guess at. Or then again, maybe it's her husband. Maybe she's been holding back little details like that as well.

But still. He believes he can tell her anything. Anything at all. In fact, he wants her to know everything about him, about his life. What the hell is happening to him? Who is this girl?

And why has Karen never asked him why he joined the police, or what he wanted to be when he was a kid, or told him he had a warm heart?

His scrambled thoughts are jarred by snarling, snapping dogs each time he passes a darkened house. He concentrates instead on trying to avoid getting bitten.

Half an hour later, when he gets back to the hotel, he still hasn't come up with any answers to the score of questions jabbing at his brain.

He walks through the gates, nods to the dozing security guard, and slumps up the dreary concrete stairs beside the empty reception. Fatigue has gripped him, delayed jet-lag and too much alcohol combining to squeeze out all his emotional and physical strength.

He opens the bedroom door slowly. A bedside light's on. Karen's sitting up, waiting. He flops down on the bed fully clothed and closes his sore eyes.

'Well,' Karen snaps at him. 'What time do you call this?

Surely it doesn't take that long to get a ...'

'Oh for God's sake, give it a rest,' he sighs back, before he plunges into an exhausted, troubled sleep.

CHAPTER SIX

Hot and cold

Karen's still not speaking to Steve. That's what she says, anyway.

Her particular interpretation of moody silences usually involves firing short, rapid bursts of complaints at him, whilst expecting him to say nothing back.

They're sitting at a table in the garden by the pool. Karen says she feels well enough to eat something, no thanks to him. A bit of toast, maybe. And some tea.

Between bites of toast and boiled egg, Steve's subjected to a long, pointed explanation of how he's ruining their holiday.

How bad the hotel is, how uncomfortable the bed is, how her illness is his fault, how his night-time desertion of her was bloody thoughtless.

Never mind the way he'd spoken to her last night.

Steve holds his tongue throughout the breakfast harangue. You didn't get ratty or argue back at a girl like Karen. Goes on a bit, but that's just her way.

Worth putting up with for a girl like her. Everybody said so.

He wants to defend himself, bat away all the accusations and misunderstandings, but he doesn't. Mainly because he knows it'll make no difference to what Karen's saying, and also because he knows what's going to happen.

She'll blow herself out in an hour or so and everything'll be fine. But there's also the guilt to take into account.

He keeps his answers minimal, his apologies succinct.

With breakfast over, and the sun starting to scorch the lawn, Steve judges that Karen's storm is finished for a while.

'What d'you fancy doing today, love?' he says, gently.

'Oh, I don't know,' she shrugs. 'Don't really feel up to much.'

Good, Steve thinks. If she'd still been on the warpath she'd have added 'no thanks to you'.

'Maybe it's best you take it easy,' he says. 'Maybe go back to bed for a while.'

'Well, I'm up now. May as well make the most of it. Maybe I'll try to sit by the pool for a little while. Maybe try for the beach later.'

'It's quite a walk to the beach, love,' Steve says, feeling a surprise jitter of panic.

'Five minutes it said in the brochure.'

'Maybe if you're walking fast, if it was a cold day or something. Not in thirty degree heat it isn't.'

Karen huffs.

'Well, it looks like the pool then. I'm not sure I'm up for a long walk.'

They go back to their room and change into swimming gear, Karen wrapping a bright orange sarong around her waist.

When they get back down to the pool, the Matlocks and Clive are already there, beached on sunbeds.

'Coo-ee,' Maureen says, waving to Steve.

He sighs, and leads Karen over to them for introductions and inane small-talk.

'Why don't you join us,' Maureen says, once they've all nodded and grinned and gone through names. 'The more the merrier.'

Karen smiles.

'Thanks very much,' she says, and takes the sunbed next to Maureen.

Steve stands there, considering, wondering if he can face it.

'Okay, now you just take it easy, love,' he says. 'I won't be too long.'

'Where you going?' Karen says, sharp but not loud.

'Well,' Steve says, an awkward smile on his face, trying to find another word. 'The beach,' he says, as if it's obvious.

'What? You're not staying here? With me?'

'You'll be fine. Anyway, it's not that, love. It's just that, well, the beach,' he says inadequately, gesturing in the general direction of the palm trees.

'I didn't come all the way to India just to sit by a pool, did I?' he goes on. 'There's a whole beach out there. A whole sea. Don't know what it's called, but it's a real one. You'll see what I mean tomorrow. When you're a bit better, love.'

He bends over and kisses her on the cheek, quickly waves goodbye to the rest of them, and strides away before Karen can say anything. He's down the drive and out the main gate before he stops, puts his hands on his hips and takes a breath.

A pretty low thing to do, leaving his sick wife by the pool while he charges off to the beach.

Very low indeed.

And why was he going to the beach? Just because it's real? To get away from the Fat Family?

Or to see Sophie.

He folds his arms and glances back at the hotel gate. He sways, considering going back to the pool, going to the beach another day, once Karen's better.

Tomorrow, maybe. When they can go together.

But then he thinks of the beach. The peace. The whispering wash of the sea. The bowing palm trees.

Sophie's smile.

He feels the ache, and starts walking down the road.

*

IAIN McMILLAN'S GREAT
HINDUSTAN ADVENTURE

Monday 28th December '98, Anjuna, Goa

I'm so hungover I can hardly breathe. It's all Barney's fault. Well, him and the large amount of poisonous beer I chucked down my throat.

Hangovers in hot countries are always the worst. The greasy sweats you normally get the morning after a session back home are multiplied six fold, with barely-diluted piss spurting out of every pore more or less constantly. How attractive does that sound.

And then of course there's the chronic dehydration. Oddly enough, it's much worse when you live in a tin-roofed sauna. I feel like I'm in Tenko. Any second now the door's going to burst open and some Japanese guard's going to do something nasty to me in a chillingly inscrutable fashion. Fuck it, he can stick as many bamboo splinters under my nails as he likes as long as he gives me a sachet of Resolve.

Anyway. Barney. He's the guy from the beach, the one who blocked my perving attempts. It turns out that, despite being posh and a perv-blocker, he's a decent bloke. Very funny in a dry, laid-back, understated way. We seem to be on the same wavelength, although I suspect we're tuned in on different makes of radios. His'll be the expensive digital one with leather trim. I've got the tinny Dixons own-brand model.

But the girl! I saw her boyfriend last night, the real one (which is just great, since it means I've two to contend with now. Although I'm not sure 'contend with' is right. 'Be pathetically jealous of from a suitably humiliating distance' probably hits the spot a lot more accurately). He's a nightmare. A Teutonic super-race left-over. I was trying to sum up last night how much I hated him, but I couldn't. I just wasn't able to find the right words. But my subconscious has been checking through all the files in my brain as I've been sleeping, and from all the words, all the phrases and insults and put-downs, all the adjectives and nouns in my vast, eloquent, educated vocabulary, there is only one word on my dry, cracked lips this morning. Cunt.

*

'And that Mrs Winters next to us, you should see what she's done with her bathroom,' Maureen Matlock says, shifting her uncomfortable bulk on the narrow sunbed.

Arthur Matlock's stretched out on one side of her, Karen on the other. Both Matlock girls are sitting on the edge of the pool, dangling thick, pink legs in the water. Clive's over by the bar in the shade, sweating in shorts and a Manchester United away top, drinking from a big bottle of Kingfisher.

'It's absolutely beautiful, that bathroom,' Maureen says. 'Gold taps, marble everywhere, a beautiful corner bath, all matching units, all done in this really light green. Oh, you should see it love. No expense spared, I can tell you. Must have cost a fortune, an absolute fortune. We're thinking of getting ours done just like it. You know, with our own personal touches. Aren't we Arthur?'

Arthur snoozes on, his grey-haired barrel chest rising and falling.

'We got ours done by Jarretts,' Karen says, her mouth set firm in a satisfied smile. 'Very well thought of round our way. Based in Carlisle. Very exclusive. It did cost a bit, I don't mind telling you, but what's money for if you can't spend it, that's what I always say.'

'Quite right, love. Quite right,' Maureen says. 'Arthur's worked hard all his life, working his way up from bus-driver to what we have now. He didn't do all that just so we could live in a small house with a pokey little garden, did you Arthur. No, we like our comforts, like a bit of luxury. Well, if you've worked hard for it, why not? Can't take it with you, isn't that right Arthur.'

Arthur is snoring, quietly but definitely.

'Not that we don't save,' Karen says quickly. 'I don't want you to think that we just spend, spend, spend,' she adds with a forced laugh. 'It's only on the important things. And if you don't buy quality, you'll only end up paying more in the long run, that's what I always say. But it's important to save as well. In a couple of years we'll be thinking of starting a family, and once that starts I don't expect I'll go on working. Steve's due for promotion again before then, but we need to have money in the bank. After all, bringing up kids isn't cheap.'

'You're right, love. It's not.'

'So we're setting some aside, a bit every month,' Karen says. 'You've got to save up to have kids, I always think.'

'And after all, that's what it's all about, the children,' Maureen adds. 'Got to make sure they've got the best. Never wanted for anything, our two. As far as I'm concerned, only the best is good enough for them.'

Maureen gazes proudly at her two girls. Over at the bar, Clive downs his Kingfisher and belches magnificently.

*

A cow has come to visit Steve and Sophie on the beach, a small brown and white cow with a sad face scarred by dog bites and barbed wire, ribs poking against its skin. Sophie is delighted to see it, Steve less so, mainly through not having any experience of how to deal with cows on beaches.

'Hello cow,' Sophie says pleasantly, as if the animal's an old friend.

'Hi,' Steve waves to it, a little uncertainly.

The cow dips its head, bulging brown eyes seeking out any scraps of fruit or paper to eat.

'I love cows,' Sophie says. 'Such peaceful animals. Always good tempered. Never violent.'

'Taste pretty good too,' Steve says, smiling, then wishes he hadn't done either.

Sophie gasps, mock horror and hurt on her face, a look that devastates Steve.

'Don't listen to him,' she says to the cow in a soft, consoling voice. 'He does not mean it.' She looks over at Steve, still trying to appear offended, but with a half-smile playing on her lips. 'You are a bad man for saying this. Looking at her as if you want to eat her.'

The cow lumbers off along the beach as it catches the smell of watermelon rind further down the sand.

'Bad man,' Sophie says. 'Cow scarer.'

'I wouldn't worry. Doubt she speaks English,' Steve says, and they both laugh.

They've been there half an hour, avoiding talking about the one thing Steve desperately wants to know. Sophie's clearly been holding back too. She hasn't mentioned anything about last night. Steve can't put it off any longer.

'So, I suppose, that man, the one you went off with,' he starts, feeling awkward.

He clears his throat, determined that his voice should betray nothing but mild interest. 'Is he your boyfriend, then?'

Sophie smiles, looking out to sea.

'Yes, that is Henrik. I suppose, yes, you could call him my boyfriend but it is not really like that. I met him here in Anjuna, one month ago.'

A long, cold knife slips into Steve's heart.

'He isn't really my boyfriend, but we are together. We stay together.'

The knife twists. Steve manages not to scream.

'He's from Sweden,' Sophie adds.

'Sweden. Right,' says Steve, speaking slowly, calmly. 'He seems, you know...' Steve searches for a word, one that he can say out loud. 'Seems very strong,' he says eventually.

'Yes. Very strong,' Sophie says, but doesn't add to it.

'So, what's the story? Are you going to travel with him? After Goa, I mean.'

Sophie turns onto her front, leaning on her elbows, not looking at Steve. She shrugs.

'I don't know,' she says. 'It is sometimes difficult between us. I do not know if it is possible for us to stay together. Sometimes he can be a wonderful man, but sometimes his heart can be so cold. He was very angry with me for talking to you last night. Some of his friends saw us together, went to find him. He knows I was with you on the beach yesterday.'

'And he didn't like it?'

'No. He is jealous, I think.'

'What did he say?'

'Many things. But he said he did not like it, and I was not to do it again.'

'Oh,' Steve says, depressed at the thought, but then realising. 'But you *are* doing it again.'

'Yes,' Sophie says, smiling. 'I like talking to you.'

Steve lies down on his back, staring at the pale blue sky, feeling the hot sand through the thin cotton of his sarong. He feels elated and sick at the same time. He doesn't understand any of it.

'Will he be angry that you're talking to me today?'

'Perhaps. But I told him I do what I like. He does not own me.'

'It sounds like he wants to, if you don't mind me saying so,' Steve says, making his words tread carefully, not wanting to appear too critical. 'A bit possessive.'

Sophie shrugs.

'Yes, sometimes maybe. But not all the time. It depends. Perhaps today he will be different. One day he can be something, and the next day something else. Perhaps today he doesn't care.'

'Doesn't care?'

'About me,' she says plainly, without self-pity.

'What?' Steve says, astonished. The thought of it's absurd. 'What do you mean?'

'It's true,' Sophie says, looking a little sad for the first time. Steve feels it sting. 'Sometimes he acts as if he doesn't even know me, pretends that I am not there. It doesn't happen often, but it happens.'

'Not often,' Steve says, shaking his head. 'Sophie, I hate to say this, and it's really none of my business, so tell me to shut up if you want, but you've only been with him a few weeks. I don't think it's supposed to be like that. That shouldn't be happening after a few weeks.'

Sophie shrugs again, her mouth in a pout.

'It is not always the same. But I can understand it when he's like that, because his passions are very strong. Sometimes his heart is hot, sometimes it is cold.'

'Sounds a bit up and down,' Steve says, hating the thought of Henrik. 'All this hot and cold business.'

'Yes, but when his heart is very hot, it makes me forget about the times when it is cold.'

She smiles at something within herself.

'But sometimes I think it is not so good. A hot and cold heart,' she says, lifting a handful of sand, watching the grains slip through her fingers in fine sprays. 'Sometimes I think a warm heart is better, not the extremes.'

'What's the difference? What's a warm heart?'

'Like yours,' Sophie says, looking over at Steve. 'I told you. You have a very warm heart. I can see it. The way you are, the way you think.' She gestures towards some of the Karnatakan beach-hawkers sitting in a group around some newly arrived tourists. 'Even the way you buy from the girls who are selling things.'

Steve laughs self-consciously and looks down at the small pile of cloth purses, bangles and a thin silk scarf he's bought already that morning.

'It's true,' Sophie goes on. 'The way you talk to them, the way you are treating them. I know you are buying for them, not for you. You buy from compassion, not from greed, not because you want to make them go away, not because you think you are getting a good deal. You are a very kind man, I think. I have a feeling for these things. You cannot hide it.'

Steve's warm heart is threatening to overheat. He's embarrassed, flattered and excited. He's also a bit scared. She's got a boyfriend. He's got a wife. In all the hours of talking, he hasn't once mentioned Karen to Sophie. It's time. If nothing else, he has to be truthful to Sophie.

'My wife might come down a bit later,' he says. 'She's been a bit unwell.'

'You are married?'

'Yes.'

'She is very sick?'

Steve's surprised to find concern in Sophie's voice. He

doesn't know why, but he didn't expect it. Some other reaction, maybe, but not concern.

'Oh, it's nothing serious. Just a bit of trouble adjusting to Indian food. She'll be fine.'

And suddenly he realises, and is flooded with shame. He doesn't want her to be fine. He can't believe it, but it's true. He doesn't want Karen to get worse, but he doesn't want her well and up and about and interrupting his time with Sophie. He'd never wish anything bad to happen to Karen. But it's there. It's been hiding deep inside his mind, leaping out to ambush him when he least expected it.

'And what does she say,' Sophie says, with a green, mischievous spark in her eyes, 'about you talking to strange women on the beach?'

'I don't talk to strange women on the beach,' Steve says, smiling but defensive, a bit shaken. 'I only talk to you, and you're not strange, you're...'

Steve realises he doesn't know what to say. The sentence dies in the warm air. Sophie gives a kind smile to Steve's troubled face, closes her eyes, and puts her head down on soft, golden arms. Steve continues to look at her, thinking.

He's in trouble. In all sorts of ways.

CHAPTER SEVEN

Periphery dolphins

'Did you hear what Max the German told me?' Crash Mary says, thumping his bulk down next to Jez in the Vibe Bar.

'That you're a fat ugly bastard?'

'Fuck off. Nah, he said that there was three of them done over at Christmas. Up in Vagator. Him and two of his mates. Benny and someone. Bosh, bosh, bosh. Cameras, Walkmans, cash, everything. Cleaned the place out. Christmas. Good will to all men, and that. Wasn't you was it, you thieving little toe-rag?'

'Nah. It's your bloody Indians, innit. Always at it up in Vagator. Anyway, that Max and his lot can afford it. Rich bastards, they are. Nah, if you're gonna nick anything, best off going for the Italians. It's something in their nature. Don't trust banks, do they. Always keep loads of cash around them.'

'What ballocks is this, then? 'Don't trust banks'.'

'They don't. It's this authority thing they've got, innit. They don't trust 'em. It's all that corruption and everything they've got back in Italy. Half the country's on the take, they've got a different government every week, whole thing's just a joke. So they keep their money at home, won't trust the banks in case they nick it. Just like here. Like the police an' all. Your Italians don't trust *their* police neither.'

And all the time Jez is thinking. A grand. He's got to get a grand together and pretty bleedin' sharpish or Hassan's going to be one very unhappy boy. A fucking grand.

Jez and Crash Mary are sitting on the low concrete wall at the front of the Vibe, right next to the beach path. Jez swings his leg, each swing ticking away the seconds of another long lazy day. He hasn't been up long. Long enough, but not long.

'Seen Nat anywhere today?' he says.

'Yeah, seen her with Kerry and that Australian bird. Don't know her name. Over at Sea Breeze, they was. What, she got the hump with you or something?'

'Yeah. Don't know what the fuck for. Just pissed off, stormed out the gaff. No reason.'

'Must have been a reason.'

'There wasn't. Just stormed off.'

'Yeah, but for her to just storm off. What I'm saying is, there must have been a reason.'

'I'm telling you. There was no reason. None. Does it all the time. Silly cow.'

'Well, what was you doing right before she stormed off.'

'Nothing. Just lying in bed.'

'Just lying in bed? Not doing nothing?'

'Well of course we were doing something. We was having a shag, wasn't we. Then she suddenly gets up, gets dressed, and storms out.'

'Yeah?' Crash Mary says, suspiciously. 'What exactly happened? I mean, in the seconds right before she storms off.'

'Well,' Jez says, a frown coming over his face. 'I'd just given her one up the poo-chute, then she's sucked me off, and then she expected me to *kiss* her.'

'Did you?'

'Course I didn't. Not bleedin' hygienic, that.'

'And then she storms off?'

'Yeah.'

Crash Mary looks at Jez for a few seconds, shaking his head in wonder at him.

'Well, can't think what it can be, then,' he says.

Jez watches a tightly clad bottom sway past. Israeli, he thinks. Muscular.

'Don't matter,' he says. 'She'll come back. Always does.'

The two of them sit quietly for a while, Jez tapping his foot against the wall to the sounds from the Vibe's powerful speakers. It's early, so they're still turned down low, but the deep throb is enough for Jez to get into. He looks around at the people inside the bar, in the shade, and the others scattered outside at the tables.

He sees faces he recognises. Sonar, Dumper, Lee and Rochelle drinking vodka and tonics, Beans, Iggy.

But there are more faces, faces he doesn't know.

'Too many freaks here,' he says to Crash Mary. 'Don't know half of them. Thought bleedin' Christmas was bad. Looks like they've decided to really cane it for New Year.'

'Yeah,' Crash Mary says, resignedly, then thinks about it and perks up. 'It's good, though. More variety and that. Makes a bit of a change.'

'S'pose.' A fucking grand. How's he going to get his hands on a fucking grand at short notice?

*

'Sometimes,' Sophie says, leaning back on her arms, gazing out to sea. 'Sometimes I think I see dolphins.'

Steve rolls over on his side to look at her. It's almost too much to bear, so instead he concentrates on the lazy waves ten feet away lapping at the beach like a tired dog.

'Dark with a fin,' he says flatly. 'Can't fail to recognise them. See something dark with a fin, then you can be pretty confident it's a dolphin. No sharks in these waters,' he says, but Sophie's already laughing. 'I checked.'

'I know what a dolphin looks like,' she says, still laughing.

'Stop taking the piss.'

'Your English really is very good,' Steve says, and they both laugh again.

The beach is busier than before, the New Year crowd arriving to set up camp. Some are fresh from the clubs of Europe, some from ashrams in Gujarat or Tamil Nadu, the Banyan Tree crowd from Arambol, the thin, naked bush dwellers of Palolem and Gokarna. From Manali, from Vrindavan, from Ko Pha Ngan, from Eilat, from Ibiza, from Borocay.

Sophie turns to face Steve.

'Do you want to hear about my dolphins?' she says. The way she says it is so cute that Steve feels hurt that she might even think he wouldn't want to. He nods keenly.

'It's just sometimes,' she says. 'I think I see them, but I am not sure. I have never seen one directly in front of me, so that I could look at it. Always they are in the edge of my eye, in my - what is it in English?'

'The corner of your eye,' Steve corrects her, but she shakes her head. He shrugs. 'Or I suppose you could say your periphery.'

'That's it, that's what I meant,' Sophie smiles. 'I always see them in my periphery. When I am looking out to sea, I think I see one of them at the side but when I look there, they are gone. And no-one else has seen them, not ever, so I do not know if they were really there. But I believe they are. They are my own special dolphins. I call them my...' She stops, working it out from the French. 'My periphery dolphins.'

'That's as good a name as any,' Steve says, laughing. 'But still, you must have seen lots of dolphins. Real ones.'

'No,' Sophie says, pouting. 'Never in my life. In photographs, on TV, yes. But never in nature. Sometimes they play out there,' she says, pointing out by the headland to the north with a lazy stretch of her arm. 'I have spoken to people who have seen them. But me? No. I would love to see dolphins. More than anything. I will see them, one day. But for now, I have my periphery dolphins.'

Steve sits up and squints out to sea, trying to catch any movement on the edge of his vision.

'I can't see any,' he says. The intensity of the sun-spattered water hurts his eyes.

'You are not looking right,' Sophie says. 'You must open your eyes. Open them up, and then the dolphin will know that you can see more than anyone else, and it is safe for him to appear.'

Steve tries a couple of times, forcing his fluttering eyelids to open as wide as they can, fighting the urge to close them tight against the glare. With one last effort, he manages to stare out to sea for a few seconds. He thinks his eyes are just about to adjust to the brightness, when an unstoppable rush builds, then explodes in a sneeze.

'Bless you,' Sophie says, laughing.

Steve, embarrassed, wipes his watery eyes with his t-shirt.

'I couldn't see any,' he says, feeling an uncomfortable throb in his sinuses, but glad that it wasn't a full-blown snottery blast. 'Did my best.'

'Perhaps they are tired,' Sophie says with a half-sigh. 'Too much jumping around, I think.'

Steve's vision is dotted with the green after-burn of sunlight on waves. He looks at Sophie. Even with green blotches, she's still beautiful.

'They've got one of those dolphin-spotting trips, a boat trip,' he says, without thinking. 'There's a poster about it up at the hotel.'

'To see dolphins?' Sophie says, sitting up, excited.

'That's the theory,' Steve says. 'Probably not much point

running a dolphin-spotting trip otherwise.'

'Oh, but to see dolphins.' Sophie cups hands over her face, almost as if she's praying, maybe too embarrassed to show how much the thought thrills her. But her body gives it away, wriggling in excitement.

'This is a local boat?' she says, taking her hands away.

'I assume so. A charter, probably.'

'If it is a private boat, maybe it is expensive,' she says, her mouth curving down.

'I think it's fifteen hundred rupees. Yeah, I'm sure that's what it said.'

'Fifteen hundred? One thousand five hundred? Oh.' Sophie's head drops, and her voice calms, the excitement fading. 'That is my money for one week.'

'Fifteen hundred? Is that all you've got? You live off that every week?'

'Yes,' she says with a shrug. 'It does not cost so much here. Fifteen hundred is possible. It is not much, no?'

'No it's not,' Steve says, letting out air. 'Fifteen hundred,' he says to himself. 'Not a lot at all.'

He shakes his head, looking out to sea. He feels a surge inside him.

'I'll pay,' he says. 'You go on the boat trip, and I'll pay.' He doesn't look at her, afraid of what he might see.

'No no no, that is not possible. Not fifteen hundred rupees,' she says slowly, denying it.

'Why not?'

'It is too much.'

'It's not too much. Trust me, I can afford it. If you get to see dolphins, it'll be worth it.'

'But it is...'

'Do you want to see dolphins or not,' he says, speaking over her, smiling.

'Yes of course, but...'

'Then it's settled. If you want to see them, you will see them. That's all there is to it. I'll get a ticket for you, then all you need to do is go along and keep your eyes open.'

Sophie smiles, but there's a slight curve of sadness in it.

'I told you - you have a kind heart,' she says. 'But this is too kind. I cannot accept this.'

Steve holds his hands out as if they're scales, weighing up one thing then the other.

'Dolphins, no dolphins. Dolphins, no dolphins. Dolphins, no dolphins,' he says. 'Which is it to be?'

'Dolphins,' Sophie says, laughing. They look at each other for a few seconds, just smiling. Steve wants the moment to go on all day. Sophie breaks off first, looking out to sea, then back to Steve.

'You are going too?' she says.

'I, I dunno,' he says, suddenly unsure of himself. 'I hadn't really thought about it.'

'If you do not go, I will not go,' she says.

'Well,' Steve says, his heart booming as he searches for some reason to stop himself saying what he's about to say. 'Looks like we're going to see dolphins, then.'

*

It's over an hour before Jez spots a likely target. He's commandeered a table in the corner of the Sun Temple, which, by happy coincidence, gives him a perfect view of the place where people park their bikes and scooters before coming onto the beach.

So far it's mostly been long-timers on their Enfields or party-heads on clapped out Bajaj lawnmower-jobs. None of them are any good to him. Too close to home for starters.

But when he's almost given up hope, the cavalry arrives in the shape of a blatant package couple. A pale, ginger-haired bloke and his dumpy girl riding two-up on what looks like a nearly new Honda Kinetic scooter. Just what he's looking for. He knows a dodgy bar-owner up in Vagator who'll give him a hundred, maybe a hundred and fifty quid for a Kinetic, depending on the condition. Not a trick you call pull off too often, but worth the risk. In the circumstances.

He watches the couple veer the scooter inexpertly along the dust path, stalling it when they reach the bike park. The two of them dismount, laughing, then the man pushes the machine up on its stand and puts the key in a black bum-bag.

How easy do they want to make it, Jez thinks. A bum-bag, for God's sake.

His eyes follow them as they walk thirty yards or so along the beach, laying out their towels near a low dune. They strip down to their swimming gear, and the man puts his bum-bag into a day-pack the woman's been carrying their beach things in. Then, just as Jez expected, they both trot down towards the sea.

Jez almost feels sorry for them. It shouldn't be as easy as this. He's rarely seen such an example of textbook stupidity. They've more or less invited him to do what he's just about to do.

He gets up from the table, leaving his warm beer to fester, and strolls down the steps at the front of the bar onto the beach. He checks to make sure they're both in the water before ambling lazily down the path which cuts behind the dunes. A thirty yard walk and he's behind their chosen dune. He creeps up on all fours, poking his head over the top. They're still in the sea, splashing and playing a good fifty yards away. And just five yards in front of him, the day-pack.

He doesn't move fast. He doesn't need to. That would only draw attention anyway, although there aren't too many people around that part of the beach to notice. Four easy strides there, four easy strides back, and he's hidden behind the dune with the day-pack in his hand.

Now he picks up the pace. A quick rummage and he's got the key. He swings the pack onto his shoulder as he jogs towards the scooter - who knows what other goodies it holds? Thirty seconds later he's buzzing down the path towards the main road on his new toy. Vagator's just a fifteen minute ride away. Suddenly life looks a bit sweeter again.

*

All the way back from the beach Steve's been going over it in his mind. He's panicked, excited, ashamed, elated, his emotions doing freeform gymnastics in his head.

As soon as he'd agreed to go dolphin-watching with Sophie, he knew he shouldn't have done it. It was wrong. Buying her a ticket was okay, but not going with her. How could he explain it to Karen? Simple. He couldn't. Couldn't? How could he not tell her? Because she'd go ape-shit, that's why.

It's no good. He'll have to tell Sophie that it's sold out, that there aren't any tickets left, let her down gently.

But the more he thinks about it, about being on a boat with Sophie and her seeing dolphins and the look on her face, the more he wants to go. And not tell Karen anything about it.

After all, it's not like he's having some sneaky affair. It's not as if he and Sophie have actually done anything wrong. There's no harm in just talking, is there? Being friendly? Two friends going out on a boat trip together to see some dolphins. As innocent as anything. It's just that Karen wouldn't understand.

But does he understand? Does he, in his heart of hearts, want it to be more than just a simple friendship?

All the way back to the hotel Steve torments himself. He knows what the right thing to do is. And he knows what he wants to do.

'When's the next dolphin trip?' he asks Mr Bandodkar, the assistant manager, pointing to the poster on the wall beside the reception desk, checking that no other guests are within ear-shot.

'The trips are running on Mondays and Fridays, sir. Six a.m,' Mr Bandodkar says, smiling.

'Two tickets for Friday then, please,' Steve says, starting to count out money from his travel wallet.

'The boat is not going on Friday, sir.'

Steve stops sorting the notes and looks up.

'What? Sorry, I thought you said Mondays and Fridays.'

'That is correct, sir,' Mr Bandodkar says, still smiling.

'Mondays and Fridays. Except not on Fridays.'

'Not this particular Friday, no sir,' Mr Bandodkar says. 'On account of New Year holiday.'

'Of course, of course,' Steve says, feeling stupid, giving himself a mental slap.

'I do not think guests are wanting to go on the boat after big party-party. I think there is *too* much drinking.' Mr Bandodkar breaks into high-pitched giggles, shaking his head furiously.

'Right,' Steve says. 'Two tickets for next Monday, then.'

'Very good, sir,' Mr Bandodkar says, still chuckling to him-self. He goes off into the office behind the reception desk, trying to find the right ticket book.

Steve stands there, glancing around nervously, his heart thumping, terrified of Karen seeing him. He can't believe it - scared of his own wife. His mind's screaming 'what are you do-ing, what are you doing, what are you doing' over and over again.

And then the tickets are in his hand, paid for in cash. He stares at the pieces of paper for a few seconds, as if he's unsure what to do with them. His mind is jammed. Then he gathers himself, stuffs the tickets in his money pouch and heads for the room.

It's settled. He knows what he's got to do. The right thing. He's going to lie to Karen and go and see dolphins with Sophie. Guilt bites at him, but desire fights it off.

CHAPTER EIGHT

Coming clean

Sophie sits reading a ragged paperback in dim light from a bare bulb. Sarongs of bright yellow suns, rich blue moons, elephants, gods and Sanskrit symbols dress the rough walls of her small, cheap room.

Incense hangs heavy in the air, two sticks of patchouli smouldering in a wooden holder on the low table next to Sophie's chair. She's sitting there, lost in the story, left foot tucked under her right thigh, absent-mindedly playing with her toes as she reads.

As she comes to the end of a chapter she looks up over the top of the book at Henrik. He's lying on his back on the bed, eyes closed, listening to a tape on his personal stereo.

That face. High cut cheekbones, a straight, strong nose, the wide mouth at turns so sensuous or so cruel. And those eyes. She looks at his eyelids, pictures the luminous blue eyes beneath.

The lids snap open, the eyes staring straight at her. Sophie starts, her heart jumping up into her throat. But then the eyes close again, slowly, the expression on Henrik's face remaining blank.

Sophie's surprised at herself. Why did she react like that? Why does he make her so nervous sometimes? He hasn't talked to her for ages, only an offhand, grunted word here and there, ever since he came down to the beach to pick her up an hour or so after Steve left. Hardly a murmur.

Then, in one long, deliberate movement, Henrik sits up on the bed, pulls the earphones off, and reaches into his dirty, patchwork waistcoat. He takes a paper cone packet from one pocket, a blue plastic lighter from the other, shakes out one of the beedies and lights it.

Sophie tries to catch the smoke's scent. She likes the smell, the mix of herbs and rough tobacco, the sweet and musky perfume of the cheap Indian cigarette.

'You were talking to that man again today,' Henrik says flatly, looking down at the packed earth floor.

Sophie lays the open book in her lap.

'On the beach?'

'Yes. On the beach.'

She flicks her eyes back to the page she was reading, trying to focus on the words.

'He is a very nice man. From England. His name is...'

'I don't need to know his name,' Henrik says sharply, cutting her off. 'I don't care about his stupid fucking name. I told you, you are not to talk with him.'

'You asked me,' Sophie says, keeping as calm as she can. 'You did not tell me.'

'I *told* you. And I am telling you now again. You are not to talk with him. I should not have to tell you this two times.'

Sophie concentrates hard on the first sentence of the second paragraph, but none of it registers. She doesn't want to argue. She hates the arguments, hates all the twisted words, the acid-raw accusations. Why does she put up with it? After only a few weeks. Maybe it shouldn't be like this.

She doesn't say anything, just keeps pretending to read her book.

'Why do you want to talk with him anyway? Huh?' His words are clipped, spat out. He's looking right at her now. She can feel the ice from his glare. 'Not getting enough fucking that you need to pick some up on the side?'

'No, Henrik.' Sophie's face breaks in concern at the sudden crack in Henrik's voice, at the wounded tone in his last few words. She puts down her book and goes over to the bed, sitting next to him, wrapping her arms around his neck.

She quiets him. Soft words and promises, soothing sounds, brushing her cheek on his shoulder, hands caressing his spine, his arms. She can't bear to see the insecurity, the deep pain inside him that bursts out in so many ways. If only she could stop it, help him heal, make the pain go away.

'Why do you say these things, baby,' she says gently, rocking him slowly. 'It's you, only you, you are everything.'

'I can't....' he starts to say, but then stops, shakes his head, and stares at the floor again.

Sophie keeps soothing, rocking, stroking, kissing his neck, his shoulders, his head. And slowly the tension leaves him, loosening his arms, his jaw, his back, his shoulders. He turns to kiss Sophie and their mouths merge. And then Sophie feels the strong, gentle hands moving over her, gliding down her back, on her arms, enclosing her. She pushes her body against his, feels the strength, the need, the intensity, the heat.

And she remembers. She remembers.

*

Steve groans when Karen tells him she's said they'll have dinner with the Matlocks. It's as if a filthy, black cloud stuffed with acid rain has covered his personal sun, blotting out all joyful brightness.

'What's wrong with that?' Karen says, turning to him from the bedroom mirror where she's putting on her make-up. Throughout the application of her foundation, blusher, eyeshadow and mascara, she's been telling Steve what an enjoyable day she's had talking to Mrs Matlock by the pool. She's clearly feeling much better, and Steve notices that she even forgets to have a go at him for spending so much time away from her.

'Let's not,' he says. 'I've already had dinner with them.'

'There's nothing wrong with having dinner with them again.'

'But I don't *want* to have dinner with them again. Once is enough to last me a lifetime. Let me put it this way – I doubt that I'll get anything more out of the experience than I got last time.'

'Oh for goodness sake, Steve. It's only dinner. I'm not asking them to move in with us. Stop making such a fuss. And you could do with a shave. Quick, hurry up.'

Steve scratches his stubble, leans past Karen at the mirror and looks at himself.

'No, don't think I'll bother,' he says. 'I quite like it like this. Goes quite nicely with all the red in my face.'

'Don't be ridiculous. It looks all messy. Go on, hurry up. We're due to meet them in five minutes. Oh, and I've said we're getting a new kitchen, so don't be surprised if it comes up in conversation.'

'Right,' Steve says automatically, then realises. 'What? Since when are we getting a new kitchen? First I've heard about it.'

'Oh Steve, you really are hopeless, aren't you. You'd be happy with those old units for the next ten years. Easily pleased, that's your trouble. Of course we're getting a new kitchen. I've been thinking about it for ages. Let's face it, if I don't think about these things, make sure the house is all nice and everything, then no-one will. Least of all you.'

And that's that. Steve doesn't argue. After all, it's how most of their major decisions are made. Karen decides something, tells him, and then they go ahead and do it. No point arguing with her. A very strong-minded woman is Karen.

He shaves while she puts on a blood-red smear of lipstick, then they go down to the hotel restaurant.

Steve doesn't say much during dinner, leaving that side of things to Karen and Maureen. He eats his chicken xacuti and plain rice slowly and steadily, speaking pleasantly when spoken to, watching the Matlock girls and Clive swallowing large wedges of pizza from the European section of the menu, Mr and Mrs Matlock devouring grilled chicken and chips.

He listens to Maureen and Karen discussing brands of dish-washers, moisturiser, the quirks of neighbours, unwise purchases by friends and relatives, soap plots, star marriages and separations, and wonders how they can talk so long and en-thusiastically about these things, subjects he has no interest in whatsoever. His mind keeps wandering. Back to the beach. To Sophie and dolphins.

But as the evening grinds on, Karen brings up his job, and both Maureen and Arthur want to talk to him about it.

'Good steady career, the police,' Arthur says. 'Good income, good benefits. A young man could do a lot worse. A lot worse.'

'Must be very exciting,' Maureen says, red face shining with anticipation. 'Catching criminals and everything. You must see loads of crime every day.'

'Yeah, sure,' Steve says, 'but it's not all chasing bank-robbers down the street, you know. Most of our time's taken up with professional criminals, people who make a living from it. Bur-glaries, car theft, drug dealing, that sort of thing. Then there's domestic violence as well, of course. You're much more likely to be attacked by someone you know than someone you don't. And despite all the scaremongering about old ladies being mugged, the people with the biggest risk of being involved in a violent incident are young men under twenty five. Though that's mostly drink related.'

'He's right, you know,' Clive says, swallowing a large gulp of beer. 'That happened to me, just before Christmas.'

'I'm sorry to hear that,' Steve says. 'Were you okay?'

'Yeah. My knuckles were a bit sore the next day, like. Right good hiding I gave him. That'll be the last time he knocks over someone's pint for a while.'

'Right,' Steve says. There's another pause, but Clive doesn't say anything else. He's too distracted by the sight of uneaten pizza crust on Angela's plate.

'But it is a fascinating job, though,' Steve says, directing it at Maureen. 'You get a lot out of it. The best bit really is helping people, keeping them out of trouble. You've got to get out there, get to know people so you can predict things and stop them from happening.'

'Oh, Steve,' Karen cuts in with a forced laugh. 'You're only a policeman. Stop trying to make out you've got to be a big psychic or something. You're not Sherlock Holmes, you know.'

She laughs again, a high, awkward titter. Maureen joins her. Steve's jaw tightens.

'Sherlock Holmes wasn't a psychic,' he says, slowly, forcibly calm. 'And anyway, that's not the point.'

But he's lost it. The point has floated off into the balmy night air on the fumes from Karen's gin and tonics. Steve looks deep into his Kingfisher as Karen tells Maureen what kind of house the Chief Superintendent and his wife live in.

*

'You go ahead by all means but count me out of it,' Barney says, holding his hands up at chest height, palms outwards, warding off Iain's suggestion.

'But I think we're in there,' Iain says, getting enthusiastic.

'That's the problem, you see. I'm not entirely convinced that *there* is somewhere I wish to be *in.*'

'Can't you at least try?' There's an edge of desperation to Iain's voice that Barney does his best to ignore. 'Make an effort with the other one. Come on. If nothing else, at least it gives us a seat. I'm fed up standing. It's too hot.'

The Pandora Cafe is jumping, revving up for the New Year. Iain and Barney have been there a couple of hours, the last few minutes of it standing talking to two vaguely hippyish, middle-aged German women.

The women spoke to them first. Or rather Martha, the more talkative of the two, had started speaking to Iain when they were both trying to get drinks at the bar. She and Judith then joined the boys by the dancefloor, Martha making simple conversation with Iain, Judith and Barney barely exchanging a word. Then Martha spotted a free table, and the women dashed off to grab it. Now Martha's beckoning them over.

'And it would be impolite not to,' Iain adds, frowning, trying to appeal to Barney's manners.

'Oh, I suppose,' Barney says with a sigh. 'Just don't expect any miracles from me.'

They weave through the dancers with their beers, trying to dodge Israelis and Italians who refuse to get out the way.

'So. Tell me. How long you are coming here?' Martha says to Iain when they're all seated. Her face is square, ruddy, carrying weight. Short, spiked, grey-blonde hair. Hard blue eyes. Hmm, Iain thinks. Maybe Barney's got a point.

'About a week altogether, more or less.'

'But your first time in Goa, yes?'

'Yes. First time.'

'Your friend also?' She points to Barney, who's doing his best to talk to Judith. Iain hears the words 'internal combustion engine'.

'No, he's been before. A couple of times, I think.' Iain nods, although he's not sure why. He can't seem to think of much to say.

'Me, I have been here five years,' Martha says, her ice-cold eyes opening wide as she holds up five stubby fingers.

'Five years? That's a long time to live here. You must really like it.'

'Sometimes I am going back to Germany for holidays. No, I am joking,' she says, in the same flat tone, with the same expressionless face. Iain tries to find the joke but fails.

'In wintertime,' Martha says, 'there is much snow in my area of Germany. I do not like this. So in wintertime for five years, I am coming to Goa for one month. It is better than cold, I think.'

'Yes,' Iain says. 'Much better.'

'I am staying at the same place each time. It is a nice place. Not so expensive. Very clean. This is important.'

'Yes. Very important,' Iain says, wondering why he can't start his conversation motor. Maybe it's her tone, he thinks. The flatness, the lack of colour in the language. It's deadening. Or maybe he's just flooded his engine with Kingfisher.

*

Steve walks past Iain and Martha's stilted conversation as he heads for the bar and buys his third Kingfisher. He escaped from the hotel after dinner, saying he needed a walk because he was a bit stiff. Bored rigid would have been a more accurate description. Karen, Maureen and Arthur got cosy at the hotel bar, while Kim, Angela and Clive continued to sit at the table in the garden, the girls drinking cocktails, Clive slugging back Cannon 10000, the strongest beer on offer.

Steve knows why he's in Pandora's. There's no point kidding himself. He hasn't arrived by mistake, happening to wander in whilst on his walk. The walk always had one destination, one motivation.

But after three quarters of an hour, she's still not there. The prospect of not seeing her depresses him. He just wants to tell her about the dolphin trip, or maybe just glimpse her from across the bar. That would be enough.

Steve pays for his beer and stands by the bar for a minute, enjoying the sensation of the cool bottle in his hand. All the beers have relaxed him a little, the soft, sticky night dampening the tension in his muscles, a gentle ease seeping into his soul. He looks around the bar. He doesn't mind the people. After all, it's not how you look that matters. No, he doesn't mind them, but he minds that Sophie's not one of them. He suddenly feels out of place again, and takes a long drink of his beer to try to soothe himself.

Scabs nudges Jez when he sees Steve standing there.

'Ain't that the copper you was telling me about? The one that was talking to French Sophie?'

Jez squints. Crash Mary jerks into life at the word 'copper'.

'Yeah, that's the bastard,' Jez says. 'Don't know what he's up to. Could be undercover or something, helping the Indians. Wouldn't put it past them. Bastards.'

'Only one way to find out,' Crash Mary says, easing his bulk up off the bench. He smiles. 'Go and ask him the time.'

Crash Mary lumbers through the crowd with his beer in his hand and stands next to Steve at the bar.

'Cheer up mate,' he says, grinning. 'You're depressing all the customers.'

Steve looks up at him, at the six foot three inch bulk of muscle and fat, the bald head, the ten earrings, the beads. Doesn't matter what people look like.

'Sorry,' Steve says with a sickly smile. 'Just thinking about something. Got a lot on my mind.'

'Haven't we all, mate. Haven't we all. Still, might never happen.'

'That's what I'm afraid of,' Steve says, and takes another long swallow of beer.

'So you over here working, then, are you?'

'Me?' Steve says, surprised. What a strange question. 'No, just on holiday. Two weeks. You?'

'Been here since the start of November.'

'Lucky for some. You travelling or something?'

'Nah, just Goa. Don't go in for all that travelling lark. Temples and stuff. Leave it to all them posh kids. Anyway, if you're on holiday, you should relax a bit. It's Goa. Don't look so stressed out.'

Steve smiles, and suddenly he feels like talking about it. He needs to talk to somebody, say it out loud, maybe make it a bit more real. A stranger's as good as anybody. Better, probably.

'Oh, it's just women troubles.'

Crash Mary nods, and looks back over to where Jez and Scabs are sitting. Nat's arrived, her legs draped over Jez's lap, whatever disagreement they had now lost in affection.

'What kind of troubles?' he says.

Steve takes a deep breath and thinks.

'Did you ever see a film called '10'? Big hit in the 80s. With Dudley Moore in.'

'Little genius, he was. Him and Pete. Yeah, I think I seen it. That the one where he falls for that American bird on the beach? Funny hairstyle. Funny name.'

'Bo Derek.'

'Bo bloody Derek! That's the one. You get to see Julie Andrews' tits in that. I'm sure it's that one. Couldn't believe it. Julie Andrews, of all people. It's like seeing the Queen with her kit off. It feels kind of wrong, but you can't stop yourself from look-ing. Incredible.'

'Yeah, well, that's what I'm in,' Steve says with a sigh. 'The Goa version of '10'.'

'Yeah?' Crash Mary's eyebrows raise. 'I take it you're Dudley Moore, then?'

'In a manner of speaking.'

'You don't look much like him, but if you say so. And your wife's Julie Andrews, is she?'

'If it was a film, yeah. But she doesn't look much like her in real life neither.'

'And that's what's happening to you, is it? That film?'

'Yeah. Bloody nightmare.'

Crash Mary thinks for a second.

'Still, look on the bright side,' he says. 'Old Dud gets to shag Bo Derek in '10'. *And* you get to see Julie Andrews' tits. Life could be a lot worse.'

Could be worse, Steve thinks. *Is* worse. And where the hell is Sophie? Just to see her, just for a minute.

They talk for another couple of minutes, but then Steve de-cides he doesn't want to go any further into his problems. He realises he's not really in the mood for company, only Sophie, and she's not there. He buys Crash Mary a beer for listening to him, then catches a motorbike taxi back to the hotel while Crash Mary lumbers back to the table and gives the others the all-clear. Just another confused package tourist.

Karen's in bed, snoring lightly, as Steve creeps into their room. He looks down at her in the half light.

Life could be worse, he thinks. A beautiful, strong wife. A woman who knows her own mind, who looks out for him, who keeps him right. A nice home, a good job, a good life. Many a man would be jealous of what he'd got. Yeah, it could be a lot worse.

Or maybe it could be a lot better. Maybe. But if he tries to make it better, if he even thinks about it, he could risk losing everything. And then suddenly it'll be worse than ever. What the hell does he think he's doing?

He undresses and gets into bed as gently as he can, anxious not to wake Karen. His muddled, drink-fogged mind seeks and finds the untroubled oblivion of sleep.

*

'How d'you mean, 'getting nowhere'?' Iain says as he pisses over a small, withered bush in the field next to Pandora's. The boys are on a tactical discussion break.

'I'm not sure there are terribly many interpretations of the term. I can't get much plainer than 'getting nowhere'.'

'But you've been talking to her for ages, that Judith girl.'

'That's not strictly true. I've been talking at her for ages. She hasn't played much of a part in the whole process. She smiles occasionally. In fact, I'd be damn insulted if she didn't. But she never quite seems to get around to actually saying anything.'

'So what have you been talking about all this time? I thought you were getting on like a house on fire.'

'Well, first of all, I've got to say that I regard my primary role here as a decoy, distracting dear Judith while you try to make hay with her chum, so I don't feel that the subject matter of my monologue is terribly relevant. It doesn't have the slightest bearing on what I'd be talking about if I was actually trying to chat her up.'

'Sorry, I think I missed the bit where you told me what you've been talking to her about.'

Barney's shoulders slump as they walk back to the main entrance.

'Oh, do I really have to tell you?'

'I'm intrigued,' Iain says. 'You've been talking to her - at her - for an hour, so, yes, I'm intrigued about what you've been saying.'

'Well, if you must know, most of the first half hour was taken up by a lecture on the history of the industrial revolution and its direct ramifications for modern day society.'

'My God. I'm surprised she's not in the bog right now removing her damp underwear.'

'Well, I told you. It was a diversionary tactic. Once I realised her name wasn't Fraulein Chatty, I knew that I'd have to do all the talking. So I thought the industrial revolution was something I could pad out for a while.'

'But the industrial revolution. I mean, come on.'

'She was damned lucky, actually. I was toying with the idea of explaining the reasons behind the collapse of planned farming in the old Soviet Union.'

'Girl doesn't know what she missed.'

'Exactly.'

They stop near the bar and check how much money they've got. Not much. A couple of hundred rupees between them.

'Anyway,' Barney says. 'I trust your seedy little scheme is progressing as planned.'

'Yes and no. The 'yes' is the horny bit. The 'no' is the taste bit. I'm kind of grappling with the concept a little. I mean, can I actually shag a woman who looks like her? But then again, I need sex desperately and she's available. That's what I'm trying to keep uppermost in my mind.'

'Is it working?'

'Sometimes.'

'That's about as much as any reasonable man can expect.'

They rejoin the waiting women. Iain's trying to think of subtle, oblique ways of asking Martha whether she wants to continue talking somewhere else. In a private room. He doesn't get a chance to ask.

'I will be coming with you,' she says, standing up.

'Oh,' he says, caught off balance for a second. 'Fine.'

They say quick goodbyes to Barney and Judith at the door to Pandora's and walk in the dark to Iain's room. Inside, Martha's eyes sweep the contents and the condition of the simple cell.

She goes over to the bed and presses down on the mattress with her hands. A satisfied smile creeps onto her lips when she feels its firmness. She sits down on it, shaking off her flip-flops.

'It is good that we have sex now, yes?' she says.

'I hope so,' Iain says. 'Absolutely.'

Martha pulls off her t-shirt and unhooks her bra. Her grape-fruit-sized breasts maintain a healthy jut, refusing to sag. Iain cheers silently. Then she lies back on the bed and slips off her pyjama-style trousers. She's wearing low-riding brown panties, which she leaves on.

'I am a very direct person,' she says. 'I hope you do not mind this.'

'No, no, not at all,' Iain says, starting to unbutton his shirt, turned on by the situation, surprised at being turned on. 'A lot to be said for directness. I won't hear anybody knock directness.'

'Some men are not so happy with this.'

'That's some men for you.'

Iain steps out of his khaki trousers and joins Martha on the bed.

'You must understand,' she says, face to face with him on the spongey pillow. 'I am very sensitive about some things.'

'Oh, sensitive is good. Don't worry about that. I'm always very careful about sensitivity.'

'I knew that you would be. I can recognise these things.'

Hurry up, hurry up, thinks Iain. Let's get to the shag bit.

'Sensitivity. Very important thing in a person,' he says.

He runs his hand down Martha's side, barely touching the skin. He's impressed with her body, despite himself. It's a bit squat, but her skin's smooth and taut.

His hand reaches her pants. He slides his fingers beneath the elasticated waistband. He's turned on even more than before. He doesn't mind admitting it. He'll still try to get it over with quickly, though. After all, it's an orgasm he's after, not a relationship.

He moves his hand round slowly. As his little finger reaches the edge of her pubes, she grabs his wrist.

'You have contraceptives?' she asks him, pushing herself up on one arm.

'Sure.'

'Let me see them please.' She removes Iain's hand from her crotch.

Iain leans over the side of the bed and scrabbles around in his shabby toilet bag. He pulls out a sealed box of twelve Fetherlites. Martha grabs them from him and examines the packaging, peering at it, turning the box around in her hand, reading all the information there is to read. Iain lies there watching her, irritated, until she slits the plastic covering with a thumb nail, opens the box and takes out two purple foil squares.

'These will work, I think,' she says.

'I certainly hope so.'

With a stretch and a wriggle, Martha squirms out of her underwear. Iain's encouraged. He stands up and hauls his boxer shorts off, forsaking the preliminaries, glad of Martha's no-nonsense attitude. He gets back on the bed and lets his fingers continue their route down her side, but he's positioned so he's looking right into her eyes from a distance of three inches. It unsettles him, so he moves his head down to her chest, pecking light kisses at the top of her left breast. His hand's almost back in Martha's crotch, his lips almost to her nipple, when she stops him again.

'Now you must wash your hands.'

Iain goes blank a second, wondering if he's too far gone, if he heard her right.

'Sorry?

'You must wash your hands,' she says again. 'This is very important. There are many germs, and I am very sensitive to these things. It is important for me.'

'Right, okay, sure,' Iain says, not understanding, trying to be nice.

He gets up, shuffles his feet into flip-flops, grabs his toilet bag and pads over to the screened-off toilet area. Techno plays somewhere in the distant dark. A dog barks in a lane nearby.

He takes out his shower gel and scrubs his hands in the meagre dribble from the tap, doing it carefully, making a performance out of rinsing and washing and rinsing again. If washing his hands properly means he'll get a shag, it's the very least he can do.

After a quick rub on his towel, he trips back to the bed. Okay, start again.

'Let me see them,' she says before he can do anything. He holds his hands out, feeling very weird, not knowing how to take the situation.

She looks at both sides of his hands, checking his nails. They seem clean enough to her.

'Okay,' she says, laying her head back on the pillow. 'Continue now.'

Iain's beginning to go off the idea. He's looking directly into her eyes again and is about to shift his gaze when she pushes her mouth against his. They kiss awkwardly, mashing lips and clicking teeth together. Iain thinks he feels stubble but tries not to think about it. He decides it's time for action. He moves his hand straight to her crotch and she opens her legs, admitting him. He plays his fingers around her entrance, slicking through her wetness, before slipping a finger into her, getting it into a slow rhythm, feeling her hips moving in time against his hand. She reaches down and starts tugging his hard-on. Doing it well, he thinks. Good technique.

They carry on for a few minutes, Martha bucking harder into Iain's hand. Then, in a flat, but loud tone, she speaks into his ear.

'You can put your finger in my anus, please.'

'What? Oh. Right,' he says, and starts to pull his finger out of her. She stops him with the hand that was gripping his erection.

'No, no. Like this,' she says. 'One here, one here.'

She positions his thumb and forefinger accordingly, each with their own entrance to play with. Iain starts to get back into his rhythm, alternating the slides from finger to thumb, finger to thumb. Martha's moaning, grinding her pelvis, gripping his hard-on too tight. He's glad when she lets go and grips onto his hand instead, helping it work into her, pulling his wrist back and forwards, his finger and thumb now slipping inside her at the same time, dual entry strokes. She pulls his hand faster and faster, bucking herself against it, moaning, clenching, gasping, reaching a pitch before the last, shuddering, slow thrusts, then stopping completely.

Her breath comes out in quick rasps as she eases Iain's fingers out of her. Her eyes are closed. Iain worries for a second that she might fall asleep, so he starts stroking her left breast.

'That was good,' Martha says, but without expression. That was bearable, Iain thinks.

'I enjoyed it too,' he says.

'Yes? This is good that you are enjoying it. Some men are not enjoying this so much.'

'That's some men for you,' Iain says, waiting for her to get her breath back, waiting for his turn.

Martha's face has a red sheen, a sunburn and exercise glow.

'And now you must wash your hands,' she says.

'What? But I've just washed them.' Iain's getting freaked-out. What the fuck's going on?

'But it is important that you wash them again. The anus has many germs. It is easy for me to catch them if you are now to put your finger in my vagina again. I told you I am very sensitive for this. That is why I am not having sex so much, because there is a problem with germs for me. It is very important.'

Iain's irritated as hell, but tries his best not to show it. He doesn't say anything, just gets up, grabs what he needs and goes back over to the sink.

Weird, he thinks. Definitely weird. Ultra-weird. Howard Hughes type weird. Almost too weird. And it's not even as if she's pretty. You can always excuse some weirdness if they're pretty enough. But this. This is definitely on the far side of weird.

He washes his hands, muttering inside his head, standing there in the dim light, starting to wonder if this is real or whether he's just smoked too much of the Manali grass he bought this afternoon.

He's not turned on like he was before. The weirdness has put him off his stride. His semi-erection's preparing for sleep.

Iain dries his hands. That's it, he thinks. Nothing else for it now. Got to get it all over and done with as soon as possible.

When he gets back to the bed, Martha notices that he's well on the way to being flaccid. She kneels up and draws Iain by the hand towards her. He lets her, although he's not all that bothered about foreplay any more. He'd be happy enough just to get on and go for it, bring the night to a quick, juddering end.

But then she sinks her mouth onto him, takes him deep, then pulls back, concentrating on the head, and Iain's face is gone in rapture, transformed by it, transported by it.

Martha works him with her mouth, her lips and tongue massaging him, bringing him up, and his horny, turned-on pulse returns. He's euphoric, his eyes closed, legs quivering, getting almost too much pleasure, feeling he could die of bliss.

She breaks off suddenly, letting him go. Iain almost cries. He can't speak, but his face says it for him. What did you stop for?

Martha looks up.

'We can have sex now,' she says blankly. 'Put on a contraceptive.

Iain does as he's told.

CHAPTER NINE

The shopping trip

Jez isn't looking forward to the conversation, but he knows it has to happen. It's been three days since he placed the order with Hassan. Two days since he got turned over. God knows how many days until he gets enough money together.

But Jez has been doing his sums. He's got nearly a hundred quid from his stash in the room, around a hundred quid he had on him that the cops missed, plus fifty or so from Nat's emergency fund, although she doesn't know it yet.

Then there's the haul from selling the scooter and the cash from the bum-bag. Another hundred and fifty. And there's the couple's camera, which he hasn't managed to sell yet but must be worth about twenty to him.

On top of all that, he's taken in a couple of hundred in new advance sales - although he's still got to supply the orders from before he was robbed.

Altogether, the princely sum of six hundred quid, more or less. A princely sum that's four hundred and fifty quid short of what he owes Hassan.

Time to start negotiating.

Hassan's sharp eyes pick him out from a distance. When Jez is twenty yards away Hassan nods at him then calmly walks away from his stall. Jez takes his time, casually turning off the main path. He knows the way well enough by now. He makes sure no-one's looking then ducks into the room where Hassan's waiting.

'My friend, sit, sit,' Hassan says, and they both squat on the floor. 'I am looking for you yesterday. Last night ektazy is coming. Top quality. Made in Bangalore. Best supplier. You have money?'

'Yeah, about the money, Hassan. Something I gotta talk to you about.' Jez clears his throat as the smile leaves Hassan's face. 'Had a bit of the trouble with the police, didn't I. Took all me money. Wait,' he says, as Hassan looks ready to explode. 'Not all of it. I've got some more. Anyway, what I'm saying is, I've already given you a hundred and fifty quid, so if I give you another four hundred and fifty now, that's six hundred. Half the money in total. So you give me half today, and I'll bring you the rest of the money in a few days' time. Then you can give me the rest of the E's. Can't say fairer than that, can you.'

'What is this you are saying to me?' Hassan says, his face like thunder. 'You don't have the money?'

'No, what I'm saying is I've got half the money. Give you the other half in a few days.'

'I don't want your half-money bullshit,' Hassan shouts, jumping to his feet. His pale eyes blaze at Jez. 'Full money. This is what I'm wanting.'

'Yeah, but I told you. Had some trouble with the cops, didn't I.'

'This is not my problem. This is your problem. And your problem is to get full money.'

'But if you give me half the E's now, I can get you the money in a few days. What's the problem? I get my drugs, you get your money, everybody's happy. That's the deal, that's what we agreed. Didn't say anything about all at one time, did we. I might have come here today, you might have only got half of them, a third, whatever. What would I have done about that? I'd've said, fair enough, give me the rest when you get them. Things like that happen in business. No point losing your temper over it.'

'You think I am a fool?' Hassan says, getting angrier, looming his barrel-chested bulk over Jez, shaking a fist in his face. 'You make big order. Very difficult, very much problem for me. But I get, and now you come to me with this half-money bullshit. You are making big trouble. You are bringing money tomorrow, full money.'

'Come on Hassan, be reasonable,' Jez pleads, watching Hassan pace up and down. 'We've done business how many times?'

'This is big business, and now you are bullshitting me.'

'When have I ever let you down before? Always paid up, always in the currency you wanted. Never let you down before, have I?'

'This is enough let down for all business,' Hassan says, eyes burning.

'Okay, okay, I'll get you the money in a couple of days.'

'Tomorrow you are bringing.'

'Not tomorrow. Two days Hassan,' Jez says firmly, trying to stare him out. It's a show. His heart's battering away like mad. You did not piss off the Kashmiris, especially not a big player like Hassan. There'd been rumours in the past about unpaid debts and people going missing. Maybe Hassan was involved, maybe not, but the overall message was clear. You just don't mess them around.

'Look, here's the first bit of the money,' he says, pulling a wad out of his pocket. 'Four hundred and fifty quid, yeah? I'll bring you the rest in a couple of days.'

Hassan counts the notes Jez hands to him. It's Jez's last card. Let him feel the cash.

'Okay, two days,' Hassan says, conceding, but his tone still sharp. 'But after that, if money is not coming, big problem.'

'And you'll give me half the E's now, yeah.'

'Not half. One hundred I am giving you.'

'Come on, Hassan, half...'

'Or maybe I not giving you anything!' Hassan says sharply, cutting him off.

Jez nods reluctantly. A bleedin' hundred. Taking the ones he's pre-sold out of the equation, that'll leave him with about twenty.

He has to hang around for ten minutes while Hassan goes off, hides his cash, gets the drugs and drops them off.

Jez leaves the hut and starts striding along the path, feeling the heat slap his naked torso. His stomach's churning with worry. At least Hassan bought the deal, and at least he's got some E's and a hundred and fifty quid left over. But it was always going to be tight getting the cash for Hassan before he got robbed. But now? Another six hundred quid. Where's he going to get that kind of dosh in a couple of days? Shit, you did not piss off the Kashmiris.

He considers his options. He doesn't have many. Borrowing money, maybe, although it's pretty unlikely. Then there's more advance sales, and of course selling the E's Hassan's given him, especially if he can avoid people he already owes them to. But there's only one option which has any hope of bringing in the sort of cash he needs to keep Hassan sweet, get the rest of the E's and maybe keep his ballocks attached to his body.

Time to go house-hunting.

*

'Baby?' Sophie says, stroking her hand down Henrik's cheek as he lies on the bed.

Henrik opens his eyes but doesn't say anything.

'Baby,' she says softly, not wanting her voice to hurt his sleep-sensitive ears. 'I'm going to the Flea Market. I said I'd help Kristina. You sleep, baby.'

Henrik closes his eyes again, almost as if he hasn't heard anything, his face set in a dull mask.

Sophie slips leather thong sandals on, puts her Rajasthani mirrored-cloth bag over her shoulder and leaves their room as quietly as she can. She walks along the red dust path through the palm trees. Her movement is languid and she's smiling to herself, her body's memory filled with last night's tenderness.

A woman sitting on a chair at the front of a small general store calls out Sophie's name as she passes. Sophie smiles, waves, and walks over to her. The woman is middle-aged, fat and greying, her features more Portuguese than Indian, wearing a shapeless, floral-patterned cotton dress.

Sophie sits and talks with her for a couple of minutes. Eventually she buys a packet of Four Square cigarettes and moves on. She likes the pace of life, the fact that nobody's too busy that they can't stop and chat for a while.

After a while she comes to a narrow tarmac road on the outskirts of the village. The day's visitors are beginning to arrive. They've travelled from all parts of Goa; day-trippers from the expensive resorts in the south, curious tourists from the hotels of Baga, Calangute and Candolim, the people crowding into Anjuna for the New Year scene, checking out the Flea Market while they're there.

Sophie loves the Flea Market - the colours, the bustle, the smells, the buzz of a bazaar with the attitude of a picnic. She follows the main drift of people, taxis, motorbikes and scooters. If she'd wanted to she could have walked along the beach and got in that way, avoiding all the hassle of the hawkers and touts crowded into the narrow lane of stalls at the main entrance. But she prefers taking it head on. It's more like going into a definite place, weaving through the stalls with everyone trying to grab the tourists' attention, then the path opening up to the wider market area with mats and informal cafes and juice bars spread out on the ground beneath the trees as far as the eye can see. Going in any other way, she feels, is like cheating, sneaking in, avoiding the sensory assault.

Once inside, she does what she does every Wednesday, walking around each section first to see the action. To a first-timer, the market may seem random and chaotic. But after a while, the organisation becomes clear. Different ethnic groups keep to set patches in the market ground, selling different wares in different ways.

First, Sophie walks past the boisterous, chattering Karnatakan girls selling sarongs, bags and cushions, rough brocades in a hundred different shades of red, heavy-chunked necklaces, wrist and ankle bracelets. Then past the impassive, no-haggle Tibetans, sitting quietly on mats while tourists pour over brass bowls, trays of rings, fine chains, bright necklaces shining with semi-precious stones, Buddhist prayer wheels and fingerbells, all spread out on coloured sheets in front of them.

Then past the Kashmiris, restless and twitchy men ready with the hard-sell at the slightest hint of Western interest, urging deals on brass Hindu gods, silver boxes with hidden drawers, garish papier mache ornaments, elephants carved from soapstone, marble eggs, fat rosewood Buddhas and cobras.

And then past the racks of clothes. Shirts, trousers, light cotton dresses, belts and t-shirts with fake labels; Reebok, Nike, Calvin Klein. Then stalls selling only baseball caps or rubber flip-flops, plastic sunglasses, marble and wood chessboards, or small, plastic boxes of bright red saffron strands.

And everywhere, squeezed amongst the tourists shuffling around the narrow paths, are the ear-cleaners, the tabla-drum sellers, the snake charmers in dirty turbans, the cold drinks vendors with cracked polystyrene cool-boxes, the ragged children tugging at shirts to beg a few rupees, the toothless, twisted old beggars hobbling along with gnarled crutches jammed under one arm, hands outstretched, eyes red and defeated.

And the smells. Incense from a thousand smoking sticks of nagchampa, patchouli, frankincense and lavender. The warm spices drifting up from cooking pots stirred by old women squatting on their haunches. Sweat and aftershave, salt from the sea, sweet, earthy smoke from fires fueled by cow dung.

Finally, Sophie reaches the Westerners' section, the three lines of stalls run by long-stayers, one-season triers, semi-permanent businesses, quick-buck hopefuls, all strictly segregated from the rest of the market. In a way, this is the section Sophie likes best. Rows of crystal jewelry, funky hats, day-glo tops, swimwear, hammocks. Ancient, grey-bearded, leather-faced men selling Hindu philosophy with their trinkets, sweet-faced hippie girls with orange garlands selling tattoos and piercings to be performed by their mad-eyed, straggle-haired boyfriends. Stalls of weird bracelets in ordered glass cases, coloured stones and burnished metal twisted into wands, chips of meteorite fashioned into necklaces, handcrafted Italian chillums, sandalwood earrings, rosewood hair-sticks, rainforest palm nuts, t-shirts printed with sunbursts, stars, moons.

Sophie smiles and says hello to some of the stallholders as she walks along one of the rows. Halfway down it, Kristina's sitting cross-legged on a mat polishing earrings made from twisted wire and blue stones. She takes them from a red velvet bag one by one, rubbing a soft cloth over them before placing them in a line on a wooden tray in front of her.

'Any business?' Sophie says brightly as she steps over the tray and sits down beside Kristina.

'Yeah, good business today,' Kristina says. She's in her mid-thirties, but has a brown, lined face suggesting she's years older. Her bright yellow, starburst-pattern lycra shorts and cut off top were probably designed for someone much younger, but she wears them with unconcerned ease. Her accent is American-English German. 'One necklace, two pairs earrings. One thousand five hundred.'

Kristina's light blue eyes scrunch up as she smiles. Her teeth are long and slightly discoloured.

'That's good!' Sophie says enthusiastically, returning the smile.

'For sure. New tourists today. They are all coming today. All white and pink and red and sweating too much. I'm putting out everything, all my stock today. I have a feeling it is going to be busy for us.'

Sophie sits back, hugs her knees, and watches the people go by.

*

Steve and Karen make love in late morning. She initiates it, waking him up with gentle strokes.

'Probably too late to go for breakfast,' Karen says, running a finger down Steve's naked chest. 'Never mind. We can have our own breakfast here.'

Steve doesn't feel like it, the edge of a hangover blurring his senses. He goes through the motions anyway, pressing all the usual buttons, waiting until she comes before upping the pace and releasing his sperm into the safe custody of Karen's birth pills.

She goes to the toilet straight away, a quick shower to wash off the grime of the act. As the blunt throb of a hangover headache starts to beat in his temples, Steve remembers something. They used to lie together after having sex, all coiled in each other's arms. He doesn't know when it'd happened last. Or why it had stopped. Or why he's only just noticing it.

When Karen comes out of the bathroom and starts getting dressed, Steve takes her place. He downs a couple of Nurofen Plus and steps into the tepid shower. He feels odd. The sex hasn't satisfied him at all. There was something about it, something too clinical, and not just on his part either. It was as if Karen did it as an aerobic exercise, just doing it by numbers.

It was the first time they'd had sex since arriving in Goa. They'd both been too tired the first night, then she'd been ill. But that couldn't explain why the sex was so functional, could it? He lets the water pour over him, just standing there, trying to get his head straight. The Nurofen will kick in soon. He'll be fine.

But why had the sex been like that? In fact, why had it been like that for a while, God knows how long? There had to be a reason. Karen was a very sexy girl. Everybody said so. Although they'd better say it with the right amount of respect if he was around or there'd be trouble.

Steve stays in the bathroom a while, pottering around, shaving even though he doesn't need to, then comes out and dresses slowly, gradually adjusting to the day. Karen's ready before him, in loose cream shorts and a black t-shirt with the D&G logo in big white letters on the front.

As they walk towards the gate leading out of the hotel compound, Karen insists they get a taxi.

'I don't think it's that far, love,' Steve says. 'Might be a nice walk.'

'If you think I'm walking for miles in these shoes, Steven Harrison, then you've got another thing coming. Getting all sweaty and tired out before we even get there. No thank you very much. It's alright for you, you're acclimatised. What about me? Been ill in bed half the time. Probably die from heat exhaustion on the way there.'

Steve can't be bothered arguing. He asks the driver of a

white Ambassador taxi parked on the road outside to take them. Five minutes down dusty roads and they're there, at the end of the path leading down to the main Flea Market entrance.

'Walking from here only,' the driver says, turning around in his seat to look at them with bored eyes. 'Car is not going.'

Steve and Karen get out, and Steve pays the driver the two hundred rupees he asks for.

Once they fight past the stalls lining the main path Karen's besieged by small Karnatakan girls holding bits of coloured cloth up to her arms, draping sarongs over her shoulder, her fresh, white pinkness acting as a beacon announcing her recent arrival in the country.

'Get off. Go away,' she snaps at them, brushing the cloth off her sharply. 'Steve, do something. They're all over me.'

Steve leads her away by the hand, waving apologetically at the girls.

'No business,' he says to them.

'Only looking. Looking is free,' the high pitched calls come back. 'You look my shop?'

They walk on quickly, Karen keeping a tight hold of Steve's arm.

'What a nightmare,' she says. 'Did you see them? Filthy, those girls were. Think I'll need another shower after this.'

'Come on,' Steve says, a little annoyed at her. 'They didn't mean any harm. Only kids, most of them.'

An Indian man in freshly pressed white shirt and trousers, with a small leather case hanging over his shoulder, steps out in front of Steve.

'What?' Steve says, as the man pushes a laminated card into his hand. The card has black, typed writing on it. As Steve reads it, the man moves to the side and grips Steve's shoulder.

'Must hold still,' the man says, and Steve looks quickly again at the card. Something about ear-cleaning, trained, healthy. He feels the point of something in his ear and recoils.

'What the hell do you think you're doing?' he snaps, putting up a protective hand.

'Look, look,' the man says, holding out his hand. He wipes a brown, waxy mass onto his thumb from the end of a short, thin wooden stick. 'From ear is coming,' the man says, pointing at the side of Steve's head. 'Very dirty, pollution everything. Five minutes cleaning only and good as new.'

The man makes a move towards Steve's ear again, but Steve backs away.

'Not a chance, mate,' he growls, raising a warning finger at the man as he and Karen move off, the ear-cleaner pursuing them for less than ten yards before seeing another potential customer. He wipes the dirty wax back onto the stick.

Steve and Karen edge along the busy paths through the stalls, Steve more interested in looking at the people than what they're selling. He takes in the sad, impassive Tibetans, the urgent anxiety of the Kashmiris halfway to a sale, the broad smiles and attempted English slang of the clothes sellers.

'All very samey, a lot of it,' Karen says, turning her mouth down, examining the glass case of jewelry at yet another stall.

'I'm a little bit hungry, love,' Steve says. 'Reckon I'll get a quick bite to eat. Just a snack or something.'

'You're always thinking about your stomach, you are. It's not long till lunchtime. You can wait till then or you'll spoil your appetite.'

Steve's not sure what annoys him more - being treated like a child or the misplaced accusation that he's always thinking of his stomach. Karen's forever saying things like that, and he doesn't know why. And it hasn't really bothered him that much until now.

'Just a snack, though,' he says. 'Thought I might get one of them samosas,' he says, pointing to a pile on a sheet of newspaper next to an old woman with a gas stove and wide, smoking pan of dark oil.

'Oh, don't touch those,' Karen says with a sour face. 'They're not hygienic. You don't know what sort of germs you'll get off them. That pan doesn't look too clever for starters.'

'Doesn't seem to bother everybody else.'

'Well, they'll regret it later, believe you me. Just wait. Wait till we can have a proper sit down and get something nice. It's not long till lunchtime. You'll survive,' she says with what she thinks is sarcasm. Steve just finds it patronising.

They look around more stalls, Karen asking Steve what he thinks of this dress or that necklace for another half hour until she's made her stand, until she says they should look for a place to eat.

Makeshift cafes, little more than a scattering of a few tables and chairs, hide under cloth canopies amongst the stalls. Karen eyes a couple of them.

'Don't look too clean,' she decides out loud.

They come to a more permanent structure in the middle of the market, a cafe with waist-high walls, a roof and a door. Karen sticks her head inside, but doesn't like the look of the busy, gloomy interior. She's just about to shake her head at Steve when Maureen calls out from a table set over to the side.

'Coo-ee. Karen. Steve. We're over here.'

Karen smiles and goes over to the table where Maureen and Arthur are slouched in plastic chairs fanning themselves. Angela's sipping at a bottle of Pepsi through a straw.

'Been doing your shopping, have you?' Karen says, sitting down. 'You must be worn out.'

'Ooh, there's some lovely things here, Karen love,' Maureen says, her face flushed and glistening. 'There's some rugs over there would go perfect in our front room, wouldn't they Arthur. And there's this beautiful wooden statue of a deer. I can just see it now on me sideboard. I'm quite taken with that, aren't I Arthur.'

Arthur looks like a red balloon, ready to burst. He's staring out through the wire mesh that passes for a window.

'So you haven't bought anything yet?' Karen says.

'No, love. Had a look round, but thought we'd best rest up a bit. Get our strength for all this bargaining. We were just about to get a bite to eat. You had your lunch yet? I didn't see you at breakfast. You must be starved. Mind you, I'd willingly starve meself if I could get a figure like yours. Beautiful figure, hasn't she Arthur.'

'Beautiful figure,' Arthur repeats. Maureen looks at him in surprise.

Steve doesn't doubt it. A beautiful figure. Everybody says so.

He sits down next to Karen who's already talking about more potential purchases with Maureen. A waiter comes with menus. When everyone else has given the waiter their orders, Steve asks for samosas. Five of them.

He has a charge of rebellious delight when he sees where the waiter gets them from. From an old woman hunkered down over a gas stove and a pan bubbling with black, black oil.

*

'I mean, I'm as clean as the next man,' Iain says, shaking his head, sitting next to Barney at a table on the other side of the cafe from the Harrisons and Matlocks. 'You won't find me being lax when it comes to personal hygiene.'

'I should think not,' Barney drawls, stretching out on his chair.

'Especially in hot countries. You've got to watch your smell and filth levels in hot countries. I'm very particular about that.'

'Goes without saying.'

'Five times!' Iain holds up splayed fingers at Barney. 'Five times she made me wash my hands. That's not clean. That's bonkers mentalism.'

'Really,' Barney says, acting disgusted. 'That's no way to talk about your girlfriend.'

'She's not my... listen, that was a one-off. No more. No thank you.'

'So it's safe to say it wasn't the ultimate sexual experience?'

'Might have been if I hadn't spent half the time scrubbing layers of skin off my palms. To be honest with you, it was much better than I expected. Not great, but not as bad as it could have been.'

'Well, she certainly looks like she's had plenty of time over the years to perfect her technique.'

'Ach, I know. I doubt whether anyone's used the words 'spring' and 'chicken' to describe her recently, but seriously, the sex was okay. I wasn't too keen on the kissing bit, though.'

'God, please, spare me the details,' Barney says, shuddering. 'I really don't want to get a picture of it in my mind. That sort of thing can scar you for life.'

'Oh come on. She wasn't that bad. I mean, I know she was no looker.'

'No looker? My dear chap, she had the grace of an ingénue and the face of an engineer. I don't think whether she was a 'looker' or not is even an issue here.'

'Yeah yeah yeah, alright,' Iain says defensively. 'At least I had sex. At least I didn't shake the woman's hand and send her off into the night like you did.'

'Well, I certainly wasn't going to attempt to seduce her. I

have standards, you know.'

'Yeah, and I have an empty sack today and I've very chuffed about it, thank you very much.'

Barney shrugs and finishes his drink.

'Come on,' he says. 'Let's go look at more of the tat. There's much worse to come, I assure you. You haven't seen the half of it.'

They pass through the clothes stalls, bamboo racks packed with hundreds of shirts and dresses, then through a tented area of sarongs. Then into the Western section. Past crystals, day-glo, hammocks, piercings.

'I think some of the old guys here must have taken way too much acid in the '60's,' Iain says out of the corner of his mouth to Barney, who laughs.

'When we were children,' Barney says, 'we were told that acid was a truly terrible thing because it would make you think you could fly, and that you'd climb up to the top of a multi-story car-park and jump off. But from a cursory examination of this lot it seems that the only really dangerous long-term effect is making you think that sitting around selling quite outrageously stereotypical new-age trash is somehow a worthwhile and fulfilling existence. Although I suspect that doesn't apply to her, of course. Her existence is extremely worthwhile whatever it is she's doing.'

'Who?'

'Up there on the right. Sitting next to that harpy.'

'Ah. Her. Yup, I'm with you.'

They slow their pace. Iain stops at the stall, glancing down at the tray of jewelry, trying not to stare too blatantly at the girl. Sophie looks up at him and smiles. Iain feels weak.

'Hi,' he says in a thin, reedy voice. He hates himself for it. 'Hi,' he says again, much deeper this time, then feels pathetic.

'Hi,' Sophie says back with a light laugh.

Barney takes Iain's arm.

'Come on,' he says, and leads him away.

'What did you do that for?' Iain whispers at him urgently as they go. 'I might have been building up to something there.'

'And were you?'

'No, but that's not the point. I might have been.'

'We couldn't stay there. I don't know if you managed, in your clearly smitten state, to actually take in what her stall was selling.'

'Yeah. No. Jewelry or something.'

'Exactly.'

'So?'

'Women's stuff.'

'So?'

'So you're either looking at the jewelry for your girlfriend back home, your girlfriend here on holiday with you, your cross-dressing self, or your tranny lover. Which may or may not be me. Which, may I just say, I am less than delighted about. Or none of the above, which will lead her to the inevitable conclusion that you are, in fact, just having a blatant perv.'

'I think I'm still at the 'so?' stage,' Iain says, sneaking a look back down the path at Sophie talking to another potential customer.

'So, none of those scenarios are likely to impress her. Which admittedly is irrelevant unless you actually attempt to seduce her at some point.'

'Which is still a theoretical possibility.'

'As is time travel.'

'I see where you're going with this.'

CHAPTER TEN

Eight annas a peg

Jez is crashed out on a mat in the Western section of the Flea Market behind a stall stacked high with cheap tapes. The home-made mixes have names like 'The Goa Vibe', 'Trancing Anjuna' and 'Bamboo Forest Full Moon Party' written in black on orange paper covers.

He's minding the stall for Ramrod, who's off somewhere getting something to eat. Jez doesn't have much to do. His main role is to make sure no-one nicks the tape player which is pounding out samples of the music on sale.

'It's not a selling job as such,' Ramrod had said to him. 'If they like it, they'll buy it. If they don't, they won't. There's no real selling to do. Think about it more as a security position.'

Jez is relaxed and feeling relatively secure, his head resting in Nat's lap. But there's something nagging away at the back of his foggy mind.

'Hear about that poor bastard Roberto?' he says to Nat. 'Italian geezer. Long hair.'

'What about him?'

'Came off his bike, didn't he. They took him to hospital in Panjim, completely out of it. And then he wakes up, and they've only gone and cut his arm off, haven't they. In England, they'd probably have given him an aspirin and he'd have been fine. Here, they chop your bleedin' limbs off. This fucking country, I'm telling you. Barbarians.'

'That's really awful. Poor bastard.'

'Yeah, you're telling me.'

Jez smokes for a while, soaking up the music, but there's

something still bugging him.

'Nat,' he says, looking up at her with concerned eyes. 'What would you do if I lost me arm?'

'Help you find it, I suppose.'

'No, but seriously,' he says, raising his head up so he can look at her properly. 'What'd you do?'

'What sort of a question's that? That's a really sick question, that is.'

'No, but just considering. What'd you do?'

'I'm not getting you. What you mean, 'what'd I do'?'

'I mean, would you stay with me an' that?'

'Course I would,' Nat says, reaching out a hand to touch his arm, giving it a reassuring stroke. 'Take more than that to drive me away from you. Way I look at it, it's one less arm for me to worry about.' She laughs lightly. 'Course I'd stay with you, don't be silly.'

'Oh. Right,' Jez says, and puts his head back down on her thighs. Nat brushes her fingers across his dreads.

'Same as you'd do for me, really. Silly question,' she says.

'Nah, sorry babes,' Jez says, his face wrinkled in disgust. 'I love you an' that, but I really cannot stand amputees. Gives me the creeps, it does. Spooks me right out. Nah, you're on your own on this one. You lose an arm or a leg or something and you wouldn't see me for dust.'

By the time Jez picks his head off the ground and rubs it, all that's left of Nat is the red, swirling dust from the path she's just stormed along.

'What now?' he says, confused. 'What bloody now? She's gone and done it again! I don't believe this.'

He looks across the path at Crash Mary who's sitting at a stall strewn with carved stone chillums, talking to the craftsman, Pieter from Holland.

'Oi!' he shouts over, raising his voice above the music. Crash Mary looks up. 'She's only bleedin' gone and done it again. Pissed off. No reason.'

Crash Mary stands up, lumbers across the path and thumps down beside Jez.

'Just pissed off?' he says.

'Just pissed off,' Jez says, fiddling with the volume control on the tape player, knocking it down a couple of notches. 'What is wrong with that girl?'

'Well, it's full moon tomorrow, innit.'

'What's that got to do with anything?'

'Probably on the rag, in't she.'

'Nah, that's just the thing. I thought of that. She's not. Definitely not.'

'Probably coming up to it, though.'

'Maybe. I dunno. What's all this got to do with the bleedin' full moon?'

'It's women, innit. Some of them, like, all start spilling their beans in tune with the lunar cycle.'

'The lunar bleedin' cycle? What you on about?'

'Phases of the moon, innit. They tune into it somehow. The full moon's when it all comes on. Happens all the time, apparently.'

'Why's that, then?'

'Dunno,' Crash Mary says, shrugging. 'Tides an' that, innit.'

'Sounds like ballocks to me. Where d'you hear that, then?'

'You told me.'

'Did I?' Jez thinks for a few seconds, his face set in concentration. 'Mind you, it's got a plausible ring to it, dunnit. The moon. That must be it, then. That's why she keeps getting the hump. She's a bleedin' werewolf or something.'

*

Maureen and Karen want to go off and shop. Karen's been getting excited by Maureen's descriptions of haggling, convincing herself she'll be a natural at it. Steve's not so sure. He doesn't feel like traipsing around on a shopping expedition, but feels even less like staying in the cafe with Arthur and young Angela for company. He decides he should get Karen a present, something nice to make up for the way his mind's been betraying her.

As both women make a move towards the stalls selling carved wooden ornaments, Steve says he thinks he'll try the other way.

'What for?' Karen says.

'Just, you know,' he says, shrugging. 'See what's around. Maybe do some haggling of me own.'

They agree to meet later. Steve kisses Karen on the cheek, winks and smiles at her, then leaves the women to their shopping.

'Silver,' Karen says, putting her head next to Maureen's, watching Steve make his way through the crowd. 'Bet it's something silver. He knows I can't wear gold. I'm allergic to it. It doesn't matter really, because I've always thought gold's a bit tacky. Not your stuff, obviously, Maureen. Looks lovely on you. Just in general, I mean.'

'Oh, I know what you mean, love. On some women, gold just makes them look dead common.'

Steve wanders through the stalls, idling, not having any clear idea of what he's doing or what he's looking for, just letting his eyes drift across anything that comes in front of them. He notices several stalls selling chillums, ingenious pipes, large cigarette papers. The sweet scent of grass hides behind incense, but not well enough that Steve can't spot it.

More or less legal here, he thinks. The police seem to take a very relaxed view towards hash and grass. Still, it doesn't seem to cause any trouble. Rather be in the middle of a flea market with stoned-out hippies than in the middle of a meat market with pissed-up lads.

Steve is surprised to see a couple of stalls manned by Westerners. And then he realises they're all Westerners, all the stallholders, right down the line. Old guys with beards, young tanned men with short mohicans, pierced eyebrows, dreads, tattoos, young women in tiny tight shorts and flame red hair. And Sophie.

Sophie. His ears roar. His heart hammers. His brain flips.

She's sitting on a mat behind a glass case, reading a book, one finger tucked absently into her mouth, gently biting on it as Steve watches. He finds the scene devastating to look at. He's nervous, almost scared, but it's not enough to stop him going to her.

'Hi,' he says, with an awkward grin. 'See you've got a shop, then.'

'Steve!' she says, looking up, taking her finger from her mouth, smiling wide and bright. 'I am so happy to see you. Come, sit with me.'

She pats the mat beside her. Steve doesn't need to be asked twice. He steps over the jewelry trays and joins her.

'So this how you make your living, is it?' he says. He feels hungry for any little detail about her life.

'No. This belongs to a friend. She has left me in charge. I make a good boss, no?' She puffs herself up, arching her back. Steve forces himself not to look at her chest, but it's difficult.

'A very good boss, I'm sure,' he says, smiling.

'And I am very good to all my workers. I let them take breaks whenever they want.'

'I bet you're very popular.'

Sophie smiles.

'So,' Steve says, trying to appear light. 'Quiet night in last night?' He doesn't want to know the answer, but asks the question anyway.

'Yes, very quiet. We didn't go out at all.'

'Oh?' Steve says, hating the thought of it, hating the 'we'. 'It's a pity. I thought I might see you in that Pandora Cafe place again.'

'That would have been nice. Maybe I would have gone if I knew that you were there,' she says, her face sympathetic. Steve wants to believe her. He aches at the thought of it.

'Oi-oi,' Jez says to Crash Mary, looking over. 'I see old Mr Coppernob's trying to get Sophie into his manacles again.'

'Where do you come up with all that ballocks?' Crash Mary says. 'Do you lie awake at night and try and think it up or something?'

'Inspiration, Crash me old love. Can't help it. A poet's soul, I got.'

'So,' Steve says, his nerves melting away in the easy warmth of Sophie's presence. 'Do you think you'll be there tonight?'

'No, not tonight. Always after the market everybody is watching the sunset from the steps of the Sun Temple, on the beach. Then there is usually a party somewhere afterwards.'

'Oh. What, like a private party?'

'Oh no, it is a party for everyone. Lots of dancing and music. It will be very good tonight, everyone practising for the New Year tomorrow.'

'So where is it, this party?'

'You are going?'

'I don't know. I might,' Steve says, caught off balance. 'If everybody's invited, it'd be rude not to.'

They smile at each other.

'And your wife?' Sophie says, polite interest on her face. 'She will be coming too?

Steve shrugs, searching about for words, uneasy at the thought of it.

'Oh, I don't know. She's, like, it's not her kind of thing, really. I wouldn't have thought.'

'Same as Henrik. He doesn't like to go because of the music.'

Something's on Steve's lips, something he wants to say to her, but he can't.

'Well,' he says. 'That's probably as good a reason as any not to go to a party. So where is it tonight?'

'I don't know yet. They always say very late where it is. Sometimes there are problems with police.'

'What, because of the noise?'

'No, because sometimes the people running the party cannot find enough money to pay them.'

'Pay them for what? A permit?'

'No,' Sophie laughs. 'A bribe.'

'A bribe?'

'Of course.'

'How often does this happen?'

'Every time.'

'And doesn't anybody report the police to their superiors? Their bosses?'

'Their bosses are taking some of the money too, I think. This is the way things work here. If you want to have a party, you pay the police. If you want to sell drugs, you pay them. If you get caught with drugs, you pay them not to arrest you. If you want to sell clothes on the beach, you pay. There are very many bribes.'

'Bloody hell,' Steve says, running his hand over his hair. 'Some of the cops here must be pretty rich.'

'Many of them,' Sophie says. 'But the richest are here in Anjuna. The bribes are much bigger here. I was told that if a policeman wants to be transferred to Anjuna, he must first pay the man in Panjim who decides on the transfers. Maybe up to two hundred thousand rupees.'

'Why?'

'Because the boss knows that the bribes are bigger here and that the policeman will get rich, so he wants a share of the money in advance. If not, no transfer.'

'But.... but that's outrageous,' Steve says, genuinely shocked.

'Perhaps,' Sophie says, shrugging. 'But it is the way things are done.'

'Even taking money from drug dealers?'

'Of course. Many of the Kashmiri people you see in Anjuna selling things near the beach, this is all a facade. Their job is to sell drugs. Each of them pays a policeman nine thousand rupees a week to let them do their business in peace.'

'Good God. I never knew it was like that.'

'Goa surprises everyone,' Sophie says, smiling at him, her head angled slightly to one side. 'Just when you think you are beginning to understand it, it surprises you again. But I don't want you to think badly of this place. It is not all corruption and drugs here. There is much beauty, many good people in Goa. I love it here.'

'I can see why,' Steve says. 'I think, I mean, me too, love, all that,' he stutters out, surprised that he's choking on the words. He swallows, clears his throat, and recovers himself.

'It's a pity you don't know where this party is,' he says. 'I don't fancy wandering around half the night trying to find it.'

'Yes, but I'll know later. If you meet me I could show you.'

Steve is sure his heart has stopped beating. Either that, or time is standing still. Nothing seems to be working. Not his brain, not his mouth. Before he knows what he's doing, he's speaking again.

'Yeah, that'd be great,' he gushes out, then starts panicking at what he's doing. He knows he shouldn't be doing it. He knows it's madness. He knows, but none of it seems to matter.

'I could meet you at the Vibe,' Sophie says. 'You know where that is?'

'Top end of the beach, isn't it? Lots of really bright colours. A bit weird.'

'That's it,' Sophie says, smiling. 'We could meet, maybe, eleven o'clock?'

'Fine, yeah, good,' Steve says. His sturdy moral walls have been breached by the brush of a butterfly's wing.

Kristina comes back. Steve stands, smiles, says hello. Kristina sits down next to Sophie and starts telling her about the vegetarian food she's just had. Steve feels awkward again, suddenly left out. He looks down at Sophie. She looks up at him and smiles, a smile so bright that he feels like running, shouting, cheering.

'Eleven o'clock, then,' he says during a break in Kristina's description of falafel and potato salad. 'The Vibe.'

Sophie nods, still smiling.

'See you,' she says.

'Yeah, see you.' He smiles at her one more time, unable to help himself, not wanting to leave her, but forcing himself to walk away. He moves slowly down the path, trying to control himself. He's excited and terrified at the same time, his nerves tingling, a joyful euphoria swelling his chest.

How can it be wrong, he says to himself. How can it be wrong if I feel like this? So alive. More alive than I've ever been in my life. And she feels the same, you can tell. She was the one who suggested meeting up. She feels it too, she must do. It can't just be my imagination.

Steve suddenly realises that he forgot to tell Sophie about the dolphin trip. He thinks about going back, but he's worried that it'll look like he's hounding her, using any excuse to be in her company. Which might not be far from the truth. He'll tell her later.

He's getting near the centre of the market, near to where he suspects Karen and Maureen will be, when suddenly he remembers. He has a quick glance around and spots a small Kashmiri jewelry seller. He goes over and points down to the nearest bracelet.

'How much is that one?'

'Five hundred. Very good piece of craftsmanship.'

'Yeah, sure. There you go,' Steve says, handing him five one hundred rupee notes. He pockets the bracelet and walks away. Then he remembers something else. He steps back a few paces.

'Is this silver?' he says, holding out the bracelet.

'Silver, silver,' the man says, nodding quickly.

'Right,' Steve says, not sounding convinced. Then he puts it in his pocket again and strides on.

*

Iain's seen enough of the Flea Market. There's only so much tourist junk a man can take, he decides, before running the risk of losing his lunch over someone's flip-flops. Besides, he wants to avoid bumping into Martha. Barney's just surprised at how much bigger the market's got in the last few years.

'Of course, the prices have gone up a lot as well,' he says as they walk through the slow crowds towards one of the beach exits. 'I overheard a few sales being made for quite ridiculous amounts. It's all to do with the package tourists, you see. They've got a lot more money than your average traveller, so the stalls inflate their prices accordingly. Added to that, the tourists are less willing to bargain, or don't bargain hard enough. Oh, and nowadays you get all this sort of thing coming in as well,' Barney says, sweeping his hand over to where a man in white is squatting down poking a stick in the ear of a fat, pink, crop-haired young man sitting on a stool.

'The ear-cleaner wallahs. Only they don't so much clean the ears as give them a quite nasty infection, often needing hospital treatment. It's all a matter of sleight of hand. First they pretend to have taken some rather filthy wax out of your ear, then, believe it or not, they keep finding little stones in there as well, and charge you around 250 rupees for each stone they take out. The stones are in their pocket all the time, of course. It can be quite amusing to watch, especially if the customer refuses to pay the amount asked, because then old Mr Ear-cleaner wallah tries to put the stones back in.'

Barney walks up to the customer. It's a worried-looking Clive, gripping Kim's hand.

'I'm terribly sorry,' Barney says, smiling. 'I don't wish to appear rude, but I was just wondering. Why would you let a complete stranger poke a long wooden stick into your ear, very close to an incredibly sensitive instrument, namely the eardrum? Hmm? Why on earth would you do that?'

Barney stands in front of Clive, rubbing his fingers back and forth across his chin, impatient, making it clear he expects a proper answer.

'Well, it's India, innit,' Clive says, confused.

The ear-cleaner makes two sharp twists with the stick.

Clive's eyes and mouth jerk wide open in response, but it doesn't seem to affect him otherwise. 'When in Rome, and that. Get your ears cleaned.'

'He's not trained, you know,' Barney says quite cheerily, his grin growing. 'Doesn't have a clue what he's doing. You don't see many Indians getting it done, do you?'

'Well, Mr Know-it-all,' Kim says, indignant, taking exception to Barney's tone and accent. 'If 'e's no good, how come 'e's dug out three stones from there already? More trained than you'll ever be. Poor Clive could've gone deaf, walking round with all them stones in his ear.'

Barney laughs, then the laugh gets louder and he has to move away. Then it's booming out of him and he's almost choking, coughing, holding his stomach, then holding onto Iain, who's laughing too. Clive and Kim stare after them, bemused.

Then Clive's eyes and mouth stretch wide twice more. The ear-cleaner's found another stone.

*

'Bloody good sunset,' Jez says as the last segment of orange slips down past the horizon. He's sitting outside the Sun Temple on broad steps leading down to the beach. Back behind him in the bar large speakers herald the sunset with hardcore. Nat's sitting on the step behind Jez, her arms around his neck, their tiff long forgotten.

Jez hands his joint back to Nat, who passes it on sideways to Becky without taking a drag. Her good mood has returned, but she doesn't want a smoke just yet. All around them, joints, chillums and pipes salute the sun's last glow, a hundred columns of thick white smoke swirling in the soft, warm breeze.

'What you doing tomorrow, then?' Nat says to Becky, who's staring ahead, nodding to the music.

'Dunno,' she says, her voice nasal and whiney. 'Sunset here, then the party I s'pose. Dunno.' She shrugs, her bare shoulders shining like rich wood.

'Sounds like tonight,' Nat says and giggles.

'Yeah. Like tonight I s'pose.'

'But we gotta do something different. It's New Year an' all that.'

'Yeah. Full moon an' all, innit.'

'What we gonna do tomorrow night?' Nat says to Jez, leaning forward so she's looking at the top of his head. 'For New Year an' that.'

'Do what you like, girl. Come twelve I'll be so off me face I'll be past caring.'

'Useless, he is,' Nat says to Becky. 'But we gotta do something. Make an effort. Like we did at Christmas. 'Cept not so Christmassy.'

Iain and Barney thread their way through the bodies on the steps, past the lounged form of Jez and the offhand chattering of Nat and Becky, past the speakers, which make Iain's chest vibrate in a way he finds particularly unpleasant. They get to the bar and shout for two beers.

'You know what we should do?' Nat says. 'We should climb that hill over there, watch the sunset from there.' She points over to the hill at the south end of the beach, the outcrop of land separating Anjuna and Baga beaches.

'Don't be stupid,' Jez says. 'What we wanna do that for? Means coming down in the pitch bleedin' dark. Packs of wild dogs and everything. No thank you. No chance.'

'Yeah. S'pose,' Nat says dreamily. 'Be nice, though.'

Back in the bar, Iain and Barney drink their beers, then order two more. The music's too loud for effective conversation, so they peoplewatch instead. Iain's not too impressed with the people that he can see. Barney's not all that bothered.

Fires are being lit on the beach in front of the Sun Temple, light to dance by in the warm-up to the bigger party later. The sun's barely gone, but a velvet darkness has draped the scene already.

Let's split,' Iain shouts in Barney's ear. 'Too loud to perv. Ruining my concentration.'

They drink up and go, picking their way down the steps with

more difficulty than before, the meagre light from the fires making it hard to see stray fingers, toes, ankles. They make it to the beach without causing anybody serious physical damage. As they walk away, people are dancing, building up the vibe. Barney stops and looks back at them.

'You know,' he says. 'I do like to see young people having a good time.'

*

A thin figure shuffles slowly along the dusty tarmac road, a slightly bandy gait giving the impression of a tired-out cowboy. The long white hair spilling out from under his brimmed hat, the chaotic beard. Jesse James come down from the hills at last, after all this time, to turn himself in. All this time.

The Doc spits a well-chewed cardamom pod into the red dust beside the road, the pod joining faded cigarette boxes, crushed plastic bottles, ripped bags and rotten fruit, an all-you-can-eat buffet for the all-consuming rib-ridged cows wandering around.

He walks past small shops, the tiny travel agent's office, then the restaurants and hotels by the crossroads. Starco's, Jose's House, and the ugly concrete box of the Beach Bay Hotel. The Doc looks up at it.

'Goddamn bastard built that should be shot,' he mumbles to himself. 'Goddamn rat-shit architects. Antichrists, what they are.'

He strolls past the crowd of motorbike taxi riders, past the half-clad Westerners doing their evening food shopping at the tiny shack-like grocery store. Then down the beach road, past new hotels and half-built bars, around the corner, past the clatter from the cafes near the bus stop, then down the dirt path towards the beach, past Mermaid's Guest House. He nods to it, the recognition of one old timer to another. Then along the trail through the palms, past Sonic bar and restaurant, past the sparse, tatty gardens of the Palm Beach Resort, dim lights flickering on the long verandahs. The Doc scowls at it.

Used to be just palm trees, all of it. From here on down to the beach. Nowadays it's all busy-business stalls and tourist souvenirs and hard sell 'buy buy buy' consumerism. All poisoned, all of it. Whole area sick with poison. Couple of houses before, that was all. And the bar, course. The old bar.

When the Doc reaches the Vibe, he just stands outside looking at it for a while. It's been a year, maybe two, since he last set foot inside it. He can't quite remember.

The day-glo paintings, the rough seats, the anti-drugs poster above the bar, the ambient sounds, the straggle-haired refugees from the Sun Temple. The old bar, but not like the old bar.

He walks in and sits at a table by himself. A man behind the cashier's counter motions to the small waiter.

'The old man is here again,' he says. 'The Doc. You tell him. No funny business. I am not having him upsetting customers again.'

The waiter slips down the steps from the back of the bar and walks towards the Doc's table. He's nervous. Something about the old man scares him. Something in his eyes.

'Okay,' he says, leaning over the table. 'No trouble from you, okay? Boss say you causing trouble, you go outside. Okay?'

'Trouble,' the Doc snorts. 'Ain't no trouble. Bring me a beer. Cold one.'

'He meaning it, okay? You are not upsetting customers. Boss meaning it.' The waiter's wagging his finger at the Doc.

'Boss?' The Doc turns in his seat to look at the cashier, who's looking somewhere else. 'You mean little Victor? Known that boy since he was knee-high to a piss-ant. Wouldn't know trouble if it came up and bit him on the ass. Used to run around this place butt naked when he was a kid. His old pa used to run this place. Fisherman's bar. No name. Just everybody called it Hector's, after Victor's old man. None of this 'Vibe' trash. What kinda name's that for a fisherman's bar? Old Victor'll be turning in his grave. Fisherman's bar, cashew feni eight annas a peg. Didn't know that, did you? Too young, I guess. I was drinking cashew feni here long before you was even supping on your mama's milk.'

'No trouble, okay?' the waiter says, not sure what the Doc's talking about. He wants feni, maybe?

'No trouble, no trouble,' the Doc says back, parroting him. 'Didn't need say nothing 'bout trouble in the old days. Slightest sign you were getting out of hand, old Hector hisself would pick you up, throw you right out the door till you sobered up. Okay, okay, no trouble. Just bring me a beer. Cold one.'

Trouble, the Doc thinks. Thirty years. When have I ever been trouble? It's the new one's brought all the trouble. With their designer beers, wailing for wholemeal bread and pancakes and real honest-to-God coffee and cornflakes for breakfast and sit-down toilets and hot showers and Western music bars and concrete hotels with satellite TV's and swimming pools and bottled water and as many souvenirs as they can stuff in their greedy bags. They brought the trouble, not me. They *are* the trouble.

A couple of young men come up to the table, cracking the Doc's brittle concentration.

'Anyone sitting here?' Iain says, pointing at two empty chairs. The Doc waves a hand, mumbles, and stares off into the middle distance.

'I think that's a 'no',' Iain says quietly to Barney, a grin on his face. 'Or at least we can sit here until some-one bigger comes along.'

They fill the chairs, drink their beers, and the Doc gets back to rambling around in his mind.

Trouble. The Doc huffs. Nobody asked me about trouble. Nobody ever asked if what they were doing was troubling me. And the rest of us. Nobody ever said, did we mind if they crashed the party. Nobody ever asked if we minded that they shipped the bricks in, built up concrete bunkers, called them 'resorts' and started kowtowing to any whim of any greed-eyed home-comfort Westerner that came shuttling in. Nobody ever asked us if we minded them changing it, twisting it, poisoning it, letting it get stuffed full of puffed-up, trough-fed consumers here to claim their God-given right of two weeks in the sun on their terms and to hell with what the country was like before. Them others no better. Goddamn rich kid play actors. Playing at being hippies, dressing like it was just some fashion state-ment. None of the values. No beliefs. Just one more consumer disposable fashion trend. All of them in this bar. None of them got any belief in the purity of life, of the self, of existence.

'Not one Goddamn one of them,' he says, hardly realising he's said it out loud.

'I beg your pardon?' Iain says politely, turning to him.

'Not one Goddamn one of them know shit about the old days,' the Doc says, a cold, grey fire in his eyes. 'Time was, just six of us here, maybe seven. Drinking with fishermen, real men, risked their lives every day. Just us and them and a bar. Eight annas a peg. Maybe the radio playing if old Hector was feeling frisky, little bitty dance music, pure Portuguese. Just talking, liv-ing pure and simple. None of this look-at-me poison-ass, rat-bastard, fashion-freak parade shit. Not in the old days.'

'You were here in the old days?' Iain ask, interested. He can tell the man's angry, but he's not worried. As far as he can tell, the anger isn't directed at him.

'Old days,' the Doc huffs. 'The only days. This was a fisherman's bar. Thirty years ago maybe. Only bar in Anjuna. Anjuna for me. Some heads got hip to Calangute, Baga. Not me, no siree. Anjuna. Always was. Dug the village, the fishermen, the palmtappers, all the dudes. Still stay with a fisherman now, sweetest dude you ever did meet, heart big as a lion's. Just a simple man with a simple life. All of them then, sweetest people on God's great green earth. Bit of life about them. Smiling, laughing, singing. Just sweet living and the sound of the sea. Cool and wide. Cool and wide.' His face falls and his voice hardens. 'Before them rat-ass bastards came in and done poisoned the whole scene.'

'So,' Barney says, leaning forward, arms on the table. 'I take it that you're not a terribly big supporter of the changes here.'

'Changes?' the Doc snaps, eyes shooting out ice chips. 'Carnage, what it is. Carnage. Concrete, pancakes, Coca-Cola, hot water, rat-ass poisonous Goddamn murderers. Can't move for some dude trying to sell you some shit, tourist shit, whatever. Everywhere. Hurry hurry hurry, money money money. Change dollar, change dollar, you want this, you want that? Place so crowded with faggots and fools that they're queuing up to get on the beach. Time was, that was just the place the villagers took a shit in the morning. No houses, rooms, restaurants. Just one big sandy shit-house.'

Up at the cash desk, Victor's keeping an eye out. The old man seems to be getting excited again. As long as he doesn't start shouting and throwing things like he did last time, he'll let him be.

'Still,' Iain says, feeling a bit of sympathy for the Doc, wanting to cheer him up a bit. 'Look on the bright side. It must have improved the Goan's standard of living a bit.'

'Living?' The Doc glowers out from under his hat. His voice is hoarse, but sharp and urgent. 'The way they living now better'n the way they was living then? Bull-shit. From the high bows of Eden to the sewers of Soddom. Wrapped up in the sins of consumerism, married to that big, fat dollar whore. Now a man's got to stress about his satellite TV, his souvenir business, how much money-money he can make for his brand new fancy car, the competition, the money man. The money man has taken the throne. Back then, all a man had to worry about was whether he caught enough fish. Or drowned. Better or worse. The game ain't the same. You don't know shit about the old days,' the Doc says, his voice rising, his eyes blazing. 'You don't know! You weren't there, man! You weren't there!'

'But everything changes,' Barney says, laid back and wrecked, refusing to be fazed by the old man's anger. 'It would have been impossible to keep Goa the way it was. The world doesn't work like that.'

'Nothing but a Goddamn zoo now,' the Doc says, spitting the words out. 'The freak show outta no-where. Not one decent bone left. Picked clean by all them bastard scavengers. Nothing but posers and frauds and shit-stealing head-fiends, sucking up the vibe and spitting out horse-piss.'

'Hmm,' Barney says, fingers rubbing his chin. 'Just out of interest. This simple, secret paradise you and your friends found all those years ago, the one you wanted to keep just as it was. How many people did you mention it to?'

*

Quarter to eleven. It's the fifth time Steve's looked at his watch in the last ten minutes. Quarter to eleven. Can't leave it much longer, he thinks. Not if he's going to get down to the Vibe in time.

He's sitting in the chair in their room, supposedly reading his book. Karen's in the bathroom getting washed, unpainted, moisturised, ready for bed.

All through drinks at the bar and a mind-numbing dinner with the Fat Family, he's been torn about what to do. He shouldn't have agreed to meet Sophie. He knows he shouldn't. Under calm, rational analysis, it was stupid, irresponsible, dangerous, disloyal, immoral, all of it. So why did he keep trying to think of excuses to go and meet her? Why was he able to think of little else? It's all too much. Way too much.

Karen comes out of the bathroom wearing a patterned silk nightgown. She ruffles his hair as she passes him. He hates it when she does that. It makes him feel like some kind of pet. He watches her as she gets carefully into bed, lifting up the one white sheet and bringing it down over her.

'You know what, love,' Steve says, standing up. 'I feel a little bit stuffy. Think I'll have a little bit of a walk. Clear me head a bit.'

'Why don't you just turn the fan up. For what little good it'll do.'

'No, I think just a little walk. Do me good. Help me sleep a bit better.'

'Hope you're not coming down with something,' Karen says, picking up one of her magazines from the bedside table, flicking through it. 'I've had enough bother with illness this holiday already. Don't want you getting all sick and mopey as well. You know what you're like when you're ill.'

'No, it's nothing like that. Just want to clear me head a bit, that's all.'

Karen continues to flick through her magazine, not looking up at him.

'So I can expect you in the early hours, can I? Reeking of

booze? Like the last two nights?'

Steve's stuck for something to say. He hadn't expected her to make a big deal out of it. He didn't even think she'd really noticed, let alone minded.

'Come on, love,' he says, his hands out from his sides, almost pleading. 'I'm on holiday. Something wrong if a man can't have a few beers when he's on holiday.'

Karen says nothing, still flicking the pages. Steve makes towards the door, only to be stopped short by the whiplash of Karen's tongue.

'It's my holiday as well, you know. Although you wouldn't guess it by the way you've been carrying on. Might be nice if we went out together at some point.'

Steve looks at her, but she's still examining the pictures, ignoring him. She's said her piece. There's nothing more to be said. He knows it.

He takes a deep breath to concentrate his mind.

'Won't be long, love,' he says, and walks out the door, closing it gently behind him, trying not to think of the look she's probably giving him. He pads down the dim corridor to the stairs.

Down in the deserted reception area, he sits in one of the cushioned chairs and holds his head in his hands.

Madness. Utter madness. What is he doing? What does he think he's playing at, going off in the middle of the night for some secret liaison with a beautiful girl? A beautiful girl who isn't his wife. He must be absolutely mad.

What about Karen? Lying there, fuming at him. What would she say if she knew the truth? Why is he even thinking of going off to meet Sophie? It's a holiday. Holiday romances are what you do when you're in your teens, your early twenties, when you're single and free. But they're not the sort of things worth risking a marriage for. And who said anything's going to happen anyway? Maybe she's just a nice, genuine, friendly girl. Of course she is. And he's just a nice, genuine, friendly man.

So why have his thoughts been dominated by her from the first day, from almost the first second he met her?

He rocks as he sits in the chair, trying to still the storm in his head.

And when it comes down to it, what does Sophie think of him? He doesn't know, he just can't tell. What does she feel when she sees him? Anything? What does she want from him? What does he want from her? It's all madness.

Steve sits for a couple of minutes more, waiting for his brain to come up with some answers. But the questions continue to whirl and twist and mash in his stretched-out mind.

He takes a deep, deep breath. Then he gets up. He walks, slowly and decisively, back towards the stairs, back up to their room. Each step is heavier than the last as he climbs. Step by step by heavy, plodding step. Madness. Sheer, utter madness.

CHAPTER ELEVEN

Little fluffy clouds

'Maureen says there's a trip to see dolphins. That might be a bit of entertainment.'

Steve's heart drops down into his stomach, landing with a squelch on the pool of boiled eggs, toast and tea he's just had for breakfast.

'Is there?' he says, raising innocent eyebrows across the table at Karen.

'Maybe we should take a break from the sun. At least for one day. Maybe go see them next week or something.'

'Hmm. Maybe,' Steve murmurs, going back to this morning's copy of the Times of India, pretending to concentrate on the international news page. 'Yeah, saw something about it. Wednesday or Thursday or something. Doesn't sound up to much.'

'Might make a nice day out,' Karen says. With precise, careful bites she finishes the last corner of her toast.

*

'But it's going on all day,' Nat says as Jez stands and brushes the dust off his baggy trousers.

The sun's up, but the party's still pumping, ready to pulse through the day towards New Year. Jez wants to go, get some sleep, sort things out, get ready for the big scene. Prepare.

'Things to do, girl. You stay if you want. I'm gonna try and get some kip an' that.'

Nat pouts but stays, going off to dance in the palms with

Sasha. Jez ambles away through the tangle of bikes and scooters parked at the edge of the party area. A different route home for him this morning. Things to work out, then sleep. Sweet.

Jez wants to check out his targets while it's still early and relatively quiet.

He sweeps around to the back of the village. The Goans are awake, readying themselves for the day. Some of the Westerners too, just a handful, slowly rising from their huts and houses, others flopping home to crash out after the party.

He's interested in three particular rooms at the edge of the village, a little cut-off from the rest of the scattered accommodation.

He walks past the front of them first. Three basic, red-clay bricked, tiled-roofed huts.

Then he slips around the back, looking at heights, structure, window size, access, easy routes there and away. He keeps walking, never stopping, acting casual, not drawing attention to himself.

Satisfied, he moves on down the path again, the long route to his own room. He feels a surge of confidence.

Everything's under control again.

At the party he'd had to give some of the E's to customers who'd already pre-paid, but he'd avoided most of the bastards. So with last night's sales and some more orders, as well as the hundred and fifty quid he kept back, he's only about three hundred and fifty short of being able to pay Hassan.

Shouldn't be a problem, not with what he's got planned for tonight.

Right, time to hide the money. After all, you can't trust anybody these days.

*

IAIN McMILLAN'S GREAT
HINDUSTAN ADVENTURE

Hogmanay '98, Anjuna, Goa

Thought I'd better write early, because I've got a feeling tonight's going to be a particularly messy one.

Hogmanay in a hot place. Sex, drugs and sweaty techno.

Just the sex by itself would be fine, really, although I suspect that my somewhat less than outrageously impressive hit rate so far makes it much more likely that I'll spend most of the night sitting around, out of my tree, sweating like a coolie. Staring at unattainable women. Sobbing like a bed-wetter.

Similar to last night, in fact, the high point of which was when me and Barney were wrecked as hell talking to this furiously old American man who claimed to be one of the first hippies to come here about thirty years ago. He wasn't enjoying himself. I think it had something to do with the passage of time.

The times they are a-changing indeed. Pensioners used to moan about the price of bread, those immigrants next door, lack of respect from young people, and the fact that there wasn't National Service any more.

Now they complain that the drugs aren't as good as they used to be. I blame the parents.

*

Sophie watches a young Indian couple in the surf and smiles. The man's in tight brown swimming trunks, almost the same colour as his skin. He's in the sea up to his knees, beckoning to his sari-clad wife, encouraging her to come into the water. The bottom of her sari is wet from the surf bubbling around her ankles. She walks unsteadily towards her husband, shrieking giggles as the fresh Arabian Sea licks its salty tongue up the back of her legs. She reaches out to her grinning husband for support, but instead he pulls her sharply out towards himself so that the water's almost up to her waist. She squeals, but doesn't seem to mind.

The couple laugh at each other, and Sophie decides they're drunk on love.

She's suddenly aware of someone standing next to her, a few feet to her right, not saying anything. She thinks it's probably another Indian tourist out to gape at naked Western flesh. Sophie usually ignores them, but this time something makes her look up.

'Hi,' says Steve sheepishly, an uncertain smile on his face.

'Steve! I didn't think you would come,' Sophie says, her soft, clean features carved with concern. 'Sit with me, sit.'

She moves over on her sarong, sitting cross-legged, making room for Steve to kneel down in front of her. They both start talking at the same time.

'About last....' 'I am so sorry.....' 'Things were just.....' 'It was difficult....' 'I hope you didn't....' 'And I thought.....'

'Hang on. Hang on,' Steve says. 'Why are we both apologising?'

'Because of last night,' Sophie says. 'Because I didn't meet you.'

'Yeah, but it's my fault. It was me who didn't turn up. You've got no reason to apologise.'

'I wasn't there,' Sophie says, biting her bottom lip, looking guilty, then realising she shouldn't be.

'You didn't show up?' Steve says, surprised and slightly worried.

'No.'

'Why not?'

'You first,' she says, with a hint of tease in her smile.

'Well. Oh, it was just. You know. Something back at the hotel. I couldn't get away. I mean, I wanted to, it wasn't that, it was just, you know, things got in the way, time dragged on and before I knew it, it was too late. So, you know, what about you?'

'Henrik wanted to go to the Vibe. That's where he meets his friends sometimes. I didn't think about it when I said to go there. I'm sorry, I should have. Last night, I thought it would not be so good if you came to meet me and he was there as well. It would not have been so relaxed, I think. I persuaded him to go with me to the Sun Temple instead. I was worried that you were waiting for me. I'm sorry.'

'As I said, nothing to apologise for. I think you were right. Yeah, I'm sure it wouldn't have been so 'relaxed', as you put it. He sounds like the jealous type, this Henrik.'

'Oh yes. Very jealous. Too jealous. But it is because he cares about me. I know this is why he gets so jealous sometimes.'

'Must be difficult to put up with, though. I mean, sometimes.'

'Sometimes, yes. But he is a man of strong passions, strong emotions. It is only to be expected that jealousy is one of them.'

'I don't know about 'expected',' Steve says, aware of having to tread carefully. 'You can have a lot of good strong emotions without jealousy barging its way in.'

But can you? he asks himself. If so, why does he feel this jealousy towards Henrik gnawing away inside him? Is it really that bad an emotion?

'Maybe,' Sophie says, shrugging. 'It's difficult. I've been thinking about what you said, that it shouldn't be so difficult so soon. Who knows, maybe I will not be with him for much longer.'

Steve waits for her to say more, his heart aching for some reassuring words, some balm for his wretched pain. But Sophie's looking out to sea, thinking, keeping her thoughts to herself for the moment.

They're only inches away from each other, legs almost touching, skin almost pressed against skin. Steve closes his eyes. He can still feel her presence, feel heat radiating from her. It's too much. Way too much.

'Well,' he says, opening his eyes again. 'I'm glad you didn't show up. Only because *I* didn't,' he adds quickly. 'Under the circumstances. It's not that ....well, you know what I mean.'

He trails off. Sophie turns her gaze from the sea to look at him. Her deep green eyes bathe him in a soothing light.

'I know,' she says quietly, a little smile creeping onto her face. 'Are you going to stay on the beach?'

'Well, if you wouldn't mind some company,' Steve says.

'Of course. I would like that.'

Steve spreads his sarong out on the sand next to Sophie's, takes off his t-shirt and flip-flops, then lies down. He turns on his side, propping his head up with his arm, and looks at this wonderful girl in front of him. This exciting, intoxicating, happy, thoughtful, beautiful, fascinating, wonderful girl. He'd be happy to lie there looking at her for days. Or until his arm cramps up.

'There are clouds in the sky,' Sophie says, looking out to sea. 'Little ones.'

Steve looks out at the clouds, nods 'yeah' happily to Sophie, then goes back to just gazing at her.

'Some people don't like clouds. Do you like clouds?' she asks him, her mouth in an involuntary pout.

'Sometimes, I suppose. Not too keen if they've got lots of rain in them.'

'I love clouds,' Sophie says. 'When I was a little girl, I used to love watching the clouds going across the sky. When they went quickly, I thought it was because the world was speeding up and going round very fast. I thought the clouds stayed where they were, like trees when you see them from the window of a train.'

Steve laughs, delighted at it.

'It's true,' Sophie says, smiling. 'I was very young. It seemed to make sense. I could stand and look up at them and feel I was going very fast too. I could feel it, really I could, like I was going at hundreds of kilometres an hour. And I'd get this very strange feeling.'

'Dizzy?' Steve guesses, expectant smile on his face.

'No, not dizzy. Not like that. It's too difficult to explain. It was something inside of me. It's a feeling I had never felt before. But I have not had it since I was a little girl. I didn't know how to explain it then, and I can't now. Many times I've tried to get it back, this feeling. I've stared up at the clouds until my eyes hurt, but the feeling never comes back.'

Sophie looks up towards the clouds again. They're hardly moving at all. The world is going slowly today.

'When I was a kid,' Steve says, 'I used to love getting dizzy. I used to love going on those roundabouts you get in playgrounds and try to get them to go round faster and faster. Then I'd jump off and be dizzy as hell. I used to love it. But I could never get quite dizzy enough, not as much as I really wanted to. I'd always feel that there was a little bit further I could go, that I could get that bit dizzier if I really tried, that it'd feel even better. But I never got there. I nearly did once, when I was spinning round and round in my front garden, just spinning on the spot. Then I lost my balance and fell into a rose bush.'

Worry flashes across Sophie's face.

'Were you hurt?'

'I cut my eye,' Steve says, leaning over, closing his left eye and putting his finger on his upper eyelid, pointing to a tiny sliver of a scar. 'I was six years old. Two stitches that needed. I was awake right through the operation, apparently, though I don't remember anything about it now. But my mother told me that for months afterwards if I saw her or anyone else holding a pair of scissors I'd scream the house down. Because of the stitches, you see. But I don't remember any of the screaming either. I've just got to take my mother's word for it.'

'That is a very sad story,' Sophie says, her face and voice draped with sympathy. 'Are you still scared of scissors?'

Steve thinks about it and laughs.

'I am, actually, now you come to mention it. Never really thought about it before, but yeah. Not scared, exactly, but I'm not too keen on them. I don't like using them, although you've got to sometimes, obviously. God, I've never actually thought about it before. I've never actually sat down and thought, are you a bit uneasy using scissors, and if so, why? But that's it. That's all it is. It's just from the stitches, twenty years ago. Can you believe it? I'd never connected the two in my mind before. Fantastic.' He laughs. 'Now I can live my life free from the fear of scissors. I'm a new man. I can dip my hand in the sewing box any time I like. Thankyou. You've cured me.'

They laugh together, then just talk aimlessly for a while. Eventually they both lie down on their backs to let the sun bake them.

'The world's spinning faster,' Steve says, staring at the clouds.

'Really?' Sophie says, excited, sitting up and looking over at him.

'Yep. No, it's gone now. Only felt it for a second or two.'

'What did it feel like?' Sophie asks him urgently.

Steve pulls a face and makes a dismissive wave with his hand.

'Too difficult to explain,' he says.

Sophie leans over and gives him a playful but hard punch on the arm.

'You are a very bad man,' she says with a deliberately sad pout, trying hard not to smile. 'Taking the piss out of me.'

'Are you sure you didn't go to finishing school?' Steve says and laughs, and Sophie tries to hit him again but can't because she's laughing too.

'But it's true,' Steve says eventually when their laughs have faded and Sophie's stopped pouting at him. 'I'm not taking the piss. I actually felt it for a second, that the world was going round really fast, almost like it was spinning out of control. I see what you mean. It was weird.'

'Good weird or bad weird?'

'Oh, good. Definitely good,' Steve says. 'But definitely weird.'

*

The Doc stands at the gates to the Coconut Grove Hotel looking in. A lethargic khaki-clad guard sitting on a chair at the side regards him halfheartedly, then looks away.

From where he's standing, the Doc can see the squat concrete bulk of the hotel's front, the expanse of lawn with shrub-bordered paths, an edge of the swimming pool where ranks of white plastic sunbeds are sprawled with their occupants. A man in a white shirt and black trousers is ordering lungi-clad workers around the garden, supervising the arrangement of coloured lights and electric cables in the trees. Over to the left, others are constructing a low stage on the grass.

The Doc snorts. Used to be fields, is all. Buffaloes wading through paddy. White herons straight as an arrow. Trees shading small houses, farmers places, scraps of land with chickens, a few pigs maybe. All torn up and raped in the name of Mammon. Playground for the fat and greedy. Isolation tank for the scared rich.

'Goddamn chicken-shit tight-ass black-heart vibe-sucking bastards,' he mumbles, then spits in the dust and walks on. The guard gives him barely a glance.

At the swimming pool, Karen and Maureen are lounged on their sunbeds, chatting. Arthur's flaked out next to them, a newspaper draped over his face.

'And d'you know what she said to me?' Maureen says. 'Right to me face, she said it. She said she wouldn't be seen dead in a new house. She did, that's what she said. The cheek of it.'

'Some people,' Karen says, shaking her head.

'I know. And I'll tell you something else - I've seen where she lives. A crumbling old barn of a place, it is. Not fit for cattle if you ask me. Costs a fortune to heat, no doubt, rot in half the beams, and there's her trying to tell me that it's better than the house we've got on the new executive estate. Well I'll tell you something, new's always better in my book. At least you know what you're getting.'

'Oh, you're talking to the converted, Maureen,' Karen says. 'When we came to buy our place, well, Steve was toying with the idea of an old house near the centre of Cockermouth. He wasn't serious, it was just one of these ridiculous ideas he gets sometimes. Almost falling down, it was. Character, Steve said it had. Not the sort of character I want to get to know, I told him. No, I made him see sense eventually. I mean, our place isn't brand new, but once we've got the new kitchen you'll hardly be able to tell. No, you're absolutely right, Maureen. It's all a matter of quality, isn't it. You know what you're getting. It's always better to get something new.'

*

'I feel like a new woman,' says Sophie as she lowers herself back down on her sarong, her body shining with water.

You're not the only one, Steve thinks, then gives himself a mental slap for being so cheesy. He's had a wonderful couple of minutes just watching Sophie splash about in the waves, cooling herself off. He found it difficult to take his eyes away from her, especially when she came walking back up the sand towards him, her body glistening and taut from the chill of the sea. He'd wanted to go in the water as well, but decided he'd prefer to just lie and look at her instead. He can always have a swim later.

Stray drops of cold water sting Steve's skin as Sophie rubs her hair with a towel. He doesn't flinch from it. The sensation thrills him.

The afternoon drifts in slow, easy luxury. Steve delights in all the sights and sounds around them; the calls of the hawkers, the rumble of waves, the bright saris of the fruit-sellers, the gently swaying palm trees, the way Sophie's skin dries quickly in the heat.

And then the question comes up. He's been expecting it.

'Have you been married long?' Sophie asks him, a look of simple innocence on her face.

Steve shifts uneasily. One part of him doesn't want to talk about Karen, doesn't want her to intrude when he's with Sophie. But another part of him wants to tell her everything, confess all, tell her every little bit about himself so she'll know him intimately. His strengths, weaknesses, hopes, fears, motivations, values, and the wild turmoil his mind's been in for the last few days.

'Three years,' he says.

'Oh. That is not so long.'

'Well, we went out together for three years before that. Living together for two of them, more or less. Marriage was the next obvious step to take. Seemed to make sense.'

'You do not make it sound very romantic,' Sophie says, her voice soft but serious.

'Oh, I suppose the day itself, that was romantic enough. It snowed. Karen had very specific ideas about how the day would go, how everybody would be dressed, how the church would be decorated. Wanted it all to look like a fairytale, she said. I suppose it did. Not that she had any control over the weather, of course, but it worked out alright in the end.'

'And you were the fairytale handsome prince?'

Steve laughs.

'Hardly. To be honest, I didn't feel part of the whole thing. It was like I was a spectator, watching somebody else getting married. Except it was me. But it was Karen's day, really. It was the way she wanted to do it. So the day itself, with the flowers and the Rolls and the reception at Moresby Hall and her dress and everything, I suppose it was romantic. I've never told anyone, but I just wanted to get the whole thing over and done with. All that worrying and organisation and fuss. Anyway, once we'd had the holiday, the honeymoon, it was just back to normal, really.'

'So you are not very romantic? You surprise me. You seem like a romantic person.'

Steve thinks about it for a moment, staring off at the sparkling water.

'I don't know, really. There's some things I suppose I find romantic, but they're just things that tend to happen, not things that are all planned out. Like, I found the snow at the wedding romantic, but that wasn't planned. But all the rest of the stuff, no, I didn't really find it romantic at all.'

'So you didn't get married for romance? It was not really a fairytale wedding?'

'Not really. As I said, we'd been going out for a while and it just seemed to be the next logical step.'

'But what about love? Love and romance. Don't they always go together?'

'Dunno,' Steve says. 'Maybe for some people. I wouldn't say for most, definitely not. Not these days, anyway. I don't know if they ever did. Marriage is about a lot more things than love and romance. There's security and getting settled. Lots of things.'

Sophie plays around with the dry sand beside her sarong, drawing small figures of eight.

'Can I ask you a very personal question?' she says, not looking up.

'Sure,' Steve says, not feeling sure at all. 'Anything you want.'

'Do you love your wife?'

The question takes Steve by surprise, and he opens his mouth to give an automatic answer. Then he stops and considers it, which shocks him even more. It's not something he should even have to think about.

'Well, yes,' he gets out eventually, flustered. 'I mean, she's my wife. I married her.'

'You are very much in love with her?'

'Well, it depends, you know, on what your definition of 'in

love' is.'

Sophie shrugs.

'What it has always been,' she says.

'Well, it wasn't some big, passionate affair, if that's what you mean,' Steve says, wondering why he's even talking about it, wondering what he's going to say, beginning to resent the questions. 'We met, we had a few dates, we started going out, then we lived together, then we got married. It's what people do. It's life.'

'And what about love?'

'Well, obviously, that's something that happens in time, isn't it. You get used to somebody first, then it grows from that. That's the way it works, usually.'

'Perhaps,' Sophie says. 'Maybe that is one version of love. But it doesn't sound like you were ever in love. When love is crazy, and intense and passionate. When it is like a sickness. It is very powerful. Have you never been in love like that?'

'Well, it's difficult to say,' Steve says, as sick as he can ever remember. 'I mean, does anyone really know when they're in love? I don't think it's that easy just to be able to point to it and say, there it is, that's love.'

'Do you believe in love at first sight?'

I can't take this anymore, Steve thinks to himself. It's too much. I don't want to talk about it. I'm not sure I can handle this.

'I'm not sure,' he says, swallowing, struggling with it. 'Maybe it can happen sometimes. But very rarely. Not to everyone.'

'What will you do if it happens to you?'

Sophie's looking right at him, her eyes cool and warm at the same time, confusing and reassuring. Steve searches them, trying to read what she's feeling, where it all leads.

'I don't know,' he says. 'I really don't know. In a situation like that. It's not, it's not a normal situation. It's not easy to judge.' He feels himself getting nearer to something, like being drawn towards the lip of a waterfall. 'I suppose it depends on the circumstances. And on me. And on the other person. It'd depend on what they thought, I suppose. To a degree.'

'And if they thought the same way as you?' Sophie says gently.

Steve tries to find the words, tries to look Sophie in the eye. He fails at both. He shrugs instead, hating himself, every fibre in his body sick, crazy and aching intensely.

CHAPTER TWELVE

Blue moon rising

'Do you think it's a real full moon, or what?' Iain says to Barney, both of them deliciously wasted on top grade grass, sitting on the veranda outside Barney's room looking up at the bright white orb hanging over Anjuna.

'You mean as opposed to a counterfeit one?'

'No. As opposed to it being the last day of a full moon or the first day of a full moon.'

'Well, considering they only usually last one day, I think it's about as real as you can get. Of course, there's one precise moment in the day when it's absolutely full to the brim, when it can't get any fuller. The Indians are particularly keen on knowing the exact time, whether it's at 9.07 in the evening and so on. Something to do with all that astrology nonsense they're into. But to the naked eye, it doesn't make a huge amount of difference for a few hours either side. This one's blue, you know.'

'What?' Iain says, eyes flicking from Barney to moon and back again. 'No it's not. That's about as white as white gets.'

'Yes, but it's a blue one as well. The second full moon of a calendar month. Very rare. Hence the phrase. I'm surprised you don't know all this, you being a country boy, and all that.'

'I'm from Perth. It may not be the big metropolis, but it's not exactly inbreds and banjoes either. Anyway, you know what us Scots are like. When we were kids we were far too busy trying to steal stuff so we could score smack. No time to go around staring up at the sky.'

'Really?'

'Of course not. With us, it was more 'Sheepshagging' than

'Trainspotting'. Anyway, I don't know what the big deal is about the full moon. Happens loads of times. I can't understand why people get so worked up about it.'

'Oh, the full moon's incredibly important.'

'Don't tell me you're going all New Age on me.'

'Anything but. You can happily ignore all the hocus-pocus mumbo-jumbo. There are some compelling, scientifically measurable reasons for watching out for the full moon. The tides are affected, of course, that's the most obvious one. But it's also been accepted for centuries that it sends some people mad. Hence the term 'lunatic'. In fact, it used to be enshrined in English law. And there are usually more violent crime at full moon, more complaints to the BBC, more attempted suicides. Some surgeons won't operate at full moon because patients' blood flow increases, or something like that. Once you see all the statistics about these things, it's pretty difficult to deny that the full moon has a surprisingly powerful effect on us.'

'So the message is, if the raving loony doesn't kill you outright it doesn't matter because you'll bleed to death anyway?'

'Pretty much.'

'That's a disgrace. I'm going to phone the BBC to complain.'

'Get to the back of the queue.'

Iain sparks up a Gold Flake, takes the smoke in deep. He's more wrecked than he'd like to be, considering he's got a heavy New Year's Eve ahead.

'I've just thought of something,' he says, exhaling through his nostrils. 'We're just about to wander around in the dark, out of our tits, not knowing where we're going, and now I'm going to worry about lunatics with blue moony eyes hiding up every palm tree. You really do wonders for a man's paranoia, you know. Great Hogmanay this is turning out to be.'

'And a 'Hoots Mon, the Noo' to you too.'

*

'Well, it's not much of a party if you ask me,' Karen says, her lips pursed, arms crossed, holding her gin and tonic high on her left breast. In the corner of the hotel garden a sweating, dinner-jacketed trio plink-plonk their way through 'Bridge Over Troubled Water'. Couples slouch at tables dotted around the lawn, their drinks, meals and shining faces flickering in candlelight.

'You never know. It might liven up bit,' Steve says, putting on a positive tone.

'Couldn't liven this lot up if you put a bomb under them,' Karen says sourly. 'Come to think of it, a bomb's probably the best thing for them. Maybe we should have gone off to that other party Maureen was talking about. Couldn't be worse than this. Honestly, Steve, I really think you should have booked an extra star up. I know it was more expensive, but it'd have been worth it. Some of the people here. There's only one word for it. They're common. Me and Maureen were listening in to a couple from Liverpool today. Common as muck, they were. And they were openly boasting to another couple about how much they'd paid for their holiday. Two hundred and forty nine pounds! For two weeks! Last minute deal, they said. A fraction of what we've paid. No wonder we're getting that sort of people here if the tour company's going to sell off the holidays that cheap. No, I think it'd have been much better if we'd paid a bit extra and gone to one of the bigger resorts.'

'What, like one of those ones we saw in the brochure? Places with three different swimming pools, four different bars and restaurants, their own bit of beach? Their own shops? Places so big you never need to go out the front gates? What'd have been the point of that?

'The point is that it'd have been a sight better than this.' Karen stops short of saying 'dump', but Steve sees it on her lips and resents it.

'If we'd been stuck in one of those resorts, we'd never have seen anything,' he says, controlling himself. 'At least here we can mix with the locals, see a bit of local colour.'

'I can do without the local colour, thank you very much. I'm on holiday. I'm not David Attenborough, you know. I'm not filming some wildlife documentary. I've no intention of mixing with locals, thank you very much. If I'd wanted to hang about with a bunch of Pakis, I'd have gone to Bradford.'

'Karen!' Steve snaps, shocked, angry and embarrassed all at the same time. 'That's not a very nice thing to say, is it. And anyway, they're not 'Pakis',' he says, lowering his voice at the word. 'They're Indians.'

'Same bloody thing when it comes down to it. It wasn't high up my list of reasons for wanting to come here.'

'Oh, so you did want to come here, then?' Steve says quickly, an edge of sarcasm scratching his voice.

'What d'you mean? Course I did. What you going on about?'

'It's just that the way you've been going on about it, anyone would think that you'd been dragged here, that maybe I specif-ically booked this holiday and this hotel just to annoy you in some way.'

'Oh, don't be so stupid,' Karen says sharply. 'What are you getting all sorry for yourself for? You're always thinking of yourself, you are. You'd think it was you who'd been laid up ill in bed hardly able to move, the way you're going on.'

There's a pause as Steve takes a breath, tries to calm down. The band are struggling with 'Mrs Robinson'.

'When?' Steve asks flatly, the word and his tone antiseptic, scrubbed of anger and irritation.

'When what?'

'When exactly am I always thinking of myself? You're forever saying things like that. So I just want to know, when am I always thinking of myself? When haven't I taken you into account, or put you first? When haven't I been thinking of us? In six years, just tell me one time.'

'Oh for God's sake, stop being so ridiculous and watch the band. I quite like this one. You're spoiling it.'

She taps a finger on her glass in time to the music, looking over at the sweating trio.

Steve glowers at her, swallowing ever-unspoken arguments, scared they're becoming too sickly and bitter to keep down much longer.

*

The Doc perches on the edge of his chair on the verandah, stroking his wild beard, looking up at the full moon burning a white hole through the palm leaves. He's switched off the glare from the bulb hanging overhead. He wants to see the world by moonlight.

'Bad moon rising, alright.'

Beside him, Cyril nods in half slumber.

'That's one bad moon,' the Doc says. 'Course, you don't need me to tell you that. Fisherman like yourself. A wild moon. A real nevergone moon from nowhere. Mark my words, old buddy. That's a moon no good's ever gonna shine out of. You mark my words good. Seen moons. Seen many moons in a man's life. But it knows, you see. It knows just what trash and evil it's shining down on. And sometimes this moon, she ain't so happy with what she sees, ain't too inclined to shoot the good vibes down. Just keeps reflecting back the poisoned vibes, intensifying them and spitting them right back down at us. The old days, on the beach, just a fire and some good smoking and a few of us with guitars and drums, maybe someone with a see-tar. Then you could feel it. The good stuff. Showering you, shaking you with all these pure, sweet vibes, powering you, making you truly alive. Unless the acid got all mussed up and it turned into Attack of the Killer Dolls. Too weirded out for a sane man and no shit. But that big old thing up there? That's a bad moon rising. You mark my words.'

Cyril marks them, stamping them with a slumbering, blubbery nod.

*

The Matlocks stand on the edge of the party ground, surveying the scene. They see avenues of large palm-frond mats laid out, each one occupied by an old Indian woman squatted under folds of saris, cooking up tea on small stoves for the Westerners lounging there. At the far end of the long rows of mats lies an empty, marked-off area of day-glo painted palm trees, swirly-patterned banners stretched between trunks, a sound-deck with pulsing lights, and three DJs on hand to keep the music pumping out. It's too early for the crowd to get into dancing. This is just the intro music.

Clive is first to spot the bar, a few trestle tables underneath hanging gas-lights over in one corner. The family waddle towards it.

'Nobody's dancing,' Kim says, once they all have drinks in hand, beer for the men, Bacardi and cokes for the ladies. 'They're all just sitting around. Boring or what? I thought these parties were meant to be really wild.'

'Maybe they're just a bit shy,' Maureen says. 'Sometimes it needs a group to liven a party up a bit. To get it going.'

They stand drinking their drinks in silence, looking around

at the sprawl of freaks, clubbers, travellers and tourists drinking tea, water, smoking Four Square and thick joints, Gold Flake and chillums.

'I can see I'm going to have to do something about this,' Maureen says, taking responsibility for the party. 'Come on, Arthur. Let's get them started. You too, Angela. You like a nice dance, don't you.'

She leads a swaggering Arthur and reluctant, trudging Angela to the deserted dance area. Maureen and Arthur mash-potato and fifties jive themselves to the throbbing techno groove. Angela shuffles her feet out of time.

Chillums and joints drop to the ground as a hundred lungs cough thick white smoke in head-fucked amazement.

*

'I just want to know why.'

'Henrik, I hate it when you are like this. There is no 'why'. I talk to who I like. I am friends with who I like. You do not control me. Don't be like this.'

'Of course, yes,' Henrik says, his eyes and jaw hard. 'Yes, this is all just me. I am being unreasonable, not you. You see nothing wrong in your behaviour, only in mine.'

'Henrik, stop this. Please. Why are you like this?' Sophie stands in the middle of the room looking down at Henrik. He's hunched over, tense, on the edge of the mattress. 'You act like I am your wife or your slave sometimes, that I should do all the things you say. You were not like this when I met you. I know it is not you. It is something inside you that makes you do it. Please, baby. I don't want us to fight. It's New Year's Eve. We are going to the party. Please don't fight.'

Sophie's tone is soothing, calming, but her face betrays worry.

'I don't want to go out,' Henrik says, staring down at the earth floor.

'But it's New Year's Eve. A full moon. It's the biggest party tonight, it's going to be wonderful, everybody will be there. Come on, baby,' she says, moving towards him, resting her hand on his rigid shoulder. 'Let's go to the party. We will have a good time.'

'No.' Henrik shrugs her off. 'You can go. Maybe your 'lover' will be there. You can have a good time with him instead.'

'Henrik, please. Don't be like this.'

'So I am not allowed to tell you what to do, but you can tell me? Is that how you are planning for things to be? And this is fair?'

Sophie hangs her head, feeling exhausted for a second. She doesn't like the sensation.

'Everybody will be there,' she says softly, trying to smile. 'It will be fun. It's New Year.'

'No. I am not going. You go,' he spits out, still not looking at her. 'I don't want to go with you. Sometimes being with you makes me feel sick.'

The words stab into her. Sophie can't reply. She doesn't know whether to shout at him, cry, run away, laugh or slap him. Her mind staggers, hurt and confused. She stares at him as he examines the floor, his hands clasped tight between his knees. Then, as coolly as she can, feeling ill and off-balance, she puts her small cloth bag over her shoulder and slowly walks out of the room, closing the door quietly behind her without a word.

*

'Do you think we should get some ecstasy?' Iain says to Barney. 'With it being New Year and all that.'

'Be rude and churlish not to,' Barney says, shrugging from his sprawled position on a mat at the edge of the party. 'Although to be quite frank with you I'm not terribly experienced as far as E goes.'

'Neither am I. Taken it, what, a couple of times. I'm not into the whole clubbing scene, so the chemical generation thing passed me by.'

'Well, it is Goa,' Barney says. 'And as that nice young man with stones in his ear would say - when in Rome, take drugs of dubious quality and provenance.'

'Do you want to get them or shall I?'

'Oh, I think you'd better go,' Barney says in an even, reasonable way. 'Because I'm either hallucinating or there are three very pink people who've been inflated almost to bursting point trying to do some sort of rain dance on a completely empty dance floor. I suspect I'm hallucinating. Besides, you have that aggressive Scottish charm which I'm sure goes down much better with drug dealers.'

'Of course. There is that,' Iain says. 'Okay, give me all your money.'

'All of it?'

'Six hundred of it. Which, yeah, is pretty much all of it, I reckon.'

'Don't they have anything cheaper? 'Not Quite Full-on Ecstasy But Pretty Pleased' at three hundred? 'Mildly Amused' for a hundred?'

'Nah, I was checking out the prices with a couple of guys earlier. Just out of interest. Six hundred seems to be about the average.'

'Better be really bloody ecstatic.'

Iain takes Barney's money and gets up, walking down one of the mat-bordered alleys, casually glancing at the people lying around in various states of bliss and sloth. He spots a couple of vaguely familiar faces from the Vibe.

'Excuse me,' he says to the nearest one, kneeling down beside him. 'Any idea where I can get a couple of E's around here?'

'Sorted, mate,' Jez says, taking in Iain's clothes, manner, potential wealth and experience in a second. An amateur. A mug. A soft touch. 'How many you want?'

'A couple. Two,' Iain adds unnecessarily, then struggles to suppress a wrecked giggle.

'Eight hundred each.'

'Eight hundred? That's a bit steep, isn't it? I was looking more at six hundred.'

'Yeah, but these are top drawer, mate. None of your shitty Indian rubbish. These are pukka European. Not easy to get hold of.'

'Oh. Right,' Iain says. Eight hundred each. Sixteen hundred. All Barney's cash, plus almost his entire, saved-up, planned-out New Year budget. 'Fair enough, then.'

He digs the money out from three hiding places and hands it over to Jez. Jez glances at it, slips it into a pocket on his trouser leg, then hands Iain two small white pills.

'Pleasure doing business with you,' Jez says, grinning. 'Have a nice day.'

It's a small victory for Jez, a good profit, but it's only on a couple of E's. He's had to give quite a few away to some bolshie bastards he'd been hoping to avoid who'd paid him up front a few days ago, so the amount of hard cash he'll get from sales tonight has dipped dangerously. Still, at least he's got his fallback plan.

Iain gets back to the mat he and Barney are sharing with a middle-aged Dutch hippy couple and a quiet Belgian called, if Iain had heard him right, Stan.

'I need another couple of hundred off you,' Iain murmurs to

Barney, subtly slipping the E into his hand.

'Another two hundred?' Barney says, sitting up, holding the pill out in front of him. 'What on earth did they put in them? Tiger jism?'

Iain pulls Barney's hand down, shushing him.

'No, but these are good ones, though.'

'And how do you know they're good ones?'

'The boy who sold them to me said they were,' Iain says, then starts to giggle at his potential naivety.

'Oh, in that case, it's *bound* to be true. And did you haggle?'

'Not with a great deal of ferocity, no.'

'In that case you probably owe me money,' Barney says, taking a long, elegant puff on his king size Gold Flake.

They both laugh at it for a few moments. Light, happy, wrecked sniggers.

'But seriously,' Barney says. 'I'll have to give it to you tomorrow. I've only got two hundred left on me.'

'And I've only got Bugger All left on me. No, hang on, that's a lie.' He rakes through pockets, pulling out change. 'I've got twenty two, twenty three, twenty five rupees left. To last maybe eight or nine hours. For fags, water, tea.'

'Here's a hundred, then,' Barney says, handing a note over. 'So we're both relatively poor now.'

'Never mind,' says Iain. 'At least we can be happy and smiley and poor. Down the hatch.'

They both pop the E's in their mouths, crunching away at them. The sharp, sour chemical flavour slashes into their taste buds, screwing up their faces. They both urge the old woman to give them tea and fast, both willing to pay a hundred each if that's what it takes.

*

'Well,' the Doc says, rising from his chair with slow, creaky effort. 'Reckon I'd best be going.'

Cyril nods, half asleep, until he realises what the Doc's said.

'Going? Going where? At this time of night? It's past eleven o'clock.'

'I got me a party to find,' the Doc says, straightening his wide-brimmed hat and smoothing down his waistcoat. 'Been a long time. Figure I better go and spread some of that old-time vibe around.'

Cyril watches in mild disbelief as the Doc swaggers across the verandah, down the garden path to the gate, double checks that his hat's sitting properly, then walks down the dark road, picking his way by the light of a furious moon.

*

'It's getting near time,' Karen says, flicking her gaze down at her watch. 'You'd best get the drinks in. Don't want to be caught out at the whatchamacallit.'

'New Year,' Steve says tonelessly.

'New Year. Exactly.'

Steve gets up and goes over to the bar, not wanting to risk the potential wait involved in being served at their table. Also, if he's being honest with himself, he wants to be away from Karen, even if just for a moment or two. She's been knocking back the gin and tonics, getting into the New Year spirit. Getting on Steve's nerves. The alcohol seems to have sharpened her tongue. It always does.

'Kingfisher and another gin and tonic please, Sandeep,' he says to the barman. Sandeep waggles his head and repeats the drink order to his assistant, while Steve takes a rest on one of the stools.

He looks around at the party, the quiet couples or foursomes at the dimly-lit tables in the garden, the sweating band, the buffet table, the barbecue, the fairy lights hung up in the palm trees, the people shuffling on the temporary wooden dancefloor in the middle of the lawn. Very sedate, very middle-class, he thinks. Very middle-aged.

When he gets back to the table with the drinks, Karen's tapping her feet and nodding her head to the band, dancing a little in her seat to a country and western-style version of the Beatles' 'Help'.

He notices the relaxation in her facial muscles, the way she's leaning back in her chair, and he recognises the signs. She's a little drunk. Another drink or so and the full-blown mouthiness will come on. After that, the fast descent into exhausted inebriation. That's why they rarely go out drinking together, Steve preferring to go out with his mates, Karen sticking to the occasional girls' night in with a couple of bottles of wine. And even when they do go out, especially in company, Karen usually stops after just one or two.

Lovely girl, but she can't hold her drink. Everybody used to say so, until it became normal for her to be sober all the time.

But not tonight. Steve doesn't mind. He can put up with the mouthiness for a while. It suits his plans.

'This is nice, isn't it love,' he says, smiling, raising his glass to her.

'It's very different,' she says, grabbing her gin and tonic and swallowing a mouthful. 'God, it's bloody hot tonight. I could drink a gallon of these. Just keep them coming.'

*

'I told you,' Jez says, raising his voice to match Nat's whine. 'I won't be long. Just nipping back to the room for something.'

He's a little annoyed with himself. He thought he'd be able to slip away unnoticed, but Nat's been hanging onto him all night. He should have created a diversion or something earlier, not left it so late that he's got to rush. In fact, he shouldn't have mentioned it to her at all, but he's a bit off his face and didn't think.

'Promise me,' Nat says, pleading.

'I promise.'

'Promise on your mother's grave. You'll be back here for twelve.'

'Don't be stupid. Course I will. New Year an' that, innit.'

He kisses Nat on her forehead, just beside a little butterfly bindi she's stuck between her eyebrows. She looks at him like she doesn't believe him.

He picks his way through the crowd towards the south end of the party ground. He's nearly at the informal bike park when some-one grabs his arm.

'Oi! I've been looking for you!'

Jez spins around. It's Marky, a big lump from Brighton.

'Where's my fucking E's, then?' Marky says, none too happy. 'Three fucking days I've been waiting.

'Yeah, I been looking for you an' all,' Jez says, thinking fast. 'Where the fuck you been? Someone said you went off to Arambol.'

'What the fuck I want to go to Arambol for?' Marky says, put off-centre for a second. 'Who was saying that?'

'Spike, I think it was. Him or that Essex boy. Whatsisname.'

'Alex?'

'Could've been. Anyway, good to see you're here. You don't want to miss this one. Not New Year in Anjuna. Gotta go. Bit up against it time-wise.'

Jez tries to leave, but Marky catches hold of his arm again.

'And I'm a bit up against it not-off-my-head-wise. So where's me fucking E's?'

'Oh yeah. Well, there was a bit of a problem with the supplier. Unreliable bastard, but what can you do?'

'You can give me my fucking E's, that's what you can do. Or give me my fucking money back.'

'Yeah,' Jez says, wiping his nose on his forearm. It doesn't look like he's got much option with Marky. He's a big bastard. 'What did you ask for? Five, was it?'

'Five? Fucking ten, it was.'

'Sorry. Yeah, ten. I remember now.' He takes a small plastic bag out of his pocket. He's got twelve left. He thinks of maybe trying to fob-off Marky with five now and the promise of five later, but reckons he won't go for it, not in the mood he's in. So he takes two pills out of the packet, stuffs them in his Gold Flake box, and hands the rest over.

As he heads through the palms at the edge of the party ground he curses himself, stamping down on the ground harder than he needs to. Fuck fuck fuck fuck fuck. He's going to have to do the calculations again, figure out how much he needs. It's getting so confusing, having to change the sums all the time. He tries to work it all out in his head as he sweeps the parking area with a cheap torch, searching for the Bajaj scooter Iggy's let him borrow for a while.

Once he finds it he drives carefully along the winding, dusty track. The low light from the scooter's front lamp barely hints at the roots and potholes hidden in the deep shadows carved by the moon's sharp glare.

Back at his and Nat's room he works quickly, dumping most of the cash he's got on him, collecting his cloth bag and a few other items he needs. Then the door's locked and he's back on the scooter, all in a matter of a couple of minutes.

He guides the machine onto the road and heads north, getting further away from the party. After a couple of miles, he cuts down a side path and parks the scooter out of sight behind a clump of bamboo. Then he just stands there, listening, waiting until his eyes adjust to the moonlight. It doesn't take long. Now he's ready. He creeps through the trees, picking his way slowly, deliberately, as quietly as he can. It's nearly midnight by the time he gets to the first house, a shack he checked out earlier in the day.

He grins at himself in the cold, dead light. Time to get to work.

CHAPTER THIRTEEN

Like it's 1999

The tuxedoed man has his mouth close to the microphone.

'Ten,' he says. Steve sighs.

'Nine,' booms a NASA-style countdown over a mellow ambient beat. Nat looks around for Jez.

'Eight.' Kim gulps back her drink, ready to toast the New Year with a fresh one.

'Seven.' Jez examines the padlock, a cheap Indian one.

'Six.' Iain smiles at Barney in happy wasted glory.

'Five.' Karen holds her glass up.

'Four.' The Doc stares out from the trees.

'Three.' Clive's eyes glaze.

'Two.' Sophie smiles.

'One.' The padlock snaps.

'Happy New Year!'

Shouting, cheers, feedback and streamers. Steve and Karen kiss, the Matlocks clink plastic tumblers, the band strikes up, the hardcore techno bursts into life. Iain shakes Barney's hand, flooded with wellbeing. Jez slips into the room and flicks on his torch. Sophie hugs friends around her, and then the dancing starts for real, the music pulsing out, the vibe kicking in.

'I think I might need a lie down in a little while,' Karen says once the band's stopped playing 'Auld Lang Syne' and started slaying a Prince classic. 'This has quite gone to me 'ead. Are you drunk, Steve?'

'Not really,' he says. He shakes sweaty hands with a grinning older couple from the next table.

'I think I'm drunk,' she says. 'Come on, I'll have a lie down after we've had a bit of a dance.'

She gets up from her chair a little unsteadily. Her short white skirt has risen up her thighs a couple of inches, but she doesn't bother to sort it out. She waits until the band finishes off '1999' and starts strumming the opening chords for 'Simply the Best' by Tina Turner. She holds her hand out for Steve to take.

'You know I don't like dancing,' Steve says.

'You don't like anything, you,' Karen says, her tone slurred but bitchy. 'Come on. On your feet. No point pretending you can't dance when I know very well that you can.'

She reaches down and grabs Steve's hand, tugging at it. He reluctantly allows himself to be pulled to his feet.

'I'm not pretending I can't dance,' he says, almost apologetically. 'Just saying I don't like dancing. Or Tina Turner, for that matter.'

'What's wrong with Tina Turner? Come on. Not having you sitting there being a party pooper. Come on!'

Steve follows Karen, tied to her hand as she weaves to the centre of the dancefloor. He forces his feet into the rhythm, determined to do his best. And then Karen starts to sing along with the chorus as loud as she can. Lovely girl, but she can't hold a tune. That's what everyone on the dancefloor thinks. Steve closes his eyes and prays for the last couple of gins to kick in.

*

'That's it, then,' Iain says, buzzing, soaring. 'Officially. We're in the future. Space 1999 and all that. Martin Landau cast adrift in the deep black unknown only to find out his spaceships are made from rejected bits of Airfix models. Although he did have that tremendously sexy girl with the dodgy eyebrows for company. I used to think Martin Landau was a huge star, but it was really only because he was American. I don't think I've seen him in anything else apart from dubious 1970s made-for-TV films. Until 'Ed Wood'. And think about it, think about 1999 itself. When I was a kid watching the series on the telly, it seemed obvious that by 1999 we'd have moon stations and spaceships and phaser-type guns and all sorts of silly one-piece clothes made of magical material. I mean, 1999 seemed like it was hundreds of years away. I thought I'd be ancient by 1999, or maybe I'd be dead or we'd all be taken over by aliens. But here I am. In the future. Officially.'

'Yes, this ecstasy is a bit speedy, isn't it,' Barney says. 'Got a cigarette?'

'Aye, sure.' Iain says, handing him a Wills from a fresh pack.

'But it's true, though. We're actually in the future. Can you believe it? I mean, think about it. The last year of the millennium. One year to the big Two Oh. And another couple of 'oh's.' He giggles.

'Yes, I'm quite sure we're going to have hours of tedium this year,' Barney says. 'Newspapers, television programmes, countless books wanking on about what the year 2000 means, what state society's in, asking how far we've come in human development, what changes are going to happen in the next 1000 years. Personally I'm dreading having to put up with a whole year of it all.'

'But that's it,' Iain says, getting more animated. 'Whether you like it or not, this is going to be a big year. People are going to make a big deal out of it. Events will happen, people will do things specifically because it's the last year of the millennium. It's history in the making. This could turn out to be the biggest year of our lives.'

'Oh, there's the Armageddon brigade, I suppose,' Barney accepts. 'I'm quite sure we're going to see plenty of cults setting off bombs and poisoning people in order to fulfil some half-baked prophecy or other. But as for the rest of the world, when you get past all the flummery associated with what the end of the millennium means, most people won't actually give a monkey's. The vast majority of people will continue to have their time, their thoughts and their energy dominated by the same things they've always been dominated by.'

'Which are what exactly?'

'Sexual and emotional relationships and how to get in or out of them.'

'The world can't be that shallow, surely.'

'Really? It's a universal theme. As far as I can see, it pretty much sums up most people. Including, quite definitely, you. Of course, old people tend to be more preoccupied with thinking about death and where they've left their teeth. But apart from that, I'd say most people. At a rough guess.'

'Nah, there's got to be more to it than that. There's probably going to be all these important things happening,' Iain says, agitated, twitching his feet to the music without realising. 'History. Major events. I mean, even as we speak, Clinton's about to get thrown out of the White House. The President of the United fucking States of America getting kicked out because he got his knob gobbled!'

'For *lying under oath* about getting his knob gobbled. There's a difference. Anyway, it still proves my point. Even the President of the USA isn't immune from it, although in Clinton's case he's preoccupied with sexual, emotional and *inappropriate* relationships and how to get *away* with them. This year, next year, last year, any year you care to choose, people are preoccupied with themselves and their urges and whether they should or shouldn't act on them. And that's really all there is to it. All the rest of the wittering on about the end of one millennium and the start of another is just dinner party tittle-tattle, all self-important posturing and speculative nonsense, PR bullshit, style over content. It's 'Tomorrow Never Dies', 'Godzilla', 'Batman and Robin'. All hype and no substance. You think you're going to have a spectacular time, but blink and you'll miss seeing Uma Thurman in rubber. It's harsh, it's cruel, but it's life. The world will change, but it'll stay exactly the same, and there's nothing you nor I nor anyone else can do about it.'

Iain nods frantically.

'You're right, you're absolutely right' he says, chewing his cheek. 'It *is* a bit speedy, isn't it.'

*

Just the essentials. Cash, personal stereos, cameras. Traveller's cheques if they're there, but he can take them or leave them. Sometimes more trouble than they're worth.

Jez works efficiently, the plastic torch held in his mouth, scanning the room with the beam. He doesn't hurry. Panic breeds carelessness.

Hiding places, that's the thing. Unlocked backpacks, drawers, between book pages, in clothes pockets. And always, always look under the mattress. He can almost hear their reasoning in his head, a thousand voices saying 'Nobody would ever look there. It's too obvious. The perfect hiding place'. Yeah, right.

So far he has an Aiwa personal CD player, an Olympus compact camera, forty pounds and around a hundred US dollars cash, a nearly new Swiss Army knife, a Grundig travel alarm, and a watch that may or may not be worth something. And he's only just started. This is just his second room. There are plenty more potential treasure chests to visit yet.

On party nights, Jez can be pretty sure that most people in Anjuna will be out, their rooms unguarded. Not always, so he had to be careful.

But at New Year, at twelve o'clock, it's a pretty safe bet where everyone will be, and that's definitely not at home. If they are, it's probably because they're sick, so they're not likely to be in any fit state to kick up much of a stink anyway. Not a risk even worth mentioning.

The only real danger is bumping into other thieves who've got the same idea.

As Jez rifles through an unfastened daypack, he thinks about his haul so far. Good money. Well-chosen targets. He's not sure if he'll be able to shift the travel alarm, but as his old man used to say; if in doubt, nick it anyway.

Which is probably why he didn't see much of him when he was a kid. Don't get caught; that was another one of his. If only he'd practiced what he preached.

Once he's checked under the mattress, where he finds three crisp twenty dollar notes and a bunch of rupees, Jez decides he's stripped the room of anything worth taking. He clicks off the torch and gently pulls the door open.

He waits for a moment for the slight adjustment his eyes need, then walks at a steady, unhurried pace to his next target.

Bastard. A Yale lock. Best of British. Not a chance with the mini crowbar he's got. Piece of piss with the tinny Indian padlocks, but a Yale?

Still, there's more than one way to skin a cat.

Jez walks around to the back of the hut and stands on a palm stump. Gently, as quietly as he can, he reaches up and starts sliding the red clay tiles from the low roof. Fort Knox it ain't.

*

'I'm not drunk,' Karen says, holding onto Steve's arm as she stumbles through reception towards the stairs. 'I just need a little lie down.'

'I didn't say you were drunk,' Steve says, thinking she's the most drunk he's seen her for years.

'But you're thinking it. I know exactly what you're thinking. You don't think I can, but I can. You're thinking, 'can't hold her drink, needs to bloody lie down after a couple of drinks'. Don't tell me you're not, because you are.'

'Eight,' Steve says flatly, guiding her up the first step.

'Five or six at most,' Karen says sharply through her slur, hating contradiction.

'I don't think you were counting on the same scale as the rest of us.' He helps her navigate the landing. 'I told you that you were drinking too fast.'

'And I told you,' Karen says, firm. 'I'm not drunk. I was thirsty. Just need to lie down for half an hour or so.'

'Do you good,' Steve says reassuringly.

When they get to the room, Karen sits down heavily on the bed. She regrets it immediately, the thump on the hard mattress juddering up her spine.

'Bloody torture chamber,' she mutters, then starts trying to undo the buttons on her blouse. Steve stands watching her. He thinks about trying to help her, but reckons it's probably a bad move. With only a little difficulty she manages to get all the buttons undone, then stands with her back to Steve as she pulls the blouse off her arms.

'Make yourself useful,' she says in a bitter tone over her shoulder. 'Get me a glass of water or something.'

Steve is overcome by an urge to salute her naked back, but he restrains himself.

By the time he's picked out a clean glass and filled it with chilled, bottled water from the fridge, Karen's already under the single sheet, eyes closed, snoring the tiny clotted snores of the gently drunk.

Steve sets the glass of water on the table at her side of the bed. He's about to leave the room when he changes his mind, goes back to the fridge and takes out the bottle of water, leaving it beside the glass. Maybe he shouldn't have bought her those last few doubles. He looks at his watch. Nearly one. Still time. Maybe.

There's only one taxi at the hotel gate.

'To the party,' Steve says, jumping into the back seat.

'Which party you are wanting?'

'*The* party! *The* bloody party!' he says, surprising himself and the driver with the note of panic in his voice.

They drive for fifteen minutes or more through dark, sandy roads, through extinguished villages then along the side of a small river shining black in the moonlight.

Then he sees the lights, hears the thump of raw energy beating its way into the taxi. He gives the driver three hundred rupees, and makes his way through the trees, his path lit by strobes and spotlights, his heart tuned in to the throbbing, pulsing vibe.

*

Regiments of them, all lined up. Conscripts of the Weird Battalion, Stormtroopers of Babylon, the 3rd Army of the Righteous Gone.

The Doc surveys the ranks as he passes down the matted avenues of tea-sellers and lounged-out partiers.

Look at them, all neat and laid out in rows like they're queuing up to have a good time, to have sacred hightime manna handed out to them, put right there in their baby little flesh hands, passed along the lines, choice cuts for the chosen few. All too Goddamn black-tie and bushy-tailed. No flow, no vibe, no happening. Too organised. This is my space, you keep to yours. Everyone keeping to their special little gangs and cliques and secret brotherhood bonds of mystic passwords. What the hell's wrong with mixing it up a little, getting into the Goddamn flow of it, moving with it, getting the vibe all fired up and skating across the sky like magical stars and just being there, being in it, feeding it, feeding off of it?

'What in the Goddamn hell is wrong with that?' he says out loud.

'I'm sorry?' Iain says, stopping, on his way back from the bar to get a bottle of water. He'd hoped the Doc wouldn't recognise him.

'With Goddamn mixing it.'

'What? Mixing what?' Iain's confused.

'The vibe, man. The Goddamn vibe. Mixing it up a little. Get a real fired raging one going, not some Goddamn plastic trash dinner-by-numbers hat 'n' tails phony sonofabitch ratbastard fashion parade.'

'I'm very sorry,' Iain says, smiling but shaking his head. 'I don't mean to be rude, but I'm afraid I can't actually *handle* you at the moment. I'd love to stay and chat, I really would, but maybe some other time, yeah? When I'm not so out of my tits. Cheers.'

Iain lifts the bottle of water to salute the Doc and walks on, getting back to the mat with relief.

'I've just met the Angriest Pensioner in the World again,' he says to Barney.

'So I noticed. What was he angry about this time?'

'Not sure. I think he was talking about creating a riot. Went on about wanting to 'mix it up' with somebody. At least, I think he was. I'm so off my face that he could have been telling me a recipe for vanilla sponge, for all I know.'

A skinny, bald, middle-aged Austrian hippie with hairy cheeks leans across the mat and hands Iain a fat joint.

'You know him? You know the Doc?' he says, seeming awed.

'What, the old guy?' Iain says, taking a draw. 'Don't know his name. Don't know him at all, actually.'

'He is the Doc, he is famous,' the Austrian says. 'This is the man. This is the man who first brought acid to Goa. He is a legend, this man. He's it. No acid, no Goa. No Doc, no acid. That is the man, man. That is the man.'

The Doc walks on through the people, the posers, the wild childs from Nevergone, remembering another time, another movie.

*

Sophie turns at the touch on her shoulder, her face breaking into a shocked smile.

'Hi,' Steve says. 'Happy New Year.'

'Bonne Annee, Happy New Year,' she says, throwing her arms around him. They hold each other tight. Steve wants it to go on forever. Somehow he recognises the feel of her body, as if he's always known it, even though it's the first time they've touched. Relief, joy and desire flood him. The curve of her back, the smell of her neck, the warmth against his chest. It's too familiar, like a memory from another life.

The hug lasts a couple of seconds longer than politeness dictates, as if they're both reluctant to let go. When they eventually unwind from each other and move a few inches apart, they keep holding onto each other's forearms.

'I didn't think I'd find you,' Steve says, trying to wipe an adolescent grin off his face, feeling lighter and happier than he can remember feeling for a long time.

'I'm so happy that you have,' she says. Her green eyes shine. 'I hoped you would come, but I wasn't sure. After last night. And I thought maybe today I upset you. Maybe I was too personal, asked you too many questions.'

'Of course not, don't be silly,' Steve says, shaking his head. 'You can ask me anything you like. So. Are you with...are you alone?'

'Yes. More than you think. And you?'

'Yes,' he says, relieved. The worry, the strain, the nerves of the evening and his journey to the party ooze away, Sophie's presence filling him with blissful euphoria. They both stand and smile for a few seconds, absorbing each other, until a delayed thought hits Steve.

'What do you mean, 'more than you think'?' he says.

Sophie's face goes serious.

'I have made a New Year promise to myself,' she says.

'Yeah? What kind of promise?'

She stares down at the ground for a moment, as if she's unsure of herself. But when she looks back up, she's smiling.

'I will tell you later. But first I need to get water. I am so thirsty. Stay right here, okay? Sit on this mat with Preema. She's a nice woman, she'll give you tea. She has the best tea of all the ladies here. Don't go away, I'll be back in one minute.'

She backs off, smiling, slipping her arms out of Steve's. His whole body tingles as her fingers brush the insides of his arms, his wrists, his palms.

'Wait,' he says, hurriedly, catching onto her hands before she can fully let go. He takes a deep breath. 'There's a tradition in my country. I don't know about France, and I don't know about India, but in England it's good luck to kiss at New Year.'

'In France too,' Sophie says softly.

They move back together slowly. Steve's ears roar. The music, his heart, the wail of straining nerves, the mournful howl of conscience. This is it, this is the moment, the danger zone, the point of no return, the acceptance of eternal madness. Steve's mind screams at him, shouting warnings, egging him on, holding him back, urging him forward. His heart, his nerves, his insane mind.

And then the touch of her lips, fitting his exactly. Warm and honey-sweet. Steve feels a surge of panicked desire.

They break after a few seconds, a minute, a thousand years. Steve doesn't know how long. They stare at each other. Steve's sure she feels it too, the power, the electric charge, the mad sickness. She must do. It's far too strong. It can't just be him.

Neither of them has any words for a moment, then Sophie gathers herself and smiles.

'Don't go away,' she says. 'I will be with you very soon.'

She backs away, letting go of Steve's hands slowly, then hipsways through the loungers and dancers and out of sight towards the bar.

Steve feels dizzy. He looks up, but he can't see any clouds blemishing the bright, pin-pricked full-moon sky. He knows that if there were any, they'd be travelling very fast, because he can feel the world spinning at one hell of a rate. It takes him all his will to keep from falling.

She's going to leave Henrik. That's her resolution. It must be. That's why she says she's more alone than I think. She's going to leave the bastard. If she hasn't done it already.

Steve suddenly feels scared. The reality. This is it. Everything's just been theory before, full of fantasies, what-ifs and maybes, hopes and possibilities. But now, maybe this is it. Now's the time he's got to face himself, make some final, irreversible decisions. He has to examine his conscience, his morals, be true to himself and his life and everything he's ever wanted and strived for and missed out on and craved. Marriage, love, obsession, belonging. If something's going to happen, he has to be sure.

He's very sure of one thing. If something starts, he won't be able to stop it. He's not after some one-night stand fumble, some easy gratification. The idea of it, being allowed one night with her and no more, after all his mind's gone through, is more than he can bear.

If something's going to happen, he'll have to be honest with her. Tell her the truth. Tell her everything. Say the words out loud, the words he's been too frightened to say to himself. The three words that could turn his whole life upside down.

He'll tell her. As soon as she comes back he'll tell her. She has to know the truth, before they go any further. He'll tell her, and maybe she'll tell him too.

Thirty yards away, standing at the back of a group crowded around a crackling fire, Henrik drags his flame-filled eyes away from Steve and watches Sophie, trailing her passage towards the bar.

*

'What?'

'I said, what time is it?' Kim says loudly to Clive, standing at the bar.

'What?'

'Oh, it doesn't matter. Get us another drink.'

'What?'

Clive looks blankly at her, sweat running down his round, red face.

'Drink!' she shouts at him, holding out an empty plastic tumbler.

'Alright, alright, don't need to shout. Not bloody deaf, you know,' he says in a huff. 'Mind you,' he says, leaning into Kim, putting his finger in one ear and twisting it around. 'Think I'll go back to see that ear-cleaning boy. Don't think he got all them stones out.'

*

Jez is satisfied. Five rooms, and only once has he had to go in through the roof. By his reckoning, he's now got about a hundred and twenty quid, a good stack of rupees, maybe a couple of hundred dollars, and gear he should be able to offload for up to two hundred quid. Not bad for a night's work. And tax free. But most importantly, combined with the cash he's got back at the room, he's now got enough to pay off Hassan and free up the rest of the E's. Assuming he can sell the cameras and shit, that is.

What the hell, just one more. While it's there, just to be on the safe side. It'd be a shame not to, what with the opportunity and everything. These rooms, almost asking for it.

He takes the short metal jemmy bar out of his bag and moves towards another block of low, tiled-roofed rooms. When he gets to the door of the nearest one he looks around carefully.

The world is grainy black and white, the full moon peering through the wrecked umbrella of palm leaves above him. Fathomless shadows lurk beside houses, by tree trunks, by bushes. Jez can make out a couple of cows sleeping next to a house over to his left, but there aren't any people around as far as he can tell. In the distance to his right he can see a light on in a house, belonging to one of the locals, probably. It's too far away to worry about.

He snaps the lock with ease, darts into the room and flicks

on his torch.

Not much stuff. An open backpack on the floor, some clothes strewn around, not a lot else. A complete waste of time, most likely.

Jez searches through the pockets of a pair of trousers lying on the bed. Nothing. He rummages around in the backpack. A medical kit, toiletries, books, more clothes. Pointless. There's a zipped pocket on the inside flap. He opens it, feeling about inside. Papers. Insurance documents, travel details. And traveller's cheques. No. Not worth it. Not tonight.

He scans the rest of the room. His torch rests on a small bedside table with a single drawer. He slides the drawer out, peering inside. Candles, mosquito coils, matches, empty cigarette packets, Rizlas, and - hang on, what's this - more or less a full tola of hash.

Don't want to leave that just lying around. That's illegal, that is.

Jez stuffs the hash in his pocket, and turns to his final target. He lifts the corner of the mattress and smiles. There it is, a little black nylon wallet. He rips the velcroed flap and pulls out a wad of rupees. Better if it was dollars or pounds, but there you go. As his old man always says; burglars can't be choosers.

And then, as he stuffs the cash in his back pocket, he hears it. A motorbike. Getting nearer.

Shit. Time to scarper.

He doesn't know yet whether the bike's on the nearby road or on the path through the trees, but he doesn't want to take any more chances. He switches off his torch, edges out of the door and stands still, trying to judge where the sound's coming from.

It's on the path. Definitely not the road. Shit. Louder and louder. Closer and closer. Heading his way.

He slides along the wall to his right, risking a quick, furtive look around the corner. He can see the bike's headlight bouncing through the trees about a hundred yards away. The question is, which side will it go, to his left or right?

The bike gets closer and closer, the engine's growl beginning to fill the still night air. It's a big one, probably an Enfield.

Time for action. Gotta move, gotta get out of here quick, just in case. But which way to go, left or right?

Left. There's a bunch of palm trees, and just next to it a well the locals get their water from. Jez keeps low, checking around the edge of the building to make sure the headlight's not pointing in his direction, before scurrying over to the well and crouching down behind it. He'll wait until the bike passes then head though the trees to the scooter, get back to his room then back to the party. One close shave in a night isn't bad going, after all.

The bike gets nearer, its beam now dancing in the bushes behind Jez's head. He tries to make himself as small and flat as he can, willing the bike to go faster, to pass him by and let him escape.

It can't be far away now. Thirty, forty, fifty yards tops. Hurry up, you bastard. Things to do, places to go, people to see.

And then the bike stops. The engine stutters into a low coughing fit, then cuts out completely.

All I bleedin' need. Shit, hope they're not going to one of the knocked-off huts. Shit shit shit.

Almost immediately the voices start. Jez's heart leaps. Have they realised they've been broken into? He gets ready to fly. A crappy old Bajaj scooter against an Enfield 500. Shit. But hang on, it's not that.

The voices. Talking English. Loudly. An argument.

It's a man and a woman. He can't see them, doesn't try to look, but the voices are getting nearer, angrier. Wakened dogs start barking, one after another taking up the call. The voices. Does he recognise them? He's not sure, what with all the noise from the mutts and everything, but for a moment there.

Shouted accusations, furious, tearful denials, a chorus of dogs yelping, growling. Jez doesn't care. He wants to get out. The voices are moving away from him now. Time to go.

He peers around the side of the well. Can't see them. Good. He eases out of his hiding place, staying low, pulling the bag up onto his shoulder. The voices change. Not an argument anymore. A fight. Jez hears slaps, crying, shouts. He keeps his head down. The trees aren't far. He can be at the scooter within a few seconds.

The fight's getting worse. Sobs of fear and pain now. The ugly rasp of punches finding soft flesh.

Jez has almost made it to the trees when the scream freezes him. A terrified, helpless, blood-stained wail. He almost turns around. And then, with a dull, thumping crack, the scream stops dead.

Jez's skin chills. Shit. The deepest shit. Instinct takes over, and he charges into the trees, running as fast as he can in the dim light, kicking out at snapping dogs, crashing though bushes, desperate to get away.

He jumps onto the scooter and races back to his room, forcing the machine at top speed along the rutted, winding road. He dumps the bag beneath a pile of ragged clothes, stuffs the money in his special stash, then sits on the bed to skin up.

He's breathless. His heart's hammering.

The scare, the shouts, the violence. The scream. He's got to calm down.

By the time he gets back to the party and Nat's fury, he's managed to lock it all in the back of his mind, in a dark, high-security cell reserved for everything he thinks it's best not to think about.

*

Steve waits for an increasingly anxious half hour where Sophie told him to, then spends three quarters of an hour scouring the party, walking amongst the mats, checking out the people lying there, checking amongst the dancers, checking back in the gloom by the trees, his heart jumping every time his eyes catch a flash of blonde hair. But it's never her.

He trudges, his head filled with uncertainty, feeling foolish, sick and very alone. Aside from anything else, he's narrowly avoided bumping into various Matlocks twice. It's getting far too risky. If he's seen, and if they report it back to Karen, then his life probably won't be worth living.

It's time to go. There's no reason to stay. Sophie's gone. She's avoiding him. She doesn't care. He's mistaken all the signals, read more into it than there was. All because of his stupid, childish infatuation. He's been blinded by it all, by his dumb, pathetic fantasies. But now he knows. Now he knows. His chest feels crushed. An oily, black depression soaks into him.

He's about to go when he sees Crash Mary's muscled bulk squatting on a mat near the edge of the party with a group of others. He goes over to him.

'Hi there,' he says, a little uneasily.

'Allo, allo, allo,' Crash Mary says back, a suspicious smile on his face.

'You remember me? From the bar?'

Crash Mary nods.

'Dudley.'

'Yeah, well, I was just wondering. Do you know Sophie? French girl.'

'Sophie? Yeah. What about her?'

'You seen her about?'

'Nah, not for ages,' Crash Mary says, taking a few short drags on a mostly finished joint. 'Left with that boyfriend of hers, didn't she. That Henrik geezer.'

Steve feels lead drop into his guts.

'Oh. Right. Thanks,' he says, his voice dull and drained.

Twenty minutes and a motorbike taxi ride later, he climbs into bed beside a still-snoring Karen and switches out the light.

Happy New Year, he says to himself, and remembers the feel of her body against his, her scent, the warmth of her lips. He hates himself. Then he hates Sophie. Every last tender, aching memory of her.

CHAPTER FOURTEEN

Downer

Grey steel water washes Jez and Nat's feet as they walk along
the dawn beach on the way back home from the party. Nat's
forgiven him for not being with her at midnight. She doesn't
know what it is, but she can never stay angry with him for long.
Somehow he always gets around her, sneaks back into her good
books when she's not paying attention.

The beach is ghostly in the dull pearl light of early morning.
Up ahead some worn-out partyheads trip along, splashing in the
edge of surf. Back behind them the throb from the party fades
to a murmur as they drift further away.

A skinny black dog trots down from one of the dunes and
falls in behind Jez and Nat, keeping a few feet behind them but
matching their pace. Jez turns his head to suss it out, check its
intentions. Tail's wagging. Tongue's out. Don't mean no harm.
He decides to let the mutt tag along for the meantime, refusing
to worry about it.

Instead he concentrates on his present situation, trying to
ignore the distant echo of a bitten-off scream bouncing around
in the back of his mind. Best to pretend it didn't happen. Nothing to be gained from thinking about it. But the sound of it,
though.

Jez shudders, only partly because of the morning chill.

No. Best not to think about it. Think about something else.
Like right now, like how sweet life can be.

Right now. There's nothing better than doing a successful
operation, having a bit of a knees-up, then walking back home
along the beach to have a shag and some kip. Sweet.

Well, obviously there are better things. Blagging a bunch of jewels, having a knees-up, then getting into a supermodel sandwich with Helena Christiansen and that Wonderbra girl, Eva whatsername. That'd be pretty hard to top. You can tell a lot about a man from the supermodels he'd choose to be sandwiched between. Some geezers just don't appreciate the fuller curves of a girl like Helena. I mean, it's suggestive, innit. But some blokes are into all them hip bones and the Ethiopian rib look. No-one, no-one is going to tell me that is sexy. Be like having it off with one of them anorexic jobs. No thank you.

And then Jez thinks about the money. Yeah, maybe there's a bit of a problem there, especially if he's got to shift the gear. Might not find too many buyers today, and today's when the goat-eyed bastard wants his dosh.

Whatever. No point dwelling on it. It'll sort itself out. Just think of the moment. The right here, right now.

They slosh along, enjoying the sharp bite of the waves. Nat leans her head to the side, resting it on Jez's chest. The dog stops and watches them walk away. They're moving into another dog's territory, and it's way too early for a fight.

*

'I think it's safe to say,' Iain croaks, hating talking, 'I'm well into the comedown.'

He and Barney are both crashed out on a mat, eyes red and bulging, mouths sour and dry. The tea budget ran out hours ago.

'I suppose we should go,' Barney drawls back at him, not looking or sounding too enthusiastic about the prospect of moving his body anywhere.

'Yeah. Anyway, if all the girls here have managed to resist me so far, they're not about to give in now.'

Iain takes a lazy look around the dying party, the weak sun-light revealing the debris of humanity strewn around him. The music's still going, people are still dancing, but the night has taken its toll. Some people are flat out asleep, catching a few hours recovery before doing it all again. Not a huge amount of females left. There had been one Israeli or Italian-looking girl he'd been quite keen on earlier, but she's nowhere to be seen.

'You did manage to stay pretty aloof from them, I have to say,' Barney says.

'I wasn't being aloof,' Iain says, slightly irritated. 'Just inde-cisive. About loads of things.'

'Which had pretty much the same effect, as I recall,' Barney says, then yawns. With tremendous effort he slowly bends his long, thin frame up to sitting position.

'Anyway, at least I was up dancing,' Iain says, not wanting to let it go. 'At least I made a bit of an effort, tried to talk to some of them. More than could be said of you.'

'I don't dance, and the devil don't scuba-dive,' Barney say, confusing Iain, crashing his train of thought. 'Come on. Might as well go now the sun's up.'

Iain's too tired to argue. He follows Barney through the rem-nants of the party, feeling the ache in his muscles, the cramped tightness of a long, sleepless, debauched night. They split at a crossroads, wishing each other goodnight and exchanging weak 'Happy New Year's' again before trudging off their separate ways.

As he gets to his room, Iain feels the throb of an ampheta-mine headache coming on, pulsing in time to the music still beating faintly way back behind him. He bolts the door and slumps down on the hard bed in the corner of his cell.

He undoes the belt on his trousers, but doesn't take them off. He just lies there, the pounding in his head building, min-gling with the vague self-loathing he feels at not really trying very hard to score with any of the hundreds of girls at the party.

Sleep won't come. He tries. He's exhausted, his body craves and pleads for it, but the speed in his system just won't let him escape.

He turns over on the mattress and grabs an emergency Four Square cigarette from the drawer of his cheap, wobbly bedside table. He inhales deeply, but the cigarette tastes stale and harsh, and he rushes the smoke out between clenched teeth, trying not to cough. He stubs the end out carefully, then reaches for his stash of grass.

He skins up with two papers, crumbling the dry, dull green leaves into the tobacco salvaged from the Four Square, before lying back on his bed and lighting up.

So many women, he thinks. All those Eurobabes. So many beautiful, young, smooth-thighed, high-chested, beautiful, curve-bellied, lush-haired, beautiful Eurobabe women. So many. And what had he done about it? Almost nothing. What was he in Goa for? More than that. One would be enough. Just one.

*

Karen doesn't want to go downstairs for a late breakfast, early lunch, whatever.

'Think I'll stay in bed awhile,' she says, hand draped over her eyes, protecting them against the light leaking in through the curtains. 'Don't feel too well. Must have been a dodgy ice-cube or something.'

Steve can't help sniggering. He's dressed, washed, shaven, feeling like shit but determined not to show it.

'What?' Karen says, taking her hand off her eyes but still shielding them, her face screwed up. Not looking too pretty this morning, Steve thinks.

'I was just thinking,' he says. 'You had so many ice cubes in all them drinks it'd be difficult to prove which one it was.'

'Ha bloody ha,' she says, drained of humour, and covers her eyes again.

'I was thinking I might go down the beach after,' Steve says. 'I don't suppose you're feeling up to much sunlight today.'

Karen doesn't say anything, just turns on her side and pulls the sheet over her head.

'See you later,' Steve says, kindly, and closes the door gently after him.

He walks through reception and out into the garden. Half the tables are occupied already, people gingerly picking at sparse breakfasts, all evidence of the party the night before swept away by a team of ragged cleaners in the early hours. He's about to sit down and order something to eat when he sees the Matlocks and Clive filling their fat faces at a table nearby.

'Coo-ee,' Maureen calls out to him, waving unnecessarily. 'Come and join us.'

Steve wanders over, determined to get the encounter over as soon as possible.

'Thanks, but I don't feel much like breakfast this morning,' he lies, trying to put on a polite smile.

'Make a night of it, did we?' Maureen says, chewing a good mouthful of something.

'You could say that.'

'Stay here at the hotel, did you? Any good, was it? Karen enjoy herself?'

'Fine, yeah. You know. Quite quiet, but alright.'

'We went to a super party,' Maureen says. 'Right enjoyed ourselves, didn't we Arthur. A bit weird, and the music wasn't up to much, but it were very different. Made a nice change. Amongst all the coconut trees, it was. Clive thought he saw you there, but I said he was seeing things. Must have been all that wacky backy, in't that right, Clive?' Maureen chuckles.

'What?' Clive says, face screwed up in confusion, biting down on a banana.

'Glad to see you're taking the healthy option for breakfast,' Steve says to Clive, grateful for the opportunity to change the conversation.

'What?'

'I think the music was too loud for him last night,' Maureen says in a raised but sympathetic voice.

'What?' Clive says, then shakes his head violently and sticks a finger in his ear.

'Well, you all enjoy your breakfast,' Steve says, keen to get away. 'And Happy New Year.'

'Happy New Year,' chime Maureen, Arthur and a bored-looking Kim. Angela just mumbles something. Steve waits for Clive to say 'what?' but he doesn't, too focused on cramming all of the banana into his mouth to notice anything else.

Steve walks out of the hotel compound, down the road to-wards the beach. At the crossroads a few post-partiers buy rolls and crisps from the small, open-fronted grocery store. He passes the bus-stop and the cafes, keeping half an eye out for Sophie, just on the off-chance, but he can't see her anywhere.

He wanders without any plan, just wanting to get far away from the hotel, the Matlocks and, if he's honest with himself, from Karen. Just a bit of breathing space, some time to think, to sift through the wreckage of his mind. He follows the dirt path winding through sparsely-set palm trees beside the sheer, red-rock cliffs at the north end of the beach, stopping at Sonic res-taurant. He gives a young, sleepy waiter his order and takes a table right at the edge of the shore, shaded from the sun by young trees. As he waits for tea and toast, he stares out at the lazy sea, wondering, lost.

Maybe there was a good reason for her going off. Maybe she'd got sick or something, ate something she shouldn't have, taken something she shouldn't have. After all, they haven't discussed drugs. She could be heavily into them for all he knows. She could have taken some bad ecstasy, some bad acid, anything, then got sick and had to leave.

Or maybe. Maybe it's all in his head. His imagination's been running wild. Just because she's been friendly to him, he goes and assumes that she's attracted to him, reading all sorts of things into every word, every gesture, when all it comes down to is that she's probably just a decent, friendly, open-minded girl who likes to talk to people. So instead of taking it for what it is, he goes and blows it out of all proportion and makes a fool of himself, stumbling around after her like a stupid lapdog. He's kidding himself, that's what he's doing. To think that a girl like Sophie would fancy him. Ridiculous.

But the signs. Surely he couldn't have imagined them all. He's sure he saw it in her face after they'd kissed, the connection between the two of them. She felt it too, she must have done. And she said she was coming right back. She more or less said she was going to split with Henrik. But maybe she was just telling him as a friend. Maybe she's not splitting with Henrik in order to go out with someone else, least of all him. Maybe she just wants to be by herself. There's no rule that says she has to go out with anybody. Maybe she doesn't have any intentions towards him at all. But then there's all the time they've spent together, the way they get on. It's all so relaxed and natural and easy. And she likes him, he knows she does. Didn't she say he had a warm heart?

But then again, she also said that Henrik was a man of passion. Maybe, when it comes down to it, she just changed her mind, decided that the fiery promise of passion was far preferable to the modest charms of a warm heart. Simple as that. Or maybe he's reading too much into it all.

Steve shakes his head at himself, smiling through his tortured misery. There he is, the great detective, priding himself on being able to work people out. But when it comes to Sophie? Not a clue.

Steve Harrison, he says to himself. You're an arse.

His thoughts are jarred by the arrival of his breakfast. Strong, black cardamom tea and lightly toasted white rolls. He smiles at the waiter, who doesn't smile back.

But Sophie, Sophie, Sophie. He can't rid his mind of her. He knows he should. If nothing else, last night should have proved it to him. She went off with her boyfriend. Her boyfriend, for God's sake, not him. She had the choice, although maybe she didn't realise it. No, that's rubbish, of course she did. She'd have to have been blind not to notice something like that, the way he was behaving.

He should be breathing a sigh of relief. He's a married man, after all. He shouldn't even be thinking about it. He should be breathing a sigh of relief and thanking God that he's had a narrow escape from nearly, possibly committing adultery. It was a temptation that had been put before him, but luckily he'd managed to survive it, even though it was through no great effort of his own. It was a lesson, that's how he should look at it, a lesson that he can learn from. He's maintained his vows, his moral wall is still intact, he hasn't given in to temptation. But then again, he's already been unfaithful to Karen in his mind, and that's just as bad, isn't it?

He shakes his head again, but doesn't smile this time.

He has to go and find her, talk to her, find out the truth. The whole truth, and nothing but.

Steve finishes his breakfast, pays, then walks down the path to the beach. The Kashmiri stalls are bare. It's Friday, the Muslim holiday. A couple of clothes stalls owned by Karnatakans are set up for business, but they don't even bother to ask Steve to look.

And then the beach. The stretch of sand, the jagged curve, the emptiness. He walks along to the usual spot, but there's no Sophie. He'd half-expected her to be lying there, smiling up at him as he arrived, ready with an excuse that he'd readily accept.

He spreads his sarong, takes off his t-shirt and lies down on his back. The palm leaves behind the dunes rattle in the soft breeze. The full moon tide pushes its swell up onto the sand in wet rumbles. Steve lets the sun soak into his body. And waits.

*

Mrs Maria Rodrigues makes one last check that everything is ready. The steaming pots of rich, sour-smelling curries, the mountain of fluffy, white rice cooling in a bowl, the freshly baked pao breads on their plate, the onion salads, the tomatoes and chillies, the tarka daal, chickpeas and coriander. All laid out on the long wooden dining table. She's pleased. A celebration feast by any standards. She smiles at her daughter Margarida.

'I think it's time,' she says. 'Go get your brother and sister. I'll find your father. Which won't be too hard.'

She goes into the kitchen, takes off her white apron and smooths down her floral-patterned cotton dress. She makes sure her graying hair is set just right, then goes outside to the verandah, where Cyril is sitting in his chair.

'Cyril, lunch is ready.'

Cyril looks round at her.

'Thank goodness,' he says. 'You have been driving me crazy for two days with all those wonderful smells. You've got me so hungry that I could eat a horse. Although I sincerely hope you haven't cooked one.'

Maria smiles.

'You know perfectly well exactly what we are having. Hurry up, or it'll get cold. Go and get your friend.'

She shuffles back inside as Cyril hauls himself out of his chair. He limps down the verandah steps, his left leg not fully woken up yet, and goes around the side of the long, Portuguese-style house. He ambles over to a brick shed at the back of the building and knocks on the wooden door.

'Doc? You ready for lunch yet. Maria has been cooking us something very special. I don't know what it is, but she promises me it's not horse.'

The door opens and the Doc's standing there in a freshly washed and pressed white collarless shirt and his best jeans.

'Right with you, old buddy. Just a few final adjustments and I'll be right with you.'

Cyril wanders back to the house, up the steps and into the dining room. As he expected, everyone's already sitting at the table waiting, eager to get at the food. Xavier, at the opposite end of the table to him. Then Margarida and Anna, his beautiful, beloved daughters, Anna home from Bangalore for the holidays. A pity her husband Ajay couldn't come. Something to do with insects in the computers, Anna had said. Oh well. And in her place by his side, Maria, the love of his life. Always by his side.

Cyril beams at them all and eases himself into his chair. The food in front of him has his mouth watering already. Of course he knows exactly what they're having. He knows the smells by now. And hadn't he bought the pig himself?

The women are sitting patiently, but Xavier looks restless.

'Something the matter, son?' Cyril says softly.

'Nothing,' Xavier mutters back.

They wait for a couple of minutes in silence until the Doc comes in, wearing a new, dark blue satin waistcoat buttoned up over his shirt, his beard combed into submission, his hair controlled in a plaited ponytail.

'Mighty fine. Mighty fine,' he says, surveying the table, taking the spare seat next to Xavier. 'The wonders you do, Maria my sweet. The wonders you do.'

Maria nods at him, smiling modestly.

'Let us say grace,' Cyril says. They all bow their heads. 'For the food we are about to receive may we be truly thankful to our Lord, and may we ask him for guidance and protection in the year to come, as he has guided and protected us in the year past. Amen.'

'Amen to that, old buddy,' the Doc says. 'Guide and protect, yes indeed.'

They all help themselves and each other to food, passing plates and bowls and dishes around the table. Cyril reserves the right, as head of the household, to pour the wine, one of several good bottles he bought in Panjim before Christmas. He's been looking forward to it, enjoying the ritual, the sound the wine makes as it glugs out of the bottle into a glass, then admiring the colour, sniffing it, although he's really just checking it hasn't turned to vinegar.

'Mighty fine, Maria,' the Doc says, fork in the air, mouth full. 'Surprised you folks don't serve more fish. But I s'pose, you see it all day, you don't want to take your work home with you.'

He chuckles at his own joke. Xavier makes a face at his father. Cyril ignores him.

'Yup,' the Doc says. 'Spend all day catching them, risking your life, you don't want to be reminded of it. A good thing you're doing there, boy,' he says, slapping Xavier on the back, causing the young man to cough out a bit of pork. 'Continuing your daddy's work. A trade. Something a man can be proud of.

Ain't nothing finer, being out on the waves. Just you and the sea. Which one wins, that's in your hands and God's hands.'

'Actually,' Xavier says, recovering himself, 'I am not a fisherman.'

Cyril thinks he sounds pompous. He shoots his son a warning look.

'Actually,' Xavier continues, fed up with humouring the old man, putting up with his delusions, 'I am a businessman.'

'Call it what you like,' the Doc says, shrugging. 'All the same to me. Modern times. But fishing's not a business like any other business. Hell, don't need me to tell you that. It's bare hands, pulling them suckers up out the water, risking everything, a man's job. No disrespect to you ladies, just saying the truth. A man knows he's a man when he's floating on forty fathoms of the big blue. I know, your father knows, you know yourself. Call it what you like. Business, whatever, ain't nothing to be ashamed of. Most honest job a man can have. Something to be proud of. Did me some time on a trawler up Nova Scotia way. Nothing like what you're doing. Not raw, man and the sea kind of scene. This is a big boat we're talking, sturdy, built to stand the gales. And you get some Goddamn wild storms in the old Atlantic, I'm telling you for sure, waves bigger'n a three story house. But the size of the boat, it don't matter. It just don't matter. You know when you're out there. You know. It's as much life as a man can take. I swear this to you, that's the closest I ever came to God. 'Cept that time got a bum trip from some half-assed Berkeley dead-head. Spent two days communing with the Big Guy himself. Knows a thing or two about fishing, that man, and no lie. Gave me some tips on how to catch sea bass. Wouldn't think he'd have the time on his hands, what with all the universe to look after and everything. But, hey, s'pose he invented it all. If a man knows the best way to reel in a sea bass, gonna be the dude dreamed up the damn thing in the first damn place.'

*

IAIN McMILLAN'S GREAT HINDUSTAN ADVENTURE

Friday 1st January '99, Anjuna, Goa

Can't sleep. Been up twenty four hours, dancing half the night, out of my tree, raging like a mad thing, but I can't sleep. It's all my fault, of course. Well, me and the dodgy bastard who sold me a big dollop of speed in what was supposed to be an ecstasy tab. Oh, I'm sure it had some ecstasy in it, but it got a little bit overwhelmed by the severe onslaught of cheek-biting, nail-shredding, chain-smoking speed-related shit it had in it. It was good fun, though - don't get me wrong. It's just that I had visions of being all loved up and feeling delicious at midnight. Instead I was fidgeting around nodding my head and going 'yeah, yeah' a lot to anything Barney said.

Anyway. The first day of 1999. It's the end of the world as we know it. And I feel shite.

Worse than shite, actually. Like some disgusting parasite living in a steaming lump of shite. A shite parasite, that's what I am. What a marvelous, self-esteem enhancing way to start the last year of the millennium. Happy bloody New bloody Year.

I'd forgotten just how nasty a speed hangover can be. My body feels like it's drenched in a thick, gooey poison. I want to sleep so badly that if I had a million pounds on me, I'd willingly give it to someone if they could tell me some fail-safe, dead-cert way of getting to sleep right now and for the next ten or twelve hours. Well, maybe not the whole million pounds. I'd haggle, of course. I mean, this is India, after all. I'd probably get them down to a tenner.

And there's the self-loathing of the (allegedly E-tinged) speed hangover as well. I'd forgotten all about it. This stuff just eats away at you, grinding down every bit of respect and hope and honour that you've got, mashing it into a rancid mush which it consumes slowly, bit by bit. It's nasty and horrible and far too expensive. I'll have to save up for ages for my next one.

So, other than the fact that today I feel like the runt of the litter from a dysfunctional family of shite parasites, how was the party? The famous Anjuna parties, the main reason why a big bunch of European pseudo-hippies spend months and months here every year. Anjuna, the beating heart of the new Bohemianism, the New Age nerve centre where anything is possible, life is free and easy, and the parties never stop.

Well, they played loads of techno. And there seemed to be an awful lot of people who were quite clearly up their own arses. And, er, that's it. Oh yeah, and I didn't get a shag. Not that it's coloured my impression of the whole evening or anything. I'm sure I could have got a shag if I'd wanted one. Yeah, okay, I did want one. In that case, I'm sure I could have got one if I'd tried. Okay, if I'd tried really, really hard. Or begged. Or drugged someone.

Fuck it, I didn't stand a chance. What the hell, I hardly fancied any of them anyway, and with so much speed in my system I doubt whether I could have got it up even if I had managed to convince one of them that I was worth five minutes of their time. Although five minutes is probably far too ambitious at the moment.

I suppose there's always the Elderly German option again if I get too desperate. No, scrub that. To coin a phrase.

Och well, I'll just have to keep myself pure, save myself for the right woman. Which is any young, non-Teutonic woman that'll let me shag her, basically. Not that I'm obsessed by sex in any way at all, you understand. Buttocks, buttocks, buttocks, buttocks. I WANT TO GO TO FUCKING SLEEP! LET ME SLEEP, YOU CHEMICAL BASTARDS!

*

Steve's been on the beach nearly two hours when he hears the scream. He looks to his right, to where the sound came from, but he can't see anything strange right away. There are a few sunbathers lying there, some in the water. That's all.

But something about the scream bothers him. It wasn't a playful yell, one of the normal background sounds of a beach, people fooling around. There was an edge of fear in it.

A couple of sunbathers stand up, making towards the low, red rocks at the northern end of the beach. Steve hears someone talking excitedly, but it's faint. He can't make out what they're saying, but there's an urgency to it. He recognises the unmistakable tone which tells him something is wrong.

More of the sunbathers are standing up now, pointing out at something in the water. He can hear a girl crying above the sound of the waves, but everything's happening just too far away for him to work out what's going on.

He gets up, out of simple curiosity at first, but then a sense of duty takes over. If something's wrong, he feels he should at least try to help.

He picks up his day bag and sunglasses, leaving his sarong

where it is. He walks up the beach, trying to look casual, the way he's been trained to do when approaching an unknown situation, using all the time to assess what's happening.

A young, dark-tanned man with long hair dances carefully over the sharp rocks near the top of the beach. He stops, looks at something in the water, gets a little nearer to it, then rushes back to his friends, saying something, pointing back to where he's just been.

As Steve gets closer, he sees that a girl is sitting down on the wet sand is the one who's crying. Maybe she's the one who screamed.

Others have joined the group of four or five sunbathers, all standing now, all listening to the long-haired man, all staring and gesturing out at the rocks. Steve can't make out what they're looking at. As he gets nearer, he thinks he can see a hint of a dark shape in the water. A dolphin, maybe?

He gets up to the group. They're talking English.

'What's going on?' Steve says to a shaven-haired man nearest him, nodding out towards the water.

'Shit, man,' the man says, fazed. 'Sammy found a body in the sea, yeah? Shit. Just, like, out there.' He points to the rocks

'A dead body? Which one's Sammy?'

The crop haired man points to the girl crying. Another girl is with her now, an arm around her naked shoulders. Steve goes over and crouches down next to her.

'Are you alright, love?' he says, his voice soft and reassuring.

She looks up at him, sniffs and nods.

'Yeah. Just a bit of a shock, you know?'

'Yeah. Course it is,' Steve says. 'Best to keep sitting where you are. Don't get up for a bit. It can be a bit of a shock to the system. Just take it easy for a while. It's probably a fisherman or something. I've been told that it happens from time to time around here. You'll be okay.' Steve smiles at her.

'Yeah,' she says, eyes still watery, sniffing up the tears, her friend rubbing her shoulders. Steve stands up.

'Not a fisherman, though,' she says. 'A girl. A Westerner.'

'What?' Steve says, sharper than he'd have liked. 'Out there?'

The girl nods again. Steve moves over towards the rocks, his stride quickening as he goes. He clambers over the low, red, volcanic mass, scanning for easy footholds in the pitted stone to speed him along, getting faster and faster the nearer he gets to the sea. A dark shape in the water. Dark and white, soaked clothes, long blonde hair, face down.

The water level's a foot below the edge of the rocks. Each new wave bumps the body against them. He reaches out as far as he dares, managing to grab hold of an icy arm. He strains, getting into position to haul the body up, jamming his feet in fissures for purchase. A wave comes in and he heaves. The body scrapes up over the edge of the rocks and down beside him. He turns the body over, sees the black, bashed side of her head, the fine eyebrows, those lips.

A surge of raw terror overwhelms him as he looks down at Sophie, her face made ugly by death, her body bloated, destroyed and obscene.

He lets go, horrified, dropping her arm and stumbling back. A few feet away he knife-jacks over and retches his heart out.

CHAPTER FIFTEEN

This is India

Steve's sitting on a hard wooden chair in the Anjuna office of the State police. He's not impressed. A couple of desks, a counter, paper lying everywhere, ledgers piled at random on tables pushed up against stained, flaking walls, and two well-fed cops swinging back on their chairs underneath the ceiling fan, both of them smoking, talking to each other in a rapid language that Steve can't understand. Talking to each other, but refusing to talk to him.

For most of the afternoon he's been in a numb, sick daze. He'd managed to convince one of the local restaurants to call the police, tell them about Sophie. An hour later, a solitary policeman came down to have a look, more or less just a glance, to confirm what they'd been told on the phone. He'd refused to answer any of Steve's questions. Then, after another hour or so, a couple of labourers in dirty loincloths trundled down onto the beach in an ox-drawn cart, manhandled Sophie's body into the back of it and covered her with sacks. Steve had watched it all with a stunned emptiness, unable to take it all in.

But then the anger appeared. His fury grew, and with it a determination. He'd taken a motorbike taxi to the police station and demanded to see the officer in charge. And then the two fat cops, sitting at desks piled high with folders and reports, had ignored him.

Eventually, hours later, a car pulls up outside, crunching to a halt on the sandy gravel. Three policemen in khaki uniforms stroll in, the first one talking loudly to the two fat cops. They

immediately swing themselves upright and put out their cigarettes, a mark of grudged respect on their faces. The boss, Steve
suspects.

The boss looks at Steve, then barks a few more questions at
the fat cops. One of them mumbles to him for twenty seconds,
until the boss shuts him up. He turns to Steve.

'Can I help you?' he says politely.

Steve stands up.

'Are you in charge of the case about the dead girl?' He hates
saying the words, but does it anyway, keeping the words steady,
professional, controlled.

'Yes. I am Inspector Gupta, from the Calangute station. How
can I help you?'

Steve reaches into his wallet and takes out his ID, his photo
warrant card, handing it to the Inspector.

'I'm Detective Sergeant Steven Harrison. From England. I'm
on holiday here, but I've come to offer you any help I can.'

Gupta studies the warrant card, both sides, before handing
it back.

'I do not see how you can be of any help,' he says.

'With the case,' Steve says, feeling useless, unsure of himself. 'I might have some important information that'll help you.'

Gupta laughs, a short cynical snort. He takes off his cap and
runs a hand through oiled black hair.

'We have all the information we need. I think we can get on
very well without the help of Her Majesty's Constabulary.' He
says the words with a sneer that makes Steve instantly dislike
him. 'These drownings happen all the time. Believe me, we have
plenty experience of fishing out Westerners who've been
drinking too much or taking too many drugs and think it's a
good idea to go swimming. There is no case. We have far more
important things to be dealing with.'

'Hang on, just wait a minute here,' Steve says, his voice rising. 'She didn't drown. Have you seen the body? Have you seen the marks on her neck? The injury to her head? You don't get them from drowning.'

'These things are of no consequence. We are...'

'They're of every consequence,' Steve says loudly, cutting Gupta off. 'There's every reason to suspect that she was killed. Murdered. It doesn't take a genius to work it out. And while you lot piss about here, the man who did it might be getting away.'

Gupta fumes. He doesn't appreciate being told in his own district how to do his job, especially by some rich foreigner here on holiday. He holds his temper, only just.

'And just how would you be knowing this?' he says instead, a sarcastic smile fluttering below his thick moustache.

'Because she, she was a friend.'

'You and your wife, you were both good friends with this lady?'

'What d'you mean?'

'Come on now, DS Harrison,' Gupta says, looking pointedly at Steve's wedding ring. 'We are all men together here. This friend. You were fucking her?'

'What?' Steve says, shocked by the question's offhand cruelty. 'No! What sort of question's that? Of course not. She was ... she had a boyfriend. She was having trouble with him. We talked about it. A Swedish bloke. Henrik something. I've seen him, I know what he looks like. She left the party with him. There's a witness who saw them leaving together. They leave in the early hours, then a few hours later she turns up dead with injuries consistent with a violent assault. We're not talking about a drowning. This is murder. The least you should do is bring this Henrik bloke in for questioning. He's the obvious and only suspect. I can help you catch him.'

'Yes, well. Maybe you can help us, DS Harrison,' Gupta says, then barks in Hindi to one of the fat cops, who shuffles over with a notepad and pen. The Inspector grabs it from him, barks something else and the fat cop retreats. Gupta turns back to Steve. 'What was the deceased's good name, please?'

'Sophie,' Steve says, then stops. 'I ... I don't know her last name.'

Gupta looks up at him, impatience on his face.

'And at which address was she staying?'

'It's, it's not a hotel. It's in one of those rooms. In the village, she said. With Henrik, her boyfriend. The one I'm telling you about. I'm not sure where it is exactly.'

The Inspector slowly puts down the pad and pen on the desk next to him. He stares at Steve with hard eyes.

'Then it does not seem that you can be of much help to us at all. No name? No local address? We will find out in time. We'll put the word out. The room owner will find her things soon enough. In my experience, these type of Westerners rarely pay more than a few days in advance. The owner will bring us her things. Or maybe her boyfriend will come to report her missing. As I've already said, these things are not unusual. After that, we can contact her embassy. There is no need for you to trouble yourself any further.'

'She's French,' Steve says quickly, then realises the useless-ness of it. Gupta is already picking up papers from an in-tray on the desk.

'Yes, well, once we get her passport we will pass it on,' he says. 'And now you must leave. We are very busy here.'

'But I can show you this Henrik bloke. The murderer. He's still out there, for God's sake. I'd have thought you'd at least want to bring him in for questioning. Even if you don't believe me, you should at least do that. It's standard procedure.'

'I have had enough of this!' Gupta snaps at him. 'I have no

time to listen to your theories and whatnot. We are quite able to decide for ourselves what is a murder and what is a drowning. This is a drowning. Do not forget where you are, DS Harrison. This is India. You do not rule us now. You cannot come here trying to throw your weight around, telling us what we should and should not be doing.'

He starts talking loudly in Hindi to one of his junior staff, one of the men who came in with him. The officer gets up, takes Steve's arm and hustles him to the door, out into the dusty light of sunset. The firm wooden door closes behind him.

Inside, Gupta shrugs, brushing his moustache with his fingers. Arrogant English bastard. Drowning. Lovers tiff between hippies. What did it matter? Nothing could be changed now. Play it low-key, like the Chief wants. Get on with the real role of police work. Keeping order. Keeping things under control. There's another party in a few nights. He hasn't found out who's running it yet, but he's working on it. He's working on it.

*

'Jesus Christ, Nat! Nearly scared the living shit out of me,' Jez says as Nat barges into the room, only just giving him time to stuff a personal CD player under a bunch of dirty clothes.

'Sorry, darlin',' she says, bouncing down onto the bed, a little breathless, eyes wide and scared. 'But I just heard. They found a body at the beach. Becky was there, wasn't she. They reckon it's that Sophie girl. She was ever so upset, Becky was.'

'French Sophie? Aw, shit, poor cow,' Jez says, shaking his head. 'Lovely girl, that Sophie. Fuck, where was this, then?' He pulls Nat close to him, hugging her.

'Up near the Vibe. Just at those rocks at the top of the beach. She was just floating there in the water, Becky said. Bleedin' awful. What a thing to happen. New Year and everything.'

'Cops'll be looking for that Henrik, then,' Jez says, releasing Nat. She keeps hold of one of his hands. 'Not that they'll find him, I wouldn't think. Well scarpered by now, I reckon.'

'Whatcha mean?'

'He'll have pissed off, won't he. Hundreds of miles away by now, probably. Him and that bike of his.'

'What's he gonna piss off for?'

'Well, he did it, didn't he. He's not going to hang around after something like that. He'll be well out of here.'

'Whatcha talking about, 'he did it'? Didn't do nothing. She drowned, didn't she. That's what they're saying. He's probably destroyed by it. Too upset to go anywhere.'

'Yeah, right,' Jez says, licking a cigarette paper, starting to skin up. 'Sounded really fucking upset when he was beating the shit out of her last night.'

'What? Whatcha talking about? When was this, then?'

'Last night. I'm telling you.' Jez stops to lick another paper, sticking it onto the other. 'Right going over he gave her from what I could hear.'

'What? At the party?'

'Nah. In the village.'

'And you saw them?'

'Not exactly saw them. Heard them. Didn't see them.'

'And he was beating her up and you did nothing about it?'

'Couldn't do nothing, could I. Didn't know it was them, not until you just said. It just clicked, two and two together. I mean, I thought I recognised the voices and everything, but there was a lot going on. Dogs an' that. Didn't know at the time, did I. Anyway, even if I did, what was I supposed to do? Take on that big Henrik bastard? Yeah, right. They're having an argument, way I see it, that's their business.'

'You could have done something.'

'What, prefer if it was me washing up on the beach, would you? 'Cause that's what would have happened. Can you imagine it, me against him? You've seen him. He'd tear me bleedin' head off. What good would that've done?'

Nat folds her arms, her face set, considering Jez.

'Right,' she says, flat and matter of fact. 'Well, you've got to go to the police, then.'

'Police? Leave it out,' Jez says, putting the finishing touches to the joint, snipping off the twisted paper end between thumb and forefinger. 'What the fuck I wanna go to the police for?'

'To tell them about it,' Nat says, her voice on the edge of pleading.

'So, yeah, right, I go up to the Old Bill and say, "Excuse me officer, but while I was out doing a bit of thieving last night I was witness to a murder. No, I didn't actually see it, I was too busy hiding my stash at the time and hoping they wouldn't see me. But I heard it". No,' he says, lighting the joint, staring at Nat through a cloud of thick smoke. 'I do not think so.'

'You wasn't thieving again, was you? Oh, Jez.'

'I wasn't thieving.'

'You just said you was.'

'I wasn't thieving. Just borrowing.' Jez leans back on the bed, taking a long drag of sweet smoke. 'It's like me old dad says, innit. Redistribution of wealth, an' that. Taking from the rich - the Italians - giving to the poor - us.'

'Jez, you promised.'

'S'alright. Just needed a bit of capital, that's all. Got to accumulate before you can speculate, in't you. Anyway, we've got to eat, haven't we? We've got to have somewhere to stay. What we gonna do if I don't provide, eh? Don't see you doing much in that direction. Nah, it's just in me nature, innit. I'm a hunter-gatherer. Just that it's easier to carry a CD player than a wilde-beest.'

Nat doesn't say anything, just stares down at her folded arms, at her sandals, her ankle chain, her toe-ring, studying them. Jez smokes the rest of the joint in peace, Nat refusing it with a sharp shake of her head.

'Still think you should go to the police,' she says quietly, after a while.

'For God's sake, will you stop harping on about it,' Jez says, sitting up. 'We've been through this. I'm not going. End of story. Leave it.'

'Just saying. It's the right thing to do. For Sophie, and everything.'

'Look, she was a lovely girl, right? And that Henrik shouldn't have done what he done, okay? No-one's saying he should. Bang out of order, that was. But it's done now, right? He'll have pissed off, and the Old Bill probably know it's him anyway. What good's it going to do me getting mixed up in all of it? I don't know nothing they can't work out for themselves. Me getting involved'll just end up causing us a lot of grief that we don't need. A lot of grief. So you're not to say a word of what I've said to anyone, right? Not anyone, not Becky, not no-one. Right? Right?'

Nat nods, still looking down at her feet.

'Right,' Jez says. 'So let's hear no more about it. What's done is done. Nothing we can do about it now.'

He stubs the roach out on the packed earth floor.

'Still,' he says. 'Right shame about that Sophie girl. Quite fancied having a cheeky fumble with her meself.'

'Jez!' Nat shouts, throwing a mirrored cushion at him. 'You can be a right bleedin' pig sometimes, you know that?'

She jumps up and rushes out the door, slamming it behind her.

'What?' Jez says, arms out, wide blue eyes staring at the

closed door. 'What?'

*

'What?' Clive says to Kim. He rubs his left ear. It's red, inflamed, irritated. His right ear doesn't look much better.

'Do, you, want, another, drink,' Kim says slowly and clearly.

Colin looks at her for a few dumb, open-mouthed seconds.

'Kingfisher,' he says eventually.

'And a Kingfisher,' Kim says to Raju the barman. Raju finishes writing down the order and walks back to the hotel bar. He starts getting the drinks together at a sedate pace.

'How's your ears doing, love,' Maureen says over the table to Clive. A pause hangs in the warm evening air as he stares at her.

'Kingfisher,' he says.

'That's nice, dear.'

The four Matlocks and Clive sit at the table in silence for a while as they wait for their drinks to arrive. Arthur's half asleep. Kim appears angry, but she's just feeling the effects of a dry hangover in a hot land. Angela looks like she's been switched off, her dull eyes resting on the leg of someone's chair at the next table. Clive's fidgeting, his face veering between blank incomprehension and outright pained confusion.

Maureen checks out the other people sitting in the garden. That top doesn't suit that girl from Sunderland. Impulse buy, obviously. And those shorts on that lady from Birmingham. Shouldn't wear shorts like that with those legs. Not a pretty sight. Some things are best left covered up.

'Oh, look, there's Maureen and family,' Karen says as she and Steve walk out into the garden. 'Let's go and join them.'

'No,' Steve says firmly. 'I'm not sitting with that lot tonight.'

He walks off and sits at a table for two at the opposite side of the garden. Karen stares after him at first, stunned, then marches across to the table, pulling her chair out a little too sharply. She sits down, arms folded, tight-faced. Steve doesn't pay her any attention.

Raju comes up to give them menus and take their drinks order.

'King's beer, please,' Steve says, his voice neutral but polite. 'Karen? Bucket of gin?'

Karen glares at him, her eyes firing icy blue shards.

'You want gin tonic?' Raju says. 'Slice lemon?'

'No. Just mineral water,' she says, not taking her eyes off Steve.

They both study the menu as Raju goes to get their drinks.

Steve looks halfheartedly down the list of options. Kingfish fried with chips. Tunafish steak with chips. Pomfret fried with chips. Shark fried with chips. Tiger prawn and chips. Chicken and chips. Egg fried with chips. Various sizzlers and tandooris, then chicken and fish curries, added almost as an afterthought. He's not interested. He closes the menu.

Raju comes back with his beer and Karen's bottle of mineral water, putting them down on the table with the greatest of care.

'You are ordering now?' he says, straightening up, showing teeth.

'Is the tuna fresh?' Karen says, sounding like she won't believe the answer anyway.

'Fresh today, madam,' Raju says, stifling an urge to bow. He finds something about Karen's manner intimidating.

'I'll have tuna fish and chips, then,' she says. She looks over at Steve.

'Kings beer please, Raju,' he says.

Both Raju and Karen wait, but after a few seconds it's clear he's not ordering anything else.

'Is that all you're having?' Karen asks him, disbelief edging her voice up a couple of notches. 'You're not having any food?'

'Nope,' Steve says, not looking back at her. 'Just Kings.'

Raju waggles his head and walks away. Karen continues glaring at Steve.

'What you think you're doing?' she says, folding her arms tighter.

Steve shrugs.

'Feel like getting drunk.'

Karen says nothing. She continues to watch Steve as he looks around the garden, at the people, the trees, the rich, dark blue sky. Anywhere but at her. There's something about him, something about the way he won't look her in the eyes. The minutes pass as they brood in silence. Steve drinks his beer, taking long gulps at it. Finally Karen can't stand it any longer.

'Well, don't expect me to carry you up the stairs when you're flat out paralytic.'

'Yeah, that's my job, carrying drunks, isn't it,' Steve says back, his face like stone.

'I don't know what's got into you today,' she says sharply. 'Been in a funny mood all day, you have. And with me feeling delicate and everything.'

'Yeah yeah yeah,' Steve murmurs. He takes another long sip of cold beer from his glass.

'What's got into you, Steven Harrison? Because whatever it is, you can shake yourself right out of it, because if you think I'm putting up with you in a mood all night, you've got another thing coming.'

'You really want to know?' Steve says, his mouth twisted in a sickly smile. 'Do you? Well, since you didn't ask, I'll ask it meself. "So, dear, how did your day go?" Well, dear, basically I spent the afternoon pulling the dead body of a young girl out of the sea and then trying to get the fat-arsed police to actually do something about the fact that she was murdered, but it doesn't look like they're going to. That's how my day went, if you really want to know.'

'Well there's no need to take it out on me. I've had a pretty bad day meself, you know.'

'Oh yeah, right,' Steve says, a sneer coating his voice. 'Lying in bed with a little hangover. Dreadful day. *Much* worse than mine. What on earth was I thinking of?'

'Don't start trying to get all sarcastic at me,' Karen bites back at him. 'I'm warning you. Don't start.'

Steve looks away, shakes his head, then takes another long gulp of beer. He's not going to start. He doesn't feel like talking. Not to Karen, anyway.

He looks around the garden again. The Fat Family are slugging back drinks, not yet fueled-up enough to attack the menu. Christ, the sight of them. And all the rest, the couples, the families, the young, the old, all of them sitting like him and Karen, not talking, just sitting there lifeless, devoid of conversation, personality, intimacy, almost like they don't know the people they're sitting with. Who are they all, this awkward looking bunch of misfits? Is he really one of them? When they look back at him, do they see what he sees?

Tense minutes pass. Steve still can't bear to look at Karen, guilt and repulsion playing equal parts in his avoidance of her eyes.

'A girl, did you say?' Karen says eventually.

'Yeah.'

'A tourist? Or, you know, one of the locals?'

'Tourist. Well, traveller really. A young girl. Battered and dumped in the sea. Murdered. Not a good day.'

'I'm not saying I'm the only one who's has a bad day,' Karen says, her voice less strident now. 'I mean, it doesn't sound like a nice situation to be in. I'm not saying that. I'm just saying. You shouldn't always go thinking of yourself.'

'There you go again,' Steve says, incredulous. 'I don't believe it, there you go again, saying I'm always thinking of myself. Where do you get all that from? If the focus of attention isn't always on you, if I stop rushing around trying to do things to make you happy for just one second in the day, suddenly that means I'm always thinking of myself. Well I'll tell you what, maybe it's time I did start thinking of myself a bit more. Seems to work for you.'

Steve makes to sip his beer, but Karen's tone freezes him.

'How dare you! How dare you speak to me like that!' she hisses at him, then stands, her face pinched with fury. 'Get drunk for all I care. But you can do it on your own. How dare you!'

She turns, spinning away, marching back towards reception, past a confused Raju who's holding a tray with her dinner and Steve's beer on it.

He walks up to the table and is about to put the plate down when Steve stops him, plucks his bottle of beer from the tray, and gives Raju fifty rupees to take the food up to Karen in their room.

'And after that,' Steve says, grim-faced, 'you can bring me another beer.'

*

'I'll give you twenty five dollar. Top price,' Shahid says, holding the CD player near to his face, examining every minute detail.

'Will you ballocks. You'll give me forty,' Jez says right back. He tries to look his fiercest, but isn't sure the low light in the room shows it off to best effect.

He's up in Vagator with one of his Kashmiri contacts, one

he's almost sure doesn't know Hassan. He thought it was best to get out of Anjuna for the day just in case Hassan's snooping around looking for him. If he can get the money together today then fine, he'll go see him. If not, best keep out of his way and deal with the consequences tomorrow.

'Twenty five,' Shahid repeats, pouting, raising his wide shoulders. 'Good price. I am selling for thirty five only. Maybe forty. Twenty five is good price.'

'You'll sell it for a bleedin' sight more than that, you lying toe-rag,' Jez says, cracking a smile. 'Sixty or more, I reckon.'

'Okay, maybe I get fifty, fifty five. I give you thirty dollar.'

'Fine,' Jez says, reaching out to take the machine from Shahid's hands.

'Plenty of others who'll give me forty at least. Thought I was doing you a favour showing it to you first, but if you're not interested.'

'Wait, wait my friend,' Shahid says, pulling the CD player away, holding it out of Jez's reach.

He examines it again at arm's length. Very new. Top model.

'I cannot get more than sixty, sixty five dollar for this,' he says.

'So what? Give me forty for it.'

'Thirty for you, thirty for me. This is fair.'

Shahid holds out his hands, a look of submission on his face. Jez isn't fooled.

'Forty for me, twenty, maybe even thirty for you.'

'But thirty-thirty is fair.'

'Who got it?' Jez says. 'I done all the bleedin' hard work, didn't I. All you've got to do is sit on your arse and sell it. Practically bleedin' sells itself. Brand new, almost straight out the box. You're getting over twenty, maybe over thirty dollars for doing sweet fuck all.'

Shahid shrugs. He looks at the CD player again.

The smooth lines. LCD. Very modern. Top model. Very nice. Very nice.

He dips into a battered black leather wallet hands four notes to Jez.

'Thirty five dollar. Last price.'

Jez nods and stuffs the money in a pouch inside his trousers.

'Sweet, me old son,' he says.

'Now. What about this watch? Don't see many of these in India, do you?'

*

'Bloody good New Year,' Iain says, then tips back his warm beer. He and Barney are wrecked, lingering over Kingfishers in the Vibe bar. The slight chill issued to their bottles by the Vibe's refrigerator has long since disappeared into the hot, humid night.

'And the best part of it,' he says, putting the bottle back down on the table, 'is that I didn't have to wear a kilt.'

'You don't like it?' Barney says, surprised.

'Hate it. Horrible, scratchy thing.'

'Really? I thought you Jocks loved getting the old tartan skirt on.'

'It's not a skirt. It's a kilt. And anyway, I'm not a Jock. I'm Scottish.'

'Oh, come on,' Barney says, face stretched in astonishment. 'Didn't think you'd be touchy about a little thing like that. It's just an affectionate term. It's like Taffs. Or Paddies.'

'Notice you didn't mention a name for the English there.'

'True, but we're hardly likely to think up one for ourselves. Anyway, you've got one for us. Sazzafrazz or something.'

'Sassenachs.'

'There you go. Exactly.'

'It doesn't mean English. It's a name the Highlanders gave to anyone from the Lowlands. Covers people from Edinburgh and Glasgow as well. No, there's another name we use for the English.'

'Which is?'

'Cunts.'

'Very witty.'

'Although we don't tend to say it to their faces any more. After all, it got us in a hell of a lot of trouble with the English in the past. I mean, you know 'Braveheart'?'

'I'm familiar with it, yes.'

'Well you know it was mainly fiction, don't you?'

Barney scratches his chin.

'I understood that perhaps they'd tinkered with one or two of the facts a little, just to tidy things up a bit, as our Hollywood friends tend to do. But I thought it was mainly based on fact. Of course, with a bit of a bias towards William Wallace's side. It's safe to say that the English point of view was never really examined.'

'It's all fiction,' Iain says. 'Okay, there's maybe a couple of historical facts in it. But mostly, complete fiction. For instance, that big scene where Mel Gibson rides around the troops giving that speech about "they may take our lives, but they'll never take our freedom", just before they go into battle with the English?'

'I remember it, yes.'

'Well, according to reliable witnesses at the time, that's not what he said at all.'

'So what did he say?'

Iain puts on a fierce accent, making it even more Scottish.

'C'mon, let's get these cunts!' he says, then falls back in his chair sniggering.

'Really?'

'No,' Iain says, shaking his head, laughing.

'Bastard,' Barney says, starting to laugh too. His eyes flick around the table. 'Damn. I can't find anything to throw at you. So this is your New Year resolution, is it? To lie at every possible opportunity?'

'You started it.'

'It was a joke,' Barney says, holding his arms out. 'One little innocent lie about me fighting and killing a King Cobra. It was just a bit of fun to pass the time, entertain you a little, perk you up. Since then you've tried to get me to believe that the Dalai Lama's a piss-head "which is why you don't see him out all that much", that Gorbachev is dead - which I think was in very poor taste, by the way - and then this Braveheart nonsense. I see what you're doing. You've turned it into a game. To test each other's gullibility. Except you didn't tell me, so now you're winning three-one.'

Iain grins and nods.

'Yip,' he says.

'I see. A gullibility game,' Barney says, massaging his chin with the tips of his fingers. 'Oh, by the way, you know, of course, that they've taken the word 'gullible' out of the new edition of the Oxford dictionary.'

'Have they?'

'Three-two.'

'Bastard,' Iain says, then takes another warm swig from his bottle. He looks around the busy bar. At a table behind Barney he sees a starey-eyed man with short, messy hair gesticulating to some-one, saying 'and with the time, with the hours and everything, with the huge pressure, I just, you know, I just, I just, I just lost my perspective.'

'I should have known you were up to something,' Barney

says with an enlightened smile, 'when you came out with all that nonsense about Cat Stevens being forced to change his name when he converted to Islam because the Muslims don't like cats.'

Iain laughs.

'You just wouldn't go for that one, would you?'

'Well, it's such blatant tosh. I mean, of course I know that you have to change your name to a Muslim one when you convert. But I've read the Koran. A couple of times. I'm sure I'd remember if it had anything about not liking cats in it. In fact, if I remember correctly, old Mohammed was quite fond of them.'

'You've read the Koran?' Iain says, a little warily, remembering the game.

'Of course.'

'Is it any good? Don't tell me what happens in the end though, just in case I decide to read it someday.'

'It's rather an odd book,' Barney says, choosing his words carefully. 'There are lots of grand statements in it. Lots of rules. Lots of 'do this, don't do that'. But oddly enough, there's very little on spirituality, and very little reasoning given for all the rules. Perhaps that's why Christianity has managed to cling on in the West, due to the influence of the European school of reason. You can reason with Christianity, you can make compromises with it, adapt it to suit you. But with Islam, there are no grey areas. You either obey the rules to the letter, or you're fucked. Or stoned, probably.'

'So why did you read the Koran?'

'Oh, I had to,' Barney says, a heavy sigh escaping from him. 'Comparative religion. Part of my degree.'

'Comparative religion? So what was your degree?' Iain frowns, trying to work it out.

'Theology.'

'Theology?'

'What's so surprising about that?'

'I don't know. I mean, theology. I just never had you down as a theology man. Some arts degree maybe. English Lit or whatever. You just don't seem like a theology-type person.'

'It's a fascinating subject.'

'I'm sure. It's just that you don't strike me as being a terribly religious person.'

'You don't have to be religious to study theology,' Barney says, lighting a cigarette.

'But don't you become a priest in the end, though.'

'Only if you didn't learn anything. No, I think you're confusing it with Divinity. That's the priest factory. Theology is the study of religion generally. You don't have to be a signed-up Bible-basher. Or Koran-basher, for that matter. In fact, it's far better that you're not. It's terribly important to have an open mind on these things when you're studying them. But I do come from a religious background. My grandfather was a priest.'

'Really?'

'Three-three.'

'Bastard.'

*

Steve wants to drink until his eyes bleed, until he howls like a dog, until he drowns his pain.

He's perched on a barstool, an empty glass held out in his hand. There's no-one else in the bar, just him and Sandeep, the way it's been for the best part of an hour.

'Another,' he says thickly.

Sandeep would normally have closed up by now, but the Englishman's promised him a one hundred rupee tip to stay open.

He pours another large peg of Honeybee brandy into Steve's glass, then puts it back down on the bar. Steve's hand is a little unsteady as he picks it up. He stares into the dark, golden brown liquid for a few seconds, before slamming half of the drink down his rough throat. He grimaces, before putting the glass back down with exaggerated care.

It's helping. It's helping to focus the pain, to dull the rest of his body, so that all he has left, all he can feel is the centre of the ache. He can isolate it, sense it throbbing away like a tumour, feeding off his energy.

It's helping, burning an escape route for the agony, easing its way. Steve folds his arms on the bar and puts his head down on them. First the rush of hot tears, then the shakes. And finally the thick liquid sobs as the pain seeps out.

Sandeep stands staring at him, drying a glass with a clean cloth, saying nothing, just like he was trained to do.

CHAPTER SIXTEEN

A Cassady or a Kesey

'Probably on a mornin' not dissimilar to this,' the Doc says, clutching a cup of coffee to his skinny, bare, nut-brown chest. The sun's easing up the morning sky on the far side of the house. The Doc and Cyril are safe in the shadows of the cool verandah, watching the day wake up. Roosters crow loud and arrogantly, scrawny dogs slink out of sunlight seeking shade, the first straggle of scooters and motorbikes putter along the road, taking people to work, taking people home.

'A way's different, course,' the Doc adds. 'Colder. A whole world colder'n this. Freeze a man clear through to his bones. And that was him, poor Neal. On a mornin' not a million miles from this time of year, he just wakes up dead. The wickedest cat I ever knew.'

The Doc smiles, digging into his memory, trying to piece a few fragments together.

'Only met him once, towards the end 'n' all. Heard plenty, rumours, legends, lies, but once was all. But, man, I'm telling you, once was enough to know. Man, what a high-tailed, wire-gone cat! Charging that bus, not hitting those brakes, not once in more'n a thousand miles. Straight across, and him just whoopin' and a-hollerin' like the Fourth of July. He had the belief, see? He knew what it was like to go. Now that was a cat. That's what these kids ain't got. They ain't got a Cassady or a Kesey. They ain't got the vibe in them for it. They're all nine-to-five and tucked up in bed, thank you ma'am, and don't trouble me and I won't trouble you, and keep it quiet and rules and no risks. A game is what they're playin'. They don't know how to live it. They don't know the feel of it in their blood. They wouldn't know a true vibe if'n it came up, stung them in the cojones. Not like good old Neal. Fireball revved-up crazy-man. Man, what a cat. Now he knew, he knew that when the vibe was buzzin' there weren't nothin' you could do but let it have its way. Yup. Must've been a morning like this, just woke up dead, froze beside the railway tracks. But he lived, man, he lived. Lived five, six times more'n these Goddamn green-ass daisy-biter half-balled sonsofbitches messin' up the whole place now.'

Cyril yawns, a wide, fly-trap funnel of a yawn. Early morning mosquitos dart away in fear.

'Life can be hard,' Cyril says lazily. 'And sometimes too fast.'

'Too fast? You're Goddamn right, old buddy. Too fast. If'n a man's gonna live, really live, he's got to have the speedfreak mania of Cassady, take it all the way to the red, see what I'm sayin'? Get it revved up there howlin' and screamin' and don't even wait for the flag to drop, just bowl on outta there. Voom!' the Doc says, shooting a flat hand out into the air, nearly spilling coffee down his front. 'Goddamnit!'

'Susegad,' Cyril says, almost sighing it. His eyelids begin to anticipate a siesta later on. An early one, maybe. 'Susegad.'

*

Steve knows there's no point starting until the afternoon. There won't be nearly enough people on the beach until then to make it worth his while. He sits in the garden drinking black tea, waiting. Aside from anything else, his hangover needs some time to react to the two sachets of Resolve he took earlier, dissolved into a bottle of cold water which he'd sipped down with slow, sensible regularity.

The pain in his guts is the worst bit. His headache's more or less cleared, saliva's returned to his mouth, the sweats are reducing. His muscles still feel stiff but they're beginning to loosen, and his throat's on the healing side of raw. But the guts, the bowling ball of pain lying heavily in the pit of his stomach. All that Honeybee. Bloody poison. Bloody guts.

In a way, he's almost glad to have the hangover, welcoming its presence. It's a distraction, making him focus on physical faults, his attention almost entirely taken up with his body's internal problems, no time for examining his mind. But the guts.

Steve puts down his tea, stands up as quickly as the rapidly building pressure in his abdomen will allow, and hobbles over to the toilet by the bar, slamming the lock home with one hand, scrabbling at his shorts with the other, just making it to the toilet bowl in time for the foul explosion.

*

The grand total. Three hundred and forty quid, and a hundred and sixty five dollars. And maybe fifty or sixty quid's worth of rupees.

Jez counts it all again, but the numbers remain the same. Not as much as he thought it'd be. Not as much as he needs, and he's been through all his best contacts, even tried flogging stuff to some of the Westerners, ones he could more or less trust.

Sure, he got rid of the knife and the CD player and a couple of decent watches, but the cameras were shittier than he thought, and one of the personal stereos turned out to be a cheap Indian 'Sunyo', not worth the plastic it was made of. No-one wanted the travel alarm, not even at knock-down price. Who needs an alarm when waking up is free?

Jez stares at the notes, doing the figures. He reckons it's about five hundred quid's worth, assuming Hassan will take the rupees, which is a big assumption because he prefers to do all his deals in foreign currency. Which is why their deal was specified in sterling. Shit.

Mind you, he'll be okay with dollars. But still, even if Hassan accepts the rupees as well, that still leaves a hundred quid-sized hole. A hole that was supposed to be filled yesterday. A hole that might end up in his head. Double shit.

There's got to be a way out of this, Jez says to himself, feeling the nerves shaking his hands as he rolls the money up tightly, putting it in a small black plastic bag. He scrapes some dirt off a flat stone in the floor in the corner of the room, lifts it out, puts the bag in the hollow underneath, then puts the stone back, brushing the earth back over it with his foot.

There's a heavy knock at the door. Jez checks around quickly, making sure everything's safely hidden. He notices the alarm clock lying on the bed, and chucks it under the sheet before walking to the door and pulling back the bolt. Harsh light floods the room, Crash Mary washed in with it.

'Wotcha.'

'Alright, Crash.'

Crash Mary slumps down onto the bed, the wooden boards creaking under his weight.

'Where's Nat, then,' he asks.

Jez shrugs.

'Dunno. She told me where she was going, but I wasn't paying attention. Details, y'know?'

He makes an airy-fairy gesture, waving his hand vaguely.

'Yeah,' Crash Mary says, absently, staring at the floor. Almost immediately, he perks up. 'Got any spliff?'

'Is that all you came round for? Scrounging bastard.'

'Nah, nah, came round for the conversation. Obviously. No day of mine would be truly complete without the benefit of your pearls of wisdom.'

'Yeah, I've got a bit left. Just on me way to get stocked up again.'

'Ran out last night, didn't I. Been smoking Scabs' stuff till four. Tell you what, if you're getting a bit, can you lend me some?'

'Lend you some?'

'Yeah, just while I get a couple of things sorted out. Just a couple of days or something.'

'Until what?'

'Just a couple of things that's happening. Go on. It's just a bit of hash. Just a tola, or something.'

'A tola? Taking the piss, you are.'

'Half tola, then. Just a few hundred roops. Not a lot to ask.' Crash Mary sounds almost hurt, his large, shaven-headed frame taking on a submissive posture.

'You're telling me you can't get together a few hundred roops?'

'Yeah, but I need to eat, though, don't I. Wouldn't want to see me starve, would you?'

'Maybe I can get you a bit, then,' Jez says, not wanting to admit the extent of his own cash-flow problems.

'Well, come on, then,' Crash Mary says, standing up. 'No time like the present. No present like the time. Want to buy a clock for the wife?'

He produces Jez's stolen alarm clock from under his t-shirt like a magician, a hopeful smile spread across his face.

'Give me that, you tart,' Jez says, grabbing it, throwing it back onto the bed. 'Thieving bastard.'

'Ooh. Pot calling the kettle. So you expect me to believe that you actually bought a brand new Grundig, world time, programmable, multi-function alarm clock are you? You? Funny, I always had you down as a Matsui man, meself. Unreliable. Hardly ever works. Cheap. Won't even lend his mate a measly tola.'

'Half tola or nothing. What you think I am? Mr Moneybags or something?'

'No,' Crash Mary agrees, then grins. 'You're Mr Grundig. Tell you what, you could sell that,' he says, pointing to the clock. 'You could sell that for...nah, fuck it, it's hardly worth the effort.'

'Piss off. Perfectly good clock, that. Quality make, Grundig. Worth about forty quid, that is.'

'That why you couldn't sell it for a fiver yesterday is it? People frightened off by how good it was? BJ said you was going right to the base line.'

'Well BJ should keep his fuckin' gob shut,' Jez says sharply. 'What's he think he's doing, going round mouthing off?'

'He wasn't going round anywhere. Just told me.'

'Still. It's the principle, innit. I'll need to have a word.'

'Come on, then,' Crash Mary says. 'No point standing round here all day. Let's get down the Vibe.'

'I'll meet you there. Got some business to take care of first.'

'Just as long as you don't lose track of time. Still, how can you when you've got a lovely clock like that.'

'Quarter tola do you, will it?'

*

'Not much talent,' Iain says to Barney as they lie side by side on the beach. Iain's been careful to make sure there's a decent, heterosexual two feet space between their sarongs. Close enough for communication, but not close enough that people - specifically *female* people - get the wrong idea. The comfort zone of the independent male. He and Barney are not on the beach *together*. They're just there.

'It really depends on your definition of talent,' Barney says, a lazy, melted drawl oozing out of him. 'For instance, that girl over there. The one with the long red curly hair. Looks a bit like she's got flames trailing back from her head.'

'Yip. That's the exception to the 'not much' I'm talking about,' Iain says, nodding, getting enthusiastic.

'Well I suppose she is sort of pretty. But then there's the question of character, you see.'

'And what question would that be?'

'Well, look at her. Admittedly, she's pert, well-proportioned...'

'Perfectly proportioned.'

'...she holds herself well. She's clearly quite fit...'

'Clearly, clearly,' nodding.

'...but there's the question of character. Look at the stance.'

'I'm looking extremely carefully.'

'The things she's wearing, those briefs cut high on the thigh...'

'I see them, I see them.'

'...the way she struts, the way she talks to people around her. Italian, I'd suspect. Even from here, analysing what little information I can gather from her, it's quite obvious that she's terribly vain. A remarkably high regard for herself.'

'Yeah. I still don't see your point.'

'Well, you don't want to spend time with a vain girl. Far too much like hard work. Always centred on themselves, always concerned that they're looking just right, that they're being seen to do things just so. Especially in that scene, the party scene. Very strict rules in that particular little clique. A uniform and code of behaviour all of their own, but no less strict than in other societies. I mean, look at that dreadful tattoo stretching across her lower back. I mean, really.'

'Okay, the tattoo lets the side down a bit, but not seriously enough to relegate her out of the talent league.'

'But the character.'

'I don't care about her character. On a beach, character is not a factor in the Perv Ratings. Whether I'd have a fantastic time bouncing up and down on top of her for a few minutes, now that's a factor. I don't want to marry her.'

'Hmm, yes. I do find character, intelligence and personality terribly important in determining whether someone's attractive or not.'

'Oh, it's important,' Iain says, examining the redhead again. 'Definitely important. But that's not what I'm talking about. I'm talking about lust. The base motivation. The biological imperative. Do I want to lick her inner thigh? Yes. Do I want to discuss particle physics with her? Hardly at all.'

'But what about that girl over there?' Barney says, nodding in the opposite direction from the Italian girl. 'The one in the mauvey kind of swimsuit.'

'The mousey-haired one?'

'It's not mousey. It's delicate brown.'

'I think you'll find that's mousey. Definitely mousey. I've seen mousey. That, as I'm sure any hairdresser worth their salt would tell you, is officially, undeniably mousey.'

'But look at her. Willowy, sensitive, thoughtful.'

'Big nose,' Iain says, then catches Barney's hooked profile. 'Not that there's anything wrong with that. Essentially.'

'And just by the way she holds that book,' Barney says, getting wistful. 'You can tell it's not some trash fiction. She has a certain calmness to her, a balanced, quiet confidence. Assured but not arrogant. Cerebral yet humane.'

'You haven't had sex for ages, have you?'

'Nine months and fourteen days.'

'You should get out more.'

'I do try.'

'Maybe you should try a bit harder.'

'Not terribly convinced it would make much difference.'

They both sink into frustrated silence, idly scanning the beach. Four pink skinheaded Westerners lie sprawled in a line to their left. A misshapen, pale girl with long dreads searches in the sand at the edge of the surf, maybe for a shell or something she's lost, or maybe she's just looking at the tiny, nervous, transparent sand crabs scuttling in and out of their holes. The fruit-sellers walk slowly, precisely, with huge, heavy baskets of pine-apples, bananas, watermelons and grapefruit pressing down on their heads. The Karnatakan girls with their bangles, chains, sa-rongs and henna-painting gear troop wearily from one sunbather to another, the afternoon heat washing them with sweat. Skinny massage-wallahs in baseball caps crouch by splayed, shiny bodies chanting 'good massage, cheap price, back head neck shoulder feet, good massage, good feeling, good power'. The cold drinks sellers carrying dirty white polystyrene boxes are doing good business. The droning drum sellers are not. The Westerners dot the beach in ones and twos, then in small groups over by the Sun Temple, the scene building up as the afternoon wears on.

'I think it's just the types that are here,' Barney says.

'What d'you mean?'

'Oh, you know. The party crowd. I can't really see what I could possibly have in common with them. They come here, stay a few months, then go straight back home. Rarely venture outside Anjuna, most of them, never mind Goa. Not the slight-est bit of interest in the rest of India. They're not here because they want to travel. They're here because they think it's just one big private club, where it's hot and cheap and they can take as many drugs as they like in relative safety. I find it fascinating how they can be in a country like India and not be affected by it, almost acting as if the rest of India isn't there. For all their New-Agey spoutings, they continue to act like the very worst of colonialists. They flounce around, ignoring local customs and sensibilities to such an extent that it's not just rude, it's downright insulting. Which is why I am less than troubled by their potential as sexual partners.'

'There's always the Goddess, though,' Iain says.

'Ah yes, of course. The Goddess. But she doesn't count. She has humanity. You can tell. She's not like the rest. She's more of a nouveau hippy than a rave-head anyway. And she has timeless, peerless grace and beauty. No, she's not like the rest at all.'

Iain nods, and lets his eyes drift around the beach.

'She's not here today.'

'I noticed.'

'But she's always here.'

'Not necessarily.'

'Yes she is. We see her every day.'

'We didn't yesterday.'

Iain frowns.

'We weren't on the beach yesterday.'

'Exactly. So we don't know if she was here.'

'Ooh. Mr Pedantic.'

'Just stating a fact.'

'Well, she's usually here, then.'

'Maybe she's gone.'

'Don't say that.'

'It's possible.'

'Don't. I refuse to believe it. On principle.'

'The principle being?'

'I want to letch at her some more.'

'Oh, *that* principle. Still, it's possible.'

'Maybe,' Iain says, looking along the beach. 'Although her

boyfriend's still here.'

'The blonde chap with the great body?'

Iain stares at Barney for a couple of seconds.

'Well,' he says. 'I don't know if I'd call it a great body. A relatively good physique, I'll give him that. Don't know if I'd use the word great. Or body.'

'But it is a great body. It's undeniable. He looks like a Norse god.'

'Look, women have great bodies. Men don't. They've got something else. You don't say it's a great body.'

'Why ever not?'

'Well. It sounds a bit, well, gay-ish really. A bit homo-erotic. You know - appreciating another man's body.'

Barney pushes himself up on his elbows.

'Nonsense. I think it's perfectly within my capabilities to determine whether a man has a good body or not without developing the slightest hint of an urge to sodomize him.'

'Still,' Iain says, not convinced.

'Oh, that's just your uptight Presbyterian upbringing.'

'Probably. Anyway, it's not him. It's the other one with a great body. Short hair.'

Barney peers way down the beach, following Iain's pointed finger.

'So it is,' he says. 'Her reserve boyfriend.'

'Thanks. Seriously, thanks for reminding me,' Iain says. 'Appreciate it.'

'Don't mention it. Always on hand to pop that old ego. Just keeping you sane.'

*

Back to the first basic rule of investigation. If you want information, you ask questions. And of as many people as you can.

Anyone you might have seen her with, seen in the same bar as her, people who were around at the party. Try to remember. Any vaguely familiar face, ask them.

Steve works his way along the beach, the same questions coming out again and again. Do you know Sophie, French girl, blonde? Henrik, her boyfriend, big with long hair? Know where he is, where they stay?

The same questions, the same negative answers, the same disinterest, the same suspicion. Why do you want to know?

He feels people are being very guarded. Not in a sympathetic way, not cautious in case he's a friend and hasn't heard that Sophie's dead. No, it's more like they're guarding themselves, guarding against the reality of it, protecting their paradise fantasy, wanting nothing to do with anything bad or ugly or real and brutal. Half the beach without a scrap of information.

But then two results in a row. A girl with her head shaved at the sides says they live in a room at the north end of the village, then a long haired guy from Nottingham says he thinks it's near Da Souza's restaurant.

But no-one saying where Henrik is. No-one.

Two results, though. Steve decides to act on the information, slim as it is, as quickly as he can. Henrik's probably not around, but there's always a chance. He cuts up through the dunes beside a beach-shack and heads for the village.

'Boyfriend's gone,' Barney says.

'Reserve boyfriend,' Iain says back.

Steve talks to the late lunch crowd in Da Souza's, a party crowd, a goateed, sideburned, wild-haired crowd. He asks in the local shops, he asks people lounging outside houses, he asks people walking through the palms. Within an hour, he's narrowed the possibility down to five red-brick huts.

He knocks on the door of the first one. After he knocks again he hears the sound of shuffling from inside. The door opens slightly. A straggle-haired, sleep-faced girl looks out.

'Yeah?' she say.

'I'm looking for Sophie and Henrik's room. French girl, Swedish man.'

'Yeah, that one on the end, I think. Don't know if they're still there. What you wanna know for?'

'Sophie's dead,' Steve says flatly, routinely, sparking a jolt of shock into the girl's face. 'I'm trying to find Henrik.'

'Shit, yeah? What - doesn't he know?' the girl says, becoming more awake with each second.

'Oh, I'm pretty sure he knows. It was probably him who killed her. That's why I'm trying to find him.'

'Shit,' the girl says. She looks uncomfortable now, as if she wishes she or Steve were somewhere else. 'Shit. Well, good luck, then,' she says slowly, without conviction, and closes the door.

Steve goes to the end room. The bolt's across the door, but it's not padlocked. So, he thinks, no-one's in. He shunts the bolt back, pulls open the door and walks in. It's too dark to see anything. He feels for a switch by the door and flicks it on. A weak bulb hanging on a cord from the centre of the low ceiling throws a dim light onto the room, showing the rudimentary wooden bed, the small table, the chair. A simple room, but not spartan. Lived in.

Steve takes a deep breath, sucking in the room's musky odour. Incense, earth, clothes. And, then, just for a second, he catches it. The smell of Sophie. The rich, lush perfume of her. Patchouli and tea-tree oil, sandalwood and coconut sun-cream. His chest aches, his heart beating a fast rhythm, and he has to force himself to calm down.

He looks around. Hangings on the wall, colourful mystical

signs, patterns of elephants. A small brass figure on the table. Ganesh. The elephant god. Sophie must have liked elephants. She never mentioned it.

Clothes, some on the red bedspread, some on top of a battered green rucksack. He sees a top he remembers her wearing, but tries not to think about it. A cloth bag hangs from the back of the chair, as if waiting for her to pick it up at any time. Steve feels a potentially overwhelming surge of sadness coming on and fights it. This is no time to weep. This is business.

He starts searching. The rucksack first, checking for pockets, for pouches, for anything that might hold papers. Then flicking through the books, lifting the mattress, scouring all around. He notices that there's nothing which obviously belongs to Henrik. He's gone. No surprise there.

Ten minutes of thorough examination bring him relative success. A money-belt, a diary, a small pile of documents. In the money-belt, a few travellers cheques, health insurance papers, and a passport.

Steve's head throbs as he holds the passport. His hands suddenly feel cold and weak, as if chilled through to the bone. He opens the cover slowly. The photograph. Her long blonde curls, the warm red of her lips, the rich, green glow in her eyes. The suppressed smile. The life.

Twenty years old. Born in February, her birthday just over a month away. Her twenty first.

Emotion wells up again, but he resists it. Control. He must remain in control.

Steve wipes angrily at his damp eyes and puts all the documents into the cloth bag that's hanging from the chair. He slings the bag up onto his shoulder and goes out the door, walking quickly to a small general store fifty yards away. He buys a padlock, goes back, fits it through the loop on the bolt, makes sure that it's firm, then heads back towards the hotel. He needs to go through the documents first before handing them over to the police. Check them, and make some arrangements of his own.

*

Chill, for fuck's sake. Just chill. Jez stands in the middle of his room, arms folded, leg twitching, tapping out an irregular rhythm on the hard earth.

He's trying to stop the adrenalin getting to him, but it's not working. It's a fucked-up mess and he knows it. Being a hundred quid short might not sound like a lot, but in India it's a fortune. Hassan's not going to react well, unless he can come up with something really smart.

And there's the problem. Jez has been going through loads of ideas, but none of them appeal. There's trying to avoid Hassan, or nicking some more stuff, or buying some Es off Aziz the Afghan and selling them quick for an okay profit, enough to cover the debt.

But each solution has its own problems. He can't avoid Hassan for much longer, he's already taken too many risks with knock-off gear, and he doesn't trust Aziz as far as he can spit.

He could always just run away, of course, but where would he go? He's not planning to leave Goa until March, maybe even April. Although he needs the Es to fund his stay.

So there's only one workable way out. Face up to Hassan, hand over the cash, and hope for a miracle. Which is why his leg's juddering and his upper lip's sweating.

Fuck it, he's a Kashmiri. As soon as he sees the cash, he'll crumble. What's a hundred between business colleagues anyway? Hassan knows he's good for it, bound to let him off with a couple of more days.

Jez pumps himself up, convincing himself to go down the

path and head straight for Hassan. Head up, chest out, no fear.
You can do it, you can do it. Come on!

He padlocks the door behind him and sets off. The midday
sun throbs through the palms as he winds along the dusty track,
past cafes crammed with crashed-out freaks easing into the day
with banana pancakes and sweet lassis. Jez walks fast, his pace
keeping time with his heartbeat. Come on, you can do it. Come
on!

Hassan sees him almost as soon as he's on the main path, as
if he's been waiting for him the whole time. He raises his arms
wide, his face open and uncomprehending.

'Where are you?' he shrugs at Jez. 'Day before, not coming.
Today, not coming. Where are you?'

'Yeah, sorry Hassan. Bit of a problem, parties and everything. Time, an' that, yeah? Just gets away from you. Here now,
aren't I.'

Hassan, blank-faced, flicks his head toward the side alley
through the shacks. Jez leads the way, ducking into Hassan's office. Hassan follows him in and stands in the middle of the floor,
hands on hips, waiting, seeming to Jez like he's almost filling the
room.

'So this is the situation, right,' Jez says, keeping his voice
calm. 'We've got a deal, and there's no way I'm backing out...'

'Money, money,' Hassan says, holding his right hand out,
clicking his fingers.

'Yeah, that's what I'm saying to you. What I'm saying is,
you've got Es you don't want to be holding and I've got cash I
don't want to be holding, so the best solution for both of us....'

'What is this? Why you are talking talking talking every
time?' Hassan says sharply, moving towards Jez, poking his finger at him. The room suddenly feels smaller and hotter. 'You
have my money? Yes, no?'

'Yes. Yeah, most of it, yeah. That's what I'm saying. Here.'
Jez pulls the roll of notes out of his trousers and hands it to Hassan. Hassan looks at it a second before going to the door,
opening it a crack and giving a short, sharp whistle. He stands
back as two more burly Kashmiris enter the room. He hands the
wad to one of them, muttering something, before standing back
in front of Jez with hands on hips again while the other man
counts the cash. The third Kashmiri stands with his back to the
door. None of them are smiling.

Shit.

'Look,' Jez says, raising his voice. 'We're supposed to be doing business, yeah? So what the fuck are these goons doing here?
I'm coming to you in good faith, with a decent proposition, and
you're coming on all heavy. You're the one always going on
about how business is done. Well I'll tell you something for
nothing, this is not how fucking business is done.'

Jez faces up to Hassan, hands on hips, aping him, trying to
stare him out.

The man stops counting the cash and says something to Hassan.

'This is not enough money,' Hassan says, barking the words
out.

Jez spreads his arms wide.

'That's what I'm saying. If you'd only listen to what I'm trying to say to you instead of...'

Hassan's fist slams into his guts before he sees it move. Jez
jerks over, the wind blown out of him. A kick sends him to the
ground. One of the men keeps him down by putting a foot on
his chest while Hassan crouches and grabs Jez's hair, forcing his
head back.

'I am sick of this bullshit,' Hassan says, low and threatening,
right in Jez's face. 'You think you can cheat me? You try to be
big man and cheat Hassan?' he says, slapping Jez hard with his

free hand. 'I could slit your throat, you sister-fucker. Who would know? Who would care? You come here with half money bullshit, then you don't come, now you come with more bullshit. I don't care about bullshit. I care about money.'

'Hassan, Hassan,' Jez wheezes, trying to catch his breath. 'I'm not trying to cheat you. I'll get the money.'

Hassan slaps him again.

'But you've got the money!' Jez whines. 'I've given you over a thousand quid! I'm not asking for nothing, not until I give you the rest.'

'You want me to trust you? You break all promises, now you want me to forget everything? I pay much money to supplier, and all I get is bullshit bullshit.'

'I'll bring you the money, I swear it.'

'There is no deal. Price is changing. I cannot trust you, so I am finding another buyer.'

Jez tries to get to his feet but the man's foot presses harder on his chest.

'Hassan, for fuck's sake. We had a deal. We agreed the price, we shook on it, everything. I've given you most of the money and I'll get you the rest tomorrow. You can't back out of this.'

'Still the big man,' Hassan sneers, then backhands Jez's face again. 'You are in no position to make deals. Okay, you bring rest of money tomorrow, then I give you half of ektazy. You want more, you pay more.'

'No way. I pay for everything, I get everything.'

'Or maybe I give you nothing,' Hassan says sharply. 'You making big problems for me. Maybe I take the money and go. Nothing you can do. What you do, go to police?' Hassan laughs.

'I'm telling you, you don't want to be starting a war. I'm fucking serious, Hassan. Don't even start thinking about fucking crossing me.'

Hassan lets go of Jez's hair and gets up, saying a few words to his henchmen. Then he turns back to face Jez, looking down at him as if he was staring at a pile of cow dung.

'You bring money tomorrow. Maybe we talk,' he says, and then he's out of the door, leaving Jez to pull himself upright. The two henchmen leave slowly, the last one eyeballing Jez as he goes.

'What the fuck you looking at,' Jez says to him, his blood up. 'You want some, do ya? Yeah?'

Jez makes as if he's going to rush the Kashmiri, but the man rushes him back, shoulder down, sending Jez sprawling into the corner. The man kicks him, then slams a vicious punch into his kidneys.

Then he leaves, closing the door behind him, and the room's quiet. Except for the sound of Jez, curled up with his head in his hands, fighting for air, fighting tears of humiliation.

CHAPTER SEVENTEEN

Australia's sunsets

'There,' Steve says, slapping down a pile of papers on the front desk at Anjuna police office. He points at it as he makes each clipped, forceful point.

'Her name, passport, address in France, letters, a diary. Her boyfriend's name. Henrik Andersen. And a key to the room they shared.'

The plump, bored policeman sitting behind the desk gives Steve a lazy stare, then reaches out and lifts the key. He drops it in a drawer with half a dozen other loose, unmarked keys. Then he flicks through the papers, opening the diary at a couple of pages, staring blankly at them.

'This is not English,' he says.

'Obviously,' Steve says with an irritated sigh. 'It's French. She was French.'

The policeman pushes the documents off to one side. Then he picks up his copy of the Konkan Times and goes back to reading the sports page.

Steve stands waiting, arms folded, looming over the desk. A sense of determination and authority swells within him.

'Well,' he says, snapping it out. 'What are you going to do now?'

The desk sergeant turns down his mouth, his moustache stretching at the corners. He doesn't bother to look up at Steve.

'We will do what we do,' he says.

'You have everything you need there,' Steve says, adamant, pointing to the pile of papers. 'More than enough. You can contact the French and Swedish embassies, send out information for border checks.'

The sergeant puts down his newspaper again and fixes Steve with a look of contempt.

'This is not changing anything. We are telling the embassy in good time. There is no big hurry. The facts are still the same.'

'This stuff gives you new facts. The man's name. Where he's been in India. It's in her diary. I've even marked the pages for you. My French might not be up to much, but even I could get that much out of it.'

The policeman starts to raise his newspaper, but gets jolted by Steve's harsh tone.

'Don't you lot even know how to conduct a simple murder investigation? You have a prime suspect, a motive, the means, his name, description, even his recent movements for God's sake. Do you expect him to arrest himself?'

'There is no prime suspect in drowning,' the desk sergeant says back, even louder. One of the other cops lounging at the back of the room gets up and walks to the front desk, sitting on a corner of it, staring at Steve. 'There is only victim, and we have victim so stop wasting our time.'

'Why the hell do you still keep saying it's a drowning? I saw the body. You don't have to be a forensic scientist to see that it wasn't a bloody drowning. It's clearly murder. It's obvious. What tests have you done? How much water was in her lungs? Why was there no mucus around her mouth and nose? Have you even bothered to check anything? What's the matter with you lot? Too much work for you? Not enough time for it in your obviously busy day?'

The desk sergeant starts yelling angrily in Hindi, springing the other policeman into action.

He rushes round the desk, grabbing Steve's arm, pushing and pulling him out the door, blocking the entrance until he's satisfied that Steve's walking away.

Steve strides down the road, feeling jittery with adrenalin. He's pleased with the result of his visit. He didn't expect them to be working on the case. He just wanted to get them annoyed, hassle them, maybe provoke them into action.

Now, he thinks to himself. Time to up the pace a bit.

*

'Bloody shame about that Sophie, though,' Crash Mary says.

There's four of them around a table in the Vibe, waiting for sunset. Jez is sitting beside Crash Mary, sore and depressed, trying to smoke himself out of it.

Ming and Dobs are across the table from them. Their ketamine's kicked in, and they loll and sway and blink slow, heavy eyes in a waking sleep, their long messy-haired, rough-bearded heads drooping, nodding.

'Bloody shame,' Jez agrees, licking a cigarette paper, skinning up in his lap. He told Crash Mary an hour and a half ago what he'd learned about the real circumstances of Sophie's death, although he'd omitted the source of the information, namely himself, just to be on the safe side. Crash is a mate, but mates have mouths.

At first, Crash Mary was angry, wanting to go searching for Henrik and do him in, but Jez - and four joints of the hash Jez stole on his late night shopping spree - has managed to calm him down. Besides, Jez is in no shape to back him up.

'Beautiful girl,' Crash Mary says. 'Lovely girl. Wouldn't't've thought it, that Henrik geezer. Doin' her in, an' that.'

'Why not?'

'Well. Swedish, isn't he. Neutral. They're into all that nicey-nicey stuff. Saunas. Safety. They're pacifists, ain't they, your Swedes.'

'Yeah,' Jez says with a snort. 'Apart from the psycho ones.'

'That's what I'm saying. Wouldn't've thought you got your psychos in Sweden.'

'Course you do. Get 'em everywhere. Cuts across national boundaries, dunnit, being a psycho.'

'Your Uncle Harry's a psycho, isn't he?'

'Nah. Old Harry's a schizo. Different thing completely.'

'Yeah? What way?'

'Well, your schizo's just a nutter. Your psycho's a dangerous nutter.'

'So if your Uncle Harry's not dangerous, how come they locked him up in that loony bin, then?'

'It's not a loony bin. It's a loony *hospital*. Anyway, he's not locked up, not really. They keep him there, but it's not a prison or nothing. They had to put him there. No-one in the family wanted him. Always been a right pain in the arse, Uncle Harry. None of us liked him. It's too much hassle having a nutter around all the time.'

'What about that 'Care in the Community', then.'

'Yeah, they talked about that. Trouble is, we didn't care. We wanted nothing to do with him, and he wouldn't go and live on his own. If you ask me, the community's got enough problems caring for itself without having to worry about looking out for nutters an' all.'

Jez holds the lit joint across the table towards Ming. Ming takes a while to get his hair-curtained eyes steady on it, then reaches out a slow, wavy arm, eventually gaining a loose hold on the smouldering white tube.

'Look at those reactions,' Jez says. 'Like an Olympic athlete at the peak of his form.'

'So, lads,' Crash Mary says, leaning his big face over the table. 'Where are the Ket-head Twins Gymnastic Team gonna perform tonight?'

After a few silent, head-drooping moments, Dobs' right hand bobs and weaves up, his middle finger extended in a lazy crook.

'Charming,' Crash Mary says, reaching out and snatching the joint from Ming's hand, forcibly excluding Dobs from the round.

'Nah,' he says to Jez, taking a long drag. 'What happened to Sophie, crime of passion an' all that, you don't expect that from the Swedes. That sort of thing, that's what your Italian's get up to. Hot tempered an' that.'

'The Italians? Nah. Not this lot anyway. The only thing they get worked up about is if they get a dirty mark on their trousers or something. It's all fashion with them, innit, the way they go around. It's like they're on some bleedin' catwalk. Like all their clothes have been designed for them or something. They try to get this look, this waster-type look, but it's too perfect, too clean, like they got it off some picture in a magazine or something. You can tell they've put a lot of thought into exactly what they're wearing, exactly how they look. Just sit in the German Bakery and watch them sometime. Ponces, the lot of them, all sitting there checking everybody else out, what they're wearing an' that.'

'Still,' Crash Mary says. 'It works, though. Some of those Italian birds. Stunning.'

'Yeah, granted, some of your Italian birds, very sexy. But in all that gear they've specially picked out, hours in front of the mirror trying to look as natural as possible. It's a joke. It's all put on. It's like the blokes. Their hair just right, their sideys shaved and shaped, so they end up looking like a cleaned-up Frank Zappa or something. And all them silk shirts. Open nearly to the waist, hairy chests out. Surprised they don't have bleedin' medallions, some of them. Probably would have done if this was fifteen years ago. Nah, you wouldn't get any of them lot getting violent. Come from rich families, most of them. Rich kids playing at being hippies, pretending to rough it for a while. I tell you what, you wouldn't find any of that lot within a mile of a commune.'

'Mind you,' Crash Mary says, handing the joint back to Jez. 'If I thought some of them Italian birds did live in a commune and not in some posh flat in Rome, I'd give up all my worldly goods and join tomorrow. Fuck it - today!'

'You haven't got any worldly goods.'

'Got some. Maybe not very worldly ones, but they're goods.'

Ming's head thumps down on the table, just missing Crash Mary's bottle of Kings.

'Oi!' Crash Mary shouts, grabbing the bottle. 'Have a word with yourself, my son. Might have done yourself some damage. Or I might have.'

'Waste of sperm,' Jez says, looking at the greasy crown of Ming's head. 'Nah, if I was a betting man, I'd have said it was more likely to be one of your Israelis who'd do someone in.'

'But you are a betting man.'

'Yeah, but you don't go betting on someone else when you know the result, do you. When you already know someone else done it. I'm just saying. If there was violence to be done, my first thought would be - Israeli.'

'Why's that, then?'

'Well, talk about your hot tempered. They've got it on a stick, your Israelis. Arrogant bunch of bastards, ain't they. Like that lot you see at them Israeli cafes on the Mapusa road. Wouldn't give you the time of day, most of them. Never mix, that lot. Always pushing and barging their way around, in the shops an' that. Racing about the streets on them big Enfields like they're God's gift.'

'God's chosen people,' Crash Mary says.

'Exactly what I'm saying. Swanning about like they're God's chosen people or something. Real bleedin' attitude problem, they've got.'

'That's a bit anti-Semitic, innit?'

'Ballocks. That's what Nat says, innit. "You're just anti-Semitic, you are", she says. Ballocks, I tell her. I'm not anti-Semitic. I'm anti bleedin' Israeli. There's a difference. Trained to kill with their bare hands, this lot. It's their national service, innit. They've all done it. One wrong move and they'll snap your spine soon as look at you.'

'Like to see them try,' Crash Mary says, puffing himself up, bulging his thick, muscly bull neck.

'I wouldn't,' Jez says. 'Hand to hand combat? No thank you.' He stares at Dobs and the top of Ming's head. 'Think there's any danger of these two specimens buying us a drink?'

Crash Mary examines them, Ming's wasted slumber, Dobs' lazy, puppet-on-a-string impersonation.

'About as much danger as them remembering their names.'

'Go on, then,' Jez says. 'Get them up and at it.'

'Oi!' Crash Mary says, leaning over the table again, getting close to Ming's ear. 'Drinks! Drinks! Money! Get your roops out, you lazy bastards!'

He raps Ming on the back of the head. It makes a hollow sound.

Neither of the Ket-heads pay him any attention, not seeming to notice him at all.

'Well,' Jez says. 'As they always say. When the diplomatic route fails, the best way to solve the crisis is through direct action.'

He leans over and starts rummaging in an oblivious Ming's shirt pocket, retrieving a few crumpled ten rupee notes.

'I don't know where you get that ballocks you come out with

sometimes, I really don't,' Crash Mary says, shaking his head. 'There's something wrong with your brain.'

Jez stands, ready to make his way to the bar, trying not to show the pain that mocks his every move. Another secret he's kept from Crash. To cover a wince, he winks at him.

'You're just jealous because I'm an intellectual, innit.'

*

Karen's kept her anger with Steve simmering all day. Anger at being spoken to like that. Anger at the suggestion that she might be selfish. Anger at his lack of sympathy for her illness. Just trying to ruin her holiday, that's what he's doing.

She sits on a sunbed, the back of it raised high, turning it into a long chair. Her skin's been browning, her lipstick standing out as a thin slash of red across a tan face. She's flicking through a magazine, one that Maureen lent her, scanning the articles on interiors, ideas for gardens, latest breakthroughs in skin cream, fashion rumours about next season's clothes, celebrity gossip. Her Jackie O-style sunglasses mask her hard eyes.

She's kept the anger simmering, not letting it boil over and be wasted on froth and steam in Steve's absence. She hasn't seen him all day, not since first thing in the morning. She didn't see him come back briefly in the afternoon. He made sure she didn't. He had important, secret things to do.

She simmers away. All day he's been gone. Not hide nor hair. Another ingredient to be slipped into the bubbling cauldron.

The last of sunset's honey-peach glow turns the sky to a velvet purple behind the jaggy silhouette of the palm trees. At the bar, Raju flicks switches to light the frosted bowls hanging from trees in the garden. Almost as if it's a signal, Karen stands up, wraps her sarong around her waist, and walks over to the open-plan bar area, taking a cushioned seat in the concrete interior beneath a gently turning fan.

'Gin and tonic,' she says when Raju comes over to take her order.

'Big peg? Small peg?'

'You what?'

'You want big peg gin? Small peg?'

Karen's flustered. She doesn't understand what he means.

'I don't know,' she says. 'Just normal.' She starts flicking through her magazine again.

Raju goes back to the bar, where Sandeep's cleaning a glass.

'What's normal for that one? Big peg? Small peg?' Raju says in Hindi, gesturing with his head to Karen.

Sandeep tries to remember what Steve's ordered in the past.

'Big peg,' he says, a little uncertain.

'Okay. Big peg gin tonic.'

*

Steve walks in the front gate of the hotel nearly an hour later. He's weary, hot, sweating from the activity. First of all at the steaming local travel agency office, the only place he could find with a photocopier. Making the poster with the blown-up copy of Sophie's passport picture, writing the information out, making all the copies at the touch of a button and a wad of baksheesh. That hadn't been all that difficult.

Walking around the bars, the restaurants, the shops, the phone bureau, asking for permission, explaining, pleading, sometimes getting his way, sometimes not, sometimes slipping over cash, sometimes failing in fury - that had been the hard bit. Spreading the message around, widening the net, scouting sites in south Anjuna near the German Bakery, others in the north near the Vibe bar, the Guru bar, Sonic. Then near da Souza's, the Oxford stores, anywhere in the village that was suitable for a poster. Then the crossroads, then out by the Israeli cafes, then up to Pandora's and the Primrose near Vagator.

Poster after poster after poster, making sure he put them up himself, not trusting waiters or owners to do it if he just left them there. It got a bit easier once he hired a willing taxi driver to take him around some of the further-flung areas, but it's been a long day. An exhausting day.

And still more places to go, people to talk to, maybe this evening, maybe tomorrow, maybe the next day. Find that big bloke who saw Sophie leave with Henrik. Get him to give a statement. Keep hassling the police.

He sees Karen in the bar before she sees him. In one way, he feels comforted seeing her. In another, because he'd really prefer to see someone else sitting there, a girl with long blonde hair and deep green eyes, he feels it's a slap in the face. Which he knows he stands a good chance of getting anyway.

Steve signals to Raju to bring him a beer, then sits down opposite Karen at her table. She looks up, but Steve can't see her eyes. They're still hidden behind the sunglasses. But he doesn't need to actually see her eyes to read her mood. The thin tightness of her lips tells him all he needs to know. She puts down her magazine.

'Well?' she says. 'Where have you been all day?'

Steve doesn't want an argument. He's too tired. He just wants to sit, have a beer, blank his mind for a while. He knows it's probably impossible.

'Just following up some leads in the murder.'

'What murder?'

'The French girl. I told you about it last night.'

'What d'you mean, 'following up leads'? What's it got to do

with you?'

'I'm kind of helping the police a bit.'

'What for? I'm sure they're quite capable of doing it themselves. Don't see why you should get involved. We're supposed to be on holiday, in case you'd forgotten.'

Raju places Steve's beer in front of him. Steve takes three greedy mouthfuls from the chilled glass, then takes a deep breath, trying to cool the air in his lungs.

'Local police aren't going to do anything unless I help them with it. They're happy for it to go down as a drowning, which it isn't. If I don't do something, nobody will.'

'Well if they say it was a drowning, it probably was. Not surprising, what with all the drugs you hear about.'

'She didn't drown. I saw the body. Credit me with some intelligence at least. I know the difference between someone who's drowned and someone who's been violently attacked.'

'So what? Leave it to the Indian police. The Indians can sort it out themselves. It's not your problem.'

'It is if I can do something about it. She deserves it. The man who did it deserves to be caught. Punished. I don't know why, but the Indians just want to sweep it under the carpet. A Westerner killing a Westerner. They don't think it's their problem.'

'And it's not yours either. I don't see why you've got to run around ruining our holiday over some stranger.'

'She's not a stranger,' Steve says, then falters. 'I, I knew her.'

Karen takes off her sunglasses. Her eyes are cold and sharp.

'You what? What d'you mean, you 'knew' her?'

'I met her on the beach. Talked to her a couple of times.'

'So this is what you've been up to, is it? The moment my back's turned you're off gallivanting around, chatting up girls on the beach? Taking advantage of me being ill. The cat's away and all that. I see. I see what you're on about now.'

'No you don't,' Steve says softly. You don't have it in you, he thinks. 'You didn't meet her. She was a really nice girl. She deserves better than to be stuck in a box with 'drowned' written on it and forgotten about. She deserves justice at least. The only way to do that is to make sure this boyfriend of hers, this Henrik Andersen, make sure he's caught. It's the right thing to do.'

Karen lets out a cynical laugh.

'So you're going to go off and catch him single-handed, are you? The big brave detective leaping into action? Getting carried away with yourself, you are.'

'I didn't say I was going to catch him,' Steve says, controlling his breathing, trying not to let Karen's jibes get to him. 'Just do some of the groundwork. Maybe provoke those lazy bastards in the local police station to get off their arses and do something. If I can do some of the preliminaries, maybe it'll make it easier for them to catch him.'

'Very presumptuous, I must say.' Karen folds her arms. 'What do you owe her that you need to take all this upon yourself? Anyway, how d'you know she'd want you to catch this bloke? Maybe she brought it on herself. Maybe that's the type she was.'

'Oh, that, that is rubbish,' Steve says, forcing the word out, like it's the worst swear he can think of. 'You don't know what you're talking about. That is complete rubbish. And anyway, Sophie was about as far away as you could imagine from this supposed 'type' of yours. She was...'

'Yes?' Karen snaps, cutting into him. 'You're very quick to defend her, I must say. For someone you've met once or twice. Go on. You were saying? 'She was...' She was what? Go on, tell us, since you obviously knew her so well. What was she like? Because she must have been really something to ruin a holiday over.'

'This is just...' Steve can't find the words. Anger, frustration and grief clog him. He stands up and makes for the stairs up to their room. Karen waits, arms folded, finger tapping on her arm. She thinks about following him up. Then she thinks about not doing it. She decides to stay and finish her drink in her own good time. She's not running after anybody. She watches the condensation on Steve's abandoned glass run onto the table in the warm evening air.

Ten minutes later, Steve walks out of the hotel again, not stopping to acknowledge Karen on the way past. She stares at his back, her jaw tense.

*

'I'm not sure I believe this,' Iain says, standing beside Barney at the bar in Starco's. They'd only meant to pop in for one on the way to Pandora's, but got chatting to a mixed table of travellers out in the garden. Now they're getting a round in, Sandpiper beer for everyone.

For the first half hour the conversation spread around the table between the five of them, all the normal sort of touchstone traveller's tales about getting lost or collecting obscure bowel disorders. But for the last hour there's been a polarisation, Barney talking to Jonathon and Gaby, a couple from Cambridge, whilst Iain's been engrossed by Jules, an Australian girl the couple met in Bombay. And what Iain can't believe is that she seems interested, almost keen.

'And she's pretty and everything,' he says, grabbing two of the barely chilled, light-green bottles from the bar. 'And I'm not even trying. Seriously. I can't believe it.'

'Must every conversation you have with a female be evaluated purely on its potential for sexual gratification?'

'Not every conversation, obviously. But when it's a conversation with a doe-eyed, deep-tanned, full-chested babe from

Brisbane then you're damn right it does.'

'Have you considered that she might not like you in that way? She's Australian. In my experience they have a rather open nature. She may simply be - gosh, it may be controversial, but I'll say it anyway - friendly.'

'Well, at least she's not being offhand or downright hostile, which is a pretty much the reaction I've been getting in Goa so far.'

'True,' Barney admits, cradling the rest of the bottles in his arms. 'Except from your feisty fraulein, of course.'

'Christ, don't remind me.'

They head back to the garden and hand out the beers. The night air is damp and warm. They're all relaxed, happy to talk light-hearted nonsense as jazz drips out the speakers and a per-fume of spices drifts across the tables, mixing with grass-smoke and sandalwood incense. Barney's laughing with Jonathon and Gaby about some weird experience they had up in Jodhpur, and Iain's listening with increasing delight to Jules' description of life back home.

'And this line in the national anthem, it's now "Australians let us rejoice", but in pre-PC days, when I was at school - this is when I was little, right - the line went, "Australia's sons, let us rejoice", and I swear, for three or four years, every time we sang it at school, I sang "Australia's sunsets, ostriches".' She starts laughing, throwing back long, curly dark hair. 'I honestly thought that's what the line was.'

'I think I prefer your version,' Iain says, grinning like a fool. 'Got a much better ring to it. Our national anthem in Scotland used to be 'Scotland the Brave', but nobody knew the words, not even the wrong ones. Every time they played it at a footy match or a rugby match, people just used to hum along.'

'How did it go?'

'I'd rather not. I think it might spoil the moment.'

Jules laughs again, showing plenty of straight, white teeth.

I'm in here, Iain thinks. I'm definitely in here. She enjoys talking to me, she thinks I'm funny. And she's Australian. They'll shag anybody. They probably think it's a sport.

They all talk on for a while, as motorbikes prowl past on the road and tables empty, the crowd heading for Pandora's or the Primrose or the late-opening bars up in Vagator and Chapora. Eventually Barney notices they're the only ones left.

'Think we'd better leave,' he says, scraping his chair back on the sandy grass. Their drinks are finished anyway. 'Who's for Pandora's?'

'Yeah, absolutely,' Jonathon says, Gaby nodding.

'Be rude not to,' says Iain, getting up, smiling at Jules.

They all head out of the garden onto the road, Barney, Jonathon and Gaby in front, Iain and Jules following behind.

'Guys, I'm going to call it a night,' Jules says loudly to the four of them. Iain's heart stops.

'But it's early,' Barney says, looking at his watch, as the couple urge Jules to come with them. Iain just stands there, plotting frantically.

'Nah, gotta get up early,' Jules says, pushing her hair back off her face, as Iain thinks, arrange to meet her tomorrow, dinner or a sunset drink or something, anything. Don't let her slip away. 'My flight's at half eight.'

'Your what?' Iain blurts. 'Your what's at what?'

'My flight. I'm off to Kerala tomorrow, Cochin. Do the backwaters and everything.'

Iain tries not to look like a puppy that's just found out it's to be put down, which is how he feels. Then he realises that if he does look like that, Jules might take pity on him and let him snuggle in to be comforted. But the moment's gone, and he realises he can't just summon up Death Row Puppy Face at will.

The couple say fond goodbyes to Jules as Barney shrugs at Iain, his expression a mix of I-told-you-so and Better-luck-next-time.

'Actually,' Iain says, panicking, 'think I'll call it a night too. Haven't really got over New Year yet, to be honest.'

'Are you sure?' Barney says with an innocently mischievous look on his face. 'Come on. Come for one at least.'

'No, seriously,' Iain forces out through gritted teeth. 'Just need a good night's kip and I'll be fine. You go. Seriously.'

'Well, as long as you're sure,' Barney says motheringly.

'I'm sure.'

The three of them walk off, Jonathon and Gaby waving at Jules and making her promise to e-mail them. Then it's just Jules and Iain, standing at the side of the road by a late night stall selling fried eggs and rolls.

'Well,' Iain says, his arms swinging absentmindedly. 'Walk you home?'

'Aw, that's sweet, but there's really no need,' Jules says, touching Iain's arm. 'I only live down there,' pointing down the lamp-lit side road next to Starco's.

'No bother at all. It's on my way.' In a roundabout fashion. 'Anyway, there's dogs and stuff. Safer to walk together. Then I can use you to distract them while I run off.'

'The last of the gentlemen,' Jules laughs.

'Damn right. Very well brought up, us Highlanders.' That's good, get the Highland bit in, very exotic in a cold, northern way. If not strictly true.

'Come on, then,' she says brightly, leading the way.

They walk past Starco's, Iain asking Jules where she's staying in Kerala, how long she's going to be there, but she hardly has time to answer. Thirty yards, and they're outside her guest-house.

'Ah,' Iain says. 'So when you said you lived just down here, you really meant just down here. Like, a matter of seconds down here.'

'I told you,' Jules says smiling.

'Well,' Iain says. 'I suppose...' he lets it trail off.

Jules looks down at her feet, then back up at Iain.

'I'd invite you in,' she says. 'But.... you know.'

'What?' Iain says, feigning ignorance.

'Well, it's late.'

'I'm not as tired as I thought I was.'

'Yeah, but....you're a very sweet man, d'you know that?'

'I'd always suspected that, but I was never quite...'

But then Jules pulls his head to hers and kisses him deep and long. The warmth of her body through flimsy linen has Iain's loins springing into action. He reaches an arm around the small of her back, pulling her closer, but then Jules backs off.

'I wish I'd met you a week ago,' she says, slightly breathless.

'I know, I know,' Iain says, stroking her upper arm. 'But you've met me now.'

'Yeah,' she says, looking at him sadly. But then she backs away. 'Thanks,' she says, although Iain's not sure why. 'Guess I'll maybe see you around India sometime.'

Jules opens the gate to the guesthouse's garden, and is about to climb the steps to the front door when Iain panics again.

'I...I could just come up for five minutes,' he says, and as soon as he says it he knows how strained and desperate and crass and pathetic his voice sounds. In that instant he loathes himself.

Jules turns. Her face isn't sad now. Just slightly disappointed

'Sorry, mate. Never been good at that one-night-stand thing.'

And then she's through the door and gone from his life, and

Iain's left standing alone in an empty, dirk-track street at midnight with a lump in his trousers and a brain full of mince.

Iain looks down at the semi-erection pressing against his chinos, then gazes up at the guesthouse.

You really know how to make a woman feel special, McMillan, he says to himself. You really do. You really know how to pick your moment and say the right thing. You knob.

*

Jez fires up another joint and watches Nat moving on the make-shift dancefloor in Pandora's. Good dancer, he thinks. Bloody good dancer. Not as good as that Becky, but then Becky's got the body for it. To dance right, you've got to have the body. It's a posture thing. If you don't have the posture right, then the dancing's just not right. He nudges Crash Mary.

'You know how to tell if a bird's going to be a good dancer or not?'

'What you on about?'

'I'm just saying. It's easy to tell whether a girl's going to be a good dancer or not. You can tell in advance.'

'How?'

'The way she walks.'

Crash Mary stares at Jez for a second.

'You've been taking them 'ballocks' pills again, ain't you.'

'Yeah yeah yeah. Whatever.'

Jez is trying to act calm, trying to be his normal self, but inside he's shitting it. That bastard Hassan. Doesn't know what he's fucking messing with. Pushing him around. Giving orders. Threatening. Who the fuck's he think he is?

Still, the man's got a reason. Jez knows it. How would he feel if someone was dicking him around on a deal, coming up with a bit of cash here, a bit of cash there, dodging meetings and spewing out excuses? But that's not the point. The point is Hassan's been well out of order. Putting his dirty fucking hands on me, fucking slapping me, the bastard. He'll pay for that, one way or another.

Yeah, but there's the little matter of paying Hassan the cash first. Jez has managed to get a loan of twenty quid off Bangs with the promise he'll get it back tomorrow, and he's sold some of the hash he found for a tenner. And that's it. Seventy quid short, and all his wells have run dry. And some of the pre-paid customers are getting right fucking uppity, the ones he's seen. He shouldn't really be in Pandora's. Too visible by half. But fuck it, it helps take his mind off things for a bit.

Seventy quid short, surrounded by paupers, and about twelve hours left to come up trumps.

Jez takes another hit on the joint, drawing a huge lungful in as far as it'll go, letting it out in a long, smooth rush.

Fuck's sake. What's seventy quid? You've done it before, much more than that, and you can do it again.

But no matter how many times he tells himself everything's going to be all right, he still feels worms of doubt squirming in his stomach. Shit, man. Deeper than deep.

Fuck it. Smoke your J. Watch the dancers, watch Nat and Becky. Life will go on. Maybe.

*

Steve can't bear the night-time vision of the ceiling much longer. He's not that tired any more, but he wants to sleep, wants to bring the shutters down on a busy day before he thinks about it too much. He hates lying there, at the inactive mercy of remorse, guilt, longing, emptiness.

Karen's in bed next to him. She was there when he got in

from asking questions in the bars.

He can't tell if she's asleep or not. She's not moving, but it doesn't mean anything. Her breathing is steady, but that doesn't mean she's asleep. He can almost feel a vibration of wound-up tension coming from her.

But that doesn't necessarily mean she's awake. He's been getting that feeling from her more and more. He's not sure for how long.

He wants to get up, go out and drink until he can't drink any more.

He wants to sprint along a deserted beach as fast as he can.

He wants to shout, kick doors, punch walls.

He wants to sink exhausted into sleep, shut his mind down, sedate his heart.

Instead, he lies in the semi-dark, tracing a crack in the ceiling. It looks like the coast of France.

CHAPTER EIGHTEEN

Standing and staring

And then Sophie smiles. Steve feels a warm rush of helpless pleasure surge through his body, through every strand of hair, through each vein and artery, through his fingernails, through his bones, filling the void of his soul. She smiles, green eyes alive and unbearable, and Steve can feel her, touch the sleek beauty of her arms, her neck, her face. She smiles and fades and Steve wakes to a room stained soft yellow by sunlight soaking through the drawn curtains.

The dread arrives. The heavy, aching dread of another day without her. Another day with the brutal, sick knowledge of her stark death.

Steve looks over at Karen. She's still sleeping, as far as he can tell. He gets out of bed carefully and starts to do his exercises, his daily rhythm of stretches, sit-ups, press-ups, a disciplined routine he forces himself into. It gives a shape to the day. Without the routine to cling onto, maybe he'd want to stay in bed all day, stay in the room refusing to talk to anybody, refuse to accept an outside world that doesn't contain Sophie.

Focus. Discipline. Motivation.

Karen wakes as he finishes the last of his straining press-ups. She yawns.

'I'm going to take a shower,' Steve says.

Karen nods sleepily. She yawns again and rests her head back down on the pillow.

She gets out of bed when she hears the water stop running, and starts to pick out her clothes for the day. All the time she's thinking. She's thinking as she chooses a t-shirt, as she compares two bathing suits, as she takes Steve's place in the bathroom. Thinking how to get control of the situation again. It's sliding away from her, and she doesn't know why.

But she knows she needs to regain control. And never lose it again. She's learned her lesson.

*

'Caaaaaark! Caaaaaark! Caaaaaark! Caaaaaark! Caaaaaark! Caaaaaaark!'

Fuck, that *noise*! Iain's snaps out of sleep, his eyes wide open with fear. He doesn't know where he is. Then he realises. His room. So that's okay then. But that noise!

At the slatted glass window set high on the wall, a skinny crow peeks down at Iain from the sill, cocking its head.

'Caaaaark!' it croaks again, then flaps off in a blur of black feathers.

Iain's head's thundering, pain jagging through his temples like he's been wired up to an electric-shock machine for full-on mentalists.

And then he notices. His arm's dead. Because someone's lying on it. He turns his head slowly, trying to find out who it is without waking them up.

The low brow. The spikey crew cut. The hard mouth.

Oh Christ.

It comes back to him in bits. The horny disappointment of the night before. The lonely trek to Pandora's to catch up with Barney and the couple. Not finding them. Finding beer instead, getting drunk, trying to talk to strangers, being ignored. And then a friendly face. If you can call it that.

Good morning, Martha.

Oh, for fuck's sake, McMillan, you didn't, did you? He looks down his body. He's naked.

You did.

He examines his free hand, sniffs it. It's very clean.

You definitely did. So how are you going to get out of this one?

On the bedside table lies Iain's shiny new Swiss Army knife. He wonders whether it would be possible to saw his arm off without Martha noticing, grab his stuff - one-handed - and escape, leave Goa, head for somewhere far away. Kerala, maybe.

Not a chance. Martha stirs, making a sound halfway between a snore and a snort, and opens her eyes. It takes her a second to focus those eyes on Iain. Then she smiles.

Oh God, Iain screams to himself. If she tries to kiss me, I'm gonna blow chunks. Fuck it, I'm gonna spew anyway.

He wrenches his arm from under Martha's neck, scrambles out of bed, and hits the sink with a projectile hurl of stale lager. Classy.

*

'So what I'm saying is, I don't know what's caused all this, and I don't want to know,' Karen says, teacup poised in front of her face. 'I don't care about handing out blame, and who did what and who said what. That's not what this is about. But we've got less than a week of our holiday left, so let's just put the first week behind us, and get on and enjoy our holiday. We deserve a nice break. We've both been working very hard this year, so we deserve it.'

She stops and takes a sip of tea, then smiles at Steve. They're having a light, early lunch in the garden under the shade of the palms.

It's her tone. The lack of accusation, the calmness, the quiet reason that makes Steve stop and think. She's been fine all morning, acting almost as if nothing's happened. And then this.

What have the last few days been like for her? The way he's been treating her. Maybe she's right after all. Maybe he does think of himself too much. All the time, she hasn't had a clue what's going on, just that her husband's been acting weird, that he'd almost deserted her. What on earth has he been doing? Was he trying to wreck his marriage? Why had he been so stupid? Why had he let himself go so far? They're meant to be on holiday. They've been saving up all year for it.

Steve feels shame redden his face. She's being so reasonable. If she knew the truth, she'd have every right to act as unreasonably as she wanted. He hasn't been behaving the way he should. After all, he's got a duty to her. He's her husband. What's going on isn't her fault, yet she's being made to suffer for it.

'Yeah, of course,' he says, smiling back at her. 'Yeah, I'm sorry love. I know I've been acting up a bit. It's just, well, you know what I'm like. The way the police here are acting. You know I hate to see cops not doing their job properly. It just gets me going, that's all.'

'Well, then. Let's say no more about it,' Karen says, still smiling. 'We haven't had the chance of a proper holiday yet, what with one thing and another. Look at you, you're worn out. You've been working so hard for this promotion, you deserve to have a bit of a rest.'

'Hang on,' Steve says, grinning. 'It's not in the bag yet.'

'Exactly, but it'll come. I've got faith in you. The way you've been going, you deserve to be promoted. They'd have to be blind not to notice. But it's best to get you in good, relaxed shape for the year ahead.'

'Yeah, you're right,' he says. 'We both deserve a break. Can't have been all that easy for you, this past year, with me working so hard.'

'It'll all be worth it in the end,' Karen says, patting his hand on the table. 'It's all for the best, that's the way I look at it. Working for the future.'

'Yeah. Let's concentrate on having a good holiday.'

He squeezes Karen's hand, feels the hard edge of her diamond ring.

Good, Karen thinks. Back to normal. Just a matter of knowing how to treat them the right way, that's the secret. When to pull, when to push, when to leave well alone. That's what it's all about. She could charm the birds off the trees when she felt like it. Everybody said so.

'And I think the first thing we should do is work on the tan a bit,' she says, laughing, looking down at her light brown arms. 'I'm not going back and showing this off. People will think we went to Grimsby, not Goa. We'll go down to this beach of yours this afternoon, work on getting a proper tan going.'

Steve smiles, but the thought of going back, of being on their beach, makes him feel sick to the bone.

*

'All I'm saying is, it's out of order. That's all I'm saying,' Jez says, looking away from Crash Mary and out to sea from the shadows of the Vibe.

'What's out of order about it? Girl can do what she wants.'

'Nah, nah, I'm not saying that. Not saying she can't do what she wants. I mean, this is the nineties, innit. We're not cavemen.'

Crash Mary looks at the ragged, hairy figure of Jez, then considers his own bulk. He shrugs.

'What's your point, then?' he says.

'The point is, what I'm saying is, right? Is she should have asked my opinion first. Before she went and done what she done.'

'And your opinion would have been what?'

'My opinion, and this is just my opinion, right? My opinion is that there was no way she was getting it done, 'cos it would look bloody stupid, all them beads in her hair. What did she think she was doing? That's bleedin' fundamental, that is, changing your hairstyle like that. That is a fundamental shift in what somebody looks like. And Nat looks bloody stupid with all them bleedin' beads and plaits an' that.'

'Did you tell her this by any chance?'

'Course I did. Soon as I saw her.'

'And it was just after this that she stormed off, was it?'

'Yeah, right after. I mean, there I was, giving her a bit of constructive advice, trying to have a discussion about something, like you're supposed to, and right in the middle of it she pisses off.'

'Can't think what it can be, then,' Crash Mary says, looking at Jez in disbelief. 'Anyway, it's good to hear you've started getting into this discussion thing. New man and everything.'

'Well, you've got to, ain't you. Talking things through, an' that. When I tell her 'no', I want her to know why I'm telling her 'no'.'

'Very considerate of you.'

'Exactly, that's my point. And hopefully then she'll consider it and learn from it, and she won't do it again. It's psychology, innit.'

'You could be a professor with that brain of yours,' Crash Mary says. 'Professor of Thick at the Stupid University.'

'That's your jealousy showing through again, Crash. Very ugly emotion, is jealousy. Mind you, it suits you, 'cos you're an ugly bastard.'

'Weasel.'

'Sumo.'

'Ratty.'

'Buddha.'

'Knick knack.'

'Paddy wack.'

'Give the dog a bone, son.'

*

By the time Iain meets Barney on the beach, he's feeling re-freshed. Throwing up has helped his hangover, getting rid of a stagnant pond of lager that's probably been sloshing around in his stomach for days.

Being sick also helped get rid of Martha, who nipped off sharpish once she realised Iain wouldn't be up for any morning-after sexual aerobics. The fear that he might have some bug was another possible motivation for her quick departure. All those germs lurking around. You couldn't be too careful.

He doesn't tell Barney that's how he spent his night, though. He tells him about the Jules knock-back, which is humiliating enough, but he's in no mood for the slagging that would inevi-tably follow if he confessed about Martha.

Instead, he lets Barney tell him about his night. He says they popped in to Pandora's but it seemed lame, so they'd headed up to the Primrose instead. He shares a few of the couple's anec-dotes, which Iain finds amusing enough. Then they concentrate on crashing out and getting some rays.

After twenty minutes, Iain gets bored and sits up. He looks around the beach, checking out the action, seeing the straggling groups of fully-dressed Indian men strolling around with bot-tles of Kingfisher and whisky.

'Awful lot of Indians about today,' he says.

'Hmm?' Barney opens an eye and squints at Iain. 'It's Sunday. This is Indian tourist day. They come on day trips from Karnataka or wherever. Bus-loads of them. It's when the tables are turned. We become the tourist exhibit. The Indian tourists come to look at us.'

'What'd they want to look at us for?'

'Well, not specifically you and I. They mainly come to look at the breasts. Naked, female, Western breasts.'

'Bloody perverts.'

'We do exactly the same thing.'

'Yeah, but not so blatantly.'

'What does it matter,' Barney says, reaching into his bag for a cigarette. 'They're fed on stories about loose Western women who'll have sex within seconds of meeting you. I don't know where they get their ideas from, but I suppose we do seem relatively promiscuous to them. They get this image in their heads, so they hire buses and jeeps, get a bit drunk, and come on down to get an eyeful of tit. Look at the strange Westerners. Stare at them.'

'Piss them off.'

'Yes, it does tend to annoy a few people, especially if the perving gets too blatant. For instance, if the Indians are standing right at a girl's feet and trying to take photographs of her. That can cause a little smidgeon of irritation. But when you think about it, what do the Westerners expect? They're lying about, virtually nude, in a sexually repressed country. I have no sympathy for people who get upset by it. If you're going to completely ignore the customs and attitudes of a country, you've got to be prepared to put up with the consequences.'

'Yeah, but you can't just go around blatantly perving, staring at people. It's not on.'

'It is for the Indians. It's not rude to stare in India. If it wasn't for cricket, the national sport in India would be standing and staring. That, and forming crowds. Usually crowds of people standing and staring. You see it everywhere. In streets, markets, fields. People just standing and staring at someone else doing something. It's a normal part of Indian behaviour. Why should they moderate their behaviour in their own country, when the Westerners aren't doing anything to moderate theirs in a foreign country? For Westerners who don't like it, I've only got one piece of advice. If you don't want to be stared at, don't lie on the beach semi-naked.'

'Fair enough,' Iain says as a group of four Indian men walks by staring down silently at them. 'Can't argue with that. Maybe I should cover up my tits.'

'Probably best for everyone's sake.'

*

'Are you sure it's clean?' Karen says, looking down at the sand, some beige, some reddish, some blackened from night-time fires on the beach.

'It's fine,' Steve says, not feeling too fine himself. 'Perfectly fine.'

'We'll just stop here, shall we?' Karen says. They've only just got onto the beach. 'Don't want to go hiking all the way along.'

It's too near where Steve pulled Sophie's body from the water. He can't face being so close to the rocks.

'It's much better along a bit,' he says. 'Nicer sand. Not so many rocks in the water.'

They walk hand in hand along the shoreline, past the Crab Key restaurant, past the Reggae bar, past the small concrete temple, all the time getting nearer and nearer the spot where Steve and Sophie lay and talked forever a million years ago. Emotion wells up, but he beats it down. Control. He must keep control.

'This'll do,' Karen says. 'It's quite nice here.'

It's too near the regular place. Steve doesn't want to lie there, but there's nothing he can say. No excuses come to mind. Karen starts laying out her towel, smoothing it down as best she can on the ridged, dry sand.

'See he's got another one, then,' Barney says to Iain from their vantage point thirty yards away.

'So he has. Maybe the Goddess has gone after all.'

'Definitely. Blown your chances.'

'That's life.'

Steve puts his sarong down on Karen's right, but she stops him.

'No, put it on the other side,' she says.

'Why?'

'Because it means when I'm talking to you I can be facing the sun. I don't want to be lying on my side with my back to the sun half the time. You know how sensitive my back is.'

'Is it? Don't remember you mentioning it before.'

He thinks about mentioning *his* back, that it'll get burned instead, but since he doesn't feel like talking much, he doesn't bother. He picks up his sarong and lays it on Karen's other side. He lies down on his back. The world doesn't seem steady enough for him to sit up. It's too close. The memories are barging into him from all sides.

Karen starts putting on her sun-cream, a healthy smear of it all around her two-piece green swimming costume. She gets Steve to do her shoulders and back. A thin, tawny dog with a drooped face comes slouching over towards them, dragging lazy paws through the sand, tongue lolling out in the heat.

'Quick, Steve, look, a dog,' Karen says, a high note of panic in her voice. 'Get it away! Get it away!'

Steve looks at it. It seems harmless, but for Karen's sake he gets up and makes a shoo-ing motion at it. The dog shies away sharply with a guilty, nervous look, then trots off down the beach.

'Filthy mutt. Did you see it?' Karen says, rubbing her arms. 'Mange all over the place. Should be put down, if you ask me. Letting dogs run all over the place. Probably got rabies and everything.'

'It hasn't got rabies.'

'How d'you know? Might have.'

'It's just a normal dog. No different to the rest of them around here.'

'I don't care. It's dangerous, letting dogs run wild on the beach. They shouldn't let them.'

She settles back down, once she's satisfied that the dog isn't coming back. She closes her eyes to the sun, arms rigid by her sides.

Steve looks over to the patch of sand where only a few days ago...but no, he tries not to think about it.

Block it out. Get your focus elsewhere.

He lies down on his back again and tries to concentrate on the calming sound of the waves rushing onto the sand, the warmth of the sun pricking his skin.

It's impossible. It's impossible not to think of her lying there, stretching out, laughing, or looking out to the edge of the sea, searching for dolphins. The more he tries not to think of her, the more she invades his thoughts. The beach, the smells, the sounds, the heat. It's all infested with her presence. Steve's mind twists and turns. All he needs to do is open his eyes, and she'll be there beside him, warm and languid, her green eyes shining at him.

Steve sits up and opens his eyes.

'I'm going for a swim,' he says, without looking down at Karen.

The water's tepid. He wades out until it's up to his waist, then falls forward into a crawl, pushing through the oncoming waves, hearing the roar in his ears as he forces himself against the tide. He keeps going, feeling the strain in his arms, getting out to the calmer waters where the breakers are born. The water's cooler out there. It pulls against his arms and legs, pours into his ears and nostrils, stings sour salt into his lips and gums and eyes.

He treads water, taking in full, chest-burning breaths. He faces the horizon.

An endless continent of water. He can see a couple of small boats far out to sea, but nothing else. What would happen if he kept going, if he swam until his arms were too weak to move anymore, his legs paralysed, numb with cold and cramp, his lungs stripped of breath?

It's too horrific to contemplate.

He turns to his left and starts swimming down the beach, parallel to it, heading south towards the Flea Market ground. He swims about a hundred metres then turns into the shore.

He stands in the shallow surf for a while, letting the water drip off him, before walking back up the beach. He hasn't gone far when he hears the screech.

It's Karen.

His eyes dart immediately towards her. Karen's scrabbling to her feet, grabbing her towel up and holding it in front of her like a protective shield, a magic garment to ward off cows. The cow's staring at her, slowly chewing the cud like a bored teenager, a couple of feet from where Karen's towel used to be.

The cow dips its head towards her straw beach bag and Karen yells again, more of a squeal this time.

'Honestly,' Barney says to Iain as Steve walks past them. 'You'd think some people had never seen a cow on a beach before.'

'Steve, Steve, quick,' Karen shrieks to him. 'It's going to eat my bag.'

Steve jogs over reluctantly. As he gets near, the cow tosses its head and wanders off at a slow, steady, nodding pace, searching the sand for anything else which resembles food.

'That's it,' Karen says, gathering in her stuff as Steve sits back down on his sarong. 'I'm not staying on this beach one minute longer. Animals roaming all over the place. Full of diseases. And while you were off swimming I was getting stared at by all these men. Indian men. Just walking right past, staring at me. And you nowhere to be seen. They could have raped me or anything. This is a madhouse, this beach. And do you see the way some of them are dressed over there? Matted hair, probably haven't washed for a month. Bloody hippies. Weirdoes, the lot of them. Come on, we're going back to the hotel.'

Steve looks up at her. He feels calm.

'You go on ahead. I'll see you later.'

He lies back on his sarong and closes his eyes.

Karen stares down at him for a few seconds. She thinks about saying something, but stops herself. She puts her bag over her shoulder.

'Well,' she says, keeping her voice steady. 'I'll see you back at the hotel, then.'

'Yeah. See you later.' Steve doesn't open his eyes.

Karen turns and walks back the way they came, determined not to get angry, determined to keep her calm, controlled, regained superiority in place.

*

'Well you shouldn't listen to him,' Sasha says, letting Nat's beaded hair slip through her fingers. 'I think it looks lovely. Really suits you, it does.'

Nat picks up her cappuccino. The two of them are lounging in cane chairs in the German Bakery's big shaded garden. The cappuccino is Nat's expensive treat for herself, to make up for what Jez said.

'I dunno if he says these things deliberate or not,' she says. 'You just never know with him sometimes.'

'Well, he's a Pisces, ain't he,' Sasha says, flicking the ash from her Marlboro Light onto the ground. 'You're bound to get that with a Pisces. 'Specially with you being an Aries an' everything. Bound to get that happening sometimes. Communication, innit.'

'S'pose,' Nat says, staring into her frothy cup. 'But it really pisses me off, y'know? He opens his mouth and doesn't think. Could strangle him sometimes.'

'Why don't you just leave him, then?'

Nat looks at Sasha, shocked.

'Couldn't do that. Not leave him. I mean, every couple's got their problems, ain't they. Comes with the territory. You don't leave someone just for that.'

'Just saying. You're always goin' on about how he said this or done that.'

'Yeah, but I wouldn't leave him. I know he seems like a total pain in the arse, but he's got a heart of gold underneath. Mind you,' she says, her eyes focusing on the foam again, 'he probably nicked it.'

Both girls laugh, then take synchronised sips at their drinks. Sasha's on jasmine tea, no milk or sugar. Nat's feeling a bit better. A cappuccino and a thick slice of carrot cake. Special mood enhancers.

'That top that girl's wearing,' Sasha says, nodding to a dark-skinned, long-haired Italian girl standing talking to a group three tables away. 'Really nice. Really suits her.'

'Yeah,' Nat says. 'Blue's good for you, because it attracts good energy.'

'Does it?'

'Yeah. But not everyone can wear it, though. The energy, it gets mixed up sometimes if you're not the right person. Can put your energy centres right off balance.'

'Yeah?'

'Yeah.'

Half an hour later when they get up to pay, Nat skims her eyes over the posters pinned up on a board near the cash desk. Fliers advertising bars, parties and their DJs, gigs, tapes, massage, aromatherapy classes, yoga. And one headed 'MURDER' with a big black and white photo of Sophie's face underneath. She reads the message beneath the picture.

'Anyone with information about the death of Sophie La-croix, aged 20, on the night of 31st December 1998, or the disappearance of her boyfriend, Henrik Andersen, please contact Steve Harrison. Room 37, Coconut Grove Hotel, Anjuna. POSSIBLE REWARD'.

Nat stares at the poster. Sasha has to nudge her when it's her time to pay. She hands over the money and looks at the poster again.

'What?' Sasha says, seeing the photograph. 'Is that about that Sophie girl? Thought she drowned?'

'Murder, it says here.'

'Everyone was saying she drowned. That's bloody unbeliev-able, that is. You wouldn't believe that if someone told you, would you. That's sick, a girl like her. Imagine doing that to someone like her. Must be that Henrik. Never liked him. I tell you what, that's a real bleedin' shame, that is. Girl like her.'

Sasha shakes her head.

'Yeah,' Nat says, thinking. Anyone with information. 'Shame.'

CHAPTER NINETEEN

Turned off

'What?' Clive says, his face wearing the question mark.

'The cotton wool, love,' Maureen Matlock says, pointing to the tufts sticking out both of Clive's ears. 'Why've you got cotton wool in your ears?'

'What?'

Kim plucks the tuft out of his right ear and yells.

'Why've you got cotton wool in your ears!?'

She stuffs the plug back in. Clive stares at her a second, a mildly confused, surprised look on his face, then turns back to Maureen.

'The cotton wool?' he says, pointing to it. Both women nod. 'Well, it's me ears, you see.'

'What's wrong with them?' Maureen says, loud and slow. Kim reaches for the tuft again but Clive stops her, holding up his hand.

'S'alright, love, I got that one,' he says, then faces Maureen again. 'Me ears. Started getting all this yellow pus coming out of them. Horrible, it was. Cotton wool's the only thing that stops it running down me neck.'

Maureen makes a face. 'Maybe you should see the doctor,' she says, mouth pursed.

Clive looks at her blankly for a couple of seconds.

'Kingfisher,' he says, giving her the thumbs up. 'Cheers.'

*

Steve can't help himself. He tried for ages, once Karen had gone.

He tried to hold back. He tried to remember what she'd said about enjoying their holiday, getting rested, deserving it, tried to remember the way she must have been feeling the last few days. But he failed. As the afternoon wore on, he started to ask questions.

He got nowhere at first. Blank looks, shrugs and apologies from most, some not even acknowledging him. The beach took its time filling up, most people waiting until late before showing their faces. But he perseveres. The more people who arrive, the more people he asks.

He recognises Crash Mary, who's walking with Jez up the steps towards the Sun Temple bar. He jogs over the sand to them.

'Excuse me,' he says, stopping them both. 'Either of you lads seen Henrik Andersen?'

'Henrik?' Crash Mary says. 'Swedish geezer?'

'What you wanna know for?' Jez says, defensively.

'I'm looking for him,' Steve says. 'I'm a policeman. He's suspected of killing his girlfriend Sophie,' he says directly at Crash Mary.

'Haven't seen him for days, mate,' Crash Mary says.

'Any idea where he might be?'

'He's not around,' Jez says.

'Don't really know the geezer,' Crash Mary says. 'Spoke to him, what, couple of times. Just know him to see.'

'Didn't know him, as such,' Jez says.

'So no clue where he might have headed? Nothing you might have heard?'

Both men shake their heads, Crash Mary adding a shrug as well.

'Might need you to make a statement,' Steve says to him. Crash Mary looks worried.

'Me? What about?'

'You saw Sophie leaving the party with Henrik. You're probably one of the last people to see her alive. It's pretty crucial
evidence.'

'Well, I dunno,' Crash Mary says, shifting uncomfortably.
'Didn't see nothing. As I said, just saw them leaving. Didn't see
nothing about what you're going on about, murder and that.'

'But Henrik's the prime suspect and you saw him with Sophie, leaving together, probably just before she was killed.
Whether you saw anything else or not doesn't matter. You
place him with her, that's the important thing.'

'Nah, you don't want to get involved with anything like
that,' Jez says. 'Statements and everything. Like, no-one knows
for certain Henrik done anything, do they. You don't want to
start throwing accusations around. I heard she drowned anyway.'

'Believe me,' Steve says, keeping a steady gaze on Jez. 'She
didn't drown. She was violently, brutally attacked. Her skull
was bashed into her brain. Do you know what sort of a mess
that makes to someone's head? To someone like Sophie? You
know the man who did this to her. A big, powerful man who
beat Sophie to death. Sophie. You're not telling me you think
that's right, are you?'

'Nah, hang on, no-one's saying that,' Jez says. 'But getting
involved, different matter. I mean, if they was having an argument or something, it's none of our business.'

'So what did you see?' Steve says to him, keeping his unblinking stare on Jez's eyes.

He doesn't trust him, not for one second.

'Nothing,' Jez says. A cut-off scream echoes in his mind. He
forces it back into its dark prison. 'Didn't see them that night.'

'Right,' Steve says with a tight smile. He looks back to Crash

Mary. 'Think about the statement. It could be a big help. If nothing else, just think of Sophie, what she used to be like, how beautiful she was. And think of the mess she was in once Henrik had finished with her. I saw her. It wasn't pretty. Just think about it.'

Crash Mary shrugs again, but Steve thinks he can see a weakening in him. Not in Jez, though. He'll get very little out of him.

'I'll see you both around,' Steve says, then walks off, looking for other faces.

'That's all we need,' Jez says when Steve is out of earshot. 'Bleedin' Interpol sniffing around. Should have told him big Henrik went to Timbuktoo or something.'

Crash Mary thinks.

'How would he have got to Timbuktoo from here?'

'Just over the border, innit. Nepal.'

'Nep...that's Kathmandu, you dickhead. Timbuktoo! You don't even know where it is, do you.'

'Not if they've moved it from Nepal, no. Where is it, then?'

'Africa somewhere, innit. Bloody Timbuktoo!'

Crash Mary laughs, but he's trying to stop himself thinking of Sophie and what Steve said.

They walk up to the bar of the Sun Temple. On a poster on the wall he sees the bad reproduction of Sophie's photo.

'Tell you what,' he says, feeling his blood rising. 'That Henrik better not show his face around here again. Fucking telling ya.'

'What the fuck's it got to do with you?' Jez says back, nodding over at the barman for a beer.

'Just saying. If I see his face.'

Crash Mary grabs his beer, holding it tight, but he doesn't say any more. Jez doesn't ask him either.

*

Loud knocks raise Iain from his afternoon slumber. A couple of hours on the beach was all he could manage before his hangover came back, the heat and dehydration forcing him into the shade with paracetamol and a bottle of water. His eyes blink at the shaft of light coming through the window, a thick spear stabbing into the hard earth floor. The knocks come again, three raps on the rattling wooden door.

'Yeah yeah yeah. Hang on,' he mutters sourly, scrambling into his shorts. Bloody Barney, waking him up for the hell of it. Probably bored and can't find anyone else to talk to.

He pulls back the bolt and opens the door.

'Good afternoon,' Martha says, standing in harsh, sunlit glory. 'You are feeling better?'

'Yeah. Yeah, kind of. Not brilliant, but, you know,' Iain says, stumbling to find words to cover his surprise.

'That is good. I can come in?'

'What? Oh aye, of course,' Iain says, stepping back, allowing Martha past. No, he thinks, no, she can't possibly want it again. Not so soon. No way.

He leaves the door open and switches on the light as well, seeking safety in stark illumination. He suddenly feels aware of his near nakedness. He grabs his beach t-shirt and pulls it over his head.

Martha sits down on the edge of the bed, patting the space next to her, looking up at Iain. He goes over and sits a couple of feet away from her, nervous and uncomfortable.

'I was just passing by,' she says. 'I have business here. A man is cutting stone for me. He is a craftsman.'

'Stone. Excellent,' Iain says, nodding, trying to be polite and enthusiastic, but wondering what she's up to.

'Yes, he is making me a statue of Ganesh.'

'Statue, yeah? Great.' He can't think of anything else to say.

'A small statue,' Martha says, giving a polite laugh. 'I do not want you to think I am bringing a big statue to Germany. I have too many statues in my garden. No, I am joking.'

'Right. Statues, yeah?'

There's an empty silence between them which Iain doesn't attempt to fill. He can't. Nothing comes to mind.

'This room looks different in the daylight,' Martha says eventually.

'Not really an improvement, though,' Iain says, thinking the room's not the only thing which looks worse in the bright, hard glare of day. How could he? But still. That chest. Something to be said for it.

'I very much enjoyed to have sex with you,' Martha says, catching Iain by surprise again.

'Thanks. Thanks very much. I mean, yeah, so did I. With you.'

'It is lucky we are finding each other last night,' she says tonelessly. 'I would be happy for this to happen again.'

'Well, you never know,' Iain says, smiling and shrugging, deliberately non-committal. 'It might happen. Who can tell about these things?'

'Yes, I hope so.'

There's another silence. Iain thinks about having a cigarette, hoping she's not going to order him to undress.

'Where are you going this evening?' Martha says, fixing Iain with a steady, unblinking stare. He shrugs.

'Dunno. Me and Barney, probably go out later maybe. Just go with the flow. See where the mood takes us.'

'You will be in Pandora Cafe tonight?'

'Maybe. Yeah, maybe Pandora's. Difficult to say. Sometimes there, sometimes somewhere else. We don't always go to the same place.'

'If you are not in Pandora, where will you be?'

Iain panics, trying to think of any name, any bar.

'Possibly the Vibe,' he says, instantly regretting it. 'Or Starco's,' he adds quickly. 'Yeah, sometimes go there.' Then he remembers Starco's is right at the crossroads, a disastrously good vantage point for Martha to watch out for him if he tries to sneak up to Pandora's or the Primrose later. 'Or that place down near the German Bakery. Can't remember its name.'

'Okay,' Martha says, standing up. Iain stifles a relieved sigh. He can't tell whether she's happy, sad or indifferent. Maybe she's taken the vague hint, maybe she hasn't. 'I will see you later, I hope.'

She hasn't.

Iain gets up and follows her to the door.

'Yeah, maybe later,' he says, smiling.

He closes the door and stands with his back to it, releasing a rush of air. I've got to move, he thinks. She knows where I live. She's memorised it. She's stalking me. There's no other option. I've got to move. Today.

He sits back down on the bed, lights a cigarette, and realises with disgust that he's a little bit horny.

*

This is it. There's no way out of it. A couple of beers and a couple of J's have calmed him down a bit, but the adrenalin's still pumping. Jez knows it's all or nothing now.

He's got fifty five quid in cash and a Canon SLR camera he swiped from a tourist's bag in a cafe near the crossroads a couple of hours ago. He hasn't got time to sell it. It shouldn't matter, though. If Hassan's got any sense about him he'll take the deal. No more threats, no more humiliation. He'll just take the deal and that'll be the end of the story.

Still, Hassan's a cash-only man, doesn't like dealing in knock-off gear. But a Canon, though. Even Hassan can see the worth of something like that. Worth a hell of a lot more than the measly forty five quid balance.

He stashes the camera in a cloth bag which he swings onto his shoulder. It's time. Nat's still at the Sun Temple with the rest. He'll join them later once the deal's sorted, then start the long process of trailing around the bars, dishing out the Es to the customers who've already paid for them, selling others to those who haven't. Might be a couple of weeks before he sees serious profit, but there's still enough people around to sell to. The season's getting longer now. The New Year crowd will piss off in the next few days, but it'll still be relatively busy till mid-February.

The Kashmiri stall-holders are hassling tourists on their way back from the beach. Hassan's talking to a pink couple with matching wide-brimmed sun hats, trying to convince them to buy sarongs, but as soon as he sees Jez on the path he shouts to one of his mates to take over negotiations.

He smiles broadly at Jez, beckoning with strong arms, ushering him down the side path. He rests a hand on Jez's shoulder as they walk.

'Why you look worried, friend?' Hassan says. 'Be happy. Is holiday.'

What are you looking so fucking pleased with yourself for, Jez thinks. He's feeling edgy, in no mood for Hassan's false old-pals act. You better not try and rip me off.

They duck through the door of Hassan's hut, where the Kashmiri immediately sits down on the palm-frond mat on the floor, easing his thick-set frame to and fro until he gets comfortable. His grin's still wide, his arms open and unthreatening.

'Sit, sit, friend,' he says, and Jez squats down cross-legged, taking the bag from his shoulder. Without saying anything, Jez pulls out the camera and puts it in front of Hassan, following up with the notes he's hidden in his cut-offs.

Hassan's smile flickers, then regains its intensity as he picks up the Canon. He turns it over in his hands, examining it in minute detail, lifting it up, peering through the viewfinder at Jez.

'Very nice,' he says. 'Very good, this camera. Expensive, yes?'

'Best on the market,' Jez says. 'Worth a hell of a lot more than I owe you, but just call it a bonus. For all the problems. So we've got a deal, yeah?'

Hassan continues to examine the camera. His mouth turns down at the corners.

'Okay,' he says, grabbing the cash and putting it into his shirt pocket. 'I get ektazy.'

He gets up as Jez struggles to hold back the biggest sigh of relief in his life. For a second he thought it wasn't going to happen, but it turns out there was nothing to worry about. That was the point with the Kashmiris. Once they had the cash, they were all sweetness and light, and even a fat-head turd like Hassan wouldn't turn down a piece of equipment as good as the Canon.

Hassan hides the camera under his shirt and waddles out. Jez waits a couple of minutes, then the door opens a crack and three small plastic bags of white pills are thrown into the centre of the room. Jez picks them up and starts counting, checking he hasn't been ripped off. He doesn't want to stand there forever, so it's just a rough estimate, but everything seems fine. He'll do a proper count later, but it seems like Hassan's given him all of them, not the half he was threatening. He drops the packets into his shoulder bag, has a quick peek through the crack of the door, then steps outside.

He decides to go along the path towards the village, away

from the beach. Before he can take more than five paces two men move out from behind a house, blocking his way. Two men in khaki uniforms.

Jez stops dead, spins around, but there's another two behind him. And behind them, the grinning figure of Hassan. Jez realises at once what's happened. He's been set up, Hassan feeding him to the lions for brownie points. And all because of a little business difficulty.

'You cunt, Hassan,' Jez shouts as one of the policemen grabs his arm. Jez swings a fist, breaking the policeman's hold, but another's bearing down with his stick at the ready. A third cop grabs Jez's hair, but Jez jerks back his elbow, catching the man on the bridge of the nose. Jez follows through with a kick at a groin, then reels as a lathi crashes across his back, pain searing up his spine. But it doesn't put him down. Instead, his anger flares and he starts lashing out with madman ferocity. Another policeman gets a head-butt in the face as he tries to grab Jez's bag, but he keeps a firm grip of the strap. Jez pulls the other way, then reaches into the bag, grabbing the packets of Es, and lets go. The policeman falls back, tripping one of his colleagues. Another man comes at Jez, the cop with the sore nose. Jez punches him full-force in the face, but his punching hand has two packets of Es in it. A cloud of white dust explodes around the man's head, the cheap pills disintegrating with the force of impact. The man drops his lathi. Jez stoops to pick it up, getting a kick in his side as he does so. But then he's up and wielding the stick, swirling it around, cracking it against arms and heads. The path to the beach has cleared, and Jez jumps over the sprawled figure of one of the cops and sprints off, swiping at Hassan's face as he passes him, but the Kashmiri deflects the blow with his forearm.

Jez skids around the corner, onto the track where the stall-holders are. Some are shouting and waving, but they don't try to stop him as he races through. He risks a glance behind him. Two of the cops are chasing, maybe gaining on him.

A tourist with short hair's sitting on his Enfield 500 motorbike, chatting to someone at an outside table by one of the cafes. Jez grabs him by the collar of his shirt and hauls him off the bike, jumping on and kicking off with instinctive urgency, self-preservation blinding him to his actions.

He roars through the stalls, scattering tourists and Kashmiris, then cutting off the path, skidding across sandy grass, through washing lines draped with sarongs, battering the cloth away as he ducks through them.

He's travelling too fast as he reaches the dunes before the beach, and the bike takes off. Jez loses the Enfield mid-flight and they land separately, hitting hard sand and rolling over. Jez ignores the pain from his ribs and gets up quickly, looking over his shoulder. The cops are now about fifty yards behind him. Not far enough.

He pulls at the heavy bike, getting it upright, climbs on and tries starting it. It coughs, but nothing more. He tries again. And again. He glances back. The police will be on him in seconds. One more time, or he'll have to run.

The bike's engine catches, and Jez veers off at high revs, spraying up sand until he gets the machine under control. He sticks close to the water, on the compact sand, making riding easier. Swimmers and bathers dodge out the way, others on the beach standing up and shouting at him, furious at the unwritten 'no bikes' rule being broken.

But Jez doesn't hear them. He tears off down the sand, as far as the beach will take him, with fire in his eyes and fear in his heart.

*

Steve keeps asking, but all he collects at the end of the afternoon is a handful of guesses. Arambol. Karnataka. Kerala. South America. Thailand. Sweden.

Maybe that's it, Steve thinks. Maybe he's gone back home. In which case, the Swedish police can pick him up. But only if he's wanted for murder, not if he's just the ex-boyfriend of someone who drowned. It has to go through official channels, through the Indian police, the Swedish embassy, the Foreign Ministry or whatever. But for that to happen, the police have got to accept that it's murder. It's the only way to track Henrik down, get the authorities working on it so that even if he tries to get a visa for somewhere else and they check up on him, he's caught.

If he hasn't managed to get away already.

When Steve gets back to the hotel he sees Karen lying at the pool with the Matlocks, chatting to Maureen. He keeps to an angle where she can't see him, gets the keys from reception, and bounds up to their room. After a quick shower to get the salt and sand off, he opens his suitcase and takes out the rest of the posters. He goes back downstairs, anxious to grab a taxi and get going while there's still light.

Two hours later he's finished, the last poster up on the last roadside palm trunk, all the restaurants and bars he knows of saturated.

It's nearly sunset. He pays off the driver at the north end of the beach by the bus stop and walks over to a fence on top of a high, sheer, red-rock cliff. He feels exhausted. His shoulders sag. He's drained of energy, sense, emotion, life. He'd like to sit down, but has an irrational fear that he won't have the strength to get back up again. So he stands staring at the sun, into its deep orange heart as it slides down towards the horizon.

The sun's almost gone when he realises there's someone

standing beside him, a grey-haired Indian man with glasses and a neat, trimmed moustache. He's well-dressed in a clean white shirt and pressed trousers.

'Hello,' the man says and smiles, his eyes warm and friendly behind the lenses.

Steve nods back but doesn't feel like speaking. He looks out to sea again. The sun is melting into the horizon, becoming a bright sliver, then disappearing. The afterburn spreads peach and pink all over the sky.

The old man coughs politely.

'Allow me to introduce myself,' he says, holding his hand out to Steve. 'My name is Ghosh. Indian Civil Service, retired. And your good name, sir?'

'Steve Harrison,' Steve says. 'English.'

'Of course,' Mr Ghosh says as they shake hands. 'I always like to watch the sunset. I feel it gives one a perspective. In the face of nature's beauty, we are all very small and insignificant.'

'Yeah. I s'pose,' Steve says, not very enthusiastically.

'I hope you will not mind me saying this,' Mr Ghosh says after a pause. 'But you look like someone who has all the troubles of the world on his shoulders, and you are struggling under the weight.'

'I think you're probably right,' Steve says, and all of a sudden he feels like telling the man, telling him everything.

Maybe this is what he needs to do, tell somebody. Nobody except him knows about the pressure and the pain inside him. It aches beyond limit. He can't tell Karen about it, and there's no-one else he can unburden himself to in order to ease the agony. A stranger, an anonymous ear for his secret confession, a neutral judge for his thoughts and deeds. Although maybe he doesn't want judgement. The confession itself is possibly enough.

'I've just lost someone I love,' Steve says, staring out at the pastel sky. He's said the words, admitted it out loud. It's real now.

'Oh,' Mr Ghosh says, hanging his head. 'I am very sorry to hear that. Was it, was it your wife?' His voice is quiet, buttery, kind.

'No,' Steve says. 'Just someone I met. I've still got my wife. This was somebody else. A girl. Sophie.'

'Ah, you are separated from your wife?'

'No, no, you don't understand. This is the mad thing. I only just met her. Sophie. Just a few days ago. And it might sound stupid but it's true. I loved her more than anyone or anything I've ever known. All of it, in just a few days. Sounds mad, I know. And now she's gone, and sometimes it feels like I can't breathe anymore. It's got my chest that tight. It's like, I can't breathe without her.'

Steve grinds his jaw. The sky darkens to mauve.

'A few days,' he says. 'Can you understand that? How does that happen? Only a few days I had her, that's all. I love her more than I know how to explain, but she's gone and she isn't coming back.'

Steve looks out into the gloom, focusing on nothing, seeing Sophie's face.

'Gone in what way?' Mr Ghosh says softly, carefully. He thought he understood what Steve meant, but now he's not so sure.

'Dead. She's dead now. And yeah, maybe you're right, maybe I'm struggling under the weight of it all. I don't know what I'm supposed to do.'

'It is a terrible time,' Mr Ghosh says. 'The loss of a loved one. There is no right or wrong thing to do. You must do what you feel.'

'Like what? Am I supposed to mourn? How can I do that and

be honest with myself? When I barely knew her, when I only met her around a week ago. I didn't know her well enough to mourn her. It's like I don't have that right. And I don't want to mourn her. I don't want to believe that it's true. Meeting someone, someone who's so incredible it makes you feel truly alive for the first time in your life. Everything else in the world disappears. Nothing else is important, just you and her, and you love her more than you've ever loved anyone. All of it happening in just a few days, and then that's it, she's gone. No warning, no nothing. Just gone.'

'If you'll permit me to say,' Mr Ghosh says softly, 'it may be a blessing in disguise that you did not know this person so well, otherwise your pain might be much greater. And however difficult it may be for you to understand at the moment, it is possible that the short period of time that you knew her means that it was not meant to be, that fate did not hold a future for you.'

'Do you know what the last thing she said to me was?' Steve says, not really hearing Mr Ghosh's words. 'I remembered it afterwards. I'll be with you very soon, she said. Can you believe it? And I've got to go around with that burning away inside me. She said she was going to be with me very soon. My whole life was about to change, and then she was dead. It's burning a hole right through me. So yeah,' he says, with a runny sniff, 'you could say I'm struggling.'

'At least you still have your wife,' Mr Ghosh says. Steve eyes start brimming.

'Great,' he says. 'Fat lot of good I am to her at the moment. Don't even feel like I know her sometimes. I notice things about her now, things I never used to. The way she is with people, offhand, rude. The way she's always very critical of things people do, always putting them down. She blames everybody else for her problems. Everything she does and says is centred on her. I never used to notice these things.'

'But she is your wife,' Mr Ghosh says, his voice rising, firm but still kind. 'That means something, does it not?'

'It used to. It used to mean everything. But now. Now it's different. Everything's changed. It's all different. I can't pretend it's not. I'm not even sure, I don't even know if I love her anymore.'

Steve feels tears rushing him, trying to force their way out of his eyes. It's the tiredness, he tells himself. The tired, exhausted frustration. He turns his face away from Mr Ghosh, trying to concentrate on the dark horizon. Control. Discipline. Strength. He must keep himself together. He mustn't give in.

'Love. I sometimes feel the West misunderstands love,' Mr Ghosh says, following Steve's gaze. Small fishing boats far out to sea have lit their lamps. 'The West puts too much emphasis on a sexual love, on a lust of sorts, the lust of instant physical attraction. Oh yes, mental attraction as well, but it is all lust. It is not the love, the deeper belonging that develops between two people over a period of time. The lust of attraction is always temporary. Real love is something that grows slowly and endures.

'Take my case. I have been married thirty eight years. My parents chose my bride, of course. I saw her only on two occasions before our wedding day, and neither time was I permitted to be alone with her. We didn't even really talk. So we didn't love each other on our wedding day, not as you would understand it. But there was a kind of love, a love that grew because we had been chosen for one another. There was a commitment, a shared task we had before us. And as we got to know one another and discovered our strengths and weaknesses and strove to make a home together, then love did come. Slowly, yes, but it came. As we learned to rely on each other and work together to bring up a family, love grew and grew. So even now, thirty eight years later, I always feel like smiling when I see her. We are part of each other now, and that is where true love lies. It does not just blow in one day on a gust of wind.'

But Steve doesn't hear him. His eyes sting with acid tears, his chest aches from trying to deny the racking sobs, his ears roar with the sound of void. He is alone. Mr Ghosh sees his withdrawn isolation, pats him lightly on the shoulder and walks away.

*

Iain and Barney are huddled on the beach steps of the Sun Temple, sipping warm beer, hating the hardcore music. It was the only place Iain could think of that he hadn't mentioned to Martha. And he hasn't mentioned Martha's visit to Barney, so he can't explain why he doesn't want to go their usual haunts. All he's said is that he wants to try somewhere new. The Sun Temple doesn't quite fit exactly into that category, but it suits his purposes.

The crowd's mixed, long-termers, tourists and travellers all together, all split off in their own little groups. The steps are packed, Iain and Barney hemmed in by people on both sides.

'Well, this is pleasant,' Barney shouts above the music. Iain nods distractedly. He's checking out a girl dancing on the beach. Jeans so short they're almost pants. Not that he's complaining.

They've been there an hour. Conversation hasn't flowed. The music's too loud and they're both tired. Iain didn't really feel like going out, but he didn't feel like staying in either. With so short a time in Goa he feels he should make the most of it. Take whatever opportunities come his way. If any.

'Sure you don't want to try the Vibe?' Barney says in Iain's ear. He's getting fidgety.

'Nah. Not tonight. Don't fancy it,' says Iain. Too risky.

'Well, if you don't mind, I might bail out,' Barney says, clearly bored. 'An early night might not do me any harm.'

'Fair enough. Me too.'

They finish the dregs, then squeeze past the others on the steps, heading home along the beach. Iain leads the way, taking the back route, avoiding the path running in front of the Vibe, just in case. The back way to his room, down a smelly ally between houses, is much safer. They say goodnight and Barney slips off into the darkness, leaving Iain to fumble with his key.

Once he's inside, he locks the door behind him and sinks onto his bed. A dull beat thuds in through the open window.

He stares at the corrugated ceiling, checking for spiders, thinking of palaces and deserts, hill stations and brimming cities. Of Martha and techno.

'McMillan,' he says to himself, feeling washed-out and aimless. 'What the fuck are you doing here?'

*

The music's too loud for the Doc's liking. It isn't turned up high - he just doesn't like the music. Any volume at all is too loud.

'Blam blam blam headfloating pigshit,' he says to no-one in particular. He leans forward on the table, both hands protecting his stubby bottle of Kings beer.

On the other side of the Vibe, a man with long white hair swept back from his forehead jerks up.

He puts down his Hindi newspaper and turns around in his seat, fixing the Doc with large bulging eyes.

'Doc?' he says. 'Doc? Is that you?' His voice is husky, and at one time may have carried an English accent, but only splinters of it remain embedded in his tongue.

The Doc looks up. From the shadows of his hat, his pinpoint, gleaming eyes shoot towards the stranger.

At first he doesn't get it. Then his memory comes into focus. The hair, the sunken face, the eyeballs looking like they're trying to escape their sockets.

'Swiss? That you, boy? Swiss Dave?' The Doc breaks into a smile and both men stand, moving towards each other, greeting one another with backslaps and gripped hands and wild grins.

'Bloody good to see you again, Doc. Bloody good.'

'Swiss Dave. Jesus Christ, man, and tack my balls to a Christmas tree. Swiss Dave in the flesh, like a true gone son of Bee-yell-zee-bub hisself.'

'Shit, Doc. Forgotten you used to call me that. No-one's called me that in years. Swiss Dave. S'good to hear it again, seriously. Why d'you call me Swiss Dave anyway. I'm from England.'

'Your brain, boy! Goddamn brain of yours! Cheese. Ain't nothing in it but holes.'

'Oh yeah,' Dave says, grinning.

He grabs his beer and lopes over with the Doc to his table, his limbs all scrawny and brown, sticking out of his battered and faded vest top and cut-off jeans.

'So where you been, man?' the Doc says. 'Goddamn, it's good to see one of the old crowd back. All you get nowadays is kids with false masks on. Doing it for some Goddamn fashion kick, not for the life. Ain't got no conception.'

'Yeah? Scene tipped a bit on the helter skelter, has it?'

'The whole whirlpool, boy. They been sucked into that psychic jacuzzi and spat out clean and gleamin'. Ain't a soul bean drop of the magic potion left. Scrubbed off. Shee-it, good to see you again, man. Beginning to think I's about the only one left standing.'

'More or less, Doc. More or less,' Dave says, his manic eyes bulging even more. 'Most of the rest of them are either dead or crazy. Only a few of us left still got our wits about us.'

'So where you been hiding, boy? Ain't seen you round these parts in a long time. Fifteen, twenty years maybe.'

Dave shrugs.

'Was the last time I saw you before or after I went to Kashmir?'

'You're asking details, man,' the Doc says, shrugging back. 'Ain't what you might call my strongest suit, these days.'

'Well, I stayed in Kashmir a while. Mad place. Opium city, you see what I'm saying? Yeah? Yeah? So stayed there, like, a while. Then got myself across to Afghanistan. Man, that was a trip, I'm telling you. Lived with a semi-nomadic tribe for a while.'

'Semi-nomadic? How so?'

'Well, they didn't want to keep moving around. It's just that their houses kept getting blown up. Booooom! You see what I'm saying?'

'Must have been a blast.'

'The biggest, man. The biggest. They had this root they brewed up. Different plane, yeah? And I'll give you one bit of advice, Doc, I'm serious. Don't ever, ever be tripping when you're the guest of honour at a village feast in Afghanistan. When they bring out that goat? You see what I'm saying? Yeah? Yeah?'

'Ain't a vision a man wants to juggle with when he's licking lips with Leary.'

'Old Leary,' Dave nods, grinning.

'He gone too.'

'Leary? Gone?'

'Yup. Took one last trip out there and just stayed. Turned off.'

'Leary gone,' Dave says, shaking his head, looking down at his drink.

'Yup. Hadn't been for him, who knows what.'

'Just look around, look at the influence,' Dave says. 'All around you. Acid, the effect it's had on this place. Goa was built on acid.'

'That was my doing, not Leary's, not Kesey, not anyone. *My* doing,' the Doc says, adamant, prodding his bony chest. 'Leary never wanted to leave his room. Down to people like me to spread the gospel. Took it where the vibe was pure. *I* was the first one brung it here. First one. That's when the vibe really started jumping in all your heads like Jimi with his heel stamped down on that box.'

'Petals in the breeze, man. Petals in the breeze.'

'You ain't wrong.'

Both men are silent for a while, lost in a soft trip-hop throb, thinking thoughts of yesteryear.

'So where you go after that?' the Doc says, snapping back into animation. 'After Afghanistan?'

'Well recently, it's been Manali, then a couple of years in the Kathmandu valley. But before that,' Dave says, waving his hand in the air.

'A bit vague. I've lost a bit of the eighties and early nineties. Not a trace.'

'Sounds like you had a good time.'

'You know what, Doc? I wouldn't be at all surprised. You see what I'm saying? Yeah? Yeah?'

*

'Well, we'd better not have too late a night,' Karen says as a waiter takes away their empty dinner plates from the table in

the hotel garden. Steve's confused. She's been in a nice, pleasant, chatty mood all evening ever since he got back and he
doesn't know why. He's been trying to match her mood, just for
the sake of peace, but he hasn't been trying very hard, just nodding and making the right noises at what he hopes are the right
times. But what she's just said rings oddly in his head.

'Why not?' he says.

'Early start tomorrow.'

'Early start? What for?'

'Oh Steve, you are a one,' Karen says, smiling. 'I found out
this afternoon when I got back. I just thought I'd check and see
if there were any left, because Maureen had been talking about
it, and the receptionist said you'd already bought some. Been
waiting all night for you to tell me, but I couldn't hold it in any
longer.'

'Hold what in? What you going on about?'

'The dolphin trip, silly. You can stop pretending now. I think
it's a lovely surprise, really. Really sweet.'

Poison seeps along Steve's veins. He'd forgotten. The trip
for Sophie. The secret liaison that he'd been so worried and excited about. He's not sure how much more he can take.

'Yeah,' he says, trying to smile, his face almost paralysed
with sickness. 'Thought it might make a nice day out.'

'Cutting it a bit fine. We'll have to be up around four.
Thought you were never going to tell me.'

When they get to their room, Karen wants to make love.
She's keen, taking the initiative. Steve's washed out, wanting to
sleep and dream the day away, his mind dead, his body weak.
But he goes through the motions anyway, doing his duty, barren
of desire until he shuts his eyes tight and sees Sophie's face.

CHAPTER TWENTY

The Pearl of Mandovi

'Dolphins can speak, you know,' Kim says to her mother as the small coach pulls up at Mandovi harbour. Half a mile away, Panjim, Goa's capital, slumbers around a low hill in the early morning light.

'Can they, love?' Maureen says.

'Yeah. Read it in a magazine. Dead intelligent, are dolphins. These scientists got them to speak. They didn't say what they said, but I don't think it was English.'

'Fancy that,' Maureen says. She turns to her husband. 'Did you hear that, Arthur? Kim says dolphins can speak.

'I've never heard one,' he says, looking straight ahead, still half asleep.

'Maybe they'll say something today,' Maureen says, giggling at the thought of it.

'Don't work like that,' Kim says, nudging Clive awake. He's still got his earplugs in, the cotton wool beginning to take on a light brown tinge. 'You've got to have all these wires sticking out of them and put them in a tank. That was what were in the photographs anyway. Don't think it works if you don't.'

The eighteen bleary tourists get off the coach, a mix from the hotels in North Goa; the Matlocks and Clive, the Harrisons, a middle-aged couple and their teenage daughter from Vagator, a younger couple from Calangute, a group from Candolim, and a single, older man from Baga.

'Hope you've got your sea legs, Maureen,' Arthur says as they file up a railed gangplank onto a sturdy, wide-bodied boat. The Pearl of Mandovi.

'Where we going?' Clive asks Kim, but she just tugs him along after her.

The boat moves out into the wide, brown river and heads towards the Arabian Sea. Karen holds Steve's hand as they stand on deck watching the edges of Panjim slip by. A concrete tower block, the pillars and colonnades of the municipal office, the red-tiled roofs of houses stretching up the hill, the fading, thirties grandeur of the Mandovi Hotel.

Angela mumbles something to her mother.

'No, we won't see them yet, love,' Maureen says comfortingly. 'In a little while. Once the driver drives out a bit more.'

The boat chugs past Aguada prison on the northern headland, the black-stained concrete blocks of cells exposed to the damp sea air. Everyone's on deck, watching the water, scanning the smooth, swelling surface in the grey dawn. They keep going for another five minutes until the captain kills the engine. The group's guide, a young Goan man with a nearly grown moustache, stands at the front of the boat and addresses them in a quiet voice.

'Now is the dolphin time,' he says. 'Dolphins they are coming, but maybe they are not liking noise. Quiet only.' He raises a finger to his lips.

'What?' Clive says loudly. He turns to Kim. 'What's he saying?'

She slaps him on the arm. He shrugs.

'Only asking,' he says, and gets another, harder slap.

The tourists line the rails on either side of the boat, waiting, cameras poised, eyes darting. They wait. And they wait. Ten actionless minutes pass.

'They better bloody hurry up,' Karen says to Steve, quietly but sharply. 'I'm not standing about all day on a wreck of a boat waiting for them.'

Steve says nothing. His mood is darker than the dawn sea. He'd gone through it all in his mind before, when he'd bought the tickets, seen him and Sophie standing together watching dolphins swim in front of them, Sophie's eyes bright with excitement. Her eyes. Her smile. Her untamed delight. In his mind, he'd always pictured them having the boat to themselves, although he'd known that wasn't the deal. It's what he'd wanted, though.

But the reality is a boat full of fat, peeling tourists and no Sophie. The reality. Anything but the reality.

A couple of squeals from a woman standing near him greets a movement in the water fifty yards away, a split second glimpse of a dark, shining back and tiny hooked fin poking through the surface. Then two more, just further out.

Eager cameras flash, catching waves, ripples, a speck in the far distance. Then the captain guns the engines again, steering the boat out to where the dolphins appeared before cutting the clatter of the diesel once more. The boat bobs gently, rocked by the slight swell of the sea.

They wait again in the dead silence.

Then there's more of them, dolphins rising, slicing lazy arcs through the calm water, four or five of them breaking the surface in a staggered relay.

The captain keeps starting and stopping the engine, nudging the boat as near as he dares to the dolphins' swimming grounds. The cameras snap at every hint of a wave break, every ripple of black water.

'Ooh, they're lovely, aren't they,' Maureen says to her family.

'Strip you to the bone in thirty seconds, they can,' Clive says, almost shouting.

'That's piranhas you're thinking of,' the older, balding man from Baga says.

'What?'

Kim plucks the soiled cotton wool out of Clive's left ear.

'Piranhas!'

'Bloody lethal,' Clive says, nodding. 'One bite, take your leg off up to the knee, they will.'

A warm euphoria begins to spread in Steve. Each time the dolphins appear, maybe ten, maybe twenty, maybe fifty yards from the boat, he feels a sense of light happiness growing.

Each sleek wet back, each fin, each tail, each rare glimpse of nose and eyes builds the feeling more and more.

Dolphins. Wild dolphins. Graceful, assured, somehow vibrating out an indefinable peace. He can feel it.

Wild dolphins. He's seeing them for her, remembering them for her, the dolphins she should have seen, would have seen if only he'd kept her with him a bit longer after they'd kissed. Kept her and not let her go, and then maybe she'd be standing next to him now and his life would be full and perfect again.

'Not very impressive, are they,' Karen says, snapping again with her compact camera. 'Can't see very much. Bloody miles away. Why aren't they doing things? I expect more than that for me money.'

'They're wild dolphins,' Steve says, sighing. 'They don't 'do' things.'

'I know they're wild,' Karen says in her sarcastic voice. 'I've seen wild dolphins on telly. Jumping along beside boats. Right out of the water, some of them. Waste of time getting up so early if this is all we get to see. This lot aren't doing nothing. Not very wild at all, if you ask me.'

'Bloody lethal,' Clive says, nodding.

The tourists click away until there's no film left. The boat stays for another twenty minutes until the dolphins start swimming further out to sea, then the captain fires the engine and the boat putters back towards the harbour.

As they're about to board the bus back to the hotel, Steve turns to Karen.

'Just got a couple of things to do in Panjim,' he says. 'I won't be long. I'll get a taxi back up. See you at the hotel.'

'What d'you mean? What things?'

'Just things,' Steve says. Then he smiles. 'Surprise things. Now go on, hurry up. The bus is waiting for you.'

Karen gets on, still not sure what she should be thinking. The bus moves off, and she turns her head to watch Steve start to walk down the long, straight road on the banks of the Mandovi.

*

Nat's been frantic all night, not a wink of sleep. It was bad enough seeing Jez race past the Sun Temple on a bike that wasn't his. But then - nothing. He didn't show up at the bar later, not at Pandora's, nor the Vibe, nowhere. So she went home around midnight and waited there.

And waited and waited. Up all night, and still no sign of him.

So many bad things have been running through her brain. That he's been in an accident, that he's sick somewhere, that one of his dodgy deals has gone wrong and someone's done for him.

Or the most horrifying thought - that he's left, got fed up with her and disappeared without saying goodbye, not given her a chance to save it.

And that thought breeds others. If he's left, what is it she's done wrong? Why has he got pissed off with her? Does she nag him too much? Spend too much time with her friends? Is it the sex? Has he found someone else?

She feels like shit. Chain-smoking all night, nothing to do but worry. She could do with something to eat, but can't risk leaving the room just in case he comes back.

When a fist bangs on the door she nearly falls off the bed in fright. Her nerves are shot right through.

She jumps up and pulls the door open.

Crash Mary bundles in, looking harassed.

'Quick, grab your stuff,' he says. 'You've got to pack, and you've got to pack now.'

'What's happened? What's wrong? Where is he?' Nat says all at once, her voice on the edge of cracking, her heart on the point of bursting.

'It's okay. He's okay,' Crash Mary says, as if suddenly re-membering. 'But we've got to get you out of here. Where's your bags?'

'Whatdyou mean, where's my bags? What's going on? Where we going?'

'Look, Jez sent me here to get you. He'll explain everything. He's over at Scabs' place. But we've got to get out of here and sharpish, so get your head together and move it.'

Crash Mary's unusually anxious. Jez has told him all about it. He had no choice. A monsoon of shit's threatening to come down, and Crash Mary doesn't want to be caught in it. Still, couldn't just leave Nat stranded, knowing nothing.

He starts stuffing clothes in Jez's battered rucksack which he's dragged from under the bed. Nat looks at him bemused, then starts doing the same herself, her mind jamming up. They don't have many things - packing's over in minutes. Then Crash Mary goes to the corner of the room and searches for Jez's se-cret stash. It's just where he told him it would be. He pockets the slim roll of money, Jez's passport and the hash, lifts the rucksack onto his back, then helps Nat shoulder hers.

After checking the way's clear, he drags Nat outside, and

somehow the both of them fit onto a scooter he's borrowed.

It sinks low into the path as they trundle off, gaining speed eventually as they wind through the trees and head for south Anjuna. Nat almost falls off twice before they get to the small weather-beaten house Scabs shares with Weedy and Bangs in a clearing behind the German Bakery.

Nat jumps off, dragging her backpack behind her as she rushes for the door, rushing straight in without bothering to knock.

'Where is he?' she shouts at a wide-eyed Scabs, who's just about to light a major spliff. He nods in the direction of the back room, and Nat drops her bag and heads through the door.

And stops dead.

Because it's Jez, but it's not Jez.

'What have you done?' she says, angry and confused now, all the worries blown away. 'Where you been? And where the fuck's your hair?'

Jez stares up from the bed, his freshly shaven head gleaming pinkly at her, a white patch around his mouth where his goatee used to be.

'Like the new look?' he says. 'It's called the *How Not To End Up Getting Bummed Every Day In An Indian Jail For The Rest Of My Life* look. I reckon it suits me.'

'What you talking about? You gone mad or something?'

'Sit down,' he says, as gently as he can. 'Think I've got some explaining to do.'

*

Steve has a Plan A and a Plan B. He worked them out over a long breakfast at a small restaurant off the main riverside street in Panjim. He sat on the first floor balcony watching the side street traffic, the street life, early morning hawkers making their way around the colonnaded buildings, rickety wooden balconies hanging precariously over their heads. He worked it out, detail by detail, over tea, a spiced masala omelette, toast, and more tea. He considered options, consequences, bluffs, diplomacy, strategies as he walked along the diesel-ridden streets afterwards, his head clattering with the noises of buses, cars, rickshaws and trucks as they puttered and horned their way past.

And now, sitting in the high-ceilinged, dull green-walled reception of Goa's police headquarters, he's got it all planned out in his mind. He thinks.

He's been waiting in reception for an hour, left alone since he demanded, with an authoritative flash of his warrant card, to see the Chief of Police on a matter of great importance but utter secrecy.

An hour. Nothing to do but read and re-read the tattered posters on the walls. 'Goa Police Say NO to Drugs', 'Goa Police Keeping Goa Safe', 'Stop Crime in Goa'.

You must have an appointment first, they'd said. That's why I'm here, he'd said. Very busy man, they'd said. Very urgent matter, he'd said.

But he'd refused to go away.

An hour with nothing to do except read the posters, refine the plans, stare at the dirty green walls and the high-ceiling fans, and walk up and down purposefully in front of the reception desk.

Now, after the long, long hour, a young policeman in a khaki uniform comes out from the bank of desks behind the reception and marches up to him.

'You are following me,' he says.

Charming, Steve thinks. No introductions, no explanations. He follows the man down a long corridor, up two flights of stairs, then back along another drab corridor reeking of damp and antiseptic. The young officer stops at a door halfway down and knocks. A little nervously, Steve reckons.

Steve looks at the name printed in white letters on the door. Chief Inspector Bernardo Da Silva. His eyebrows arch. A Chief Inspector? Well below Chief of Police. A high-up, but not the top man.

'Come,' a voice barks out from behind the door. A strong voice, one clearly used to giving commands.

The officer opens the door and leads Steve into the room. The men exchange a few words which Steve doesn't understand, and then the younger man leaves.

'Welcome, welcome,' Chief Inspector Da Silva says, extending a hand, beaming a smile of perfect white teeth beneath his moustache. He's a tall, imposing man, middle-aged, but with very little gray in his neat, black hair. Very smooth, Steve thinks.

'Always a joy to meet a fellow officer from another country,' Da Silva says, indicating that Steve should sit in the wooden chair in front of the desk.

Steve introduces himself, showing his warrant card again.

'Of course, of course,' Da Silva says, waving it away politely, as if it's a formality not needed between brother officers. 'Can I offer you something? Tea? Coffee?'

'No. No thank you,' Steve says, settling into the uncomfortable chair. 'I think we'd better get straight down to business.'

'Quite, quite,' Da Silva says, still oozing friendly charm. Probably not for long, Steve thinks. 'What can we do for you? Perhaps you'd like to see the way we operate here, compare it to your own country. A tour of our headquarters, perhaps.'

'Well, I asked to see the Chief of Police, because I have to inform him of a very delicate matter. Something I think will concern him greatly.'

'Be assured,' Da Silva says. 'Any important details will reach the Chief. I'm sure you understand that he is a very busy man and regretfully he cannot see anyone without an appointment. But if you'd care to tell me, I hope that I can deal with it.'

'There's been a murder in Anjuna.'

'A murder?' Da Silva says, his face registering surprise. 'When?'

'New Year's Eve. After a big party. A young French girl was murdered, most likely by her boyfriend, a Swedish man called Henrik Andersen.'

Chief Inspector Da Silva's face relaxes again.

'I am afraid you are mistaken DS Harrison. There has been no murder in Anjuna recently. The last murder in the area was some six weeks ago. Well before Christmas. A worker from Andhra Pradesh died in a fight with a local man. Alcohol involved, of course. But this is all over and done with. The man is in custody.'

'How d'you know there's not been another murder?'

Da Silva laughs, not altogether kindly.

'We are the police. Of course I would know. It so happens that the Bardez taluka, the area which covers Anjuna, is my responsibility. I can assure you, I would know.'

'The police in Anjuna know.'

The Chief Inspector's brows furrow.

'Again, I am saying you must be mistaken. No murder has been reported.'

'Exactly!' Steve says, leaning forward. 'The police in Anjuna, and some officer from Calangute, Gupta, I think his name is...'

'Yes, I know Inspector Gupta.'

'Well, they know it's a murder. It's perfectly obvious it's a murder, but they're refusing to do anything about it. As far as they're concerned, it's a drowning and that's it.'

Da Silva barks at a side door to his office. Within seconds, a thin, harried-faced man in uniform comes into the room and stands in front of the desk. Da Silva barks at him some more, 'drownings' the only word that Steve can make out. The thin man waggles his head at the Chief Inspector as he's being given the orders, then returns silently to his room, closing the door behind him.

Da Silva leans back in his chair. Steve attempts to say something, but he's silenced by Da Silva raising his hand.

'Wait one moment,' Da Silva says.

It only takes a couple of minutes for the thin man to return holding a tattered manila folder, which he places in front of the Chief Inspector before scurrying back to his room again.

Da Silva snaps open the file and flicks through a few pages, his eyes resting on one in particular.

'Yes, I have it here,' he says. 'Unidentified Western female drowning in Anjuna, first of January.'

'First of all,' Steve says firmly, 'she's not 'unidentified'. Her name is Sophie Lacroix. I went and found out where she was staying, where all her things were, took them to the police office myself. It was relatively straightforward, but your lot didn't seem bothered about it. And secondly, it's not a drowning, it's a murder.'

'You keep saying this 'murder, murder',' Da Silva says, getting irritated. 'This report is very clear. It is a drowning.'

'I saw the body. She had injuries, bruising that you don't get from drowning. A large injury to her head. I know what I saw, and I certainly didn't see any evidence of drowning. What I saw was a body that had been violently attacked and then put in the sea. And there's a prime suspect. His name's Henrik Andersen. That's H, E, N...'

'DS Harrison,' Da Silva says loudly, cutting him off. He taps the report. 'This says drowning, and there is nothing here that suggests to me anything else. Maybe you don't understand the situation. The report says she was one of these 'hippy' people. Every year they are coming here, dressed like beggars, living off little money. They are not respectable people like yourself. You do not know what they are like. Every year there are drownings. These people are taking many drugs, or drinking too much, and then when they are not in control of themselves they decide to go swimming and they drown. This is a matter of fact. What can we do? This is not an unusual case. I see these reports every year. This is not the first and it won't be the last. It is to be expected with all the drugs they are taking.'

Steve's face remains hard, but inside he's nervous. He's just about to drop his hand grenade.

'Which is to be expected with all the bribes your officers take from drug dealers.'

'DS Harrison,' Da Silva says angrily. 'This is very serious accusation. Let me remind you that you are a guest here. I am seeing you as a courtesy only. Do not come here and start flying about with your accusations and slander.'

'You know it's true as well as I do. Everyone knows. Anjuna police are as corrupt as they come, getting fat on bribes from drug dealers, bars, restaurants, parties. Fifteen thousand rupees, that's what I heard the going rate is for a police bribe so that someone can hold a party.'

'Enough!' the Chief Inspector barks. 'It is time for you to go.'

He shouts out some orders, and the thin man rushes into the room to escort Steve from the building.

'Just remember,' Steve says at the door, his voice harsh, pointing at Da Silva. 'There's been a murder, I've told you about it, and you're doing nothing about it. Just remember that.'

Da Silva glares at him but says nothing. The junior officer drags an unresisting Steve away.

Once he's outside the building, Steve feels his temper cool. He's a bit disappointed with the way the meeting went, but not altogether surprised. Plan A was never the one most likely to work, not going by what he'd already learned about the Goan police.

He stands on the pavement, trying to get his bearings. Okay, time to find the offices of the Konkan Times. Time for Plan B.

CHAPTER TWENTY ONE

Even for a Romanian

'It's not that I haven't got the confidence to do it,' Barney says, handing the cheap bottle of Number 7 port wine across the verandah table to Iain. 'It's just that I can't see what I could possibly have got in common with any of the girls here. I wouldn't know what to say.'

'That, I think,' Iain says, pouring the thick, sweet liquid into his paper cup, 'is actually the dictionary definition of lack of confidence with women.'

'Hell of a dictionary.'

'*Hell* of a dictionary,' Iain nods. 'And what you've got, very simply, is one hell of a lack of confidence with women.' He takes a slug of his drink, pulls a face, and sets the paper cup back down on the table. 'And you don't have any reason for it.'

'As I said,' Barney says. 'What on earth am I going to talk to some ravey chick about? Hello, I like those incredibly tight pants you're wearing? You really must tell me where you got your belly button pierced? It just doesn't work.'

'You're just making excuses. You know fine well it's not just ravey chicks out there. There's travellers, there's tourists. Loads of people out there.'

'Oh, come on. Me? And a package tourist? Have you gone completely out of your mind? Me and Beverley sitting there drinking Malibu and coke with her telling me what she did in the office last week and who said what to who, and what she's going to be doing in the office next week once she gets back?'

'That's a bit harsh,' Iain says, affecting an injured air. 'I've shagged some perfectly nice package tourists. In fact, I've been a package tourist myself.'

'Fine. But these girls you slept with. How long did they last?'

'In terms of minutes?'

'In terms of how long did you see them for?'

'Oh, usually a night or two. I wasn't looking to start up any meaningful kind of relationship with them or anything.'

'But then again, you're into one night stands and I'm not. I don't see the point of a quick bit of gratuitous sex with a virtual stranger. The attraction just isn't there for me. I want someone I can talk to. Be with.'

'Ah,' Iain says with a knowing nod. 'A relationship man. Sorry, I didn't realise. Not too many of you around these days. Not amongst free, intelligent men.'

'Are you trying to say I'm out of date? Oddly enough, that doesn't worry me in the slightest.'

'It's not a matter of being out of date. It's a matter of not playing their game anymore. This unwritten contract that says you have to have a relationship with them before you can expect reasonably regular sex. That it's somehow this gift they bestow on you, that they own the supply of sex, and for you to get it you've got to give something to them in exchange. In the old days it was a ring, a commitment to marriage, if not marriage itself. No ring, no sex. That was the deal. It's not as bad as that now, obviously. Now it's no relationship, no sex. But it's still weighted in their favour. The sooner men stop falling for the con, the sooner women will realise that they can't hold sex over us like a threat, and maybe then we'll start to see honest relationships that work, not dishonest ones failing because they've been founded on outdated, unbalanced, flawed social concepts.'

'My God, you've got worse,' Barney says. 'I thought you were ranting a bit before you had sex. I thought it'd calm you down a bit. But it hasn't, it's made you worse.'

'The blood's up,' Iain says. 'I think I've tricked my body into producing more testosterone. Probably need it, with the amount I spent the other night. I've probably got to stock up from scratch. The cupboard's bare.'

'Don't remind me, please. Anyway, I think you need a smoke. Un-stress you a bit. You don't want to overdose on that testosterone stuff.'

'Only if you agree to come out sharking with me.'

'I've already said no. You'll have to do your Great White impression by yourself.'

'Oh, come on,' Iain says, pleading. 'It's easier with two people. Come on. We'll just go, chat to a couple of girls, and if you don't like it we can leave.'

'Promise?'

'Cross my heart.'

'Girls? Not pensioners?'

'Cross my legs.'

'I'll skin up, then.'

*

No matter how many times Jez counts, it still comes to the same number. Fifty three. Of the three hundred Es he picked up from Hassan, he only managed to keep hold of fifty three. So in total, including the Es Hassan let him have near the start of the deal, he's paid twelve hundred quid for a hundred and fifty three tabs. Nearly eight quid per E. And he'd had to sell the first hundred to fund the rest, so in a way they're even more expensive.

Jez can't be bothered to work out just how badly he's come out of the deal. It's too depressing. All he knows is it's probably the worst piece of business he's done in his life. Especially when you throw in the bit about assaulting police officers.

And it's not as if he can just pop out and sell his stock. Aside from having to keep a low profile cops-wise, some of the Es have already been paid for by customers who'd expected them long before now. In fact, if Jez admits it to himself, he's lost track of what he owes to who. It all got a bit complicated for a while back there.

He stretches out on the mattress, scratching at one of the cuts on his head. Crash Mary claimed he was a wizard with a razor, but Jez's got nicks all over his cranium. Makes him feel like some pox-ridden twat. Still, at least it means he's not instantly recognisable to Hassan and his stick-wielding mates in the Goan constabulary. No dreads. No goatee. Taken all his piercings out. A pair of dark glasses and he could be anyone. Well, anyone with a suntanned face and a pink head. He'll have to sort that out somehow.

But fifty three. Okay, say he owes twenty three, just for argument's sake. So if he sells the rest at six or seven quid a go, that's around two hundred quid tops. Which is about half of what he started with in the first place. Which is not a great bit of business, however you look at it.

Ripped off by cops, thumped by drug-dealers, double-crossed and on the run. All that just to end up down on the deal. Well fucking done, my son. Richard Branson better watch his back.

There's nothing else for it. If he's going to get any serious funds at all, enough to help pull him out of the swamp of trouble he's blundered into, he's got to sell them all. And for a hell of a lot more than six or seven quid.

Difficult, but do-able. Still plenty of wide-eyed tourists and travellers around, people who don't know the going rate for a dodgy E in Goa.

A bit of salesmanship, that's all it needs.

A plan's forming. As long he can avoid the people he owes,

it should be fine. And Hassan. And the police. And most of the people who know him. And somehow still do a sales job with the Es. Fuck.

*

'So when you get off the bus, Swiss?' the Doc says, raising his hat brim half an inch so he can get a better look. In a way he's surprised that Dave remembered to meet him. He doesn't look in great shape.

Swiss Dave never used to look like this, he thinks. It's him, but he looks like he got himself dipped in some of that liquid nitrogen. Everything about him looks frozen, with most of his blood sucked out.

'The bus? Depends on what you mean. The physical bus, or the metaphysical one. You see what I'm saying? Yeah? Yeah?'

'Either one,' the Doc says. 'Don't matter which.'

'Well, the physical one,' Dave says, skinning up on the table between the beer bottles, checking that the surface is dry before putting the papers down. 'A couple of days ago. I wasn't going to come here. Was headed for Gokarna. But I thought, hell, why not just shoot over to the old patch. Just for old times' sake. Well, the times that I can remember, anyway. Changed a bit, hasn't it.'

He looks around at the Vibe's day-glo painted interior, the mystic symbols, the trance-dripping speakers suspended from the roof.

'Changed?' the Doc says, rising out of his seat. 'Goddamn annihilated!' He suddenly seems to remember where he is, remembers his warning. He sits back down. 'Ain't nothing left of the old days. Only me and old Cyril. Remember Cyril? Skinny kid, fisherman, him and his family used to rent out rooms. Way back in the old days.'

Dave smiles but shakes his fuzzy, grey head.

'Blank, I'm afraid,' he says.

'Well, Cyril ain't so skinny no more,' the Doc says, ignoring him. 'Musta got himself hit by one o' them fat sticks.'

'Yeah?'

'Ain't jazzin' you.'

'Too much, man.'

'You're saying it. Remember the Flea Market?'

'Yeah,' Dave says, grinning, poking a triumphant finger in the air. 'Yeah, I got it, yeah. Couple of hundred dudes, buying, selling, exchanging. Just trash really. Books, dodgy sleeping bags, homemade pipes and stuff.'

'Well, multiply that by fifty, then add some more. Then drop in the names Calvin Klein and RayBan and whaddya got?'

'Who's Calvin Klein?'

'Don't matter. But what you got is a shopping mall, that's what you got. Little lanes with different sections? Specialist boo-teeks? All kinds of convenience? Goddamn shopping mall. Ain't got no soul no more.'

'Yeah?' Dave's eyes bulge in wonder. 'This I gotta see.'

'How long you putting your bag down?'

'As long as I need.'

'You'll see it.'

Three tables away, Iain's hurrying to finish his beer, not wanting to risk being around much longer in case Martha comes in.

'Slow down,' Barney says, noticing. 'You've got to be careful with that stuff. It's a very volatile liquid, Kings beer. Drink it too fast and you could spontaneously combust.'

'I just think we should be moving on,' Iain says, wiping the back of his hand across his mouth. He still hasn't told Barney about yesterday's visit from Martha, let alone the exertions of the night before. He knows keeping it a secret is a bit pathetic, a bit schoolboyish, but in some weird way it would seem a betrayal to Barney to come out with it now. Even though it happened only twenty four hours ago, to reveal that he'd been hiding it from him would emphasise the fragility of their recent friendship, point out that they don't know each other well enough for real trust to develop. And he doesn't want to get dog's abuse for shagging her again, although he knows he probably deserves it. 'No point hanging around here. It's dead. Let's go somewhere that's got girls.'

'Pandora's, then.'

'No,' Iain says too quickly. 'I mean, yeah, that's obviously an option. Just thought we might try somewhere else. Maybe Paraiso. Or the Sun Temple.'

'What, after the overwhelmingly entertaining experience it gave us last night?'

'Let's try Paraiso, then.'

'And if it's dead, we can head up to Pandora's. And if that's dead, we can go on to the Primrose.'

Iain thinks. He can check out Pandora's from outside before going in. Check that the coast's clear.

'Deal. Hurry up.'

They finish their drinks and walk out onto the path, twisting their torches on for the long, dark stretch after the Guru Bar and Vasant restaurant, a darkness strewn with snapping dogs guarding their shopfront territories.

Up the path, past Barney's place, through the palm trees and up to the bus stop.

Paraiso is dead, barely twenty people inside it, lost in the big space. Iain and Barney stay ten seconds before deciding to split.

Iain starts getting nervous as they walk up to the crossroads. What if Martha's hiding out at Starco's waiting for him to pass by? He ups the pace, raising his arm nonchalantly to cover his face as they take the left hand turn. He can hear the reggae from Starco's garden, but he doesn't even glance over. Walking along the dark road towards the Pandora Cafe, he starts to chide himself for getting uptight about it. So what if she's there? He can always tell her to go away, that twice was quite enough, thank you very much. Not a very polite thing to do, admittedly, but it would solve the problem.

Pandora's isn't all that busy either, although it's busier than Paraiso. But there are still enough people standing around to block out corners and tables where Martha might be hiding, waiting to pounce. Iain can't be sure she's not there as he peeks in from the gloomy safety of the road.

What the hell. Just have to risk it.

They go in, get beers, and sit at a table away from the bar.

'Extraordinary looking girl over there,' Barney says, nodding over towards the cluster of tables at the other side of the bar.

Iain sees her too. Extraordinary. Dark brown curls. Classic face. Standing proud and firm. Balance and poise.

'Good point. Yeah, I'm glad I decided we should come here.'

They drink, happy just to watch the girl, the way she stands, the way she laughs, tosses her hair, shifts her weight from hip to hip.

'Quite extraordinary,' Barney says.

'Even for a Romanian.'

'You think she's Romanian?'

'No,' Iain says. 'It's just an old bit of football commentary. David Coleman. It wasn't one of his famous cock-ups, or anything, but I heard it when I was a kid and I've always remembered it. 'Quite extraordinary, even for a Romanian'.'

'Yyeeees,' Barney drawls, not quite sure what to make of it. 'But she is extraordinary, though.'

'Still not attracted to those ravey types? She's got a tikka on her forehead and everything.'

'Youthful impetuousness. Nothing wrong with that. Can't really fault her.'

'Still,' Iain says. 'No point lusting after her with those uncontrollable urges you don't get. You'd have nothing to talk about. She's strictly my territory.'

'But I said I'd make an effort.'

'Not with the best-looking girl in the place, you don't. If you're starting out on a one night stand mission, you should probably lower your sights a bit.'

'Oh, I'm not saying I'd get anywhere with her,' Barney says. 'Just remarking on what a beautiful girl she is.'

They settle into their chairs, soaking up Pandora's and the ambient vibe, checking out new arrivals, looking at the established customers.

'What about them two,' Iain says, nodding over to a couple of straggle-haired, pale girls.

'Vegans.'

'How d'you know?'

'They look so ill. Dead giveaway.'

'Good call. Not sexy, vegans. Too worried that you might crush some tiny organism when you're grinding against them. Probably don't brush their teeth. 'Bacteria have, like, rights too, man'. They probably want their teeth to clean themselves 'naturally'. I mean, even monkeys use twigs to clean their teeth with, for God's sake.'

'Do they?'

'I'm not sure. I might have made it up.'

'If you got forty thousand monkeys typing away at typewriters for a year, one of them would probably type 'twig'.'

'Wouldn't surprise me. Okay,' Iain says, scouting the room again. 'What about those two over there.'

'The anorexic and the fat girl with the hair-lip?'

'*Next* to them.'

'Oh, they're alright. In a bland sort of way. Travellers, probably. Not very inspiring, though.'

'Who needs inspiration? Ejaculation's what's important. And they, if I'm not mistaken, could be exactly what we're looking for.'

'You think so?'

'I know so. My antenna's tuned in. If you can tune antennas.'

'Antennae.'

'Whatever. It's working now. It's been a bit rusty for the last while, but I'm getting crystal clear reception now. Okay, we've got to think tactics. Let me just go for a piss first.'

'Be my guest.'

Iain gets up and goes past the bar to the reeking shed at the side of the building. Someone's in it already, so he waits in the darkness, thinking of openers. Not chat-up lines, but openers. Questions that'll open up the conversation, allow it to diversify, get the girls talking about themselves, give him opportunities to drop in funny lines.

He's about to piss on a nearby bush when the toilet door opens and a plump girl with dreads comes out.

'Take a deep breath,' she says. 'It's evil.'

'Cheers,' Iain says back. 'Looking forward to it.'

Once he's finished in the hot, filthy, stinking hole, taking care not to splash on his trousers, he hurries back with some kind of loose strategy in his head. He rounds the bar, goes back to the table, and sees that Barney's gone.

Gone? Where? Maybe he's having a piss somewhere as well. Maybe outside in one of the fields. But he's taken his beer. Where the hell is he?

Iain sits down and lifts his bottle, drinking back a couple of tepid mouthfuls. He scans the bar. His eyes pop. Barney's talking to the extraordinary girl.

*

'Tell you what,' Steve says as he and Karen sit over their post-dinner drinks in the hotel bar. 'Why don't we go up to Arambol tomorrow? Be a nice change of scenery.'

'Arambol? What's that? A restaurant or something? I'm not going if it's not clean.'

'It's a place. Up north a bit. It's just miles and miles of empty beach. So they say, anyway.'

'How far's it?'

'Dunno. Ten or fifteen miles, I think. Not that far.'

'It's a bit far to go just for a beach. Which is probably full of cows and dogs and perverts anyway.'

'That's the point. There's nothing there,' Steve says, trying to smile. He wants to get Karen out of the way, just in case the shit hits the fan. Which it might, depending on what the paper does with the story he's given them. Best to be on the safe side. 'It's just miles of deserted beach. I've been reading about it.'

'How we going to get there? Taxi?'

'Thought we could maybe hire scooters or something. We can hire them here at the hotel.'

'Never driven one of them.'

'Neither have I. Can't be that difficult, though. Or I could get a proper bike, one of those big Enfields. You could go on the back.'

'On these roads? You must be joking.'

'It'll be perfectly safe. It'll be fun. It's years since I had a bike. Remember that Yamaha I used to have? You used to like going on the back of that. At first, anyway. Until you made me sell it.'

'I did not make you sell it,' Karen says sharply, but smiles

352   Rae Stewart

inwardly at the memory from the start of the relationship. It'll never last, her mother had said. Can't see you going about on the back of a motorbike for long. Don't worry, she'd told her mum. I'm sure he means to get a car soon. 'All I did was point out the practical reasons why a car would be better. Weather, that kind of thing.'

'And that if I kept it you wouldn't go out with me anymore.'

'I never said that.'

'Near enough. I distinctly remember at one point you saying how awkward it was us going out because of how difficult it was to wear normal clothes, nice clothes I think you said, when you were having to ride on the back of a bike. As well as having to carry a bloody great helmet everywhere.'

'Well it's true. Those helmets are murder on your hair. It was all just practical reasons, as I said.'

'And if I hadn't got rid of it and bought the car?'

'What d'you mean?'

'If I hadn't got rid of the bike and bought the Golf. What would you have done?'

'What d'you mean, what would I have done? The reality is that it was the best thing you could have done, getting rid of that bike. The car was far nicer. Far more practical.'

'But what if I hadn't?' Steve says, leaning forward, interested, not wanting to let it go. 'What would you have done? Left me? Gone off with someone who did have a car?'

'This is just stupid. What's the point of going on about something that never happened? It was all years ago, anyway. The reality is that you *did* sell the bike, and we *did* get a car. That's the reality.'

'I reckon you'd have gone for someone like Keith Beckinridge. He was always sniffing around. *And* he had a car. Always very friendly with him, you were. I'll admit it, it even made me

THE VIBE   353

jealous sometimes, though I never showed it. Maybe that's one
of the main reasons I bought the car, in case you went off with
him. I reckon, if I hadn't got rid of the bike, you'd have gone out
with him instead.'

'Keith Beckinridge? I don't think so,' Karen says, a little in-
dignantly. 'Look how he's turned out. Managed to drink his way
out of two promotions at that company he's with.'

'Exactly,' Steve says calmly, but feeling a ripple of realisa-
tion. 'So it's turned out alright for you, hasn't it. Just how you
wanted it. You made the right choice. But still. I wonder what
would have happened. If I'd kept the bike, where would we be
now?'

'What matters,' Karen says, seeming a little flustered to
Steve eyes. 'What matters is we're in Goa now. Alright, it means
that much to you, hire one of them bikes. But I'm warning you,
if I fall off the back, you're in big trouble.'

Big trouble, Steve thinks. I'm already in that.

*

'You're that Jock geezer from the party, ain't you,' Jez says, sliding into the empty seat next to Iain.

It takes Iain a while to place him, what with the lack of hair
and the round glasses with green lenses.

'Oh yeah, you're the, we had a bit of business, yeah?' he says.

'Had a good time that night, did you?'

'Yeah, brilliant time, cheers.'

'Told you they was top notch, didn't I. Going on Wednesday, are you? After the Flea Market?'

'Probably,' Iain says. He flicks a look over towards Barney
and the girl. They're still talking, laughing. They've been doing
that for ages. 'Haven't thought about it too much.'

'You should go, man,' Jez says, sounding enthusiastic. 'This is going to be mega. DJ Rani C's mixing it, real hardcore stuff. Should be the biggest, yeah?'

'Yeah? S'pose I might. I'll see how I feel.'

Iain doesn't feel much like talking to Jez. There's a nervous energy, a strained eagerness about him that makes Iain feel uneasy. There's just something about him he doesn't like.

'What you need's something to perk you up a bit, get the vibe going,' Jez says. 'Now, that stuff I gave you last time, that was pretty good, yeah?'

'Yeah. A bit speedy, it's got to be said, but yeah.'

'Well, I've just got some in that are even better. Straight in from Amsterdam. About the nearest you'll get to pure MDMA anywhere. Well, anywhere around here, anyway. A bit pricey, but worth it. It's your quality control and all that.'

'How much?'

'A score and a five spot for two.'

'What?'

'It's the lowest I can go, God's honest truth. That's quality for you. Most of the stuff floating around here's just flour and liquid speed. To get real Es, you've got to pay for them.'

'Yeah, but I still don't actually understand how much you're asking.'

'A score and five. Twenty five quid.'

'Twenty five quid? So you're asking, what, seventeen hundred rupees for two?'

'Nah, not rupees, mate. Got to be in English money. And no coins. Though I suppose you could call it a twenty and the balance in roops if you like, say four hundred, what with the exchange rate and everything. Bloody good deal, that is. Pay a lot more than that back home. For this kind of quality.'

'Doubt it,' Iain says quietly. 'So, twenty? Plus four hundred rupees?'

'Or a fiver if you've got it. Saves you fifty roops, that does.'

'It's still a hell of a lot, though. I'm not on a particularly huge budget.'

'Tell you what, then. Since you're an old customer, call it twenty flat. And a hundred and fifty roops, just so I can get me-self a couple of beers. Can't say fairer than that, can you. I'm not taking the piss, I can't go any lower, not with this quality. Lot of hassle getting hold of these, I'm telling you. You wouldn't be-lieve the trouble I've gone through to get me hands on them. Anyway, there's not many left and there's others wanting them. Just thought I'd give you a shout. Since we've done business be-fore and everything.'

Iain thinks for a few moments, trying to get his half-stoned head to do sums. Go for it, Jez is thinking. Be a mug. Take the crappy fucking deal, you tosser.

'Okay,' Iain says. Jez cheers inwardly.

Iain dips into the security pouch hung inside his trousers and takes out a crisp Bank of England twenty. From his pocket he unearths grubby rupees. He passes them under the table to Jez, who slips two white pills into Iain's empty hand.

'A pleasure as always,' Jez says, grinning. He jumps out of the seat and disappears into the thickening, late night crowd.

Iain examines the pills, and then realises he's just staring at them. There's nothing about them that can tell him anything, whether they're good, bad or indifferent. Or paracetamol. He puts them in his pocket.

He sits a while longer, trying not to look at Barney and the girl, wondering what he should do. A man with a short mohican and tattooed arms sitting at the next table holds a mostly smoked joint towards him.

'Just finish it,' the man says. 'I'm smoked out, yeah?'

Iain has to get out of his seat to reach the smouldering stub.

'Cheers,' he says, pulling in a grateful lungful of sweet, harsh smoke as he sits back down. It takes him a couple of seconds to realise that the seat next to him, Barney's seat, is occupied again.

'Hello,' Martha says. 'You are having a good evening?'

'Mostly,' Iain says, trying not to leap away from her.

'Good.' Her face is blank, unreadable. 'It is good that I am finding you here. I was looking in the Vibe Bar, but you were not there.'

'No. That's right. I wasn't. Kind of.'

'But I have found you here. This is good, because it means we can have sex now.'

Iain glances over at Barney and the girl, then looks at his watch and shrugs.

'Well,' he says, with dull resignation. 'I suppose now's as good a time as any.'

CHAPTER TWENTY TWO

Arambol by Enfield

'This is bad business,' Cyril says with a sad heave of his chest, reading the story at the bottom of the Konkan Times' front page.

'Any business is bad business,' the Doc mutters from his chair next to him on the verandah. Small, fragrant early morning fires burn in the lanes around the house.

'Murder in Anjuna. I didn't hear about this. Maybe I don't listen as much as I used to, but I would have thought I'd hear about this. A poor girl murdered, a Westerner, French. A month away from her twenty first birthday.' Cyril shakes his head, tutting. 'Right here in Anjuna. This is not how it used to be.'

'Say that again.'

'And the police, they are doing nothing. They are saying she is drowning, but an English policeman here on holiday saw the body and says there is no doubt that she was murdered and that the police are covering it up.'

'Figures.'

'It is not right. How can they do nothing? A poor girl is dead, and they are just standing by. How can this be right?'

'Can't deny what's staring you in the face.'

'This is very bad business.'

'Truer word never been said.'

A motorbike slows to take the bend in front of the house, the engine dropping into a deep, throbbing grumble before the driver slips down a gear and revs the bike to take it into the straight.

Steve's enjoying it. He hasn't been on a bike for a long time, but within a few minutes he feels he's been riding one forever. The roar of the Enfield's 500 cc engine echoes in Steve's chest as they tear down the shiny tarmac road through the rice fields. Karen leans forward from behind him. The balance of the bike doesn't shift by even a millimetre. It's a big beast.

'You're going too fast,' she shouts.

'Nope,' Steve shouts back. 'Just fast enough.'

The bike speeds on. Herons fly up from the fields. Sunlight cuts through the palms. The road ahead is clear.

*

As soon as Martha's gone, Iain starts packing. He pretended to be asleep for half an hour before she got up and left, scared to face her in daylight.

That's it. No more. All that handwashing stuff. In the middle of the bloody night. And she wanted me to bite the skin at the back of her neck. What the fuck was all that about?

He chucks shirts, t-shirts, trousers, wash-bag, everything into his battered backpack, forcing it all in. Towel, torch, camera, books, his personal stereo, homemade compilation tapes, Radiohead, Stereophonics, Ash, Headswim, the Dandy Warhols, packing it all in as quick as he can, just in case she comes back for more.

After fifteen minutes he's ready, his backpack strapped over his shoulders, his bulging daypack hanging by his side. He padlocks the door and takes the key to a nearby house, a long, modern, squared-off bungalow.

His squat, grey-haired landlady comes to the door wearing a faded floral dress. He explains that he's moving. It's the end of the period he'd paid for anyway. She takes the key, smiles, and closes the door.

Iain trudges off along the red dust path, homeless again, searching for sanctuary.

*

Chief Inspector Da Silva scans the newspaper story again as he waits for his assistant to get Gupta on the line.

Tourist killed. Police cover-up alleged. Detective from England. Tell-tale signs of violence. Police inaction. Prime suspect absconding. Incompetence.

It doesn't make for pleasant reading. Da Silva's already had Chief of Police Tendulkar chewing his ear off about the story, demanding he get to the bottom of it. It's not so much the facts of the case that Tendulkar's worried about, more the bad publicity.

The phone buzzes on Da Silva's desk. He snatches it up.

'Gupta?' he barks into it.

'Yes, sir. Good morning to you, sir,' Gupta says through sporadic static.

'Never mind all that bullshit. What is all this in the Konkan Times? Why didn't you tell us about this? Why do I have to learn from the newspapers what is going on in my own area? You are even quoted in this bloody story. So you can talk to the newspapers but not to me, is that it?'

'Chief Inspector, sir. I did not know they were going to make such a big fuss out of this. This is nothing. You should have the reports by now. This is simple drowning only. These newspapers, they are always mentioning a drowning here, a drowning there, a few words only. This is normal. How was I to know they would make a tamasha out of this one? The reporter asked me about it, I told him. This is normal practice.'

'You still should have told me,' Da Silva snaps. 'The Chief of Police is very unhappy with this publicity.'

'Sir, you know what the Chief is like. Only last month he is addressing us in Calangute station saying, keep things low-key, don't put off the tourists, no bad publicity, leave the tourists alone. I am only following orders.'

'Are you sure this is a drowning?'

'The body was in the water, she was dead. There is enough to say it is a drowning. It is just one of these hippy-shippies, nobody notices that she's gone. Why should we bother ourselves with this? It is not important. Low-key, the Chief said. He does not want us to make a big deal of every dead drug-addict we find. It is not good publicity.'

'And you call today's publicity good? Anyway, there's nothing that can be done about it now. We just have to live with it. But you are wrong that nobody notices that this girl is dead. This policeman, this DS Harrison noticed.'

'But I notice the Konkan Times didn't say that he was fucking her, sir. He is just being hysterical.'

'How do you know he was fucking her?' Da Silva says, surprised and suspicious.

'He as much as admitted it at the station.'

'Which station? When?'

There's a crackling pause on the line. Da Silva's worried that they've lost the connection, but it's just Gupta weighing things up, wondering if he's made a mistake.

'He reported the body,' he says eventually. 'He was in the Anjuna station when I got there, so naturally I questioned him. He as much as said he was fucking her, even though he's here on holiday with his wife. All very messy, sir, and not the way the Konkan Times is painting the picture at all.'

'If a policeman was involved, you should have told me right away. He came here to my office yesterday, but only now am I learning that he actually reported the body and was in a relationship with the girl. If I'd known this, if you had done your job and told me about everything, we wouldn't need to be having this conversation, and you wouldn't need to be thinking of an alternative career. I could have sorted this all out yesterday if you hadn't got it into your mind to keep me in the dark. The man is a foreign policeman. You didn't think this important enough to tell me?'

'Chief Inspector, sir,' Gupta says, sweating, trying to limit the damage. 'How was I to know this? He was an upset tourist. That's all I know. How was I expected to know his occupation?'

'You could have asked him. I thought you said you questioned him.'

'Of course, sir, but just the basics. He didn't know the girl's name, her address, nothing. He wasn't of any help to us. I didn't need to question him further. This is just a simple drowning only.'

'For your sake it better be,' Da Silva says. 'I have my doubts about these injuries this DS Harrison is talking about, but if you are sure it is a drowning, then we'll go with that and hope this thing blows over.'

'I think it's best, sir. These injuries, she could have got them falling over the cliff or getting battered against rocks. They mean nothing. Nobody can say this is not a drowning. You are correct to play this low-key, sir.'

'But you were still wrong not to tell me about this. If anything else goes wrong, remember that it is your head on the chopping block.'

Da Silva puts down the phone before Gupta can reply. He's not filled with confidence. Gupta isn't one of his brightest officers, but what can he do? If Gupta says it's a drowning, that's what they'll stick to.

He takes a deep breath and prepares to brief the notoriously explosive Chief Tendulkar. Words ring in his mind.

Low-key. Blow over. Cover-up. Chopping block. He has a duty to protect his own officers, but who's protecting him? As Gupta's direct superior, he has to take ultimate responsibility.

Or maybe. Maybe it's time to start putting some distance between himself and Gupta, just in case. Tendulkar wants reassurance, so maybe it's best to make it plain that all the reassurance is coming from Gupta, and that, whilst he has Da Silva's full support, he is not known to be infallible by any means. Just sow enough doubt in the Chief's mind to put the heat straight onto Gupta if anything goes wrong.

Da Silva's thoughts and worries are interrupted by the buzz of his phone. The impatient Chief of Police is waiting.

*

'Tell you what, love,' Steve says. 'You just stop here a bit, drink your drink, get your breath back, and I'll go and find out where the best bit of beach is.'

Karen nods at him. They're in a tiny restaurant in Arambol, one of several shacks scattered around forming the relaxed hub of the village.

'I think I need to stay in the shade a bit,' she says, taking a sip at the straw sticking out of her Limca bottle. 'Recover for five minutes.'

Steve makes his way from restaurant to restaurant, all of them appearing semi-permanent with their walls of palm-leaf mats and crude hand-painted signs hanging from bamboo poles out in front. He goes into each one, asking customers, owners, waiters, describing Henrik, his height, physique, the dates he might have arrived. He encounters vague suspicion and bored indifference. Once he's been around them all, the only useful information he's gathered is on the local beaches.

'They're back down the road a bit, the best ones,' he says to Karen when he returns. Her Limca bottle's empty. She seems a bit edgy. 'There's one here, but back the way we came is the best, apparently.'

'Well, you took your time finding out,' she says. 'Should have been able to find that out in ten seconds, not ten minutes. So we've got to go on the bike again, do we?'

'It's not far. A turn-off about a mile away. I think I remember going past it.' He smiles. 'Come on, you know you love it really.'

Karen gets up only a little reluctantly, smooths down her cotton skirt, and prepares for another terror ride.

*

Iain can see Barney's teeth from fifty yards away. He's sitting at a table by the shore in Sonic restaurant, looking out to sea, grinning like a maniac.

Iain orders black cardamom tea from the wizened, toothless old man behind the cash desk, then jumps down the concrete steps into the palm-shaded garden.

'Do you absolutely have to look so bloody happy,' he says to Barney, pulling out a blue plastic moulded chair and sitting down at the table.

'Good morning,' Barney says brightly. 'And how are we today?'

"'We' would feel a hell of a lot better if you didn't look so damn pleased with yourself.'

'Quite,' Barney says. 'And how's your Madchen from Munchen?'

Iain ignores him, looking out at waves breaking against the red, laterite rocks.

'Your bierkellerenjungenfrau?'

Still no response.

'Hitler's granny? Fraulein Gobbler Goebbels?'

'Alright, alright. I take it you saw her, then.' Iain crosses his arms, annoyed.

'Only that you left with her. It's a pity, really. I was just about to ask you over to join us.'

'Oh, I'm sure that would have been tremendous fun,' Iain says sourly.

'You'd adore her. India's an extraordinary girl.'

'I'm sure,' Iain says. 'India?'

'Yes. That's her name. Isn't it fantastic?'

'It's a bit, well, her parents must have been a bit hippyish.'

'Undoubtedly.'

'And what about her?'

'Oh, she has tendencies.'

'Such as?'

'Nothing much really. She's studied shiatsu, some type of Oriental massage. She's got some magic crystals. Tarot. She read my palm and told me I'd live to eighty three and have four children.'

'Where?'

'Right here,' Barney says, holding his palm out. They both examine his hand. Barney wiggles a finger at it. 'It's in there somewhere. I'm not sure where, exactly.'

'And of course,' Iain says, straightening back up, 'being able to tell someone's future from a few wrinkles on their hand is so obvious it must be true.'

'Oh, I know,' Barney says, smiling. 'But she's so sweet and innocent about it. She's not heavily into it, not overwhelmingly so anyway. I think she's just playing with it. I can't see it doing her any harm.'

'No harm? Hitching herself to a patchwork belief system full of contradictions, everything taken out of context? I don't believe I'm hearing this.'

'I don't think she really believes in any of these things. She's just experimenting, trying them on for size. But, I've got to say, an absolutely charming girl.'

'I could see that much from where I was sitting. Alone. Thanks for abandoning me, by the way. Helped a lot when it came to fighting off the Reeperbahn Strangler.'

'Well I couldn't help it. You were at the loo, and I happened to find myself gazing at India when suddenly she looked back and smiled. I'm not clear how it happened exactly, but before I knew it I was sitting talking to her and the whole world's bloody marvelous.'

'Delighted to hear it,' Iain says bitterly. 'Absolutely delighted.'

'I take it she was on quite strict form last night.'

'Move this way, move that way, put your hand here, bite there, speed up now, slow down now. Made me cut my bloody nails! I had to sit there with a nail clipper after washing my hands, and I actually had to cut my bloody fingernails! Then wash my hands again!'

'It wasn't all bad, was it?'

'Well, no,' Iain says grudgingly. 'But that's not the point, though. I'm not doing it again. I've got my self-respect to think of. I've moved to a different hut.'

'Oh, very assertive of you. Bound to do your self-respect no end of good.'

'Well at least it means she can't find me.'

'What if you see her out at night?'

'Then I'll just have to tell her.'

'Tell her what?'

'That she can't treat me like this. Like a sexual object, a plaything. That she's really fucking scary on all sorts of different levels.'

'You can't tell her that.'

'Can you tell her for me?'

'What do you think?'

'Och, I'll think of something. Some ballocks like I've just come out of a bad relationship and that I need time on my own, that I'm not ready to have that level of intimacy with someone.'

'She'll never believe that.'

'It's worked before.'

'But it doesn't sound like she wants any intimacy. She just wants you to do your sexual performing seal act whenever she tells you.'

'I'll tell her that my cock's fallen off, then. Or I could just throw stones at her whenever I see her.'

'That ought to get the message across.'

'Yeah,' Iain says, softly, distracted by the waves. 'So. Any plans for tonight?'

'Well,' Barney says, drawling the word out. 'India and I were planning to have dinner at a little place up by the crossroads. You're most welcome to join us if you like. As long as you don't bring the Monster of Munich along to make up a foursome. We don't want dinner ruined by all the villagers marching to the restaurant with flaming torches chanting 'kill the beast, kill the beast'.'

'Nah,' Iain says, turning his mouth down. 'Think I'll have a quiet night in. I have no wish whatsoever to be a gooseberry. Hang on a minute, though. She got any mates?'

'Not that she's mentioned. She must have, but we haven't really been talking about that kind of thing.'

'I can imagine. So this isn't just a one night stand thing, I take it. Did you, you know?'

'Now, now. A gentleman would never betray a woman's

confidence.'

'Oh. So you didn't shag her, then.'

'Of course I did. But I can't just tell you something like that.'

'Fair enough.'

Iain's tea arrives, and they both sit quietly for a while. Iain starts eyeing the open-mouthed crows strutting arrogantly around the garden, the bolder ones hopping up onto chairs and tables to get at left-overs before the waiter can clear them away. Hah, he thinks, staring at one particularly scrawny-looking bird. You're probably descended from the Tyrannosaurus Rex, according to the latest theory. Don't look so tough now, do you.

'Anyway,' he says. 'I think I'm just going to stay in tonight, get used to the new place.'

'Where is it?'

'Up the back. I'll show it to you. Pretty new, I reckon. A half-decent bog and shower as well.'

'Cost much more?'

'A bit. Anonymity has its price, though. Come on, it's only five minutes away.'

They both climb the steps to the main body of the restaurant. As they wait to pay, a middle-aged American woman with cropped hair gets up from her table, sticks her head through the door to the kitchen and starts yelling.

'Where's my Goddamn food! I want it right now! Jesus, this is taking an hour!'

'Calm down, dear,' Barney says, loudly and clearly, as if he's talking to a slightly deaf pensioner. 'You're in India now, you know, not McDonald's. Things take time.'

She spits a stream of abuse at Barney as he and Iain leave.

'Californian,' Barney says in a confidential tone. 'They don't travel well. They don't translate well overseas.'

'How can you tell she's Californian?'

'Oh, you can always tell a Californian. The trouble is, you

can't tell them much. It just confuses the poor dears.'

*

'Oh Steve, this is beautiful, look,' Karen says, standing at the top of the dune that seconds ago she'd been complaining about climbing. Steve comes up behind her and scans the view, a broad landscape wider than his eyes can take in. The Arabian Sea lies about a hundred yards in front of them, and between the dunes and the water there's only flat, golden, pristine sand. A couple of long fishing boats pulled up on the beach are the only objects breaking the monotony of paradise.

'Never seen anything like it,' Steve says, awed. 'Miles and miles of empty beach. Can you believe it?'

They jump down the dune in sliding steps and walk towards the sea, a thin, shimmering band of turquoise way in front of them. Delicate breakers spread lazily onto the shore.

Steve lays his sarong down on the sunny side of a beached wooden fishing boat, its name, Santana, just visible in flaked white paint on the side.

The afternoon passes in quiet luxury, lulled by the soft rush of the waves, caressed by a cool hint of a breeze. They talk, happier and more relaxed than they've been all holiday, the surroundings seducing all stress from them. They talk, they laugh, they smile. Sometimes they just lie there, content to soak up the sun and the peace. This is the way it's meant to be.

Steve's brought a book, but he doesn't want to read it. He wants to look at the eternal, infinite beach, the wild beauty, the palms poking up behind the dunes, the diamond sparkle of the sea. He wants to look at it so hard, concentrate so keenly, that it'll never leave his memory.

White-headed sea eagles swirl high over the water on their

right. To their left, the wide stretch of beach curves out of sight, the ragged, feather-hatted tops of palm trees blocking out the rest of the world, leaving them in delicious isolation.

Surely this is what people mean by paradise, Steve thinks to himself. Would it be possible, if he had the money? Just to get up, go to the beach, hang around, go back to bed. No worries, no stress, no rush. What would it be like? Would he be able to stand it? What about boredom, the lack of activity, the lack of challenge? Would it get to him? Was a simple life really possible? Few possessions, few ambitions, few responsibilities.

Other people did it. For months, sometimes years on end. Sometimes forever. Maybe the hippies, the New Agers, whatever they want to call themselves, maybe they're right after all. Maybe life can be lived without strain, without striving, without complications and the endless grind of getting through every day just to make more money so that it can be spent on new kitchens, new cars, new curtains, new furniture, new houses and a thousand other things which'll eat up even more money so that the cycle goes on and on, working harder, earning more, spending more, working harder. Surely life doesn't need to be so full of things, not when it could be full of all this.

In the distance over to his left, wobbling in the heat haze, Steve makes out a figure walking along the shoreline, the first person other than Karen that he's seen for hours. As the figure gets nearer and the haze gets less, he can make out it's a man, an Indian. A young man in blue shorts and a white vest, wearing a straw hat. He comes closer and closer, heading in a direct line to where Steve and Karen are lying. Steve feels resentment building up inside him. He doesn't want an intrusion into their private paradise, to have the fantasy shattered. But he reasons with himself. It's a public beach, a working beach for fishermen, not a playground for tourists. The young man walking towards them has far more right to be there than they do.

'I think you'd probably best cover up a bit, love,' Steve says to Karen, who's lying face down. 'I think one of the locals is coming over.'

Karen huffs, but picks up her bikini top and shuffles into it, bending her arms back trying to fasten the clasp.

The young man, thin-legged and wide-smiled, with the first sproutings of a moustache, comes right up and stands over them.

'Hello,' he says, beaming. 'Which country, please?'

'England,' Steve says, smiling back. Karen says nothing, sitting facing away from both Steve and the young man, still trying to adjust her bikini top so that it's comfortable.

'England. Very good, England,' the young man says. 'I also am learning English. I am wanting to be travel agent. Your good name?'

Just a kid, Steve thinks. A local kid, pleased to be meeting foreigners, trying out his English.

'Steve,' he says. 'And this is Karen.'

'Esteve, and Kah-ron,' the young man says, still smiling. 'My name Villi.'

'Villi,' Steve repeats, and holds out his hand. 'Pleased to meet you Villi.'

'Pleased to meet you,' Villi says as she shakes both their hands in turn, although Karen doesn't seem too enthusiastic about meeting him. 'I am sitting?'

Steve doesn't want him to, but feels it would be unnecessarily harsh to say no.

'Please do,' he says, moving over to join Karen on her beach towel, letting Villi sit down on his vacated sarong.

'First time in Goa?' Villi says.

'Yes, first time.'

'You are staying which place?'

'Anjuna.'

'Ah, Anjuna. Anjuna very famous place.' Villi's eyes brighten. 'Always I am hearing about Anjuna. Too much party-ing.' He laughs a high-pitched giggle.

'Do you go to the parties in Anjuna?' Steve asks him slowly, politely.

'No, I not go,' Villi says as if the idea is ridiculous. 'But par-ties in Anjuna, very famous. Much girls there. Really, I am hearing this.'

There's a sudden lull in the conversation, and Steve hopes for a second that Villi will go, but he speaks again, pointing to both Steve and Karen.

'You have marriage?'

'Yes, we're married,' Steve says. He's getting bored with Villi now.

'For a few years now,' Karen says. Steve can see her forced smile, see how uncomfortable she is, arms folded across her chest, sitting side-on to Villi, trying to cover her bikini-clad breasts.

There's another pause, Steve and Villi sitting opposite each other smiling, Karen turning around looking for her t-shirt, pull-ing it out of her beach bag.

'Steve?' she says over her shoulder. 'Would you brush some of that sand off me back? I'm going to put me t-shirt on.'

Steve starts sweeping his hand over her shoulder blades, wanting Villi to go but not knowing how to say it without ap-pearing rude. Dry sand is stuck to Karen's skin. It falls at his touch.

'You miss here,' Villi says, reaching out, pointing at a spot just beside Karen's breast, making as if to touch it. Steve slaps his hand away.

'Hey!' he says, his voice sharp, pointing in Villi's face. 'You just outstayed your welcome, mate. I think it's time for you to go now.'

He turns to Karen's back again, aware of Villi standing up. He continues to brush the sand away, trying to get every last grain, trying to calm his sudden flash of temper, playing for time until Villi's away. He looks to see how far he's gone, only to find Villi's crotch a few feet from him, Villi's left hand holding down the elasticated band of his shorts, his right hand pumping away on his erect penis.

'See? See?' Villi says.

An unformed word between a growl and a yell breaks from Steve's throat as he tries to scramble to his feet, but Villi's already sprinting away, back down the beach. Steve starts to go after him. He flicks a glance back to Karen. She's still got her back turned. She hasn't seen anything.

But he wants to catch Villi, punch him again and again, thump fist after fist into his young, smug face, kick his balls over and over, turning them to a mess of jelly for the insult, for the violation.

He stops, barely into his stride. Villi's still running. Steve stands and looks back at Karen again. She's pulling the t-shirt over her head. Villi's too far away now. He's got forty yards on Steve. Then Villi looks back, stops, and faces Steve, chugging away at himself again. Steve, still raging, makes a false start at running to get Villi on his way again. It works.

Steve walks back towards Karen. His muscles are tense, his teeth gritted. He tries to slow his breathing, tries to calm down, but the violent fury won't go away.

Karen looks round at him as he sits back down on his sarong and starts pulling his things together.

'He was a bit weird,' is all she says. He expects her to make a big deal of it, but she doesn't. She didn't see what he saw.

'Better get going,' Steve says, trying to loosen his voice.

'Time we got back. Don't want to be driving in the dark.'

Karen doesn't mind. They've had a good few hours on the beach. They gather their stuff into their daypacks and begin the trek across the sand to the dunes, the palms, and the thin dust road where Steve parked the bike. On the way, Karen issues orders about his driving. Steve doesn't reply. With the anger brewing fiercely inside him, he's afraid of what he might say if he opens his mouth. Karen seems to have enjoyed the day, more or less. No point in spoiling it for her now.

He guns the bike, feeling the reassuring note of power, the aggression of it. They take off, speeding through tiny villages, scattering millet laid out to bake in the sun on the normally quiet back road. Once on the main road he roars south, cutting corners as the tarmac winds over small hills, heading towards the Siolim ferry. All the way, his jaws are clamped, trying to focus all his angry energy into the engine, firing it out through the machine-gun exhausts. He sees Villi's face, his cock, feels the insult, the violation, the humiliation.

He revs the engine higher.

Karen's nervous. It's too fast. Way too fast.

'Going too fast,' she shouts forward to Steve.

They hit a straight, a raised stretch between fields. Steve slips a gear, then guns the bike faster. He sees the water buffalo at the last moment as it lurches up the bank from one of the fields, half hidden by a bush.

Steve swerves, pulling the bike onto the dirt at the side of the tarmac, nearly losing the back end as it slews through the red dust, the wheel slipping.

He pulls it back, past the thick, swinging behind of the buffalo, Karen screaming.

He gets the bike under control again as they skid to a stop. Karen's breathless.

'See!' she says, slapping him on the shoulder. 'Told you we

were going too fast! I knew something like this would happen!
I told you! Could have killed us!'

Steve readjusts his sunglasses.

'Just shut the fuck up and hold the fuck on.'

The Enfield roars, and they're off again.

*

He's had his eye on them before. Checked them out just a few
days ago. Just out of interest. Three in a row. Sturdy enough, but
some basic security flaws.

Unless Jez is very much mistaken, which he doubts, it's a
group of wealthy young Italian kids. He's seen them before,
three couples, well-dressed in off-the-peg bohemian fashion.

One of the couples is lounging outside their room. He's seen
them at the parties, at Pandora's, at the Vibe, maybe. Doesn't
know them, but he's seen them.

Well into the parties, they are. Just asking for it, really. Indian locks on the doors, from what he can remember. Cheap,
tinny shit.

Jez walks past slowly, but not too slow as to be suspicious.
Just the normal, relaxed swagger of the aimless long-termer.

Piece of piss, this lot should be. Candy from a baby. Prime
targets. *Prime* targets. Not too near the main path. Good access.
Should get them done within ten, fifteen minutes. They'll do for
starters. This lot will be at the party on Wednesday night. No
fear.

Sales haven't been going as well as he hoped. Difficult circumstances, after all. He'll shift some at the party, but it's
always worth having a back-up plan.

Jez carries on walking, shambling around, wandering lazily
through the groups of huts and small houses, window shopping.

*

IAIN McMILLAN'S GREAT
HINDUSTAN ADVENTURE

Tuesday 5th January '99, Anjuna, Goa

Ho-de-hum. Hum-de-ho. Hum-de-hum-de-hum-de-ho. I'm not bored. Honestly. Or lonely. I repeat, I am not lonely. Okay, maybe just a tad, but it's not real, official, noose-tying loneliness. It's more a general, pointless, bored kind of loneliness. What gives it that extra sharp edge of irritation, though, is that there seems to be a significant smidge of jealousy wedged in there as well.

Barney's going out with this girl he got off with last night, an absolute honey of a peach called, believe it or not, India. He said I could join them, but he was only being polite. I thought of going along just to piss him off, but I'd feel like an arse so I said no.

And here I am. I find myself at a loose end for the evening and I don't know what to do. I've just realised that since I arrived here, I've spent virtually every night going out with Barney. It's been an absolute blast. I haven't laughed so much in months. I mean, I've met loads of people in India so far, gone out with them, had a good enough time, but it was always just polite traveller-type talk. All people want to talk about is where they've been, what they've done, what they've seen, and which bowel complaints they've had. In fact, in most cases Bombay Botty and Rajasthan Runs are the only things I've had in common with these people, although I suppose it's natural that the subject matter of any on-the-road chat tends to be somewhat limited. But with Barney I've had real conversations.

Sometimes about something important like the meaning or otherwise of life, sometimes just debating which Spice Girl we'd most like to murder and dump in a skip. But real conversations nonetheless.

I realise now that it's a rarity to meet someone like that when you're travelling. I've lost count of how many bits of paper I've got with names and addresses and e-mail details of people I've met in different parts of India. Whether I'd actually want to contact them back in Britain is debatable, though. Sure, we could meet up in some bar and talk about what we've done, seen and shat since we last met, but that's hardly the basis for a meaningful, lasting friendship of any kind. In fact, after I write this, I'm going to chuck all the little bits of paper straight in the bin. Fuck 'em.

It's different with Barney, though. There was a genuine bond growing. Both of us just seemed to assume that once the evening came, we'd go out together. Or at least I did. But now he's out with that gorgeous girl from Pandora's, and I'm sitting in my room, lonely, bored and jealous. And here's the really spooky thing. I'm jealous, but not of him. If I'm completely honest, I'm jealous of the girl for having Barney's company. How fucked up is that?

So I've got nothing to do this evening except twiddle my thumbs. Or twiddle something else, but I don't feel like it. Munchen Martha's bled me dry, drained me of my masculine spirit. Och well, at least I've got a couple of top grade Es in my pocket. If all else fails, if things get just too lonely and boring, I could always pop one of those. Yeah, there's an idea. In fact, maybe I won't stay in after all. Perhaps it's time to go out and make some new friends. Preferably ones with snug puppies curled to their chests beneath flimsy, see-through cotton tops. Rock 'n' roll.

CHAPTER TWENTY THREE

The message

Steve takes a long, painfully cold draft of his Kingfisher. It's the first of many he plans to down tonight in the hope that they'll numb his hurt and blunt the razor edge of his rage.

Karen's in the room changing. She's not happy with him. He knows it, but at this particular moment, he doesn't care. She's angry about the way he drove back to the hotel, but so what? She survived, didn't she? Now she's deliberately drawing out the simple process of finding a change of clothes, making him wait down at the bar by himself.

It's probably meant as a punishment of sorts. It certainly doesn't feel like one. Anyway, she can change as much as she wants, but she'll never be able to change into what he really needs.

He lifts his glass again, the outside of it already running with condensation. Cold beer. Warm air. The clash of different worlds. He stares at the golden liquid. An anaesthetic like no other. Put the memory up against a wall and riddle it with alcohol-tipped bullets.

He looks around. He's virtually the only customer in the garden. He's not that surprised, because it's still fairly early in the evening. People are up in their rooms showering, snoozing, reading, arguing, pleading, lying, dressing. All those secret lives behind a hundred closed doors. They'll all come down later and nobody else will know anything about them, about the secret agonies they hide away from the world. They might be up there right now slapping each other, punching each other, whispering endless devotion with hands tied behind backs, snarling vile oaths in tender embraces, hating with kisses, loving with scratches, all of them twisted and sad and two-faced and bitter, all coming down to dinner with bland smiles and empty hearts and mindless chit-chat, all fresh and clean and neatly-dressed to face the outside world, a world away from their private hells. And as they chew their food primly and sip their drinks carefully they'll keep rotting away inside, a dark festering of thwarted ambition and ruined dreams invading every inch of their bodies little by little.

Steve's glad he's by himself, glad to be away from them. The worthless, fucked-up bastards, all of them. They can pretend as much as they like, but he knows that lurking inside each one of them is a potentially corrupt, vile soul. They can keep to themselves, as far as he is concerned. He wants nothing to do with them.

A young girl comes through the front gate of the hotel, and Steve watches her walk nervously up the path, head bowed slightly, keeping up a brisk pace, heading for reception.

Strange, Steve thinks. Doesn't really look like her sort of place. All silk and bangles, hippy gear. A budget traveller, most definitely.

He takes another drink and thinks of the day. The hopes he had for it. A nice day out for Karen, getting her away from seeing the newspaper story, and maybe finding some trace of Henrik. And then that incident.

He knows he should tell the police, but he can't, not now. And then there's the anger, the full-blooded fury, like he's been violated, or smeared with something filthy. He knows that the pervert wanted Karen to see his cock, not him, but that's part of the insult. A foul, rancid sexual insult, directed at his wife, but also at him. Part of the sick thrill the perv got was by tossing off in front of a woman and her husband, showing Steve he was powerless to stop it happening.

Maybe it shouldn't have got to that stage. Maybe he should have done something sooner and to hell with stupid ideas of meeting the locals and being nice and friendly to them. He should have told him to just fuck off as soon as he'd come up to them. After all, the reason they'd gone to Arambol in the first place was to get some peace and quiet, to get away from it all.

But he hadn't done anything, and then the bastard tried to touch Karen's breast and started abusing himself, almost in Steve's face. He should have chased the little bastard up the beach and beaten him to a pulp, regardless of what Karen did or didn't see, regardless of how she'd have reacted. She didn't approve of violence, but so what? This was different.

Steve takes another drink, but his throat still feels dry. The rage is burning him up.

A kicking might have taught the little bastard a lesson. What's going to stop him doing it again? After all, he got away with it today. What'd be the best punishment, the best way of getting him to stop it? A ticking off from a magistrate? Or a hefty doing over.

The young hippyish girl leaves. Thought so, Steve thinks. I knew the prices would be too steep for her. Poor kid. Late teens? Early twenties? Probably her first time away from the comforts of home. Probably crying out for clean sheets and a hot shower.

Steve looks away from her as Nat continues along the shrub-bordered path towards the hotel gates, her steps quickening all the time. Once outside, she jumps on the back of Becky's scooter and the two girls speed off, buzzing down the road.

Karen comes out of the main hotel building, heading towards Steve's table. She's wearing a tight, light blue t-shirt and dark blue, pleated, tight shorts. Good legs, Steve thinks, distracted. Everybody says that.

She sits down at the table, composing herself tidily. She's decided not to make an issue out of Steve's driving. Best to keep things light and happy. In control.

'D'you want a drink?' Steve says. Sandeep's already on his way.

Karen's mouth unfurls.

'Yeah. I don't know. It's a bit early. Bloody starving, though.'

'They're not serving food yet. I already checked. May as well get something to drink.'

'I don't know how I've lasted all day without lunch. Maybe something light. A cocktail or something. So what we going to do about dinner?'

'We could go out somewhere.'

'No, I don't fancy eating out. Not from the choice I've seen.'

'What d'you mean, the choice you've seen? You've hardly set foot outside the hotel. You've hardly seen any of it.'

'That's not true and you know it,' Karen says, a little sharply. 'Hardly been in the hotel the last couple of days, what with dolphins and motorbikes.'

'We can eat here, then. I'm not bothered.'

Sandeep stands beside the table, waiting, bending forward slightly.

'Another Kingfisher please, Sandeep,' Steve says, smiling tightly. Sandeep waggles his head. 'Karen?'

'I don't know.' She's scrutinising the drinks menu. 'Probably all rubbish, the cocktails here. How can you expect bloody Indians to make a proper cocktail? Probably water them down, or put God knows what in them. You can't trust them to be clean, can you.'

Steve's head slumps in embarrassment as Sandeep raises his eyebrows. He coughs.

'And madam would like to be drinking?' he says politely. Karen looks up, as if noticing him for the first time.

'Have you got any other cocktails?' she says, her mouth turned down. 'Don't fancy the ones here.'

'I am making special cocktail, madam. If you like, I am making you Goan Surprise.'

'What's that taste like?'

'I am not drinking alcohol madam. But my customers are saying very nice, very good cocktail.'

'What's in it?'

'Secret recipe only, madam. Very special ingredients.'

'One of those, then,' Karen says, offhand. 'And no ice. I don't want any ice in it. Full of germs and God knows what.'

She looks at Steve as Sandeep backs away.

'I'm sure he didn't understand any of that,' she says. 'I'll probably end up with an orange juice.'

*

Iain sits on his bed, elbows on knees, staring at the little white pill on his bedside table. The other one's safely hidden away in his emergency medical kit.

He considers his options.

Take all of it? No, maybe not. Not if what the guy was saying is right. Don't want to be completely out of my tits. Just a bit. A half? Maybe a quarter. Mind you, difficult to break off a quarter. A half, then. Take a half, see how it goes, go out if it's not too heavy. If it is, just stay in and have a thrash.

Iain opens the biggest blade on his Swiss Army knife and cuts the E in two. He wraps one half in a small piece of paper and puts it in his toilet bag. Then he picks up the other half and pops it in his mouth, crunching down on it, his mouth immediately soured by the violent flavour of chemicals. He grabs his water bottle, taking long, urgent gulps from it, stopping for a moment, then drinking again, trying to wash the taste away.

He reaches for his cigarettes, Gold Flake, lighting one, inhaling deeply, face grimaced. He takes another gulp of water, then moves back on his bed, leaning his head against the white-washed wall. And he waits.

*

Sandeep's put most of the ingredients in. The white rum, the coconut milk, a dash of fenny, the cream, the liquefied banana. Just one more thing before mixing.

Bloody woman. Coming here and treating Indians like that. Speaking to him in that way. And him with a Bachelor's degree in accounting. More educated than her, for sure. Looking down her snooty nose, just because he's a waiter with a dark skin.

He checks that no-one's looking. Some more guests have come down from their rooms, but they're far away, out in the garden. Sandeep ducks down behind the bar, grabs a knife that he's been using to slice limes, and starts scraping out his toenail cheese He tips his prized harvest into the cocktail glass, dribbles in some spit for good measure, then stands up to assemble the other ingredients.

Three and a half minutes later he places Karen's Goan Surprise with its special ingredients carefully in front of her, before taking an opener from his waistcoat pocket and popping Steve's Kingfisher bottle, pouring the beer into a new cold glass.

Karen takes a sip of her drink through a straw, approaching it a little tentatively.

'Ooh, that's lovely, that really is,' she says to Steve, holding the glass out to him. He shakes his head.

Sandeep inclines his head slightly, watches Karen take another sip of her cocktail, and moves away from the table, a thin smile of satisfaction on his face.

*

Iain's left leg is working to the thud of drums, his head bobbing with every thrash of guitar. He's sitting on the edge of his bed, smoking, foot going, earphones blaring 'The Bartender and the Thief' by the Stereophonics, live at Cardiff Castle.

Nothing better, he thinks. A modern classic. Once they get past the first slightly ropey verse, it's one of the greatest live performances ever. Just a guitar, bass, drums, and Kelly's raw, clean voice stripped of technique until there's only passion left. That's all you need. The beauty of simplicity. Four simple things gelled together into a song you'd be glad to see the world end to. But best on earphones, hearing the layers of sound, the position of each instrument, the surging power of it playing in different spaces inside your head.

The song ends to cheers, and Iain immediately hits the rewind button on his personal stereo, wanting to hear it again, even though he knows 'Jesus Says' by Ash follows it on his homemade compilation tape. 'Jesus Says', one of his favourite songs for years, a brain-mincing hero of a classic which he thinks everyone should listen to loud on earphones at least once a day.

He hits the play button a couple of times, but it's not at the right bit. He wants to hear it right from the start, from the introduction when Kelly Jones says to the crowd, 'this is a new song. This is called the Bartender and the Thief'. And then someone in the crowd, in the lower right part of Iain's head shouts 'never 'eard of it', and then the guitars start thrashing, and before they've hit four beats a scream rises next to where the heckler was, a blood-curdling scream as if the screamer's just seen the devil. Iain loves that bit, loves isolating the individual sounds.

He gets the tape to the right part. He mimes the shout of the heckler, then the open-mouthed scream, and then his head gets into it, his foot gets into it, and it's halfway through the song before he realises he's miming playing the guitar as well, eyes closed, straining through the solo.

He hits the stop button.

'When you start playing air guitar,' he says out loud to himself. 'You know it's time to go out.'

He stands up, crosses to his toilet bag, and takes out the crumpled bit of paper. He pops the remaining half E in his mouth and swallows, following it down with water. Just in case one half isn't enough. Sometimes you gotta go the whole way. Rock 'n' roll.

*

'I fancy another Kingfisher if you're going to the bar,' Steve says as Karen gets up from her chair.

'Actually I'm going to the toilet if you must know,' she says. 'Anway, I think you've had enough of those already. You can wait for whatsisname to come over. I mean, that's their job, in't it.'

'Yeah, too many beers, bad for the digestion,' Steve says. 'Think I'll have a large Honeybee instead. Don't you bother yourself, love,' he says, getting up, unable to keep the sarcasm out of his tone. 'I'll go and get them. After all, that's my job as well isn't it.'

Karen glowers at his back as he walks to the bar where Sandeep's cleaning glasses, then she heads for the stairs to use the toilet in their room. She doesn't trust the toilets downstairs by reception. You never know who uses them, or what you might catch in there.

Steve smiles at Sandeep as he gets to the bar and orders another round. He could go back to the table and wait for Raju to bring the tray over, but he doesn't feel like it. Raju looks busy enough as it is.

Mr Bandodkar, the hotel's assistant manager, walks through the tables in the garden, scanning, holding a piece of paper in his hand. He nods and smiles to a few of the couples sitting there, then sees Steve on a stool at the bar. He walks, slowly but surely, over towards him.

'Mr Harrison,' he says, smiling broadly, holding out the piece of paper. 'A message is coming for you. The boy should be bringing it to you but I am seeing that he has forgotten. So now I am bringing instead.'

'Thank you,' Steve says, his brow creased. A message?

He unfolds the paper, which has his name written on it in rounded capitals. Immature writing, he thinks. Blue biro.

To Steve Harrison

I saw the poster and thought you would want to know this. The Henrik your wanting information about killed Sophie. I heard them fighting and him killing her. I cant say my name because I got to protect myself and hope you understand. Since your interested I thought you should know and something gets done about this because she was a lovely girl and it didnt deserve to happen. Sorry but I think that Henrik has done a runner.

No signature. Steve reads it quickly again, his heart pounding. A witness. There's a bloody witness. He jumps off his seat and jogs after Mr Bandodkar, catching him by the arm.

'Who brought this,' he says, waving the paper at the assistant manager.

'I am afraid to say I do not know. I am asking the boy. Come with me please.'

They walk over to reception, Steve setting the pace in urgent strides. Mr Bandodkar asks the grey-jacketed house boy standing next to the reception desk a few questions, then the boy disappears through a door at the back.

'Just wait one moment, please,' Mr Bandodkar says. 'Please, sit down.'

He gestures to the cushioned chairs, but Steve stays standing.

'I need to know who brought this and when,' he says, his voice and face firm, determined.

'Just one moment, please,' Mr Bandodkar repeats. He's getting worried. He hopes the hotel hasn't made a big mistake. Mr Harrison seems very vexed.

The first boy brings back another, who's immediately barraged by quick-fire questions from the assistant manager. The boy's replies are quiet, indistinct, rarely more than a few words. Mr Bandodkar goes on at length in a harsh, interrogative tone. Finally he turns to Steve.

'It was brought about one hour ago,' he says. 'Maybe longer. The boy cannot say. By a female Western girl. Not a guest of this hotel.'

'What did she look like?'

Mr Bandodkar interrogates the boy again.

'He is just saying Western girl,' he says. 'Young girl. This is all he is saying.'

The girl. The one who came into the hotel and went straight out again. Steve tries to remember her face. Did he even see it properly? Mr Bandokar's still talking.

'Please accept sincere apologies. I hope this is not urgent message.'

'Yes,' Steve says, clipped, putting the note in his pocket. 'Very urgent.'

'Boy is saying he did not know it was urgent. I am telling him it is none of his business, that he should be bringing note to you at once. I am sorry. He is lazy and stupid. I would sack him, but he is my brother's boy. What am I to do? He is so stupid no-one else will employ him. Again, please accept our sincere apologies.'

But Steve's not interested. Plans reel in his head. A witness. One who'll confirm that it was definitely Henrik.

He nods at the assistant manager, who's still making apologetic noises and cuffing the house boy on the ear.

He strides to the bar, downs the rough double Honeybee brandy with a grimace, then sets off at a brisk pace along the path towards the hotel entrance. Karen comes back down the stairs just in time to catch a quick glimpse of his white shirt as he passes through the gates and sinks into the murky gloom of nighttime Goa.

*

Jez is hanging back amongst the trees, away from the light. Watching. Waiting. It doesn't take long. His eyes follow Hassan as he puts the last of the sarongs and brass figures from his stall into the hut and locks the door, pulling on the padlock to make sure it's firm. Then he and one of his stall-holder mates walk up the path towards the village. Jez follows, keeping his distance, staying out of sight in case Hassan looks around.

It's a risk, but sometimes you gotta take them. Especially when there's principle at stake.

Hassan and the other man stop at a flat-roofed concrete

house. Lights are on inside. The men exchange a few words, then Hassan goes in without knocking while his mate walks away, heading further in to the village. Jez waits a couple of minutes before getting closer to one of the shuttered windows. This is the dangerous bit. This is where it could all go tits up.

He edges nearer. Voices chatter from the room, set against a backing tape of Bollywood screeching. Jez keeps his head low. The shutter's not closed, and if he gets his angles right he'll be able to see without being seen. He ducks back as a shadow crosses the shutter, ready to run if someone looks out the window.

They don't. Jez creeps nearer again, keeping close to the wall on the dark side of the house, craning his neck forward until he can see through a crack in the shutters. And then sees what he hoped for. Hassan sitting at a table, talking to a middle-aged woman, probably his wife. In the background, on a settee, a boy and a girl, both teenagers.

Got you, you fucker, Jez says to himself, his face hard as stone. I know where you live.

*

Iain's on the edge of the makeshift dancefloor in Pandora's. His feet are into it, wanting to dance, but the rest of him doesn't. He just wants to stand there, getting into the music, watching the scene. He grins. It's an absolute blast.

He's been buzzing for the last couple of hours, greedy for experience, hopping from bar to bar checking out the people, chatting to strangers, humming with life, dancing, caning it. He's consciously trying to stop himself licking his teeth, downing Kings beer to wash his mouth out, take away the thirst.

Very speedy, he thinks. Very speedy, but there you are. Not

sure it's anything extra special. Not worth more than a tenner, definitely. Still, that's the way it goes sometimes.

He decides to move away from the dance area and watch the people in the bar for a while. He scouts around for a good place to sit and chill out. There's a small table nearby with only one person sitting at it. Iain thinks he's seen him before but can't think where. He goes over. The man's staring down into a tumbler. Looks like whisky. A half-empty Kingfisher bottle stands beside it.

'Mind if I sit here a minute, mate?' Iain says, loving the sound of his own voice, the reverberation of it in his chest.

Steve looks up, taking in Iain at a glance.

'No. On you go,' he says, glancing at the empty seat, then staring back down into his glass.

Iain sits down, putting his own squat Kings bottle next to the pint-size Kingfisher.

Brandy, he decides. The man's drinking brandy. Too dark for whisky. Probably that Honeybee shit. They say it's got amphetamines in it, but who knows. Mind you, it could be whisky. Some of those Indian brands only have a slight resemblance to the real stuff anyway. What was that one he had in Jaipur? The barman in the hotel was dead proud of it. Said it was the nearest that Indian whisky got to Scotch. Even had some real Scottish blends in it, he said. Whatever it was called, the barman was dead proud of it. It tasted like creosote.

Brandy. It looks like a double the man's drinking. Big peg. Or not drinking. He's just staring at it.

Steve suddenly picks up the glass in his right hand and swallows the brown liquid in one go. He puts the empty glass down gently, then picks up the Kingfisher bottle in his left hand and starts glugging at it, drinking until he has to come up for air, finishing about half of what was left.

The performance delights Iain.

'You should watch that,' he says, grinning. 'Keep on drinking like that, you're in danger of getting drunk.'

Steve's face slips into a sardonic smile and Iain suddenly recognises him. The guy from the beach. The one who was with the Goddess. And that other woman. The guy from the beach, but with his clothes on. That's why he didn't recognise him. Fit looking bastard.

'I think I'm already into the drunk bit,' Steve says.

Very drunk, Iain thinks. Still able, in control, conscious, but very drunk. He can see it in his face, the tired eyes, the sloppy movements.

Steve takes another drink of beer. Hours of searching have done him no good. No sign of the girl anywhere. Nothing to do now but sit in Pandora's and wait. Wait, rage inside, feel helpless, and get very, very drunk.

'You don't see many people drinking heavily in here,' Iain says, then wonders why he said it and tries to backtrack. 'You see some. I'm not saying it's weird or anything. I mean, I respect a good, heavy drinking session. It's in my blood. Born into it. Part of the culture.'

Steve can't work out if there's a question in there somewhere and he can't be bothered trying to find it. The boy's talking nonsense. Still, seems harmless enough.

'So,' Iain says, keen to change the subject, start another one, letting speedy enthusiasm run away with itself. 'What brings you in here, then?'

Steve looks up, a delayed movement.

'I'm looking for a girl,' he says.

Christ, you're getting a bit greedy, aren't you, Iain thinks to himself. You've had a couple of corkers already. Can't you leave some for the rest of us?

'About five four, maybe a bit taller,' Steve continues, his

head clearing a little, chanting out the task. 'Late teens, early twenties, shoulder-length brown hair with plaits and beads, green, silky-type trousers, and a tight, bluish cut-off top with some writing on it.'

'Christ, you're picky as well as greedy,' Iain says, then can't believe he's said it out loud. Then he's not sure if he did say it out loud. The man's face hasn't changed. It's blank. A hard face, Iain decides. Deceptively hard. An intelligent face. A drunk face. Staring at him, waiting. He wishes Steve would stop it.

'Well?' Steve says. 'Have you seen her?'

Iain shrugs.

'Mate, I see hundreds of them every day. Look around you. Take your pick.'

Iain gestures around the bar, the dancefloor, Anjuna, then licks the back of his bottom front teeth.

'No, it's one girl,' Steve says. 'It's one girl in particular. I don't know her name. But I need to talk to her about something. Very important.'

'Is she one of the ones you've been with on the beach?'

'What?'

'It's just, me and my mate, he's not here at the moment, but he was with me. We couldn't help noticing. First that blonde girl, then the brunette. Or dark hair. I'm not sure it was officially brunette.'

Steve looks away, into the dancefloor middle-distance.

'Dark one's my wife. Blonde one's Sophie. She's dead.'

'She's what? *Dead*?' Iain's mouth gapes. Not the Goddess, surely?

Steve nods and looks back at Iain.

'Murdered. Strangled. Several blows to the head. Not very nice.'

'Fuck.'

'This girl I'm looking for's got information. Might help send the killer to jail.'

'Fuck,' Iain says again.

'So that's why I need to find her. And I need to find her quick, before everything just slips away.' He lifts the bottle to his mouth again, nearly draining it completely. He wipes his mouth with the back of his hand. 'Except I can't find her. I've looked everywhere, but I can't. So, I'm getting as pissed as I can so that in a few hours I might be able to forget all the shit that's been happening over the last few days, and then I might actually be able to get some fucking sleep.'

The sudden intense tone surprises Iain. The single, serious, direct concentration of the words, an angry frustration breaking through them. An angry man on a mission. All very heavy. He's not sure he wants to get mixed up in it all.

'Well, good luck mate,' Iain says, standing up. 'I'll look out for her. Let you know. Gotta go. Gotta mingle.'

Iain dances, swerving through the crowd of people, relieved to get away. Too intense. Too much to handle. He stops when he reaches the other side of the bar. Safe. Then he decides he wants to dance and wanders back into the centre of the action.

But fuck. The Goddess, dead. Murdered. Maybe the man's just bullshitting, the drink talking. Maybe it's not even the same guy. He could be talking about someone completely different. But it is him, definitely him. Christ, it's unbelievable. Murdered. Shit, maybe he's the guy who did it. Maybe he's looking for the girl because she knows he did it and he's going to kill her as well. But the Goddess, dead. It doesn't seem real. She never really seemed real either. Nothing is real. Strawberry Fields. Keep on dancing, it's all too heavy.

Steve catches the arm of a passing waiter who's been collecting bottles and gives him plenty cash to bring more brandy and beer. He waits, furrowing his brow.

That kid who was sitting there. Must have only been a few years younger than him. Yet there he was, thinking of him as a kid. When did he, Steve Harrison, suddenly start getting so old? He shrugs to himself. When parts of him started dying, probably.

As Iain's dancing he sees Barney and India come in. He tries to decide whether he should go over and see them or not, but he can't. He takes the indecision as a sign that inaction is the best policy, so he continues to bounce away for a while, turning his back to them. When he eventually stops, he checks where they are first before going to stand at another part of the bar. He's in no mood to be a gooseberry.

He picks a spot where he can watch them, though. They're sitting with what Iain assumes are India's friends. Ravey types. Crusty types. Probably all went to the same posh English private school. Somewhere in the Home Counties. Wherever the fuck that is. Probably all went to the same school as Barney. Keeping it in the family, as the English, moneyed middle classes tend to do.

No, maybe that's not fair. Barney's not like that. Or maybe he is. Maybe it's that old con trick, the Scottish accent, that fooled him. The great leveler, making Iain a social enigma to the English as far as class is concerned. Maybe Barney's first impressions of him would have been completely different if he'd spoken with a Barnsley accent or a Nottingham one. Maybe his reaction wouldn't have been the same. Maybe his own reaction would have been different if Barney had spoken with a severe Glasgow accent, or one of the silly, sing-song Western Isles ones. What the fuck. It's all just headmince anyway. None of it matters all that much.

Barney and India only stay for half an hour. When they leave, Iain dances around again, talking to a couple of people for no reason, just buzzing, speeding along. He's talking to a lad from Middlesbrough when the fight breaks out.

A tall man with long blonde hair is on the floor. Steve's got his arm pinned halfway up his back.

'Got you, you fucker!' he shouts at Henrik over the music, screaming it. 'You're *fucked*! You're *fucked*!'

And he doesn't know why he does it or why he can't stop himself but he punches down hard on the back on Henrik's head.

'*Fucked*!' he shouts, punching again. 'You should fucking *die*!'

He pounds another couple of punches, until someone at the side boots Steve off and he falls to the floor, letting go Henrik's arm. The arm swings, catching him on the nose and mouth, delivering a blast of shooting, red pain. Steve scrambles to his feet and starts kicking. Henrik's still on the ground. A kick to the stomach, a kick to the ribs. He wants to keep on kicking and kicking until Henrik's a heap of crushed bones and flesh. Until he's dead. The only real justice.

Hands yank him back, grabbing his arms, his throat, a couple of punches to his head, people shouting at him. He tries to fight them off, hauling with all his strength, kicking out at Henrik again but missing.

But they've got him. His head's in a lock, his arms are pinned. People are helping Henrik up from the floor.

And it's not Henrik. Even in his drunkenness, through the madness, through the man's bloodied face, he can see it's not Henrik. He'd been sure, so sure it was, but it's not. He's not even all that much like him.

'What the fuck you do that for?' the bloodied man shouts at him, an English accent. 'Fucking prick.'

The man watches, fazed, holding his chest as Steve is dragged towards the door. Steve doesn't struggle now. Most of his strength has gone. He lets them shove him out into the night.

He feels sick, poisoned, out of his head. He staggers into the road, then starts running towards the far light by the crossroads, panicked, scared, stumbling but not falling.

The bar is reeling. The blinding flash of sudden, raw violence has snuffed out the vibe. People are standing around, not knowing what to do, talking excitedly to one another, trying to catch a glimpse of the bloody-faced man being surrounded by his friends. The shock of the aftermath. The music goes on, but everything else has stopped.

'Fucking bummer,' the lad from Middlesbrough says.

'Fucking right,' Iain says back. 'I was sitting next to that guy earlier, the guy who went psycho, I mean. I knew there's was something weird about him, I knew it. He was really tense. It was like, you know, you could tell he was one of those really tense bastards who can only hold it in so much and they blow like one of them pressure cookers but without the bit that controls the steam. Fuck,' he says, nodding to the injured man. 'That could have been me, that bloke there. If I hadn't got up and left once I realised he was a psycho that could have been me. Fucking psychos, I'm fucking telling you. Fucking everywhere. Can't turn your back these days without some bastard sticking a chainsaw through it.'

Pandora's gradually gets back to some kind of normality. People start dancing again, the tension lifts, and the focus of attention wanders away from the group who are now feeding opium-filled chillums to the injured man to dull his pain.

Iain stays another hour, chattering, dancing, speaking to a couple of girls but getting nowhere. He's restless. He wants to do something, even if it's just going for a walk. Maybe he should check out the Primrose up in Vagator. Or maybe go down to Paraiso, see if there's a party brewing. He feels up for an all-nighter.

He downs the last of his warm beer, licks his teeth, and walks out of the bar. A taxi arrives just as he's leaving. The back door opens.

'I have brought a taxi,' Martha says, getting out. 'This is good, because it means we can go quicker, yes?'

Iain looks down the dark road towards Vagator, considering. Then down towards the sea-front. He can't hear any music from Paraiso.

'Why not?' he says. Just a quick one.

The taxi takes them along the back road near his new room. They get out and start to walk through the trees.

'Yes, I discover that you are moving,' Martha says once they're inside, taking her clothes off right away. Iain kicks himself. She's seeing his new place. What the fuck. It's just a quickie. One last hurrah.

'Yeah,' he says. 'Didn't like the toilet in the last one.'

He pulls his shirt over his head and starts getting out of his dusty khaki trousers. He undresses methodically, not in a hurry, not in an urgent frenzy. He puts his clothes, almost neatly, on the room's one chair, then reaches into his toilet bag for his condom supply. Martha lies on the bed on her side, her large breasts falling towards the mattress.

If you could only cut off the face, Iain thinks. Maybe lengthen the legs a bit. Replace the personality, of course. Maybe there'd be something.

'Right,' he says, taking his wristwatch off, becoming fully naked. He gets on the bed next to her. 'I'm very sorry about this, but you're not going to get any foreplay tonight. My hands have had about as much washing as they can take.'

Martha, her head propped up on one arm, glances down at Iain's groin and sighs.

'Well,' she says, eyebrows raised. 'I am ready to begin when you are.'

For a second, Iain's not sure why she seems a little puzzled. He looks down the length of his body.

'Oh,' he says, sitting up.

It's not there. He's feeling horny, but it's just not there. It's not even approaching hardness. In fact, it looks like it's shrunk.

He jumps off the bed.

'Back in a minute,' he says and pads over to the toilet. He locks the door behind him.

He looks down at his crotch. A prawn. Not much better than a flap of skin.

He tugs at his foreskin, trying to lengthen his flaccid cock, wake it up, provoke it into action.

Shit shit shit. No no no, not now. Don't do this to me. Don't do this to me. The dreaded curse of speed. Chemist's droop. The amphetamine floppy.

'Come on,' he says to his groin, teeth gritted, tugging at himself. 'Don't let me down, boy, don't let me down. You can do it, you can do it.'

No response. His cock slumbers on.

'Come *on!*'

He tries again, stretching, jiggling, pulling, tickling, teasing, squeezing. He lets go. It just sits above his tightened scrotum, a useless, pathetic excuse for a member, looking a bit like a penis - only much, much smaller.

He lets out a long, whimpering, desperate sigh, turns to the sink and starts to wash his hands.

CHAPTER TWENTY FOUR

Dislocation

'And still they do nothing,' says Cyril with passion, slapping the front page of the Konkan Times on the breakfast table.

'What's that, papa?' Xavier says, taking a sip of strong black coffee, holding the mug just like a Wall Street hero he saw in a movie.

'The poor girl who was murdered,' Cyril sighs, looking over the top of his glasses. 'Still they are doing nothing, the police. It says it all here. And our great Chief of Police, that pompous fool Tendulkar, all he says is that Goa is safe and that any serious crimes are dealt with firmly and quickly, but he won't comment on the murder because it is not a murder. How can they know? It says that the police have not carried out any tests on the body, so how can they know if it is murder or not? I've never heard so much rubbish. And it says that Tendulkar will personally lead an anti-drugs demonstration at the Flea Market today, to prove how serious he is about fighting crime. Pah! The only crimes he knows about are tax evasion and bribery. You know he accepted a new house from Pereira, the developer?'

Xavier shrugs.

'If it is offered,' he says, 'why not take it? He's not breaking any laws.'

'Yes, but Pereira is. All the time. Building without permits, intimidating people off their land, bribing officials. But has he ever been arrested? No. And I'll tell you why. Because he keeps the police in his pocket by handing out houses and cars and such things.'

'Susegad,' Maria says, putting a fresh cup of tea down in

front of her husband. 'This is too early in the morning to be getting worked up about something you can do nothing about.'

'I know, my love, I know,' Cyril says, calming. 'It is just these fools in the police. And this poor innocent girl. What is happening to this place, I don't know.'

*

Chief Inspector Da Silva lets the phone on his desk ring four times before picking up the receiver.

'Yes,' he barks into it, loosening his collar. When will they get these damn fans fixed properly?

He stops fidgeting as soon as he hears the voice on the other end of the line. Tendulkar himself, the big Chief.

'You've seen the Times?' Tendulkar snaps, not waiting for a reply. 'Other people are also seeing the Times. Which is why I am spending half my time this morning trying to explain to our unhappy Chief Minister why the incompetent fools in my command cannot investigate a simple bloody murder case. What is wrong with you bastards that you cannot even do a simple thing like that?'

'With respect, sir,' Da Silva says carefully, fingering his moustache. 'As I explained to you yesterday, this is not a murder, it is a drowning.'

'I know that is what you said. But for the second day, the Times is calling it murder. Now all the other papers are calling it murder. Now we have foreign journalists calling up about the murder. Why does everyone in the world except you think it is a murder? I will tell you this. Chief Minister Prakash is not a happy man. Even he is calling it a murder. Yesterday I had the Home Minister and the Tourism Minister on my back. But I am telling them, don't worry, my boys have it under control, it is a simple misunderstanding, it will blow over in a day, my best Chief Inspector is handling it. Now I find I would have been better putting a monkey in charge. You are making me look a fool. Chief Minister Prakash is most unhappy about all this bad publicity.'

'But sir, the newspapers, you know how they like to sensationalise things.'

'And I have some sensational news for you. The Chief Minister wants the bad publicity stopped. Before it spreads. Before the place is swarming with European journalists writing stories about Goan police being so incompetent they can't even find their own arses in their trousers.'

'You want me to arrest the editor?'

'Bloody fool! Of course not. Don't you understand anything? Don't you listen to a word I am saying to you? It has been taken out of our hands now. The Chief Minister has been put under pressure from Delhi to get this whole bloody shambles finished with. The French embassy has been asking questions, demanding action. And so, on his own initiative, the Chief Minister has requested a team from the Central Bureau of Investigation. They are on their way from Bombay right now, as we speak. He was telling me 'as a matter of courtesy', he said, although he knows that he should have expressly consulted me first. It should have been my decision, not his, but there's nothing we can do about it now. The CBI are going straight to the morgue to examine the girl's body as soon as they land, which is within the hour. How do you think this makes us look? We are so bad at conducting our own investigations that we have to have the big boys in from Bombay to do it for us, to show us how to do our jobs properly. That is how it looks. Think what the newspapers are going to make of that. This is a bloody disgrace, Da Silva. An absolute bloody disgrace. It should never have come to this. Tell me who was in charge of this case again.'

'Gupta, sir,' Da Silva says. 'From Calangute.'

'I want you to go up there right now and kick his arse hard. Tell him it's from me. I would do it personally, but I've got to prepare for this damn rally in Anjuna. The photographers will be there to see me leading the fight against drugs. This is the sort of publicity we are wanting. Make sure you meet me at Anjuna station after you've kicked Gupta's arse. I want you there when the CBI boys arrive. And make sure they get everything they need, although I cannot for the life of me imagine what help you useless bastards could possibly be to them. This does not look good for us, having the CBI come in to clean up our mess. I am holding you responsible.'

The line goes dead. Da Silva replaces the handset, his ear ringing from the Chief's explosive rant.

He shouts to his assistant to phone Calangute police station to make sure Gupta is there, then get a driver and car ready at the front door immediately. It's time to start spreading the arse-kicking around.

*

Steve is sick. He's sitting in a shaded part of the garden reading the Konkan Times. He should be pleased. He knows he should be pleased. They could have dropped the story after yesterday, but it's a good follow-up, done on their own initiative, with their own research. Quotes from the French Embassy, from the Goan Home Minister's office, from the Chief of Police, more details about the lack of police activity, the absence of an autopsy. The newspaper's done a good job. The pressure's still on. At least the police should be paying a bit more attention now.

He should be satisfied that his plan is working, but he can't concentrate on the page. It's not so much his hangover that's the cause, although he can feel the poisonous ache of it in every part of his body. The problem is his memory.

The foggy, addled events of last night keep soaking his mind with fear, shame and an overwhelming, wretched self-loathing.

Some of the circumstances, the order of events, are muddled up in heat and colours and a heavy mist of Honeybee and Kingfisher. But one memory is clear as day. He'd done it. He'd attacked a man, started putting the boot in when he was down. He'd lost control of himself. The man wasn't even Henrik, but even if it was, it still wouldn't make it right. And since it wasn't, it makes it all the worse. He acted like the very lowest of scum.

What the hell did he think he was doing? He's not a violent man. Not one of those who gets a thrill out of that sort of thing. He's fit, he trains, he can handle himself, but he's certainly no thug. He's never done anything like that in his life before. Violence just isn't a part of his make-up. At least, that's what he'd always thought before. But now. To picture himself there, to know that he'd done it, to remember the man's face dripping with blood and terror, to have every value he holds sacred smashed by the brutal, hard fist of hatred, to know that the potential is there in him somewhere. All his certainties about himself and his character are in doubt. He feels weak. There's no excuse for what he did.

Angry at the pervert on the beach, frustrated at his own inadequacies. Bitter, furious, grief-stricken, tormented. That didn't make any of it right.

A thin, sour sweat seeps out of Steve as he folds the paper and puts it on the table in front of him. He picks up his third cup of sweet tea and, between sips, despises himself.

*

Gone but not forgotten. Iain's body remembers her. He aches

in odd places. Lots of them.

And thirsty. He's so, *so* thirsty. He stretches an arm out from his prone position on the bed, feeling for the plastic water bottle on the floor beside him, grabbing hold of its top. He lifts the bottle up towards his head, but his hand stops in mid-air as he lets out a whine.

'Bastard,' he says with a dry, rasping throat. 'You absolute empty bastard.'

He lets the bottle fall back on the concrete floor where it bounces around for a couple of seconds, mocking him with echoes.

He needs water. He needs water badly. But he's too depressed at the thought of having to pull his pathetic, speed-wrecked body out of bed, into the harsh, painful daylight, and along to the local shop to get some.

Three loud knocks boom into his door.

Christ, she hasn't come back for more already, has she?

Iain seriously considers not getting up, but he knows it's obvious he's in there, and that the knocking could go on all day. He slips on boxer shorts and hauls his legs off the bed with slow, painful effort. He stands, takes a quiet second to get his bearings and balance, then stumbles over to the door, prepared to meet his doom. He's beyond caring any more.

'Hi,' Barney says. 'Sorry. Did we get you up? It's after midday. Thought that'd be safe enough.' India, standing next to Barney, gives him a bright smile.

'After midday?' Iain says, absently scratching a mosquito bite on his arm, his face creased in pain and exhaustion. 'Great. Means I've had nearly three hours sleep. Fantastic.'

'Long night?'

'The longest of my life. D'you know,' he says, leaning forward, dipping his voice so that India can't hear. 'I think my right forearm's been dislocated. Can you dislocate a forearm? Or a wrist or something?'

'Don't know,' Barney shrugs. 'India, darling? Can you dislocate a forearm?'

'Well,' she says, cocking her head to the side, her voice light and happy but her brow furrowed in concentration. 'You can get it out of alignment. But that's probably just a reaction from your liver.'

Nice midriff, Iain thinks.

'My liver?' he says.

'Yeah, you're probably storing up some negative emotions in it. You've created a blockage and the negative energy's trying to force its way out through your arm. Except it's put your arm out of alignment, so all the bad energy's being directed back into your liver.'

'Oh, I don't think my emotions would be too keen on spending any time near my liver at the moment.'

'Does it hurt, your liver?'

'I suspect so,' Iain says, hands on his hips, arching his back. 'Everything else seems to. It's difficult to isolate any one particular pain. It's more like a 'whole body' sort of pain at the moment.'

'This could be very serious,' India says, taking Iain's elbow, turning him so she can see his naked back.

He suddenly feels very self-conscious. 'Could have knocked all your energy centres out of place,' she adds. 'You need some serious treatment. You might need weeks of shiatsu to sort all that out.'

Iain folds his arms, then cricks his neck from side to side, trying to loosen it up.

'I think I'll settle for a long weekend in a detox unit. Or maybe just a few days staying in with water and vitamin pills. Anyway,' he says, trying to brighten up but failing, 'if you've come round to go for lunch somewhere, you're going to have to count me out. I think my body's just about to burst into a million droplets of quivering jelly.'

'Er, no, actually,' Barney says. 'We're off.'

Iain notices for the first time that both Barney and India are fully dressed, kitted out for the road rather than the beach or the market. Travelling gear. Two backpacks and a smaller day-pack lean against his outside wall.

'Oh,' he says, trying not to look and sound surprised and shocked. And failing. 'Right.'

'Yes, we're going to head up to Bombay,' Barney says. 'Up to Ahmedabad, then over into Gujarat.'

'Oh, right,' Iain says, trying to be as enthusiastic and happy for them as he can be, trying to dig up some sincerity from the wreckage of his being.

'Gujarat. Nice one. Should be good. Gandhi country.'

'Is it?' India says, wide-eyed. 'Well, as long as we don't get attacked by any of them, I don't mind. That bit's his idea.'

She points a triple-ringed finger at Barney.

'Oh, I'm sure you'll be perfectly safe,' Iain says. 'There aren't too many Gandhis lurking in the jungles of Gujarat anymore.'

'Can I use you loo?' India says. 'Baba said I'd be able to use your loo.'

Both India and Iain look at Barney, Iain's eyebrows raised.

'Of course,' he says.

'Thanks. Baba says you've got a real English loo. I've been squatting for weeks. I'm fed up with it.'

'An image I wouldn't have conjured up for myself,' Iain says, standing aside for India to pass. 'But one which, I'm sure we can all agree, is oddly powerful.'

India smiles at him as she passes. Iain waits until he hears the toilet door locking.

'Baba?' he says. 'She calls you Baba?'

'Don't blame me. I didn't ask her to.'

'And what was all that about being attacked by Gandhis, for God's sake? What, she thinks there's packs of little old men in white sheets and glasses running around the countryside mugging tourists non-violently?'

'Yes,' Barney drawls, smiling. 'That was a bit of an unfortunate one. I'm sure it's a perfectly innocent mistake, though. Maybe there's some particularly vicious animal called something that sounds like Gandhi.'

'Oh, come on.'

'She's not that bad, really she isn't. She knows a lot more about this country than you'd think. She surprises me sometimes.'

'And what was all that stuff about my energy being out of alignment, and my liver and all that? What's that got to do with a middle-aged German hygiene freak using my arm as a dildo?'

'Oh, not her again. Why on earth did you let her do that?'

'I had to. I had Chemist's Droop.' He looks down at his boxer shorts and shakes his head. 'I didn't have anything like a baby's arm down there. More like a baby's penis.'

'So she used you as her personal marital aid.'

'With everlasting batteries, as far as she was concerned.'

'What a terribly ugly thought.'

'It was a very ugly reality. But that's it. No more.'

There's an awkward silence between them for a few seconds.

'So,' Iain says. 'Why you leaving so soon?'

'Oh,' Barney says, waving his hand vaguely. 'I'd always intended to leave around this time anyway. I just hadn't quite finalised specific plans, dates and so on. Besides, India says we need to go now. Something about the moon rising in Mercury, or the sun's in retrograde, or the cat's in the cradle. Something along those lines.'

'Oh, come *on*!' Iain says, grinning in disbelief.

'I know, I know,' Barney says back with an even wider smile, lowering his voice, worried that India might hear through the toilet window. 'But she's so terribly, terribly sweet. I can't help it. I'm not going to get into a huge discussion with her each time she comes out with something like that. And it's interesting. In a way. I've never spent any time with someone like her before. I'm learning things. And aside from anything else, she says she's going to teach me something tantric.'

'Ah,' Iain says, nodding and smiling. 'I don't know about its spiritual worth, but I know it involves a lot of nudity for a long time.'

'Exactly.'

The toilet flushes. Both of them stop the giggles that are threatening to break out.

'So,' Barney says. 'We're off then.'

He takes a piece of paper out of his pocket and hands it almost apologetically to Iain.

'Here's my address and things. Dates when I'll probably be back in the UK. You know, if you're ever in the area and all that.'

Iain takes the paper, looking at the neat capitals.

'I'd give you mine,' he says, 'but I don't have an address at the moment. It'll be either London or Edinburgh, but I won't know until I get back.'

'Whatever,' Barney says. 'Drop me a line. Let me know how it's going.'

India comes out of the room, brushing her hands down her sides. She goes over and hugs Barney.

'Ready?' Barney says to her. She smiles and nods.

Iain helps them on with their backpacks, then hands Barney the small day-bag.

'So what about you?' Barney says. 'When are you off?'

'Och, a couple of days, maybe. Once I feel better. Get down to Bangalore, then Mysore. There's a Maharajah's palace there with these iron pillars my grandfather helped make in a foundry near Glasgow. Must have been when he was about our age. I thought it would be nice to see them. He died years ago.'

'Well,' Barney says. 'Good luck in finding them. It's a tremendous place.'

Iain and Barney shake hands, and India gives Iain a delicate kiss on the cheek. The couple turn to go, then India spins back around.

'By the way,' she says. 'D'you know you've got a fat old German woman crashed out in your shower?'

'What?!' Iain's jaw drops.

India giggles.

'He told me to say that,' she says, smiling sweetly, pointing at Barney. 'Did I say it right, Baba?'

'From the look on his face,' Barney says, laughing, 'you couldn't have said it any better.'

'Bastard,' Iain says, releasing a smiling sigh of relief.

The couple wave at him and walk away.

'What's it mean, anyway?' India says to Barney.

'Trust me. You don't want to know.'

Iain watches the backpacks bob along the lane and turn the corner. And then they're gone.

*

'Mr Harrison? Mr Harrison, sir? I am sorry to be disturbing you.'

Mr Bandodkar is standing next to Steve's table, trying to smile but looking uncomfortable. Steve glances up at him.

'Mr Harrison, there is a visitor for you in reception area.'

Steve rises quickly out of his chair. Maybe it's the girl.

'But I am not certain that he is a very desirable visitor, sir.'

He?

'Who is he?' Steve says, starting to walk towards reception, Mr Bandodkar doing a waddling jog after him.

'He is not giving his name. But I am knowing this type. I would not be allowing him into the hotel, but he is requesting you by name. I would be very careful of this visitor, sir.'

A very thin Indian man with a sunken face, unkempt hair and tired, worn clothes stands leaning against the reception desk, a cheap cigarette in one hand and Steve's homemade poster in the other. Mr Bandodkar, with polite distaste, indicates that this is the visitor.

'You're looking for me?' Steve says. 'I'm Steve Harrison.'

The man focuses yellow and red tinged eyes on Steve. He smells of cheap alcohol.

'This yours?' the man says, holding out the tattered, poor quality photocopy. Sophie's stark, black and white face stares out from the paper.

'Yes. You've got some information about it?'

Steve waits, but the man says nothing.

'Well? What is it?'

The man takes a draw on his cigarette.

'Is saying reward. How much you are paying?'

'Depends on the information. If it helps, then yes, of course there's a reward.'

'One thousand rupees,' the man says, hissing the words out.

'Possibly. If the information's good.'

'You give me one thousand rupees, I tell you information.'

'That's not the deal. You tell me the information, and if it helps, you get a reward.'

'No,' the man says, and begins to walk off.

'Wait,' Steve says, stepping to block the man's path. 'Okay, if you've got information, I'll pay you.'

'How much you are paying?'

'I'll give you,' Steve rummages in his pocket, 'one hundred rupees now, then maybe more if the information leads to something.'

'Okay,' the man says, reaching for the note.

'Information first,' Steve says, snatching the note back.

'Money first. No money, no information.'

Steve swears to himself and hands over the cash. The man looks the note over, then stuffs it in his pocket. He puts the poster on the reception desk and smoothes it out. He points to Henrik's name.

'This one,' he says. 'Disappearing one. Ashram is going.'

'Which ashram?'

'Maybe somewhere Tamil Nadu. I am hearing these things.'

'Who told you?'

'I cannot say this.'

'I need to know which ashram.'

'Ashram,' the man says, closing his eyes, nodding slowly. 'This one, she is ashram going.'

'She? That's a 'he'. A man.'

'She, he,' the man shrugs. 'Ashram going.'

'I need to know which ashram,' Steve says slowly, trying to be patient, knowing now he's being conned but determined not to lose his temper.

'I am not knowing which ashram. One thousand rupees, maybe I am knowing.'

'What's going on, Steve?'

Karen's standing off to the side of him. He doesn't know how long she's been there.

'Nothing love. Just sorting a couple of things out.' He turns back to the man. 'Get out. Don't come back unless you've got some real information.'

Karen walks over to the reception desk and snatches up the poster. She reads it quickly, paying particular attention to the photograph.

'This her, is it?' she says sharply, not looking up at Steve.

'Yes.'

'I thought we'd agreed you were finished with all this.'

'It's only asking for a bit of information. So I can pass it on to the police.'

'Yeah, but all this,' Karen says, flapping the paper. 'Did you make this? Posters, for God's sake? Giving out your name, where we stay? I suppose you've been handing them out all over Goa. I don't know what people'll be thinking.'

'It's just in bits of Anjuna.'

'In fact I'll tell you what people'll think. They'll think my husband's gone soft in the head, that's what they'll think. Look what you've done. You'll have every beggar in Goa queuing up here next.'

'I'm just trying to help.'

'You're the one who needs help. There's something wrong with you, Steven,' Karen says, her voice rising, taking on a nervous edge. 'We come away on holiday and all you can do is sneak off investigating some made-up crime. Is that normal? Is it? I'd really like to know what you think, because I don't think it's normal at all. Something weird's been happening to you. I don't know what it is, whether it's work or what, but I don't know where your mind's gone because it's certainly not on me or this holiday.'

'But these posters are from days ago, love.'

'And what have you been doing in the meantime? While my back's turned? I don't know that I can trust you any more, whatever you say. I don't know why you're doing this, but I want you to stop right now, because I'm not sure how much more I can take of this. You're meant to be on holiday with me, not this, this...'

She hits the picture of Sophie. She wants to say more but her tears stop her. She turns and runs up the stairs to their room, locking herself in.

Steve stands dumb. He looks around. The thin man has slithered away, the receptionist is staring at him, and Mr Bandodkar looks embarrassed.

Steve feels sicker than ever, and none the wiser.

CHAPTER TWENTY FIVE

Louts and drug dabblers

There's got to be a way. Iain's convinced. He doesn't know what it is, but he's sure there must be a way somehow. All he's got to do is think practically, rationally, slowly, methodically.

He scans round his room. At the window, at the toilet door, at the door to the bright outside.

There must be a way to somehow padlock his door on the outside, to make it look like he's out, yet still manage to get inside. Make it look like he's out when he's in. So if she comes round he can keep quiet and bluff it out. Hide, if he's being honest with himself.

No way. No way is he ever, ever having sex with the German germ-freak again. Not even if she offers to pay him. Unless it's a lot of money.

He pulls on a clean t-shirt, grabs his sunglasses and goes outside. He examines the door, the barred window, trying to get his cloudy brain in gear.

There must be a way. He takes a closer look at the window, at the boxed metal grill over the angled slats of glass. He could slip the glass out from the inside, but the grill will still be there, fixed to the wall.

Hang on. Fixed to the wall. The grill is screwed onto the outside wall. All he needs to do is take out the glass slats, lock his door from the outside, unscrew three of the corner screws on the grill so that it swings around on the fourth one, then climb in. It'll be easy enough to put the screws back in from the inside, then put the slats back in the window frame.

And if she comes round, Martha will never know that he's

tucked up safely inside. Rock 'n' roll.

It's easy. Or maybe it's too easy. Maybe he's looking at it all from the wrong perspective. Maybe he shouldn't have had that joint half an hour ago.

*

'You stupid cow.'

'But Jez...'

'You stupid, stupid, *stupid* cow.'

'Jez!' Nat shouts at him, knees hunched up under her chin, squatting on a chair in a Flea Market cafe. 'You'd have done it yourself if you had any bleedin' conscience.'

'You unbelievably stupid cow. How could you have gone and done that? What if they think the letter's from me?'

'They won't. I didn't write no names or nothing. I'm not completely stupid.'

'Only about one brain cell away from it.'

He takes a nervous drag of his joint as Nat hits him on the arm.

'I was just telling them,' she says. 'Just so they'd know.'

'They already bleedin' know, don't they. Inspector bleedin' Morse has already been sniffing around asking questions about that Henrik geezer. Saying he killed her, an' that.'

'Well I didn't know, did I. You should have told me.'

'The less you know the better. Bloody liability, you are.' Jez stamps on the ground in frustration. His muscles are tensed, his shoulders tight.

'What if there's a trial or something?' he says. 'What if they want to get me roped into all that? That's about the last bleedin' thing I need at the moment. The pigs come round looking for me, realise who I am, and that's the last you'll see of me. Don't think they'll give much of a fuck about me being a witness. Do you?'

'Well I didn't think of that, did I.'

'You didn't think. That's your trouble.'

'I was only doing what I thought was right.'

'Yeah, well you was wrong, wasn't you.'

Jez gets up.

'Where you going?' Nat whines up to him.

'Not staying around here with you, am I. If someone saw you hand in that letter, which is why they probably set the whole bleedin' thing up in the first place, then I don't want to be sitting next to you when they find you.'

'Oh, Jez!'

Jez makes his way quickly out of the Flea Market grounds, through the thickening crowds, the wandering sellers, the tourists, the scabby beggars, past the stalls, sarongs, statues.

He's jumpy as hell. He wasn't going to come to the Flea Market at all, what with the possibility of running into Hassan or his mates, but he needs to shift more of the ecstasy.

He's only raised about a hundred quid so far, and that won't last long. Coming out into the open means he's already had to hand over a dozen pills to people who'd paid in advance.

And now the chance of selling the rest to the visiting tourists has been ruined.

All because of his stupid girlfriend.

Marvelous. Just bleedin' marvelous.

He pulls a borrowed baseball cap lower over his eyes as he comes out of a corridor of stalls and skips down a short flight of concrete steps onto the beach.

He ignores a couple of young boys asking if he wants a boat to Baga and heads south along the sand, his mind racing, trying to think how to handle the situation.

An Indian man in white shirt, white trousers, slicked back

hair and a small leather bag over his shoulder steps out to block Jez's way.

'You want I clean your ears?'

'You want to keep your teeth?'

*

'Oh, look at that,' Maureen says to Arthur as they walk along the road towards the Flea Market. She gestures at an old man with long white hair and beard wearing a wide-brimmed black hat and waistcoat standing at a crossroads looking puzzled. The Doc's sure he agreed to meet Swiss Dave right at this very spot, but there's no sign of him. That Goddamn memory of his.

'Poor old love's probably lost,' Maureen says. 'I don't think it's right, letting old folk come over here on holiday. It just muddles them up.'

'Too big a shock at their age,' Arthur says.

Maureen walks over and starts speaking loudly and slowly.

'Are you lost dear?' she says.

'Been lost so long don't rightly know if'n I was ever found to begin with,' the Doc says in a mumbling monotone.

'Right,' Maureen says, nodding, smiling as if she understands what he's talking about. 'You're in Goa, love. Are you here alone?'

'A man comes in alone, sure as hell leaves alone. Bit in the middle's the mystery. Better men than me's died trying to find out the secret.'

'Oh, I'm sure you've got plenty years left in you yet,' Maureen says.

She turns to Arthur. 'I don't think he's got all his marbles. Maybe we should get him back to his hotel.'

'Maybe,' Arthur says. 'Mind you, he seems happy enough.'

'Only thing worth pursuing,' the Doc says, nodding. 'That's right.'

'I think it's dangerous, just leaving him in the street like this. He must have got split up from his tour group. His Rep needs shooting.' Maureen turns back to the Doc. 'Have you got a Rep, love?'

'Like you wouldn't believe. A rep bigger'n Texas, and that's a fact. But these kids, don't know nothing. I don't know them, they don't know me.'

'He's lost his Rep,' Maureen says to Arthur, tutting. 'Some of the youngsters they put in charge of these tour groups, I don't know. They haven't got the experience, have they. Where are you staying love? What's its name?'

'Ain't no-one ever said's got a name. Give something a name, changes it into something else.'

'Well,' Maureen says, taking the Doc's arm and leading him along the road. 'You just come along with us while you try to remember. We'll have a nice sit down and a cup of tea in the market, see if it all comes back to you.'

'Always comes back. What goes around, comes around. Might not come back so as you'd recognise it, but it comes right back just the same. Just circles. Everything's circles.'

'Is that right love? I think he's been standing in the sun too long,' Maureen says to Arthur. 'I think he's a bit dizzy.'

*

The Chief of Police preens himself in the back of the white Ambassador car. He wants to look his best.

His uniform is freshly laundered and pressed, his shoes polished, his grey hair oiled and combed. There'll be photographers at the rally, waiting to take pictures of him leading the marchers, making his speech. And reporters, notebooks at the ready, eager to transcribe his words for Goa's nine newspapers.

Oh yes, everyone will see that Goa's police force is taking the fight against drugs very seriously indeed. What does it matter if the people carrying banners and placards are just a bunch of hired goondas doing what they're told? The message is the important thing. And the messenger, of course.

The tourists will see the rally, see him in charge, see the token arrests, and the message they'll take home is that Goa is not a soft touch. A brilliant idea of his, even if he says so himself. Just what the Chief Minister wants.

Tendulkar turns to Chief Inspector Da Silva on the back seat next to him.

'Will Gupta be at this rally? He better be.'

'I expect so, sir,' Da Silva says. He doesn't like having such close contact with the Chief, but Tendulkar insisted they ride together from Anjuna police station. There was no way out of it. Officially, it's Da Silva's patch, after all. 'All officers in Bardez have been ordered to attend. I'm surprised Gupta wasn't at Calangute when I got there. I was told he was earlier when I called.'

'Did he know you were going to kick his arse?'

'I don't think so, sir.'

'If he's at the rally, I'll kick his arse personally. And if he's not, I'll find him and kick it twice as hard. But don't forget, ultimately this is your responsibility. Your arse is the one deserving of the biggest kick.'

'I'm fully aware of that, sir.'

'So you should be. Now that the CBI says it's most definitely murder, there'll be a lot more arse-kicking today. Once the Chief Minister found out, he was threatening to have the whole lot of you sacked. I agreed with him but I talked him out of it, since it would mean having to promote even bigger fools. So just you remember who you've got to thank for still having a job.'

'I'm very grateful, sir.'

'Good. Now, let's see if today's as big a cock-up as you've made of this murder case. It better not be.'

'Everything will be fine, sir,' Da Silva says, praying to every saint he can think of.

*

Steve moves down one of the rows of Western stalls. He's uneasy. He's not sure, but he thinks some of the sellers are on edge too. Maybe they recognise him from Pandora's. Or maybe the mask of hate he was wearing was an adequate enough disguise. It's possible he's just imagining that some of the Westerners are regarding him with more than passing interest. It could just be paranoia. He hopes to God he doesn't run into the man he attacked.

He can't see the girl anywhere. He's been checking all around the market, circling, looking in the cafes, at the stalls, in the tattoo parlour. Not a sign.

He flicks his eyes from left to right, trying to be subtle, wandering through the potential customers, every glance at every stall returned. Paranoia, or maybe not.

The girl. He has to find the girl.

He comes down to the stall where he sat speaking to Sophie just a short, endless week ago. The German woman's sitting behind the tray of jewelry. Steve rakes his memory, trying to find her name. K? Was it K something? Karla? Katrina?

'Hi,' Steve says to her. She looks up.

'Hi.'

'I'm Steve. Remember me from last week? We met. When Sophie was here.'

'Ah yes,' Kristina says and gives him a thin, empty smile. She doesn't offer her name.

'Did you hear about what happened to her?'

'Yes. A dreadful thing,' Kristina says. She shakes her head, her face pinched. 'A beautiful girl like that. So sad. A very dreadful thing to happen. So young.'

'I'm trying to find out where Henrik might have gone.'

'I do not know this name. Who is Henrik?'

'Henrik. Her boyfriend. Surely she must have mentioned him.'

'Ah yes, her boyfriend. But I do not know him. I think I only saw him one time, maybe two times.'

'Do you know where he is?'

Kristina shakes her head.

'Maybe Sophie said something,' Steve says. 'Maybe about where they were planning to go after this? Or where Henrik planned to go?'

Kristina picks up her blue velvet bag and starts to take rings out of it, placing them on the mat in front of her.

'People say so many things,' she says, shrugging.

'And sometimes other people remember them,' Steve says, getting annoyed at Kristina's offhand attitude.

Kristina shrugs again.

'There are so many things to remember.'

'For God's sake, can't you at least *try*? I mean, what the fuck is wrong with you people? Don't you even care that she's dead? Don't you at least want to help?'

'What do you expect me to do?' Kristina says sharply. 'I meet the girl a few times. A sweet girl, but what do you expect me to do? I'm not her mother.'

'I thought, maybe, - hang on while I try to explain this really difficult concept – I thought, maybe you might just be a *friend*.

I thought that maybe you'd want to see the man who killed her put in jail.'

'This is too heavy for me,' Kristina says, waving Steve away, not looking up at him. 'I don't like to think about this.'

'I don't fucking believe you people,' Steve says, his voice getting louder, his blood bubbling. 'All this peace and love and shit you go on about, but then the minute something like this happens, when your supposed friend is lying dead, you just close your minds completely. What, you think that if you ignore it, it'll go away? That you can go around living in this make-be-lieve dreamworld you've got pretending that nothing bad ever happens? Is that what it's about? Your friend, Sophie, is lying dead in some Indian morgue, and not one of you bastards will even raise a finger to help catch her killer. Not one of you. A wonderful, beautiful girl like that, who you all seemed friendly enough with a few days ago, and now she's dead, murdered, and not one of you has the guts to do something about it.'

'Chill out, geezer, yeah?' a man with a goatee at the next stall says. 'It's a bummer, yeah? But what's done is done. You stressing people out about it's not going to change nothing.'

Steve realises that more people are listening now, sellers and customers, although Kristina's doing his best to ignore him, pretend he doesn't exist.

'What sort of friends are you?' Steve rants, almost shouting, frustration firing him. 'When one of your friends dies and it doesn't even seem to bother you? When she's murdered by someone you know, and you're prepared to just ignore it? How the fuck can you live your lives like that? It's all just a game to you lot, all this pretending to be sensitive and understanding and all the rest of that New Age bullshit. When it comes down to it, you're just as selfish and uptight as everyone else. If it doesn't fit in with your perfect little safe and cozy fantasy world you don't want to know. Don't the words 'right' and 'wrong' mean anything to you people?'

Steve's interrupted by a man in dreads sprinting down the row of sellers, bleating one word over and over as he runs, leaps, dodges his way through the tourists.

'Raid! Raid! Raid! Raid! Raid!'

The row bursts into loud activity, people pulling out stashes from their pockets, burying them in the sand by their mats, at the base of palm trees, inside samosas and cakes from the bakery, a furious game of hide the substances, the prize being freedom.

Steve stands, dismayed, his words crushed in the frenetic panic, everything he said lost as a more urgent reality consumes the Westerners. His frustration, anger and depression grip him. And then he sees her. At the end of a row, just standing staring at him, red-faced and guilty. Steve pushes through the crowd towards her, barging past bumbling tourists and scuttling stallholders. By the time he gets to the end of the row, Nat's long gone, disappeared into the hubbub of the market.

*

Chief of Police Tendulkar is pleased with what he's seen so far. A good turnout from the newspapers. The orderly march into the market by a handpicked, chanting crowd of fifty or so. The banners clear and precise. 'No Drugs In Goa', 'Say No to Drugs', 'Goa Against Drugs'. Although he's less sure about the one reading 'Keep Goa Drugs Free'.

And his officers have been demonstrating to the tourists how hard they crack down on suspected drug fiends. No doubt about it. The message is clear; Goa is a safe, clean, respectable place to come to for two weeks and spend a lot of money in. The Chief Minister and the Tourism Minister will be pleased.

Goa's police force in action. Tough on drugs, tough on the causes of bad publicity.

'Remember, no more than ten arrests, okay?' Tendulkar says to Da Silva. 'We don't want to overload the system. Just make sure the arrests are in front of the cameras.'

'My men have their orders, sir,' Da Silva says. 'Anyway, the van can only hold ten so if we catch more than that by mistake then we can always let some go.'

'If you do,' Tendulkar says, adjusting his peaked cap, 'make sure it's *away* from the cameras.'

They watch as four officers lead two long-haired, hand-cuffed Western men away from the market ground, doing it slowly enough for the newspaper photographers to get clear shots. Tendulkar smiles. The day's going well.

When he thinks the crowd of tourists has seen enough firm action to be impressed, he decides it's time for his speech. He nudges Da Silva to introduce him on the megaphone.

Da Silva ushers forward the officer holding the fluted speaker and hand-operated microphone on the end of a coiled cord. He takes hold of the mike, looks at it, clicks the switch on and off a few times, then coughs into it. The sound comes out of the speaker like a pistol shot, making one or two officers jump.

'Ladies and gentlemen, tourists to India,' Da Silva says. 'We are honoured today with the presence of Goa's Chief of Police, Mr V J Tendulkar. He will now speak to you on drugs.'

He passes the handset to Tendulkar, who clicks the switch off and on a few times, then coughs but gets no sound. Da Silva reaches over and flicks the switch on.

'Tourists of Goa,' Tendulkar says. 'What you are seeing to-day is Goan police leading the fight against that most evil of curses in the world today. This evil is drugs. Some of you may be hearing that drugs are not a serious issue in Goa. This is completely untrue and no less than a lie. Goan police are taking drugs all the time in a most serious way.'

It's not an attractive speaking voice, Da Silva thinks. Monotone and staccato. The tinny megaphone speaker doesn't help much. He just wishes Tendulkar had taken the speaking notes he'd tentatively offered him in the car.

'We are showing you how seriously we take drugs. Goan police will crack down on any suspected drug fiends, so that you may have a safe and comfortable time here in Goa. We are dealing with drugs in a most rigorous fashion. You are safe here in Goa. We are working for all you people of the world, making Goa the paradise holiday destination that you can most clearly see that it is. We are working day and night for you, never resting.'

'What about trying to catch murderers?' Steve shouts, standing at the front of a bank of mildly interested tourists.

The Chief of Police pauses, thrown for a second, then continues. Da Silva's eyes narrow.

'As you can see before you today, no-one dabbling in drugs is safe in Goa. If any person thinks that he can come to Goa and take drugs, they are very much mistaken. We are not allowing this to happen.'

'What about murder?'

'The message that Goan police are sending out is that this is a safe place for tourists, but not a safe place for louts and drug dabblers. We are devoting our time to this with utmost priority.'

'What about spending some time trying to catch murderers?' Steve shouts again.

Tendulkar tries to continue, but he's off his stride. He stares, incredulously, at Steve. Who would dare interrupt his speech?

'What about trying to catch Henrik Andersen?' Steve shouts, pulling the poster of Sophie out of his pocket, holding it up above his head, swinging round so that the tourists and photographers can see it. 'He killed this girl, Sophie Lacroix, here in Anjuna less than one week ago. Why aren't Goa's police doing anything about it?'

'Arrest him,' Tendulkar says in a barked aside to Da Silva.

'But sir...'

'Get him away. Arrest him, you fool. The photographers, man. The photographers!'

Da Silva grabs two officers and together they rush Steve.

'We are doing everything we can to fight the drugs menace in Goa,' Tendulkar says into the microphone, trying to regain his composure, keeping one eye on Steve.

'There's no bribes in murder cases,' Steve yells, trying to keep the poster out of the policemen's grasp. 'That's why they're not interested. No money in it for them.'

The three policemen get him to the ground.

'We want you to tell all your friends and family,' Tendulkar says. 'Goa is against drugs. The police are ensuring your safety.'

'Goan police take bribes from drug dealers,' Steve shouts, before one of the officers smacks him across the shins with his lathi. Steve howls, clutching at his legs. Another officer cuffs him, and the three men, led by a sweating, disheveled Chief Inspector Da Silva, pull him to his feet and drag him away out of sight, trying to muffle his shouts. Once they move away from the rallying point, Steve quietens down, offering no resistance. He only hopes the reporter and photographer from the Konkan Times were there. Especially because he tipped off the paper earlier that there might be something happening at the rally to move things along.

Chief of Police Tendulkar glares at the sparse, distracted crowd with dark, burning eyes.

'Thank you for your attention,' he says. 'Demonstration is now over.'

He shoves the microphone into a junior officer's hand, and marches away towards his car. Someone's arse is going to get an almighty kicking for this.

*

Jez scuttles quickly away from the grocery store. He's just bought two plastic bottles full of petrol from the shop, just like any normal scooter rider who's run out of fuel. Nothing necessarily suspicious there.

But he doesn't want to be seen carrying them, not with what he's got planned for later, just in case someone puts two and two together.

He cuts off the road and heads through a grove of palm trees.

The trouble is, he can't take the bottles back to Scabs' house. Too much explaining to do. He's told Crash Mary about what he was going to do, but that's it. And even though Crash wasn't keen on the idea and tried to talk him out of it, he won't spill the beans.

There's hardly anyone around, most people still at the Flea Market. He could always go ahead and do it now, but that would spoil the effect. And it's still daylight. Far too risky.

Jez spots a thick clump of bamboo. That'll do. It's not far from Hassan's house, so he can get it done quickly, once he's done the other thing.

He can see it all in his mind. The night's dark, the music's pumping out from the party, and Hassan at home counting his dirty money.

A sick smile oozes onto Jez's face.

He looks around, making sure no-one sees him dump the bottles amongst the bamboo stems. Then he strolls off south, and he starts to feel that his troubles are coming to an end, that he's on the verge of regaining control of his life. For the first time in days he feels a sense of lightness in his soul. He's so relaxed he starts whistling as he goes. Burn baby burn. Disco inferno.

*

IAIN McMILLAN'S GREAT HINDUSTAN ADVENTURE

Wednesday 6th January '99, Anjuna, Goa

I feel low. I've still got a speed hangover depression from some shitty E I bought off that same old cockney rip-off merchant and I'm not happy. And I've done something really pathetic.

I've managed to lock the outside of my door with the padlock so that if Mad Martha comes around she'll think I'm out. I had to climb in here through the window. It's not as difficult as it sounds, but it is as pathetic as it sounds.

So I've got to stay in here all night unless I want the hassle of messing about with the window again, which, to be perfectly frank, I don't. Since I'm preparing for a night of severe Manali grass abuse I've already bought in crisps and rolls and other munchies and I've got plenty water so I don't really need to go out unless I somehow set fire to the room, which I'm not planning to do at the moment. Although if the depression doesn't lift I might consider it.

I know it seems like I'm going to extreme lengths to avoid the Teutonic Tart, but you don't know her. She's not the type you can just say 'piss off' to. She'd probably think it was some dead funny joke and then order me to scrub my hands. Desperate women call for desperate measures.

Anyway. Barney left today, which was a bit of a surprise. I suppose it shouldn't have been all that odd really because he's been here longer than me, which is probably about as much as any sane person can take of Anjuna. It's just the manner of his leaving which makes it seem so sudden, mainly because I haven't really seen him in the last couple of days. If we'd talked about it, it wouldn't have seemed so sudden. Obviously.

He left with this ravey-chick he met, Trippy Headspace, or whatever her name is. I think he also packed his new found tolerance for all things touchy-feely, which is a major cop-out of the highest order. After all the things we talked about, after stripping down all the bogus nonsense that the self-styled New Age set say they believe in, after criticising all the air-headed, humour-deficient, ironically-challenged style slaves who go around with their heads stuck up their arses, he goes off with the first one who'll let him sleep with her. I thought there was more to Barney than that, but clearly I was wrong. It was all just talk. I'm very, very disappointed in him. And slightly jealous. The girl is very cute, after all. And does tantric things, apparently.

And yeah, I admit it, I'm lonely. Maybe it's just the speed depression, but it seems pretty genuine anyway. And what am I doing about it? Staying in to smoke my tits off in a locked room with a few bags of crisps, some masala peanuts and a couple of bottles of tepid water. Rock 'n' roll.

There's another thing getting me depressed as well, though perhaps it's just magnified by my chemical imbalance. I found out last night that the Goddess is dead. Murdered, to be precise, which somehow makes it seem all the worse. I didn't know her, I'd never really spoken to her, I don't even know her name, but thinking about it today has got me down. I suppose her death shouldn't be any sadder than anyone else's, but at the moment it is. Perhaps it's because she was quite exquisitely beautiful and graceful and, from my distant observations at least, seemed to be a good and happy person. Even without knowing her I felt something for her, although of course I accept it was purely superficial, given that I only once got within ten yards of her. But I watched her, and I don't just mean that I was perving (and it's impossible to think of her in those terms now anyway). I suppose I'd built up a personality for her in my mind based on what I observed, turning her into some symbol of female perfection. A goddess, in short. And to think of someone like that being murdered, to realise that all she stood for can be destroyed so easily, almost carelessly, is quite simply obscene.

When I was told last night, I was so out of my tits that it didn't really register, the blockage aided by the unreality of it all and the fact that the guy who told me was a psycho who later attacked somebody. Now it's sunk in, I'm infected with a loss that I cannot explain. I feel cheated in some way, but not because I thought I stood any chance with her, nothing as shallow as that. And since I didn't know her, I can't really make any claim to be suffering personal grief. Perhaps it's just that with her death an idea has been lost, and an image of goodness, beauty and vibrant youth has been soured and blemished. People like her aren't supposed to die young. Their existence is what keeps the rest of us going.

Apart from grandparents, death has never touched my family, and I've never known anyone young who's died. When you're in your twenties, death seems like a rumour or a theoretical possibility, something that happens way off in the future - if at all. When we're young, we feel secretly immortal. Perhaps that's what I've really lost. Today, wrapped in a cloying speed-hangover, lonely, aching and depressed, burdened with the knowledge of an obscene death, I suddenly feel very mortal indeed.

CHAPTER TWENTY SIX

Leaving it, losing it

'Still no clue, dear?' Maureen says loudly, smiling, raising her eyebrows.

The Matlocks, Clive and the Doc are sitting around a table in the lamp-lit garden of the hotel, sipping drinks after a long dinner of fried chicken, chips, pizza and lager.

'Near sixty year looking at clues enough to turn any man's mind,' the Doc says. 'Every time think you're close, just plain skeets away. That's the mystery. That's why you gotta keep searching.'

'Never mind,' Maureen says. 'I'm sure you'll remember eventually.'

She turns to Arthur beside her. He looks ready for bed.

'Poor love,' she says. 'Letting him out on his own like that. Good job we came along, or God knows where he would be. What we going to do with him? We can't keep him all night. Maybe he's got to take special medicine. At his age and everything.'

She turns back to the Doc.

'Have you got any special medicine, dear? Something you need to take?'

The Doc looks at her from under his brim for a second, then dips his hand into his waistcoat pocket.

'Best in the world,' he says. 'Kind of medicine holds your soul in its hands. Kind of medicine takes you to another place.'

'Maybe you should take some then, dear,' Maureen says, looking at the eight small, flat patterned squares lying in the Doc's palm. 'Might help you remember.'

'Hell, more'n enough for a whole party,' the Doc says, chuckling, handing the tabs out around the table.

'What's this?' Kim says, holding hers up at eye level, scrutinising it.

'Medicine of God,' the Doc says. 'Turns you from Nowhere Man to Superman. One single bound. Makes your mind bigger'n Wyoming. Get on the bus and start ringing that bell. Next stop, Psychedelic City, USA.'

'Best just to humour him,' Maureen says in a loud whisper. 'Can't do us much harm. Old people's medicine. You never know, might even bung us up a bit.'

All five of them copy the Doc's lead, putting the tabs in their mouths, chewing, then swallowing, taking a sip of their drinks to get it down.

The Doc leans back in his chair and puts his hands behind his head, a grin cracking his face.

'Spreading the gospel,' he says. 'Get some of that ol' time vibe working. Y'all hang on tight, now. We's going for a ride. Yes siree.'

*

No phonecalls, no lawyers, no nothing. Hours sitting in a cramped cell in Aguada jail with three other Western men, with no hint of the normal process of law.

On balance, Steve isn't surprised. No rights read, no explanations about why they'd been arrested, although in most cases it seemed pretty clear. All that had happened so far was having to give their names at the front desk, and that was it. Locked up, eight of them, four to a cell, straight afterwards.

The men in Steve's cell hadn't seemed all that keen to talk at first, nerves, fear, maybe even shyness stopping them. But gradually he's been drawing them out, even Enrico the surly Italian who's sitting hunched on one corner of the rope bed that's got to serve all four of them. They're taking it in shifts to use it, two at a time. Sitting next to Enrico is Wolf, a skinny German with long hair and a straggly beard. He's brightened up a lot since they were first put in the cell. He's contributing more to the conversation now, even if his English is somewhat halting and limited. The only other occupant of the cell, sitting on the floor next to Steve, needed the least provocation to talk.

'It's not that bad once you get used to it,' Crash Mary says, looking around the cell, the dirty walls, the damp ceiling. 'You'd pay three hundred a night for this in Anjuna. Not sharing with three others, obviously. But a bit of paint, maybe white, or a very light, subtle green, and yeah, you could make quite a pad out of this.'

'Bit of a problem getting down to your local, though,' Steve says.

'Yeah. If I was paying three hundred a night for this, I'd definitely want the door policy changed.'

The overhead light goes out.

'And electricity beyond,' Steve says, squinting at the luminous dial on his watch, 'eight thirty.'

'Goes without saying.'

All four men are silent in the dark for a while, the gloom of their situation pressing in on them.

'I think that settles it,' Steve says after a while. 'We're in for the night.'

'Maybe,' Wolf says, slowly, precisely, 'we could escape by digging a tunnel.'

'Yeah, but me and Steve'd have to dig it,' Crash Mary says. 'You Germans ain't got the experience of digging tunnels. It was us Brits who did all the escaping from prison camps.'

The men laugh, before falling into silence again. Steve feels he should try and keep the atmosphere as light as he can in the circumstances.

'They'll probably just let us all go in the morning,' he says. 'A slap on the wrist, then send us on our way. I get the impression they're not overly keen on paperwork.'

'I dunno,' Crash Mary says. 'It's a bit weird, this one. Mostly you can get away with paying a bribe if they catch you with something. I tried it with my lot, but they wouldn't have none of it. Very worrying, that. I mean, if you can't trust the Indian cops to be corrupt, who can you trust?'

'So what's the penalty for possession here?' Steve asks.

'For some grammes of hash,' Wolf says, 'it is ten years in prison and a two hundred thousand rupee fine.'

'For a first offence?' Steve says. 'That's a bit steep.'

'Yeah, but it's usually just a couple of years,' Crash Mary says. 'Sometimes you can be in the nick for a couple of years just waiting for the case to come up, and if you manage to get a deal to increase the fine, they just let you go.'

'They are bloody bastards,' Enrico says, spitting the words out. 'Indian police. Pigs. Their mothers are whores.'

'I hope that's not what you're going to give as your statement,' Steve says, causing Crash Mary to snigger.

'I tell them,' Enrico says. 'I tell them to their face, all the bloody bastards. They are sons of bitches. I shit on their whole family.'

'I'm sure it'll be alright in the morning,' Steve says. 'They were just doing the whole thing for show. It wasn't a real raid. You could tell.'

'Well, they found a real tola of Nepalese black on me,' Crash Mary says. 'Which is odd, because when I left the house this morning I only had a little bit of grass on me.'

'They planted the hash on you?' Steve says.

'Course. You should know all about that kind of thing. Part of basic police training the world over, planting evidence.'

'In that case, there's no way they'll go through with it. It's just a stunt.'

'You never know,' Crash Mary says. 'Stranger things have happened. Talking of which, I've still got me grass on me if anyone fancies a smoke.'

'Ja.'

'Si, si!'

'Might as well.'

*

Iain stabs out the roach of yet another joint. He's safe. He's happy. He's out of his tits.

In the darkness of his room he feels for his personal stereo, his thumb seeking out the volume control, edging it up slightly. Cerys Mathews of Catatonia purring and yelling and pleading her way through 'Road Rage', losing her mind. The proper album version, not the disgracefully truncated summary of a song which was released as a single.

Iain smiles in the dark. The only sexy Welsh voice ever. A voice husky with bourbon and Gauloises. He doesn't know if she smokes or what she drinks, but that's what it sounds like anyway. A voice smeared with the promise of enthusiastic, gasping, sweaty sex. An arrogant sensuality. Maybe he needs to get out more.

Iain giggles to himself. The line's coming up. It always gets him, the line, especially when he's had a smoke. 'Come here,' Cerys purrs at him. 'You can leave it late with me'.

And there's only one thing, just one thing Iain can ever think of when he hears the line. He can see it, Cerys lying back on white sheets, deliciously naked, one knee slightly raised, one hand behind her tousled hair, her face a little flushed, her body sheened with a thin layer of sweat, singing that line to him, and him getting on top of her and leaving it late, right to the last, critical, euphoric moment.

Oh God, he thinks. Time for a quick emergency one.

*

Karen sits on the edge of her bed, legs crossed, arms folded, fuming.

So it's like that, is it? He's off on another late bender, is he? Met another floozy, has he? And not even the decency to come back to the hotel first.

Very mature. Very mature indeed for a grown man. Well he's in big trouble now. Big trouble. If he thinks I'm letting him off lightly this time, he's got another think coming. I've been patient with him up to now, but this is it. He's going to pay for this when we get back home. I'm not going to let him forget this for a long time.

Leaving me here to eat dinner on me own. I'll get him back for it.

Karen unclips her watch, puts it carefully on the bedside table, and starts to undress.

Well, if he thinks I'm waiting up half the night for him, he can forget it.

In the bathroom she cleans off her make-up, moisturises her face, cleans her teeth thoroughly, and goes back into the bedroom, climbing under the single sheet.

Part of her wants to read, but she doesn't have any magazines left. Besides, she wants to be asleep when Steve comes back, so he can be blamed for waking her up as well. She's not going to forget this in a hurry. Not on your life.

She waits five minutes more, staring at the wall, then reaches over and switches off the light.

*

The party's pumping. Old ladies pour out the tea, chillums pass around, colours blare from lights in the trees, and the music keeps on pulsing out. The vibe is sweet. People can feel it. They're feeding off it, sucking it up.

Jez lies on a mat, head in a forgiven Nat's lap, smoking a weak joint. She strokes his stubbly crown.

He's going through it in his mind again, working out how much cash he needs to last a couple of months. After off-loading some of the Es to punters at the party, if he manages to get hold of another two hundred and fifty quid, that should just about do him.

Two hundred and fifty. Difficult, but do-able. Okay, no pissing about with dodgy gear. Just cold hard cash and anything blatantly valuable. With a bit of luck he should be able to do it in three or four houses. And then, as a farewell present, a Kashmiri bonfire. Teach them bastards a lesson they won't forget in a hurry. Anyone who thinks they can get one over on Jez the Man has got another thing coming.

He takes a look down at Nat's watch. It's nearly time.

'Going for a slash,' he says to Nat, pulling himself to his feet. He walks between the mats, avoiding staggering Israelis, young, out-of-it English girls, crashed out Germans. And the Italians, of course. He's already marked the fact that some of his targets are at the party, with no sign that they plan to leave for at least a few hours.

As he skirts the dance area he stops, looking again to make sure his eyes aren't lying.

A straight, middle-aged fat couple dancing, caning it as

much as the rest, eyes closed, grinning like maniacs.

'I can hear shapes,' a bobbing Arthur says over to his wife, blissed out. 'You've got to try and hear the shapes.'

'The colours,' Maureen says, laughing. 'The colours.'

Jez shakes his head and moves on, around the edge of the dancers, past the trestle-table bar, and out into the dark.

Back in the party, Clive sits cross-legged on a mat next to the Doc, staring open-mouthed at a palm tree five feet away, its trunk covered in day-glo paint. He suddenly sits up straight, yanks the cotton wool from his ears, and turns to the Doc.

'I've just realised,' he says, eyes wide in rapture. 'Everything's connected. You, me, the tree. It's all connected.'

The Doc cackles.

'Welcome to the real world, son.'

Kim and Angela are sitting on the mat beside them. Kim's face is blank, dumb, her mouth hanging slightly open. Angela prods her on the knee.

'D'you think we'll go back to Tenerife next year?' she says in a bright, happy voice. 'I like Tenerife.'

Kim slowly drags her eyes around to look at Angela with no clear hint that she's heard what she said. Kim lifts her hand, looking down at it as it twists in the coloured, flashing lights, watching the patterns it makes at it gradually moves over and delicately, precisely, pokes Angela's knee three times.

Angela stares at her a second, starts giggling hysterically, stops, then falls over on her back.

Jez walks steadily, not fast but not holding back. The party's quite far from the targets, which is good in one way, but it means a hell of a schlep. Still, better safe than sorry.

He gets to the room and grabs the things he needs, then starts the scooter he blagged off Scabs earlier. He sets off, taking the long route, the smaller, winding dirt roads around the edge of the village. After fifteen minutes driving he parks by a clump of trees, takes a crumpled cloth bag from the locked compartment on the scooter's steering stem and removes his small, plastic torch.

He lets his eyes adjust, then moves through the trees, sometimes getting tangled in low branches, tripping over exposed roots, stumbling into potholes in the sandy earth. He'd prefer to use the torch but it's too dangerous. For inside work only.

He crosses a ditch filled with crushed plastic bottles, dried out palm leaves, empty oil cans and cardboard, trying not to make a noise. He traces his path carefully, taking it slowly, listening out for sounds of habitation. The targets are near. In the distance he can still hear the throb of music, the vibe still flowing.

In a couple of minutes he's at the targets he's already checked out, but he does it again anyway, circling them, making sure no-one's in, that it's safe. The lights are all out. Time to go to work.

The first padlock, a cheap Indian make, snaps under one twist of his metal bar, popping open with a brief, tinny clatter. Jez puts in on the ground and creeps inside. He works quickly by torchlight, checking bags, clothes, under the mattress. One hundred and twenty dollars, a shortwave radio, a watch and some coloured stones. Maybe semi-precious, maybe not. He decides to leave them. The cash goes in his pocket. Everything else goes in the bag.

The same make of lock, the same result on the second target, but the pickings are slim. Thirty dollars and an Italian credit card. He takes it anyway, even though he doubts he'll be able to use it. Maybe he can sell it to someone who can.

He pauses at the door, checking that there's no-one around before going back outside. One more room in this row, then move onto another area.

Shit. A Yale lock on the third target. Too much hassle. Too much noise.

He moves around to the back of the building to reconfirm what he already knows. He risks a brief blast of the torch, shining it up at the low roof just to make sure. Easy. He stands on a low wall to get balance, and carefully, quietly, slides out six large red tiles, placing them on top of the wall. Then, gripping a wooden beam, he hauls himself up and slips through the hole feet first, the torch between his teeth like a high-tech pirate.

His feet touch a mattress and he's in. He swings the narrow beam of the torch around, catching Iain's face just as he yells, yanks out his blaring earphones and slaps his hand against the wall to hit the main light switch.

Iain kicks out at Jez's legs before Jez can pull himself back through the roof. He falls awkwardly to the floor, dazed, surprised.

Shit. The geezer he sold the Es to. This isn't meant to happen.

Jez tries to get up, but Iain's already on him, punching at his face, eyes wild and scared.

Shit. The guy who sold him the dodgy Es. The bastard.

Jez swings a right, catching Iain on the side of the head, making him stagger. It gives Jez the second needs to scramble to his feet. He dashes to the door but can't open it. Then Iain's on him, hands at his throat. Jez thrusts his elbow back, catching Iain in the guts, then does it again, hitting Iain's head. Iain lurches to the side in pain. Jez turns and grabs the nearest thing to him, a chair. He draws it above his head, smashing the bare lightbulb by mistake, blanketing the room in dark chaos. Iain lashes out blindly, catching Jez on the jaw, then rushes forward. Their heads clash. Jez reels, but just keeps his balance. He kicks, catching some part of Iain's body, then swings the chair. It connects with a hollow clunk, followed by a stumbling, thumping crash as Iain falls.

There's a few moments of roaring silence as Jez waits for another attack. The room's still. He picks up his fallen torch and shines the beam over at Iain. He's lying crumpled against the wall beside the bed, a dark mess seeping from his head onto the concrete floor.

Jez leaps onto the bed, adrenalin shooting through him. He scrabbles up through the hole in the roof, jumping down to the ground, catching his shin on the edge of the wall but not feeling it.

He runs as fast as he can across open ground and into the trees, not looking back. Nearby, dogs release long eerie howls in the dark.

Jez gets to the scooter, kicks it started, and only then realises he's left the bag behind in Iain's room.

Sod it. Cut and run. Like his old man always said; if it looks like Lady Luck's turning against you, piss off before she really gets the hump

He races back in the direction of Scab's house. But halfway there he slows. His work isn't finished. There's something else he's got to do. For the sake of his pride if nothing else.

Jez turns the scooter around, heading back up the road, turning off down a sandy lane. He parks, resting the machine against a palm tree. The house isn't far. Even in the poor light he can make out a narrow path, see the shapes of the houses, recognise the cluster of bamboo where he hid the bottles in a plastic bag.

After picking them up he moves quickly over to Hassan's house. He checks to make sure no-one's around. A couple of houses nearby have dim lights on, but there's no noise above the distant techno from the party.

Jez unscrews the cap from one of the bottles. The sharp reek of petrol invades his nostrils immediately. He shakes his head, holding the bottle to the side. For a second it throws him and he doesn't know what to do. Should he do this? It's pretty fucking hardcore. But he was cheated. Humiliated. Hassan wouldn't have given a shit if he'd been locked up in Aguada for life. He deserves everything he gets.

He sprays the petrol around the bottom of the walls, managing to get right around the small bungalow using just one bottle. All the time he checks the surrounding area, making sure he's not being seen. A dog barks nearby but it doesn't stop him. He's too worried about what he's just about to do. To drive himself on he focuses on the humiliation, on the beatings, on the way Hassan made him feel so small. The hatred builds. There's got to be payback.

He stuffs a rag into the open top of the other bottle, giving it time to soak up some of the petrol. He's already worked out where it's going. Through one of the open windows, through the bars. The window nearest the door, so that Hassan can't escape.

The lighter's in his pocket. He takes it out and moves into position, his heart thumping. This is fucking serious. This is asking for more trouble than it's worth. But fuck it, the bastard's had this coming.

But then. This is fucking serious.

With his thumb poised on the lighter's firing mechanism, Jez hesitates. He's not sure. What's he doing? There's shit coming down and he's hanging about, in danger of getting in deeper. He should be miles away. That Jock boy could be dead, and it's his fault. He's stupid to be even thinking of torching Hassan's place. What the fuck does he think he's doing?

But then. What about revenge? A message needs to be sent, to be received. Turning the other cheek is not an option. It's gone too far for that. Hassan was the one who pushed it too far. He's the one who has to be taught a lesson.

A message. A lesson. Jez considers it. Is there a way to carry it off without getting himself in even deeper shit? He looks down at the bottle in his hand, feels the weight of it, breathes the fumes.

There is a way. There is a way to leave a message for Hassan, a message he can't fail to understand. Would he learn from the lesson? That's up to him.

Okay, no more pissing about. Decision time. So Jez decides. He'll put the bottle, full of petrol, with the soaked rag sticking out of the top, on Hassan's windowsill. And he'll place the lighter right next to it, so that when Hassan finds it in the morn- ing he'll be in no doubt about the message. That he could be dead. That he wasn't as big or powerful as he thought he was. That he'd been spared by someone bigger and more powerful than him. Someone who'd held Hassan's life and death in his hands and decided that he just wasn't worth the fucking hassle.

It's perfect. Hassan won't sleep well ever again.

Jez takes a step towards the window. A loud, low growl stops him dead. As he spins around, the growl breaks out into a full-throated bark. The dog's in shadows but he can tell it's big, much bigger than some of the pathetic specimens he sees during the day. And he knows as well as anyone else that the dogs act differently at night, that they can develop an extreme aggres- sion and a bravery that's absent in daylight, when they lounge about all lazy and useless.

The dog moves forward a couple of feet, out of the deep shadows, snarling again. Jez takes in its scarred face, the bared teeth. Moonlight catches a hard glint in its black eyes. Jez's legs shake, his bowels flutter.

Another burst of barking, which is then taken up by a sec- ond dog off to his left, maybe only thirty feet away. Then there's three of them, and they're all coming towards him.

Jez kicks sand and dirt at the big one, the leader. It backs off a second, then barks louder. And now a baby crying. The sound seems to be coming from Hassan's house. He didn't remember seeing a baby there - he was sure there wasn't one. But the sound's there now, the wail coming out clear and strong, setting off the dogs even more.

The lead dog lunges at Jez's leg. He stumbles back, but manages to keep his balance, kicking out, catching the dog on the side of the head. It howls and spins away. But the others are coming in from the side, the sound of barking and wailing unbearably loud now. Jez doesn't know what to do. Everything's happening so fast, his heart's beating so hard. There's no time to think.

A light snaps on in Hassan's house as one of the other dogs rushes Jez, nipping his calf. He yells, more out of fright than pain. He kicks out at it, misses, then the big one comes back at him. It takes a chunk out of his other leg. This time the pain gets through. He stamps down on the dog's back with his free foot, forcing the animal back. There's shouting now, and Jez suddenly realises it's his own voice.

He's got to get out of there. It was a stupid idea. He knows it now. It's all going wrong and he's in danger of making everything worse.

He backs away, edging out of the dogs' territory. Then light floods the path as a door opens. Jez looks to his side, and there he is framed in the doorway. Hassan. Looking at him and grinning.

Without thinking, without lighting the fuel-soaked rag, Jez hurls the bottle at Hassan. The smile leaves Hassan's face abruptly as instinct forces his hands up to catch it, to stop it hitting him. In doing so he drops the cigarette he lit just before coming to the door to see why the dogs were going mad.

His hands grasp the bottle mid-air, his hard grip forcing petrol to gush out of the top, spilling over his chest and face. He yells as the fuel stings his eyes. The bottle drops just as the petrol at his feet catches fire from the cigarette. Flames spread along the ground, around both sides of the building. And then the bottle explodes, spaying fire outwards and upwards. Jez is blown back by the force, but the flames don't reach him. One of the dogs runs off yelping through the village, its coat on fire. The others scatter too.

Jez scrambles to his feet and starts to run, his heart pounding so hard he feels he might die. His head is filled with raw terror now. All he can think to do is get to the scooter, to get away as fast as he can. The fire's ruined his night vision and he blunders into trees, trips over rocks and roots. But he keeps going. He keeps running and running, as if the devil himself is chasing him.

As he gets to the scooter, he's whimpering, jabbering to himself. He doesn't look back to see the flames. He knows what he saw. He knows what he heard. The hellish screams as Hassan beat at his own face, trying to kill the fire that had burnt out his eyes.

CHAPTER TWENTY SEVEN

A few rotten grains

Chief Inspector Da Silva's ear feels like an over-fried poppadum, and he's only just picked up the phone. He knew it was going to be like this. Ever since seeing his morning copy of the Konkan Times with the unflattering photograph of Tendulkar being heckled by the English policeman, he's been rushing around trying to get ready for work much earlier than usual, but the Chief of Police has managed to catch him before he can leave his house.

Da Silva's not really all that surprised. As well as the photograph, the accompanying story wasn't particularly flattering either. A police PR stunt gone badly wrong, censorship of free speech, police brutality. And the bland quote from the Chief Minister denying allegations of a police cover-up over the murder. Hardly a ringing endorsement of the force. Combined with the revelation about the CBI coming in to take over the case, Da Silva's ears had started tingling as he read the story over breakfast. Now they are truly on fire.

'Worst kind of publicity!' Tendulkar yells at him. 'Worst kind! You men should have stopped all this happening. This is your job, for God's sake. Can't I trust you fools to get anything right!'

'But sir, we didn't know the Englishman would do something like this. This could not have been foreseen.'

'I'm just asking you to use some common bloody sense. Any fool could have guessed he'd try something like that. We need to quieten this Englishman down. Where is he now?'

'In Aguada jail, sir.'

'What!? What the bloody hell is he doing there!?'

'You told me to arrest him, sir.'

'Well, release him you fool! I didn't know it was this English troublemaker. And I didn't tell you to arrest him, I told you to get him away from the cameras. You knew it was him. You've met him. You should not have allowed this to happen. I am holding you personally responsible. We are all looking like fools because of you. You should have intercepted him as soon as you saw him, before he could do anything. The photograph in the Times makes me look like a complete bloody idiot. This is not helping your promotion prospects.'

'No, sir.'

'No, sir. Exactly. Now get this Englishman out of Aguada right away. He's caused enough trouble as it is. We don't want to antagonise him any more than we have done already, although I cannot see how that would be possible. Any more cock-ups will only bring us more bad publicity. You have let this situation get completely out of control. It is a complete bloody shambles.'

'Yes, sir.'

'Yes, sir. Indeed. The Chief Minister has been chewing my ear for the last half an hour. He wants the situation under control now. We need to get this Englishman on our side. We can't have him going running off to the newspapers every ten minutes. We are to treat him well from now on. Direct orders from Chief Minister Prakash himself. We're to keep this Englishman fully informed of the investigation, show him that something is being done, give him VIP treatment. Those are the Chief Minister's own words. VIP treatment. Fortunately he doesn't know that our VIP is locked up with the roaches in Aguada. See to it he's not there any longer. You personally take

him back to his hotel and apologise for being such an incompetent fool.'

'Yes, sir,' Da Silva says, but the phone is already dead.

*

'But I don't see why, Jez,' Nat says, her face tired and confused.
She sitting on the bed next to the rucksack that Jez has packed
for her. She's just come back from the party and wants to sleep.

'Because we just do, that's why. We've got to get out of here.
The scene's dead here. Hampi's the place. You saw the party last
night. Dead as anything. The whole vibe's moved on. It's at
Hampi, that's what everyone's saying.'

'I didn't hear anyone. Anyway, I thought it was a kicking
party. And why do we have to go right now, this very minute?'

'Because we do. We want to get an early start, don't we. Get
to Panjim, get a bus. Best time to travel, early morning. Everyone knows that.'

'You're up to something. I know you are.'

'I'm not up to nothing.'

'Why this rush all of a sudden? Why haven't you mentioned
nothing about this before?'

'There was no need, was there. Not until I saw the party.
Wasn't hardly nobody there. Anyway, there's all that trouble I
had with the cops and that. Put me right off the place. Could do
with a change of scene. Don't feel none too comfortable about
hanging out here anymore. There's Hassan, the cops - it's just
shit.'

'Well, whose bloody fault is that? Anyway, I want to stay
here. I'm tired. I haven't had no sleep.'

'Do what you want, then,' Jez says. 'I'm going to Hampi.'

He doesn't feel like discussing it any more. Both legs hurt
from the dog bites, his body aches, his mind's in a mess. The

more time they waste, the later it gets in the day, the more chance he has of getting caught. The cops are bound to be looking for him. Hand in glove with the Kashmiri mafia. Bastards. And there's all that Jock business as well. Not a fucking sensible place to be.

Nat folds her arms and takes a deep breath.

'I'm not going,' she says.

'Course you bleedin' are. What's the matter with you? Stop being so fucking stupid. Now come on. We've got to go now or we'll be late.'

He picks up his bag and slings it over his shoulder.

'What's the matter with your face,' Nat says, her eyes narrowing. 'You've got a bruise or something coming up.'

'What? Nah, it's nothing,' Jez says, wiping at it, pretending it's dirt.

'Where'd you go when you left last night? You've been getting in trouble again, ain't you.'

'You'll be in trouble if we miss this bus. Now get a move on.'

Nat takes a long look at Jez standing there with his bag, eager, pushing her.

'I'm not coming.'

'Course you're coming. It's bleedin' Hampi, innit. You said you wanted to go there.'

'Yeah, but not right now this instant. I want to stay here with my friends.'

'They'll all be in bleedin' Hampi by the time you get round to deciding anything,' Jez snaps at her. He's on the edge, he knows it. It's all getting too much for him. 'Now stop being such a silly cow and come on.'

'I'm sick of the way you treat me. It's like, your word is God or something. Why's it always me who's got to do everything you say. What about what I want to do?'

Jez raises his eyes to the ceiling.

'I just haven't got fucking time for this. I really haven't,' he says. 'Come if you're coming, stay if you're not.'

'I told you. I'm staying.'

Jez stares at her for a few seconds, but she doesn't flinch. He can't believe it. She's not bluffing.

'Fine,' he says, his face snarled. 'But don't expect me to welcome you with open arms when you roll up in Hampi with no dosh and nowhere to stay. I'll remember this, you deserting me. After all the things I've done for you. All the fucking things. I'll give you a week before you're knocking on my door because you can't handle having to sort everything out for yourself. A week.'

'Yeah,' Nat says softly. 'And I'll give you a month of Sundays before you find anyone stupid enough to put up with you like I've done.'

Jez says nothing. He gives Nat one last glare, a few seconds to change her mind, then he turns and walks out the door, leaving it open.

Nat looks at the rectangle of sunlight on the floor, thinking. The light nearly touches her feet. She can feel the warmth from it. She gets up slowly, closes the door, and goes back to sit on the bed. For a second she thinks she's going to cry, but then she doesn't.

She's about to curl up and go to sleep when there's a knock on the door. It creaks open. Jez is standing there. Nat thinks maybe he's decided to stay, but then she sees something in his hand.

'Thought you might need this if you're staying,' Jez says, holding out five ten pound notes.

Nat looks at him.

'I don't need your money,' she says. 'I've got plenty of my own.'

'Yeah, well, that's the thing. This is yours. I borrowed it from your stash to pay for something, but I don't need it now.'

Nat leaps up, grabs the money, and slams the door in Jez's face.

'Arsehole,' she says, leaning her back against the door. 'Complete and utter arsehole.'

Jez scuttles quickly along the path, shooting anxious glances from side to side, checking who's around. His swagger's long gone. He's nervous and jittery, a man on the run.

*

Steve wakes from a light sleep as the cell door screeches open. His back's sore, his legs stiff from sitting so long on the hard floor. Crash Mary's awake, but Wolf and Enrico are snoring on the rope bed, entwined.

Chief Inspector Da Silva stands framed in the doorway, a guard on either side of him. He tries to smile, but the muscles in his face won't work properly.

'Good morning, DS Harrison,' he says. 'I won't ask you if you slept well. The surroundings are not perhaps as comfortable as those you are used to.'

Steve rises painfully to his feet but doesn't say anything, waiting to see what Da Silva has to offer.

'Please,' Da Silva says, extending a hand, beckoning Steve out of the cell. 'Come with me.'

'Where to?'

'To your hotel. You are free to go.'

'What about the others?'

Da Silva looks down at the smiling Crash Mary and the two snorers on the bed.

'That is another matter, Mr Harrison. One in which I would

urge you not to involve yourself. They are facing very serious charges. You have had enough on your plate already, I think.'

Steve points down to Crash Mary.

'He shouldn't be here. He had drugs planted on him. By your officers.'

'That is not something I would wish to comment on, and it is a very serious accusation,' Da Silva say, his face firm, his voice rising. Then he remembers Tendulkar's ear-bashing. VIP treatment. He softens. 'But I will have a close look at the arrest report.'

'Cheers,' Crash Mary says up to Steve, giving him the thumbs up.

'But I am not promising anything,' Da Silva says quickly.

Crash Mary scratches the stubble on his head.

'Yeah, well. That's life for you, innit.'

'He's also agreed to give a statement,' Steve says. 'He saw Henrik Andersen leave the party with Sophie Lacroix just before she was killed. He's an important witness.'

'Yes. Well,' Da Silva says. 'That is something that we will have to consider. I'll see what I can do.'

The cell door closes. Steve, Da Silva and the guards walk along the concrete corridor, their senses assaulted by the stench of urine, stale sweat, harsh disinfectant and the sour reek of abandoned hope.

*

The clatter of yells, raised staccato voices, the hubbub of chaos. The noises rouse Iain.

He comes round, aware of the pain in his head first, an icy throb above his left ear. Then his shoulders, cramped and aching against the wall, then his dead leg curled beneath him.

It feels like the worst hangover in the world.

He pulls himself to his feet with difficulty, feeling unbalanced, using the wall for support. Once he's standing he gently touches the side of his head, feeling stiff, sticky, blood-matted hair.

The noises outside. Voices. Voices shouting. Italian or something.

He feels weak. He looks at the window.

No way. No way is he going to try to climb through there.

He takes his keys from his trouser pocket, walks over to the window and starts pulling out the glass slats from their wooden grooves.

Outside the Italians are shouting to the world, cursing, gesticulating at their rooms, at each other and the sky.

'Hey!' Iain says, trying to shout it, but the pain in his head stopping him. 'Hey!' he croaks at them. 'Over here. I'm locked in.' He dangles the key. 'Can you let me out?'

One of the Italians, a tall man in his early twenties with long dark hair and shaped sideburns, comes over.

He views Iain with a mixture of mistrust and indifference, but unlocks the padlock anyway. Iain helps himself along the wall to the now open door and takes the key back.

'Fuck, man. What happen?' the Italian says when he sees the state Iain's in.

'Got attacked,' Iain says, holding onto the door frame. 'Guy came through the roof. Think he was trying to rob me.'

'Us too! Now we are coming back from the party and everything is stolen. Money, everything.'

'I know who it was,' Iain says, seeing Jez's face, the look of surprise when he turned on the light. 'I've seen him around before. He must have locked me in once he'd knocked me out. Left me for dead, the bastard.'

Iain feels a need to explain the locked door, before it comes up in conversation. He can't be bothered with the tedious, pathetic truth.

The Italian's eyes widen. He speaks quickly to his friends, a very angry man and two distressed women, filling them in.

They come over, crowding Iain.

'Who is this bastard?' the angry man says, knitting thick black eyebrows. 'Where is he?'

'I've seen him,' Iain says, not sure if he's said it before. The world is becoming a little soft at the edges. 'Don't know his name. Know where he hangs out. The Vibe, Pandora's.'

The two Italian men start speaking rapidly to each other in murderous tones. Iain guesses what their plan is.

Go to the bars, with him in tow, and exact their revenge.

He doesn't feel up to it.

In fact, he doesn't feel great at all. He's beginning to sweat, a cold chill running through him even though the blistering sun's already climbing its way up the late morning sky.

'You are okay?' one of the girls says to him.

She's either very pretty or not at all. Iain can't decide which. He can't focus on her properly. 'Maybe you should go to a doctor.'

Iain shakes his head, immediately regretting it.

'No,' he says. 'No, I don't think it's all that serious.'

He smiles, and crumples in a faint at her feet.

*

Steve isn't looking forward to getting back to the hotel. It's been a long morning. First, the briefing on the case from Chief Inspector Da Silva, then giving his official statement at Calangute police station with officers from the CBI, the Indian equivalent of the CID, dragging up every bit of information he could think of which might help. A painful morning, thinking about Sophie, about Henrik, about everything he's gone through since New Year's Day and before.

And then the stream of assurances that something was being done, talking to the case officers, being told that they regarded Henrik Andersen to be the prime and only suspect, that the local police and the CBI were doing everything in their power to 'nab' him, as they said, before he leaves the country. But what the Chief Inspector repeated throughout the morning, and what Steve knew anyway, was the problem of hard evidence. The lack of it. Circumstantial at best, with only an anonymous note for back-up. Hardly a solid case, even if they take a statement from Crash Mary.

Without some form of confession from the suspect himself, the Chief Inspector said, it would be unlikely to reach a courtroom. But still, as Da Silva hinted slyly, there were always different ways of extracting confessions, and they always had a knack of 'finding' witnesses who could be relied upon to stick to a story.

A long morning. And here he was, pulling up outside the gates to the hotel. He'd specifically asked not to be driven up to the front door, not wanting to be seen getting out of a police car, especially with the reception he's expecting.

He's already phoned Karen from the police station, waking her, the first she was aware that he hadn't been back the whole night. She'd been too stunned and sleepy to take in what he'd been saying, and he'd kept the phone call short and to the point.

But she'll have had more than enough time for it to sink in now. Oh yes, more than enough time to build her temper up, sharpen her tongue, dip it in poison while she's waiting for him.

'Well, DS Harrison,' Da Silva says, extending a hand as the car pulls to a stop. 'I will keep you informed of any developments. And again, our sincere apologies for the little misunderstanding yesterday. I hope that there are no hard feelings.'

Steve shakes his hand.

'My back might not forgive you for a while, but sure, no hard feelings.'

Da Silva's been trying hard all morning. Star treatment, VIP status, just the way Tendulkar wants. Although he only wants it because he was being told what to do by his benefactor, the high and mighty Chief Minister, who only got his position through Pereira's dirty money. All morning Da Silva's been biting his tongue, following orders.

'But there's just one thing,' he says. 'When are you leaving Goa?'

'Tomorrow afternoon,' Steve says.

Da Silva smiles. He knows that already.

'I think that is most fortunate for both of us,' he says. 'My advice to you would be to have a pleasant, quiet last day in our beautiful state, and then go home, Mr Harrison. Go home and don't come back. I think your presence here is a disruption for both of us. Forget about Goa. Forget about everything that happened here. Go home and get back to work and get on with your life. Goa and you, they are not good for each other, I think. It would be better that you don't see each other again.'

'Maybe,' Steve says. 'But it strikes me that all the things that are messed-up here were messed-up long before I arrived. Maybe you needed me here to give things a bit of a kick up the backside.'

Da Silva tries to put on his charming smile, but he can't.

'I can assure you that we in the Indian police force are perfectly able to do our own kicking if that is necessary. And it is safe to say we can solve our own crimes.'

'Except you'd have done nothing about this one if I hadn't started interfering.'

'There was a small problem with the start of the investigation, I grant you.'

Steve snorts out a bitter laugh.

'Small problem? A lazy and corrupt police force in Anjuna. Not exactly small, by my reckoning.'

'Ach,' Da Silva rasps. 'In every bag of rice there are a few rotten grains. It is to be expected. You can pick out only so many, but sometimes they stay hidden from view. A few rotten grains do not spoil a whole banquet. You, of course, have never had corruption in your own police force,' he says, letting himself go, dripping the comment in mockery. Then he remembers Tendulkar again. He steadies himself.

'But anyway, Mr Harrison. We are getting along so well now. Why spoil it? The case is in hand now. You do not have to concern yourself about it any longer. The Chief of Police himself has asked me to pass on his gratitude for all the help you have given us. Leave it to us now, Mr Harrison. I shall probably not be seeing you again, so have a restful last day in Goa, and have a good flight back to your country. Anyway, I must be going. We are quite busy today. There was an arson attack last night. A trader from Kashmir is in hospital, very badly burned. Probably connected to a battle for the drugs business, but we must investigate it anyway. Actually, it would make our job a lot easier if we just let them kill each other.'

Steve looks at Da Silva. The insincere smile, the composure, the easy wielding of authority he's seen during the day. Lazy? Maybe not. Corrupt? Who knows?

'Goodbye, Chief Inspector,' he says without smiling, and gets out of the car.

He walks up the hotel driveway as the car speeds off. Karen's sitting in the shade near the bar. He can see she's not happy. He cuts onto the flagstone path bisecting the lawn, making his way steadily but reluctantly towards her, his body and soul dog-tired.

'Well?' Karen says, arms folded, face stern. 'Just what the bloody hell d'you think you've been up to?'

'I was arrested.'

'I know that. You told me that. What I didn't know was all this.'

She flips a copy of the Konkan Times onto the table. Steve can make out his face in the grainy photograph on the front page, standing in front of Tendulkar, pointing a finger at him.

'Well?' Karen snaps again.

'At least they got my best side.'

'I'm glad you find this funny, Steven Harrison. Because I don't find it funny at all. Not one bit. The manager showed me this this morning. And the stories from the last couple of days. Thought I'd be very proud of you. Think what sort of a fool I felt, him showing me all this and me knowing nothing about it? How humiliating do you think that was? Oh, and there's been a couple of beggars calling for you this morning. They've heard you're a soft touch for money, apparently. Handing out rupees like confetti for any old lies they can make up on the spot. Lucky for me that assistant manager got rid of them, although he's not happy about it, all these tramps coming into the hotel at your invitation. Don't know what they must think of us in this place. All morning he's been fending off these beggars, because where were you? In some bloody jail because of this bloody obsession of yours. I'm not having it, Steven. These past two weeks you haven't been the man I married, and I'm just not having it. It's high time you took a good look at yourself and remembered what your priorities are.'

All the time Steve's just been standing there slouched, no energy left to fight back with.

'And a very good morning to you too, dear,' he says, only able to summon up weak sarcasm. 'I'm off to bed.'

Karen sees the deadness in his eyes, a look she hasn't seen before. For a moment, she almost doesn't recognise him. Steve walks away in silence.

*

It takes Iain an hour and a half to work out the trick. A woozy hour and a half in the hot, teeming waiting room of the doctor's surgery in Anjuna, a room filling up quicker than it's emptying. An hour and a half before he realises what he should have done in the first place.

He mentally kicks himself for forgetting his traveller's skills.

He shuffles over to the receptionist, a scary-faced woman with thick eyebrows and grey hair pulled back in a bun.

'Any idea how much longer I've got to wait?' he says, casually sliding a fifty rupee note across the desk to her.

Suddenly, he's the next to be seen.

The doctor examines him for two minutes, writes out a note and a prescription, then tells him to go to the hospital in Mapusa.

He gets his prescription at the chemists next door to the surgery, then spends half an hour trying to find a taxi to take him to Mapusa at a decent price.

The lowest he can get is an extortionate three hundred rupees, the driver refusing to budge for less.

Bumping along the winding, rutted road in the battered old Ambassador, he tries to enjoy the scenery but feels too sorry for himself.

This healthcare business in India, he thinks. It's getting to be an expensive and time-consuming business.

Thank God I'm an emergency case.

The hospital is a long, low green building off a side road at the eastern edge of the small town. Iain negotiates with the driver to wait for him, then spends a few confused minutes trying to find out where he's supposed to go.

For ten rupees a porter takes him, ushering him into a waiting room where six Indians and two Westerners lie and sit in varying degrees of wounded distress. There are a few spare seats, one next to a Westerner, a very pretty blonde girl. That chair, he decides, is the one for him.

'Hello,' he says, wondering, Swedish? 'Is this seat taken?'

'No,' she says, smiling.

He sits down. Norwegian? Dutch?

'So what have you got,' he says, pointing at a scarf wound around the girl's right ankle. 'Did you sprain it or something?'

'No,' she says, beginning to unwind the scarf. 'I was taking a motorcycle taxi to Mapusa, and it didn't have a part to rest my foot on. But I forget, and I put my leg against, against a part of the engine. The very hot part which takes away the smoke. Like a pipe. I'm sorry for my English. I can't remember its name.'

'The exhaust?'

'Yes, that is it, I think,' she says, still unwinding. 'And this is what happened. All my skin came off.'

Iain stares at the ugly, weeping patch of burnt skin. He feels very queasy, a pained expression screwing up his face.

'Nasty,' he hisses out through clenched teeth.

'Yes it is,' she says back, but smiles. She starts winding the scarf back on. 'It is very painful, but I'm getting used to it. I'm not crying any more. And you? You do not look so well.'

'Och, it's nothing really,' he says, still trying to pick out her accent. A very nice voice, he decides. Soft, sympathetic, a bit of a Cerys husk to it. 'It's just a scratch.'

He turns his head, pointing to the dark, matted patch of hair.

The girl takes in a sharp breath, and her face furrows in concern. Very cutely, Iain thinks.

'It looks very bad,' she says. 'Are you okay? It must hurt very much.'

'Aye, you'd think so,' Iain says, a crooked smile on his face. 'But I got some painkillers from a doctor in Anjuna, and to be perfectly honest I don't feel very much of anything at the moment. Everything's a bit,' he says, looking around the room, searching for the word, 'spongey.'

The girl laughs.

'Like after too many parties,' she says.

What a lovely, sweet girl, Iain thinks. Absolutely adorable. Danish, maybe. Never heard a Danish accent before. Could be Danish.

'So what happened to you?' the girl asks, concern back on her face. 'Did you fall?'

'No. I was attacked, actually.'

'Attacked? Where?'

'A man broke into my room and attacked me.'

'Oh my God!'

'Yeah. He was trying to rob me, but he didn't get anything.'

'And you were fighting with him?'

'Oh, I had to. There was no option,' Iain says, trying to put on an understated, modest expression. 'And I probably would have beaten him as well, but he had a weapon.'

'A weapon? My God! What, like a knife?'

'No. It was more a kind of a 'chair' kind of weapon.'

The girl looks confused.

'He had a chair with him?'

'Oh, no. It was my chair. It's just that he was the first one to look at it and recognise its full potential as a dangerous weapon. I realised pretty soon afterwards, roundabout the time he hit me with it. Which is when this lovely hairstyle happened,' he says, pointing to his head again. 'My name's Iain, by the way.'

'I'm Charlotte,' she says. Iain runs over the pronunciation in his head, looking for clues. Shar-lott-eh. Definitely could be Danish.

'Hi, Charlotte,' he says. 'So where you from?'

'Germany.'

'Germany?'

'You are surprised?'

'No, no, it's not that. Well, yes, a bit. It's just your accent. Excuse me for saying this, but it's the only cute German accent I've ever heard in my life. Seriously.'

Charlotte giggles and drops her eyes for a second, coming over a little shy.

'Thank you, I think,' she says. 'Many people say I don't have a German accent, but I do. I'm from the Pfalz area of Germany, near the border with France. The accent is not so strong, I think. Maybe this is the reason. But thank you for the compliment anyway.'

It's another two hours and four hundred rupees each by the time they're both seen, cleaned, stitched and bandaged. By this time Iain's learned that Charlotte's single, 22, travelling in India by herself, intelligent, beautiful, and, as far as he can tell, has the soul of an angel. They've talked about all kinds of things, even making him forget his head-wound for a while. Charlotte is seen by the medical staff first. She waits for Iain to come out after his turn.

They leave together, Iain helping her into the taxi, delighting in the way she leans against him for support. She lives in Anjuna too, in a small guest-house on the road down to the beach.

'We should make it in time for sunset,' he says as the Ambassador bumps its way back along the road. 'I know a great bar to watch it from if you'd like to join me.'

'I'd like that very much,' Charlotte says, smiling.

Iain wants to wind down the window and cheer to the countryside. But he doesn't. Some things are better left un-whooped.

CHAPTER TWENTY EIGHT

The right thing

There's a new spring to the Doc's step as he walks along the beach road. He can feel some of that old time vibe coming back. Just a little, maybe, but it's a victory of sorts, enough to make his heart feel renewed, make his blood flow sweet and smooth. The sun's almost set, and he takes a seat in a cafe by the bus-stop, letting the golden air enrich his fading eyes. He sees a familiar figure huddled over a book at a table in the corner, gets up and goes over to join him.

'Swiss, boy? Where you been?'

Swiss Dave looks up. A smile cracks his face.

'Hey, Doc. How's it going, man?'

'Fine and dandy, boy. Fine and dandy. Expecting to see you yesterday. For the market.'

'Was I supposed to meet you, yeah?'

'Ain't no matter. Missed yourself one hell of a party, though, boy. Spreading the gospel. Getting the old time vibe working. Makes a man feel alive again.'

'Yeah, sorry man. I, like, y'know, it all just went whoosh! Yeah? I knew there was something, but I just couldn't pin it down. Yeah, it's coming back to me now. Flea Market, yeah? I was meant to meet you. Sorry, Doc. It's just the old grey cells. Must've left the handbrake on, you see what I'm saying?'

'Figured as much. Man's only got so much space.'

'And there's space, and there's *space*,' Swiss Dave says, then chuckles, nodding his head at the Doc. 'Yeah? Yeah?'

'Got a whole lot more space to play with. Been doing me some baptising.'

'Converts, yeah?'

'The world's a bigger, sweeter place today. Minds are opening, unspun minds opening up to the vibe, taking in the sun and the moon and the pure joy of being out there. Vibe may be poisoned to shit, but a man can still fight back. Every one of them who comes over to the other side makes the vibe live a little ways longer, makes the old vibe stronger.'

'The other side, yeah? Too much, Doc. They should give you a medal, all the things you've done for this place.'

'Medals? Don't want no lousy medals. Ain't pinning no militaristic tin-pan rat-ass button shit on me.'

'Yeah, well maybe not a medal, then. What about a title? Like, a name or something. The Technicolour Wizard. The Vibemaster. The High Priest of Nevergone. You see what I'm saying? Yeah? Yeah?'

'I like that,' the Doc says, smiling. 'High Priest of Nevergone. Got a ring, ain't it? High Priest of Nevergone.'

Both men laugh to themselves, repeating the title. A pale, drawn-faced junkie shambles over to bum a cigarette off Dave.

'Sure, man, sure,' he says, handing the man a Four Square then lighting it for him.

'So what you reading, Swiss?' the Doc says. 'Never figured you for much of a book man.'

'Oh, it's just a travel guide thing.'

'A travel guide? When the hell's a man like you ever needed a travel guide? On the road thirty years? Ain't got no use for a Goddamn travel guide.'

'Yeah, I hear what you're saying, Doc, yeah? It's just, I'm trying to figure out where I'm supposed to be going next.'

'Gokarna, you said.'

'Did I? Gokarna. Yeah, maybe, yeah. Maybe that's it. Wonder what I'm s'posed to be going there for?'

'Does it say in the travel guide?' the Doc sneers.

Dave flicks through the pages until he finds the right place, then reads a few paragraphs.

'Nope.'

'Ain't worth shit to you then,' the Doc says, grabbing the book out of Dave's hands and throwing it over the cafe's low wall into a pile of rotting rubbish. A cow immediately ambles over and tries to eat a couple of chapters. 'Goddamn travel guide. All a man needs is to follow his soul. Ain't got no need for books saying 'go here, go there, do this, do that'. Goddamn snot-nose college kid travel guide.'

'You're right, Doc, you're right. Nailed it right down. Boooosh! Yeah? Just hit the road and keep hitting it until it tells you to stop. You see what I'm saying? Yeah? Yeah?'

'Never a truer word, brother. Ain't no lie. So when you pulling out of town?'

A pained look comes over Dave's face as he scratches his white hair, looking up to the corrugated iron ceiling, wrenching the gears in his memory, then counting off digits on his hands. He goes over it again in his mind, just to make sure.

'Now,' he says, eyebrows raised in surprise. 'Just as well you came along. I knew there was something I had to do.'

*

Fortified by Kingfisher, codeine and a kiss on the cheek from Charlotte, Iain sets out for the police station. The combination of drink and pills are keeping the pain in his bandaged head at bay.

The kiss, the delicate press of Charlotte's lips two inches away from his mouth, is creating a new, different ache altogether. It was his heady reward for helping her hobble back to her room after watching sunset at Sonic bar. Iain had offered to pay for an auto-rickshaw for the four hundred yard journey from the bus-stop to her room but she'd refused. He didn't mind. It meant he got to hold onto her for a little bit longer.

Now, after winning a successful pitch for dinner later, he's on his way to report the assault. He knows he should have done it earlier, but what with the long process of getting his head seen to, and the delicious distraction of Charlotte's company, it didn't seem like a priority. It's still not that big a priority, but a mixture of indignant self-righteousness and the fear of bumping into Jez again makes him feel almost duty-bound to go to the police. Added to that, he wants to make sure he has a copy of an official police complaint to add to the receipts for his medical bills, just in case the insurance company gets arsey about paying him back.

There's only one policeman in the station, a sullen-faced officer hunched over a desk at the back. He barely glances at Iain, preferring to carry on making laborious entries to a big, tatty, cardboard-covered ledger. Iain stands at the front desk wondering what the procedure is, whether he should try to attract the policeman's attention or wait to be acknowledged. When it becomes obvious that he'll have to make the first move, he coughs, realises it sounds pathetic, then raps on the desk.

'Excuse me,' he says. 'I don't mean to interrupt but I'd like to report...'

'Wait,' the policeman says curtly, cutting him off.

'Or I suppose I could just wait,' Iain says, making a face at the policeman, whose attention is fixed on the ledger.

A couple of minutes pass with Iain still standing waiting.

'If it's a bad time,' he says eventually. 'I mean, if you've other, bigger police-type things to be doing, I could always come back later. If I live, that is.'

The policeman looks up, giving Iain a long, bored appraisal.

He puts his pen down on the ledger, gets up from behind his desk, and slouches over.

'What?' he says, leaning on the front desk, his face and manner oozing unfriendliness.

'I'd like to report an assault. I was attacked. A man broke into my room. He was trying to rob me.'

The policeman sighs, pulls another ledger from a pile and opens it at a flat wooden page marker halfway through. Then he trudges back to his desk to pick up his pen, comes back and sits down in the chair behind the front desk.

'When?' he says.

'Last night.'

The policeman scrawls the date in the ledger.

'Where?'

'In a room in the village.'

More scrawls.

'Your name?'

'McMillan. Iain McMillan.' He spells it out slowly as the officer copies it down.

'Which country?'

'Scotland. Sorry, Britain. UK.'

'Passport?'

'Obviously.'

The policeman looks up at Iain sharply.

'Give me your passport,' he says.

'Oh. Right. See what you mean,' Iain says, unzipping his flesh-tone money belt and taking out a battered, creased claret rectangle.

The gold-leaf coat of arms on front has nearly worn away completely. He hands it over.

The policeman flicks through it, looking at some of the visas, finds the appropriate Indian one and copies down the details, double-checking Iain's passport number.

'Items being stolen?'

'Nothing. He didn't get anything.'

The officer sighs again and puts down his pen.

'If nothing is being stolen, then it is not a robbery,' he says.

'I know. It's an assault. I told you. He assaulted me when he was trying to rob me.'

The policeman scores two lines through the entry he's just written and makes a note next to it. Then he closes the ledger and puts it back on the pile.

'Who is carrying out this assault? Indian or Westerner?'

'Westerner.'

'This is pointless time-wasting,' the policeman says. 'Nothing was stolen, so where is the harm?'

'The harm? It's right here,' Iain says, pointing to his bandage. 'I was attacked. As far as I'm aware, that's a crime in India.'

'Some tourist attacks you and you think we have nothing better to do than chase around after him?'

'He attacked me. Nearly bloody killed me. So, yes, I want you to arrest him, lock him up, throw the book at him. That one would be good,' he says, nodding at the thick ledger. 'Something nice and heavy.'

'And just how do you expect us to find him, this 'dangerous criminal' you are describing?'

'Well,' Iain says, feeling absurd and increasingly irritated. 'You're the police. I thought that's what you did, finding criminals. Anyway, I know who he is. I've seen him around, I know where he hangs out, the bars, the parties and everything.'

'And you expect us to go with you to all the bars in Anjuna to find him, I suppose.'

'Well. Possibly.'

'You think I can spare two officers to go around bars all night looking for someone just because you got in a fight? Are you out of your fucking mind?'

Iain thinks for a second.

'Probably,' he says. 'But that's only because this guy tried to pan my brains in. Look, what is the problem here? I'm telling you about a crime, I can more or less take you to the person who did it, and you can lock him up. It's pretty straightforward.'

The officer shakes his head, drawing in breath through his teeth.

'Tell me,' he says. 'How long you are staying in Goa?'

'Oh, I don't know. Not long. A couple more days, probably.'

'And you are thinking that we are catching this man, locking him up, having a trial, all within a few days? Months, this would take. And you want to stay here for months until you give evidence at trial?'

'I hadn't really thought that bit out. I suppose I could come back for the trial.'

'This is just timewasting nonsense. Go.'

He waves at Iain dismissively, and gets up to go back to his desk.

'I don't believe this,' Iain says, although mostly to himself. 'I absolutely don't fucking believe this.'

He turns towards the door, but is halted by the officer's voice.

'Wait!'

Iain turns back. The officer's coming towards him, a concerned look on his face.

'What is your profession in your country?' he says.

Iain shrugs.

'I don't have one at the moment.'

So you are not a policeman?'

'What? No.'

'Go,' he says with the dismissive wave again.

Iain leaves the police station, bemused, while the newly de-moted Sergeant Gupta goes back to making menial entries in his low-grade ledgers.

*

Steve climbs the stairs slowly, his body still ravaged by the ef-fects of his night in the concrete cell. He's managed to get a couple of hours sleep, but when Karen had come up to tell him about all the commotion, he'd dragged himself out of bed and gone downstairs to see if he could help. As it turned out, there was very little he could do except offer condolences. One of the guests had died, a middle-aged man on holiday with his boy-friend. The body had already been taken to the morgue at Panjim's main hospital, and the police had been and gone.

Steve opens the door and slumps into a chair by the window. Karen's lying on the bed fully dressed.

'Well?' she says. 'Did you find out what happened?'

'Heart attack, by the sounds of it. The poor boyfriend's out of his mind. I asked the hotel to get hold of a doctor, give him some sedatives.'

'Oh,' Karen says, sounding disappointed.

'Poor bloke. Only forty seven.'

Karen doesn't say anything, just flicks through her maga-zine.

'I'll maybe look in on the boyfriend after dinner,' Steve says. 'Martin, his name is. Just to see he's alright.'

'Oh, I'm sure he'll get over it. As soon as the next one comes along.'

'What d'you mean?'

'Well, you know what they're like, them lot.'

Steve rubs the back of his neck, feeling he's just about to get a headache.

'Not sure I do,' he says. 'Enlighten me.'

'Well, it's not like they're a proper couple, is it. Not like a man and a woman. It's all just about sex with them lot, isn't it. It's not like there's emotion involved or anything.'

'They were a couple,' Steve says. 'This bloke Martin says they were together eight years. He's absolutely devastated by the whole thing. There was certainly emotion there as far as I could tell. If you could have seen what he was like, the state he was in. I'd defy anyone to say he didn't love him.'

'But I mean, it's not like proper love, is it,' Karen says, her face pinched. 'I know they say it is, but simple common sense tells you it's just not. It just can't be the same. Probably had AIDS, more than likely, which if you ask me is what caused the heart attack in the first place.'

'I'm not sure I'm following this,' Steve says, tired and irritated. 'You're saying that there's no way he could actually love this Phillip bloke, who he was with for eight years. You're actually saying that he's not really upset?'

'Well, you've got to admit, it's a bit unlikely. I mean, they're all very "drama queen" and loud and playing-up in public, trying to draw attention to themselves. But in his mind, that's different. They've always got three or four on the go at least. All those "gay" clubs they go to, it's disgusting the things they get up to in them places. I've read articles about them. And you can't have that kind of emotion, any normal kind of feelings for people, not when you're carrying on like that. All that drama, that's just for show.'

'Why should it be? I mean, how would you feel if I died? You'd be upset, wouldn't you?'

'I'm not having my marriage compared to a couple of queers, thank you very much,' Karen says, sitting up and folding her arms. 'What they've got, them lot, there's no way you can call that a marriage. It's not legal for starters, and quite right too. It's unnatural, that's what it is.'

'I'm not saying it's a marriage or anything,' Steve says, his headache beginning to kick in. 'But eight years he said they were together. Eight years. That's longer than us, for God's sake. How d'you know they didn't have real feelings for each other? That's just ridiculous.'

'Well, excuse me for thinking that two men having sex isn't normal,' Karen says, getting indignant. 'It may not be "trendy" to say so, but I don't care, you can't possibly have proper love between two men. Not like a man and a woman. No way.'

'So what do you define 'love' as? What is proper 'love' to you?'

'What d'you mean, 'what is love'? Love's love.'

'But when you say it, what do you mean by the word? What do you actually mean?'

'That's stupid. Everyone knows what love means. It doesn't become different from person to person. It's just love.'

'Look, all I'm doing is asking you to describe the emotion you mean when you talk about love, that's all.'

'Oh, for God's sake. It's obvious what it is. It's, well, it's about, it's about things like security, isn't it. Knowing someone, getting on with them, feeling comfortable with them, being able to rely on them, needing them. It's about having the same values, wanting to get the same things out of life. Wanting to have a family, see your children grow up. And I don't care what they say, that's something those homos will never have. Can you believe it - even trying to adopt kids, some of them. Can you imagine letting a child be put in that situation, left alone with a couple of queers so they can do anything they want with them? It's all about sex with that lot, and dirty, perverted sex at that. God, it makes me sick to the stomach just thinking of it. Any of them tries to adopt a kid, they should be locked up. And if it's those lesbians, when they get one of their twisted friends to impregnate them, they should have the child taken away from them. Give it to a proper home. There's plenty of normal couples who can't have children who'd be more than willing to look after them. Ugh! Sends shivers up my spine, it really does. So don't talk to me about "love" with them lot. They don't know the meaning of the word.'

Steve doesn't say anything. He sits, examining his wife, almost as if he's seeing her for the first time. Karen's version of love; a friendship between a man and a woman based on safety, stability and shared ambition. It's not his understanding of the word. Maybe in the past, when he hadn't thought about it, when he hadn't experienced anything different, it would have been a reasonable definition. But not now.

Love. The sickness of it, the sheer, euphoric madness. Obsession and devotion brought on by a glorious fever. What part could they ever play in Karen's heart and mind? Would she even be able to stretch her emotions that far? Love. Feeling that you can't live without the other person.

'Well,' is all he says, trying to relax, trying not to fight about it for both their sake's. 'Anyway, I've told this Martin bloke if there's anything we can do just to let us know.'

'What on earth did you do that for? We're going home tomorrow, and you want to go and get mixed up with someone else's problems again. For God's sake, Steven.'

'For God's sake nothing,' Steve says, raising his voice despite himself. 'Christ, I wonder if you've got a heart at all, sometimes. You said to me that the last couple of weeks I haven't been the man you married. Well, if you think the man you married is the sort who can just stand by when someone needs help, then you must have married someone else because it's certainly not me.' He leaps to his feet. 'I'm going out.'

He clatters the door shut after him, then marches off down the corridor, anger boiling in his veins. Karen pulls the door open and calls sharply after him.

'Steven! Steven!'

He doesn't reply. He keeps going, down the stairs, past reception, along the driveway and out into the humid world of madness and euphoria.

*

Iain's sitting in the garden of Starco's restaurant by the crossroads, waiting, loitering over a bottle of Kingfisher. He's early, but he wanted to make sure he got a good table and a clear view of both entrances, the gate over by the restaurant building and the wide gap in the wall marking the start of the driveway, so that he can spot Charlotte right away. Just in case she takes a seat somewhere he can't see and thinks he hasn't shown up. Or makes him think she hasn't shown up. Neither scenario appeals to him.

He's freshly cleaned, shaved and laundered, looking the best that he can under the circumstances. The bandage around his head's causing him severe self-consciousness, but there's nothing he can do about it. It's either the bandage or a patch of shaved hair with an ugly black mess of stitches in the middle. Not the most difficult of choices he's ever had to make, although he's hoping German television hasn't shown any episodes of Rab C Nesbitt. It's not an image he's keen for Charlotte to associate with him.

Apart from the physical complaints, Iain feels good about himself.

There's a touch of the chuffed Boy Scout about him. After getting back to his room following the pointless exercise at the police station, he discovered Jez's bag of goodies on the floor.

At first he couldn't understand why he'd suddenly obtained a radio and an expensive watch, but then he saw the Italian credit card and it all clicked. He's ashamed to admit it to himself, but for a second, just for a second, he thought about keeping the stuff and dumping the card, but his conscience quickly took over and he handed everything back to his loudly grateful Italian neighbours.

His good deed was only slightly soured by the discovery that both couples had already reported the thefts to the police and now had the necessary documents to make claims on their travel insurance, an action they all eagerly planned to proceed with. Iain had reassured himself that he'd done the right thing by deciding that the watch probably had sentimental value. Maybe even the radio too.

Sitting in Starco's garden, he looks down at his own cheap watch. Charlotte's five minutes late.

Five minutes, he says to himself. Five minutes is nothing. Even ten minutes, fifteen, hardly anything to worry about at all. So when's the cut-off point? Do I stay for half an hour? No, got to give her more time than that. She's half bloody crippled, after all. An hour. Three quarters of an hour. No, an hour. At least an hour. Just over an hour, just in case she gets the time wrong and thinks that it's supposed to be nine rather than eight. But then that means starting all over again. If she thinks it's nine, I can't even think about leaving until nine thirty at the earliest. Nine forty five, maybe. Ten, just to be on the safe side. No, fuck it, nine forty five's as much as she's getting. God, I hope she comes.

He takes a nervous swig of his Kingfisher. He doesn't want to risk getting drunk too quickly, just in case he gives her the wrong impression. Or, to be more accurate, the correct one. No, he'll go easy on the drink tonight, at least until it looks like she's getting a bit drunk as well. Not that he thinks he needs to get her drunk in order to have any chance whatsoever of seducing her. But it would help. If she comes, that is.

Iain lets the evening hubbub of the cross-roads distract him. Motorbikes, scooters, taxis and cows vie for the indeterminate right of way, while weirdoes, wasters and unreconstructed hippies weave between them on foot, heading for strip-lit cafes and the small general store beside the road, or standing over a stall where a smiling Indian man fries eggs on a gas stove for a few rupees. The night has a warm, heavy quality to it. Unseen insects scratch loudly in the trees.

Anjuna, Iain thinks. It's not that bad, once you accept it for what it is. After all, it's still recognisably India, even if the Western influences and visitors sometimes obscure the fact. India is a mansion with many rooms. Goa's simply the games parlour.

He looks at his watch again. Twelve minutes past.

She's not coming. She's spent half the day with me and decided that's enough. She probably only hung about so long because she wanted me to help her get home. Agreeing to meet me for dinner was most likely a ruse to get rid of me. Right now she's probably having a whale of a time with a tall, handsome, witty bastard who's been everywhere and makes her quiver with excitement with his laid-back confidence and his worldly-wise bearing and his all-over suntan and his six-pack stomach and his...

Get a grip of yourself, for God's sake, McMillan. She's only twelve minutes late. Well, thirteen. Nearly fourteen. That's nearly a whole quarter of an hour! A quarter. A significant fraction. A crucial watershed. Well, that tells me quite clearly what she thinks of me. She doesn't like me at all. She's not coming. Fine. I'll just make my own entertainment. I'll have a couple of beers, a chicken masala, then pop home for a smoke and a monster thrash. Women; who needs them? People; fuck them all.

He looks up towards the gate and sees the familiar hair, the legs, the stance, the penetrating eyes. Martha smiles at him and Iain's guts whirl. She starts to walk towards the table.

Iain doesn't know what to do. He wants to scream, run away, hide under the table, throw menus at her.

'Hi,' Charlotte says, sweeping in through the driveway, bouncing up to Iain's table and hugging him in his seat, then pulling back to kiss him on the cheek again. 'I'm sorry I'm late. I was sleeping. I was worried that you might have gone.'

Over Charlotte's shoulder, Iain sees Martha give him a sad, resigned smile. She shrugs and turns away. He feels a little guilty, but the rush of pleasure he gets from Charlotte swamps it.

'You were lucky,' he says. 'I'd just decided that if you weren't here in two minutes time, I was only going to wait another hour.'

Charlotte laughs, a brightness in her eyes.

'Your leg seems a lot better,' Iain says.

'Yes, it's feeling good now, not so painful. How's your head?'

'Excellent. As is yours, I hope,' he says, thinking, did I really say that out loud? 'What'll you have to drink?'

*

Karen's bored. And hungry, now she comes to think about it. She puts down the magazine she lifted from reception, an old copy of Cosmopolitan, and wonders what to do.

After all, she can't go down to dinner on her own. Not again. Think of the stares, the humiliation. 'That girl's husband's off on the razz and she's got to eat all by herself. Sad, isn't it.' She can almost hear the laughs hidden behind all the hands. No, there's no way she's going to sit down there in the garden all by herself just to give other people pleasure at her misfortune. But if Steve doesn't come back, what then?

She gets off the bed and looks at herself in the bedroom mirror. Good features, there's no denying it. She turns her face from side to side, making sure her blusher's just right, perfectly balanced just below her cheekbones. Her lipstick could do with a bit of touching up, though.

She takes the correct shade of red out of her make-up bag and applies it carefully.

Maybe the Matlocks are planning to have dinner soon. She hasn't seen Maureen for a couple of days. Wonder what they've all been up to? Maybe she should go along and see her.

Karen goes over to the window and pulls back the curtain just far enough to get a good look at the diners sitting out on the lawn. She can't make out any faces. It's fairly dark, with little light thrown up by the candles on the tables, but she can see well enough to tell there aren't any groups of five.

That's it decided. She'll go along and see Maureen and have dinner with the Matlocks. After all, she can say that Steve's off sorting out some last minute purchases or that he's not feeling well or something. There's no need to go into any great detail.

Karen locks the room behind her and click-clacks down the flight of stairs to the first floor. She's just about to knock on Maureen and Arthur's door when she stops herself. She can hear noises from inside the room. She strains, trying to make out what it is. It sounds like a murmur. Like a chanting of some kind. Whatever. She knocks three times.

Immediately she hears shushing noises, then silence. She knocks again.

'Maureen?' she says loudly. 'It's Karen.'

She's not sure, but she'd almost swear that was a whispered giggle she just heard. She waits, arms folded, looking down at her shoes, but no-one comes to the door. She knocks again.

'Maureen?'

No response. Silence in the room. Karen turns and heads for the stairs again, as hungry as ever.

The whole world, she says to herself. The whole world's gone bloody mad.

*

The Vibe's less than half-full. The New Year crowd have drifted away, short of cash and time. Only a few regulars occupy the hard wooden benches, letting the gentle trance music wash over them. The Ket-head Brothers, Ming and Dobs, slumped in a corner, Scabs and Ricky hunched over stubby bottles of Kings, Pieter from Amsterdam sharing a fat joint with two bearded Germans whose names he can't remember, a strung-out, skinny, mid-thirties woman with dyed red straggly hair and her gaunt, shaven-headed lover. Not a pretty bunch, Steve decides as he sips at his Honeybee brandy. Looks might be deceiving, but not always.

He doesn't know why he's sitting there. The bar holds no memories. It's not a place he's ever considered going, other than the abortive meeting with Sophie and a short visit to put up a poster, which is now nowhere to be seen. No, it's not really his kind of place, although maybe that's the reason. Just to get away, be on his own for a little while, be somewhere he doesn't know anyone, and they don't know him. Just have time and space to sit and think.

But what's there to think about? About Karen? About the way her lack of compassion is eating him to the bone? About Sophie? About the helpless rage he feels whenever he gets near to letting go and thinking about her and the fact that he's lost her? About the flasher on the beach? About the man he attacked? About his life? About love?

No. Maybe it's best not to think at all. Maybe it's best just to have a few drinks, let the alcohol loosen his tight muscles and clear his mind of the horrors threatening to overwhelm him.

He's on his third Honeybee when Nat walks into the bar. She smiles and says 'hi' to Scabs and Ricky, veering towards their table as Steve rises from his seat.

'Excuse me,' he says loudly.

Nat turns, sees him, and tries to dash back out of the door. Steve lunges after her. He catches Nat's arm, all the time trying to reassure her.

'It's alright, it's alright, there's nothing to worry about, I just want to talk to you, you're not in any trouble, calm down, take it easy.'

Nat stops struggling just as Scabs reaches them.

'Get your fucking hands off her!'

'It's alright, I just want to talk to her,' Steve says, keeping hold of Nat's arm, making firm, unbreaking eye-contact with Scabs.

'S'alright, Scabs,' Nat says in a defeated voice. She doesn't see the point in running any more. 'Cheers, but it's alright.'

Scabs stares at Steve for a few seconds, a non-verbal warning, then goes back to his seat. Both him and Ricky watch carefully as Steve leads Nat towards a seat outside near the shore.

'My name's Steve, by the way,' Steve says as they sit down. Nat's eyeing him suspiciously. 'But I reckon you know that already.'

Nat doesn't say anything. She shrugs and looks out at the dark sea.

'Why did you bring me the note?' Steve asks, keeping his voice low and calm.

'Dunno,' Nat says. 'Just the right thing to do.'

'I'm glad you did. The police weren't going to do anything about Sophie's murder. I must admit, even I was having doubts about it at one point. I thought maybe I was going mad, that I was imagining it all. Your note helped a lot. Did you know Sophie?'

'Nah, not really,' Nat says, looking at Steve properly for the first time, her suspicion dropping. He seems okay. There's a kindness about him. 'Like, she was just around, part of the crowd. But she was a lovely girl, really sweet and everything. She didn't deserve nothing like that to happen to her.'

'Nobody ever deserves that. But especially not her.'

'Couldn't believe it. I mean, a girl like that. And, like, even though I didn't know her all that well, it was always really nice being around her. Really peaceful. Lovely girl, she was.'

'What's your name?'

Nat pauses for a second, but realises there's no harm.

'Natalie.'

'Well, Natalie, the thing is, the police are finally taking it seriously. They're looking for Henrik, he's the only suspect. But unless he confesses, there's a problem with evidence. We've already got one witness who saw them leave the party together, but that's not enough. It'd help a lot if you'd make a statement.'

'What, to the police?'

'Yeah. It's okay, I'd go with you, it'd be alright. It'd just make the case against Henrik much, much stronger. You don't want to see him getting away with it, do you?'

'Nah, it's not that. But I can't go to the police.'

'But think about it. How many other Sophies are out there? How d'you know the next girl Henrik goes out with won't end up the same way? If nothing else, think of Sophie. Doesn't she deserve some justice?'

'But I can't. It's nothing against Sophie or nothing, but I just can't. Can't you just use the note?'

'The police need to hear it from you in person. A note's no good. Think about it. Anyone could've written a note. It doesn't count, I'm afraid. And you're the only witness, as far as I know. Your evidence, what you saw, it's crucial to everything. Without you telling the police what you saw, Henrik just gets off with it.'

'But I, it's just, y'know, the note and everything. I mean, it's not true. Not really.'

'What d'you mean?' Steve says, struggling to keep his voice even, dreading the answer.

'I mean, I wrote the note and everything, but I didn't see nothing. I just wrote it so's you'd know.'

Steve slumps in his seat. So close, and now nothing.

'So you didn't see anything?' he says, his voice dulled.

'No. It was my boyfriend. My ex, I should say. He was out that night. Robbing some houses, if you want to know the truth. Anyway, it was him that saw them. Or heard them. He said they were fighting and that Henrik was giving Sophie a right going over. What got me was that he didn't do nothing about it. I mean, that's not right, is it? He should have tried to help or something. I tried to get him to go to the police but he wouldn't. Because of the robberies and everything, and maybe a trial an' that. He didn't want to get involved. But I knew it wasn't right, so when I saw that poster, that's when I wrote the note. I told him after and he had a go at me for it, but I still think it was the right thing to do.'

'And you're right,' Steve says, feeling hope growing again. If he can get to the ex. 'It was the right thing to do. Where is he, this ex of yours?'

'He's gone,' Nat says, shrugging. 'Went this morning.'

'Went where?'

'Hampi.'

'Where's that?'

'Over in Karnataka. Not far, not really. Far enough, though. Don't care if I never see him again, to be honest.'

'What's his name?'

Nat pauses again, thinking.

'Doesn't matter,' she says. 'Even if you managed to find him, he wouldn't tell you nothing. He's like that. Don't want nothing to do with the police an' that. Not even if you paid him.'

'Wouldn't hurt to give me his name, then, would it?'

Nat considers it. She knows she probably shouldn't. Jez would be furious at her. But, when she considers all she's had to put up with.

'Yeah, I s'pose not. Don't owe him nothing. It's Jez. Jeremy Chamberlain, his name is. Right poncey, innit? You'd never guess he was just a piece of shit, would you, not going by the name.'

Steve commits the name to his memory, repeating it over and over again. He'll pass it on to the police tomorrow. It might not do any good, if what the girl's saying about him is true, but at least they can try. He'll take hope wherever he can get it.

'Look, Natalie, thanks for everything you've done.'

'Haven't really done nothing.'

'You have. All the people I've been talking to around here, none of them wanted to know. None of them would help. They just wanted to pretend it didn't happen. It was like, they didn't want anything to interfere with this fantasy world they've got. Cloud cuckoo land. You're the only one who took it upon yourself to do something decent.'

'Yeah, well,' Nat says, smiling uncomfortably at the compliment. 'You do get a lot of arseholes around here, I'll give you that. Get sick of them all meself at times. But anyway, like I said, it was just the right thing to do.'

Steve thanks her again and gets up to go.

'Was Sophie a friend of yours or something?' Nat says, just as Steve turns away.

'Yeah,' he says. 'A very good friend.'

'I just ask, because I never saw you around with her. Well, once in Pandora's, I think, but that was it. You're just on holiday here, ain't you?'

'Yeah. I didn't know her very long. Not really. Although it feels like a lifetime now.'

'So why'd you get involved in all this, then? All the posters and wanting information and everything?'

'Well,' Steve says, sitting down again. 'The police here weren't going to do anything, not until I started interfering. I cared for Sophie. A lot. I couldn't just let her die and then let everyone forget about it, like she'd never been alive. She deserved better. I had to do something.'

'And you just did everything off your own back, did you? Like, getting the police to take it seriously an' that?'

'Yeah. Pretty much.'

'I bet no-one's said thank you, neither.'

Steve's never thought about it. He shakes his head, a tired sadness in his eyes.

'She was a lovely girl, that Sophie,' Nat says. 'She'd be glad you done all this for her. So, thank you. For Sophie's sake. You've done the right thing as well.'

Steve feels tears welling, but he fights them off with a tight smile.

'Thanks,' he says. He stands up again, then something occurs to him. 'With your ex going. I mean, are you alright? Do you need anything? Money or anything?'

'Nah,' Nat says, smiling wider than before, hugging herself. 'I'm fine. Better than I've been for a long time.'

They say goodbye, shaking hands, then Steve starts walking

along the dark path through the palms up towards the bus-stop and the road, the beginning of a mile's trek back to the hotel and Karen's wrath. He doesn't hurry.

Nat stays in her seat overlooking the shore, watching the white tops of waves break out of the sea's blackness, enjoying the peace, the cool night breeze, and the fresh, nervous sense of being on her own.

CHAPTER TWENTY NINE

Susegad

The white Ambassador car with the red light on its roof crunches to a halt on the sandy gravel outside the Coconut Grove Hotel. Chief Inspector Da Silva gets out of the back seat and stretches, pulling his khaki shirt away from the sticky sweat on his back. Then he and his sergeant march towards reception, the sergeant in front clearing an imaginary path for his boss.

Da Silva cuts off when he sees Steve sitting at a table on the lawn. It takes the sergeant a few seconds to realise that the Chief Inspector isn't following him anymore. He does an abrupt about-face and scurries over the grass after him.

Steve's reading the foreign news page of the Konkan Times. Clinton won't lose the impeachment vote, according to a report from Washington. Steve finds with surprise that he's not bothered about it. He'd usually be interested. Suddenly America, politics, everything seems distant, puny and irrelevant.

Karen's up in the room, packing. She's so furious that she's not talking to him. Which, as far as he's concerned, is an improvement.

'Good morning, DS Harrison,' Da Silva says as he reaches the table, his mouth stretched in a smile. 'I see you are keeping up with the news. I don't read much foreign news myself. Too much sex and scandal.'

'Good morning Chief Inspector,' Steve says, his tone cool. 'I didn't expect to see you here this morning.'

'Just passing on my way to the Anjuna station. A couple of matters to attend to. I just thought I'd drop in. I received some news this morning that might be of interest to you. Certainly more interesting than anything you'll read in the Konkan Times.'

He's looking pleased with himself, Steve thinks. Too full of himself by half. Probably just glad to see me go.

'Yeah? Well, I've got some news as well. It might help. About a witness who saw the murder. He might not be too keen on testifying, but it's worth a go.'

'That won't be necessary,' Da Silva says, raising his hand. 'You see, the news I have concerns this Swedish gentleman. This Henrik Andersen. It seems we no longer have a suspect.'

Steve's confused.

'I'm not with you,' he says, eyebrows creased. 'What, he's gone? Skipped the country? What d'you mean?'

Da Silva waits a moment. He looks off to the side, at the crows lurking in palm leaves, at the red-brick wall surrounding the hotel compound, at sparrows taking fluttering dust-baths in the dry flower beds. Then back down at Steve, at this man who's caused him so much trouble in such a short time. He gently clears his throat.

'We were informed by the Swedish embassy this morning that he was killed five days ago. A traffic accident. It seems that he drove a motorcycle through a routine police road block in Maharashtra, about two hundred miles from here. Maybe he was frightened, maybe he thought the police were looking for him.' He shrugs. 'They were not, of course. Not at that time. If he had stopped, the officers would have checked his papers and let him carry on. But instead he panicked, drove right through and crashed into a bus coming the other way. He died very soon afterwards. A very unfortunate mishap, I'm sure you'll agree, but all the same it is one which leaves us without a suspect. The investigation has come to a surprising but satisfactory end. We need take no further action. The case is now closed.'

Steve's mouth won't work. His mind struggles with the news. This is not what he expected. Not what he hoped for. He feels deflated, cheated, frustrated. Maybe it's justice in a way, but not the kind he was looking for. He doesn't know how to react. The bastard's death may close the case, but it doesn't solve anything. He wanted Henrik Andersen to pay for what he did, to be punished for the lives that he destroyed. It wasn't just Sophie's death that Steve had sought revenge for. But dying in an accident - that was no punishment at all. He's managed to escape forever.

'Thank you,' Steve says quietly, subdued. 'Thanks for coming to tell me that.'

'Not at all. But you see, Mr Harrison, for five days you have been troubling yourself and others for no reason at all. All your efforts were for nothing.'

'Maybe not all of them.'

'No? You do not understand India, Mr Harrison. Things happen differently here. You cannot expect to understand this country in such a short visit. Nothing you did changes anything. Your Western ego may prefer to believe that you did, but I'm afraid it isn't true. This is India. What goes around comes around, as my Hindu colleagues might say. A case of karma. As a Christian, I prefer to say it is God's will.'

'What goes around comes around,' repeats Steve, emptily. 'A novel approach to law enforcement.'

'Fate has a way of catching up with people. If you knew India, you would know that. You should have left things as they were. You have wasted your time in Goa, which is a great shame. It is a beautiful place, a paradise in many ways. If you had come here and concentrated on having a holiday with your wife, I am sure you would be leaving here with happy memories and joy in your heart. But now?' He shrugs again.

'Thanks,' Steve says bitterly, 'but I don't need any lessons on morality from the Indian police.'

'Not morality, just friendly advice. But I must not interrupt your preparations for departure. Goodbye, DS Harrison. I hope you have a safe journey home.'

'Well, that's probably in karma's hands too,' Steve says.

The Chief Inspector flashes an official smile, then turns to go back to his car, the sergeant trotting in front of him.

Steve tosses the newspaper onto an empty seat and stares at the sky. He feels pointless. The days have taken their toll. All the effort, all the pain, all the disruption and angry, obsessive energy. Has it really been for nothing?

He gets up. He needs a walk.

*

Iain wakes, slightly dry-mouthed. The first thing he feels is the tight throbbing in his head. The second is the soothing balm of realising that Charlotte is nuzzled into his shoulder, his arm beneath her slim neck.

He smiles as he looks down at her, curled up next to him on top of the sheet.

Smooth golden legs, the delicious curve from hip to waist, the soft, shallow breaths.

He feels something welling inside him, an urge to get up, run outside and go screaming around the village, punching the air, rushing to the corner flag to take the adulation from the crowd.

But not as much as he wants to just continue lying there, feeling her warmth beside him, listening to her breathing, smelling the sweet scent of coconut oil from her hair.

*

The lonely beach stretches out before him. Steve's feet automatically take him to the old place, the usual spot. He sits down on the sand in his beige trousers right where they would have put their sarongs, side by side, while Sophie laughed at his stupid jokes and gazed out to sea, trying to find dolphins at the edge of her vision.

Sophie. Somehow, somewhere, she got lost in all of this. In the daily battle to fill his mind and his actions with purpose, to deliberately block out thoughts of her and what she was and how he felt, she got lost.

But now that's all there is. There's no hiding from it any more. All his effort, all the activity, the anger, the obsession. He's achieved nothing, other than managing to hold his feelings in check, not allowing himself to dwell on the horror of loving Sophie, and the lost potential of life. Her life, his life, maybe even their life together. It would have happened. There's no doubt in his mind. There was something strong between them. And if she hadn't actually loved him, at least the potential was there. He could feel it.

He hangs his head, and for the first time the tears are not from anger or frustration or confusion. This time they are the hot, raw tears of pure grief. Grief for Sophie, for himself, and for everything that's been lost.

He lets the cries come, forcing their way out in silent wheezes at first, then gaining intensity, the sound pushing up from deep inside him. Desolation racks his body.

He sits crying, hands on his head, shaking with sobs until there are no tears and no sounds left.

It takes a long time for his breathing to return to normal, for his drained soul to summon up the will to open his aching eyes to the world.

The sun's getting higher, bleaching out the images before him, evaporating the shadows inch by inch.

He rubs his face, scraping off salty tear-stains, dries his nose, then sighs like a death rattle. He looks out to sea for a while, just watching the waves slide lazily onto the beach, thinking of Sophie. The way she smiled, the way she said his name, the way her eyes shined when she laughed. He wants to hold the vision as long as he can, bring her back to life through sheer force of imagination.

Something out in the sea to his left catches his eye. At first he doesn't believe it. He stares. Then he stands, raised up by astonishment, and watches the dolphin swimming along barely thirty yards out in the calm water. Gliding, taking it slow, its black body sleek and glistening, weaving up and down in the wide, gently rolling waves.

Steve smiles as he feels a flood of euphoria flow through him, his gaze following the dolphin as it swims past. Some of the other people on the beach have seen it too now, and are standing like him, stunned with delight, a mute honour guard.

Sophie's dolphin, Steve thinks to himself. The one she was always nearly seeing, the one she believed in. And now it's come looking for her, wondering why she doesn't believe in it any more. It had always been out there, just waiting. Her own secret dolphin.

He watches until it slips its fin under water for the last time and swims away unseen. Then he starts to walk back along the beach. It's time to pack.

*

'How much longer will you be in Goa?' Charlotte says, blowing cute, cooling breaths on her hot cardamom tea, big blue eyes regarding Iain above the rim of her cup.

They're in the garden at Sonic, down by the shore, tucked

up in the shade of the palm trees.

Iain tries to shrug, but it comes out wrong, the way it always does when he has to lie on the spot.

'Don't know. What about you?'

'I think maybe one week more. Then I would like to go to Hampi.'

'Suits me. I mean, that's where I was thinking of going next. At around that time as well. About a week.'

Bugger Bangalore, he thinks. Hampi's Hampi, after all.

'Really? Maybe we will be travelling together?'

'Christ, you German girls are a bit forward, aren't you?' Iain says, grinning. 'We've barely exchanged bodily fluids and here you are planning the rest of our lives. You might have at least waited until after our first lunch together, seen how that went before deciding something so important. Och, alright then. You've talked me into it.'

They both laugh, Iain the hardest, because he knows how ridiculous the proposition is that he wouldn't want to go with her. To Hampi, Hamburg, Hampden, anywhere. Anytime. For as long as you both shall live.

Watch yourself, McMillan. That's fighting talk.

He gives his fragile mind a gentle kick for getting slushy. It's just the painkillers, he decides. Maybe.

Maintain your defences. Do not give in. Do not allow such minor considerations as fantastic looks, wonderful personality and an overwhelmingly delicious sensuality distract you from the essential basic freedoms of life. Do not get fooled. It's a ploy of some kind, some underhand trick to suck you in.

Surrender, McMillan. Consider yourself well and truly sucked. And eternally grateful.

'I was quite surprised that you were attracted to me,' he says, feeling himself flush under his tan at the truth of it. 'I mean, with this cut and everything. I don't think you're seeing me at my best. It's not all that attractive.'

Charlotte smiles, but doesn't say anything for a second. She puts her cup down, then takes a long look at him, examining Iain's eyes as if she's searching for something.

'I do not think that what is outside a person, what they look like, is so important,' she says. 'It is what is inside them that matters.'

Iain's left eyebrow rises as he channels his inner Roger Moore.

'Absolutely. What's inside a person is crucial. Ask anyone you like, I've always said that to really find out what a person's like, you've just got to get inside them.'

He smirks. Charlotte's face is suddenly blank.

'And I suppose that is an example of your Scottish humour,' she says in a flat tone. 'Dirty jokes, just like a little schoolboy. Or did you think I would not understand?'

Iain's mortified, stammering in panic.

'I...I...I'm sorry, I didn't mean....it just came out. It wasn't meant...'

'One thing you must learn about the German sense of humour,' Charlotte says sternly, cutting him off. She leans forward on the table, beckoning Iain closer. 'We like taking the piss.'

She collapses back on her seat giggling. Iain releases a long breath, then starts laughing too, more out of relief than anything else.

'The look on your face,' she says between giggles. 'It was very funny. Okay, so was saying about being inside someone. You have a very dirty mind.'

'But the rest of me is absolutely spotless. Especially my hands.'

He holds them up for effect, chuffed that he gets a laugh from it.

'So,' he says when they calm down. 'Got any plans for to-day?'

'No. Just another lousy day in paradise. What about you?'

'Well, I thought I'd try hanging around you for eight or nine hours, see if I drive you mental or not. Then see how it goes from there.'

'That sounds okay,' Charlotte laughs. 'Hey, I've got an idea. We could go to Calangute. I was told there's a very good astrologer there. He could do our charts.'

'Yeah, and then I suppose we could go and get matching tattoos,' Iain says, snorting out smoke from the cigarette he's just lit. He sees Charlotte's face and stops sneering. 'And you were being completely serious, weren't you.'

'Of course. Don't you want to know your future?'

Steady, McMillan. Bogus New Age hippy-shit clap-trap alert. Mind you, that's probably what all Capricorns say.

'Och well. What the hell. Rock 'n' roll.'

*

Steve has his suitcase packed in no time at all. The choices about what's to go in the case and what's to go in his overhead-luggage-sized mini backpack are fairly easy.

He swings the backpack over his shoulder and lifts both his case and the one that Karen's left for him to take downstairs.

He dumps both suitcases at reception with everyone else's. The coach is already outside the main entrance, waiting to be loaded up by the hotel staff.

Steve walks out into the sunshine and stands next to Karen, who's still not talking to him.

'Have you packed, then?' she says in a clipped voice, ignoring him.

'Yeah.'

'About time too.'

The Matlocks and Clive appear with their luggage. Clive's got a shaven head, a nose ring, and he's wearing an orange collarless shirt of thin material with Sanskrit writing on it. Arthur's got on a patched waistcoat, silver shades and little else, tiny denim cut-off shorts the only thing keeping him nearly decent. Maureen's got beads in her hair and a long tie-dye cheesecloth dress on. Kim and Angela are both in dowdy black.

'Fuck me,' says Steve. 'It's the Munsters.'

The family troops to the rear of the coach with their cases. As Clive passes Steve, he turns to look straight at him with wide, staring eyes.

'It's all connected,' he says without breaking stride.

Twenty minutes later the coach is packed and the passengers wave goodbye to the assembled hotel staff. The coach pulls out onto the road, along the rutted tarmac, through the village, and heads south on the long drive to the airport.

In front of Steve and Karen, Clive's bent in serious conversation with Kim.

'And it's like that thing,' he says. 'What the old man was talking about. That stuff about millions of angels being able to dance on the head of a pin. They've got no form, no mass. They don't exist in space and time, not as we know it. It's an intelligence which isn't physical. They're not made of anything that we can understand.'

'Don't be stupid, Clive. Everything's got to be made of something. Even angels have got to be made of something.'

'Exactly,' Clive says, grinning. 'Exactly. You got it. They're made of something. You got it. We just don't know what it is yet. But when we find out. It's all connected, see.'

A screeching, lurching, swerving hour and the coach reaches Dabolim airport. They all get off, muscling past the swarm of porters eager to take their luggage into the departure hall for a handful of rupees.

'I'll deal with check-in,' Steve says to Karen. 'No point you standing here for hours. Go on up to that cafe up there,' he says, pointing up to a corner of the mezzanine first floor. 'I'll meet you up there when I'm done.'

He hands Karen two hundred rupees and she goes without complaint, clutching her hand luggage to her chest. Many of the other passengers have the same idea, preferring to escape the cloying swelter of the busy main hall.

Steve joins her an hour later. She's sitting alone at a table for four by the window. He goes over and sits diagonally across from her, handing over her boarding card, ticket and passport.

'Need to go through security soon,' he says. She shrugs, but doesn't say anything, picking up a cup of tea to fill her mouth instead.

They sit like that for a quarter of an hour, Karen guarding her tea, Steve looking out the window at the mechanics and catering staff and security people strolling around the runway, getting the plane ready at an unhurried, relaxed pace in the shimmering heat.

A scratchy call comes over the tannoy asking them to make their way to security for a final check before boarding. Steve and Karen both get up and head for the stairs.

'I've got to say this,' Karen says as they join the queue to go through the square-arched metal detector. 'This has not been the holiday of my dreams, Steven Harrison. You're going to owe me for this big time. There's a lot of talking to be done when we get home.'

Steve grunts, and watches the queue shorten. When it gets to their turn, he lets Karen go first.

She puts her handbag on the x-ray machine conveyor belt, then passes through the security scanner without a beep. She looks back, waiting for Steve to come through.

He takes a step to the side, standing behind barred railings, allowing the man behind him to go through instead.

Karen stares at him, puzzled. He stares back, a look on his face that she can't read. When he lets another person go through, she speaks up.

'What are you doing?'

'I'm not coming with you,' Steve says in a quiet, reasonable voice.

'You what?'

'I'm not coming with you. I'm going to stay on for a bit.'

'What d'you mean, stay on? You can't stay on.'

'I won't be long. A week or two, maybe. I just need some time to think about a few things.'

'Think about what? What's there to think about?'

'Just things.'

'Oh, pull yourself together for God's sake. Stop mucking around and come on through.'

'I told you. I'm not coming.'

'You can't just not come back. What about work?'

'Don't worry about work,' Steve says, waving it away. 'I'll talk to work. Work won't be a problem.'

'You can't just do this. You can't just leave me standing here in an airport. What d'you think you're playing at? What on earth d'you need another week for?'

He shrugs.

'Maybe I'll go looking for dolphins,' he says.

'You what? What you going on about? Have you gone stark staring mad or something? Going on about bloody dolphins. Come on, you're holding everybody up.'

'There's a particular type of dolphin, a very rare one, called a Periphery Dolphin, that you can only see when you look at it a certain way, out of the corner of your eye. Maybe that's what I need to do. Sometimes you need to look at something from a different angle before you can see it clearly.'

'I don't know what you're going on about, but I don't care because...'

'Karen. For God's sake, just get on the sodding *plane*!'

Her mouth snaps shut. She needs a second to reassert herself.

'But there's all kinds of things to consider. You can't just drop everything like this.'

'Look, the car keys, the house keys, money, it's all in your case. You've got your ticket, your boarding card, your passport. It's not very complicated.'

'But what about your case? You can't just leave your case on....'

'Look, it's all taken care of. I've sorted everything out. I've got all I need here with me,' Steve says, shrugging the daypack. 'When I sat down and thought about it, I realised I didn't need all that much. Not really.'

'But what about me?' Karen says, her voice straining, getting desperate. 'What about me?'

Steve takes a deep breath.

'Maybe I *do* need you. That's one of the things I've got to think about. In fact, I've been doing a lot of thinking already. I do love you, don't be in any doubt about that. I do, in a way. The trouble is, you see, I'm not sure I actually *like* you.'

He nudges the daypack higher on his shoulder, turns and walks away towards the exit.

He can almost feel himself getting lighter, growing taller with each new step as he sees the bright, vibrant world beyond the plate glass windows. He doesn't look back.

*

The coach takes the corner outside the Rodrigues house with confidence.

A Shivaji Travel Deluxe coach, according to the writing on the side, on its way towards the village and the big hotel. A gallery of pink, concerned faces peers out at Cyril and the Doc sitting back on their chairs on the wide verandah.

'Here they come. Here they come,' the Doc says. 'Flock of them vibe vultures just circling in. Smell the decay from here. A man can only do what a man can do. No more'n that. I spread the gospel, but it's just a piss in the ocean, my friend, a piss in the ocean.'

'Susegad,' Cyril says. He just wants to sit quietly in the shade and let his lunch settle.

'It's one big battle, my friend, one big battle,' the Doc goes on. 'For every one you turn, there's a hundred more of the bastards coming in. Even the young ones. The ones you wouldn't expect. Where's their soul gone? Where'd it go? Ain't one of them believe in nothing no more. They don't stand for nothing. They don't try to make a difference. All just sit around and eat tofu, some shit like that.'

Cyril nods slowly, his head dropping, anticipating a snooze.

'Ain't saying nothing wrong 'bout knowing nature,' the Doc continues. 'A man's gotta find his place, know where he fits in. The whole pattern. Plants, trees, air, fish, birds, animals. Gotta respect them. Don't mean to say you shouldn't eat them too. Tell you somethin', brother. All them bloodsuckers, them vultures, them Goddamn ratbastard vibesuckers. Maybe they're here now. But I can feel it. I can feel it coming. Old Mother India'll do what she's always done. Take 'em in, use 'em up, spit 'em out. Always has done, always will. Old Mother India. I can feel her rising. She ain't none too happy 'bout all them lard-ass, slack-head, Goddamn poisonous pigshit fools coming in. She's gonna spit them out. The time's a-coming, I can feel it in the vibe. Then it'll get back to the old days. They'll all be gone, and it'll be just you and me, brother. Just you and me.'

'Susegad.'

The Doc watches with keen eyes as the coach drives down the road then disappears behind the palm trees. Peace descends on the verandah again.

'What's that mean anyways?' he says. 'What is the actual, authentic translation of that 'soo-sey-gad'? Always been figuring to ask you.'

'Susegad,' Cyril says, drawing the word out sleepily. 'Take it easy, go slowly, calm down, enjoy life.'

'You shitting me? That what it mean? That 'soo-sey-gad'?'

'Susegad,' Cyril says, nodding slowly, his eyes struggling to remain open.

'All this time you've been telling me to calm down? I thought it meant 'I agree with you', or 'you're right', something like that. For thirty years you've been telling me to calm down?'

'Calm down, take it easy, enjoy life.'

'Shee-it!' the Doc says, cackling, slapping his thigh. 'Wished I'd known that in the first place. Might've saved everyone a whole lotta trouble.'

Cyril's head nods onto his chest. The siesta has started.

Printed in Great Britain
by Amazon